Man on a Murder Cycle

For Milton, life had merely started over. The light had been snuffed out for a time, and there had been blackness, and he had been faceless. But then his shadow soul had revolved out of the darkness like some alien moon, and soon it was the only face he knew. Soon he could remember, and wanted, no other. Now he could indulge himself. The whispering, vindictive part of him had come to the fore, and it didn't have to share its space with conscience and morality because those better things were gone. His evil was pure and true, for he possessed no opposite.

Also by Mark Pepper

The Short Cut

About the author

Mark Pepper was born in Lancashire in 1966. After gaining an honours degree in history, he studied for three years at RADA. He has since acted in theatre, and has appeared over a dozen times on television including roles in *Heartbeat*, *Pie in the Sky*, *Prime Suspect 3* and *Coronation Street*. *Man on a Murder Cycle* is his second novel.

Man on a Murder Cycle

Mark Pepper

NEW ENGLISH LIBRARY
Hodder and Stoughton

First published in Great Britain in 1997 by Hodder and Stoughton
A division of Hodder Headline PLC
First published in paperback in 1998 by Hodder and Stoughton
A New English Library Paperback

10 9 8 7 6 5 4 3 2 1

British Library Cataloguing in Publication Data

Pepper, Mark, 1957–
Man on a murder cycle
1. Horror tales
I. Title
823.9'14 [F]

ISBN 0 340 69624 9

Printed and bound in Great Britain by
Clays Ltd, St Ives plc

Hodder and Stoughton
A division of Hodder Headline PLC
338 Euston Road
London NW1 3BH

For Jeannifer Blankanette.
I love you, sayang.
For never giving up. For always loving.
For more than words than say . . .

ACKNOWLEDGEMENTS

Thanks to: Merric Davidson, for his unfailingly sound advice, for making me laugh when I don't much feel like it, for being a good pal and a great agent (and, believe me, I've known some lousy ones); Stephen Powell, a fine editor at the sadly defunct Ringpull Press, whose input on *The Short Cut* made it publishable; George Lucas, an English gentleman now in New York, for believing, and bringing me into Hodder; my new editor, Carolyn Caughey, for her enthusiastic acceptance of a novel she did not commission, and her insightful editing thereafter; my Mum for providing the spell-check my Amstrad lacks; my Dad for reading every draft I write when I'm sure he'd rather be gardening; both of them for their love and encouragement, and for giving me the financial freedom to pursue what might otherwise have remained a hobby; brother Dave for his multi-faceted support; Christina and Carl for understanding why the grumpy bugger in the back room needs his peace and quiet; Jim Middleton for trusting that I'm a bona-fide writer and not just some sicko in letting me view an embalming; all at Hammicks, Stockport, for suffering my bookstand and publicity mugshot in their doorway for weeks on end, especially Rachel Coaton, and the manager Rick Pennell, who happily gave their valued help simply because they were in a position to – a strange, antiquated concept; family and friends who shelled out on *The Short Cut*; *Performance Bikes* magazine for their article on the Mr Turbo ZZ-R1100; and especially Jeannifer Blankanette and our mutual friends.

ONE

***

He leaned the Honda CBR600 into another sweeping right-hander. A glance down at the speedo told him 70 mph. It was fast enough. He wasn't experienced like so many of them on the island. He couldn't imagine cornering any faster. But still they shot by him. Lunatic speeds. His whole body jolted, shocked by their sudden noisy appearance. It didn't help to check the mirrors. One second the view behind was clear, two seconds later and a sleek bright shape was past. These riders moved at warp speeds, made him feel he was in reverse. Their exhaust notes crackled, whined, snarled, and they always made him jump in his seat.

Still, in the warming sun of an early June morning he smiled inside his helmet. The dawn start had been worth the effort. He was not alone even at five a.m. In a few hours the road would be a crowded racetrack. Riders pushing their machines, pushing their limits and pushing their luck. There was no prize, except the high from tempting fate and beating it. He understood the buzz as well as the rest of them – the thrill of speed – but he had recently acquired an acute sense of his own mortality. He had fought through a long darkness to reach this point in his life; he had worked too damn hard to risk killing himself now.

Ahead, the road opened out, long and straight. He rolled on the throttle and shifted up through the gears. His eyes flicked down to the speedo. 110 . . . 120 . . . 130. What was that about risk? He eased back to a steady ton. This was the heart of biking; a warm early morning, green lanes lit by the yellow glow of the dawn sun, no sound but the wind's roar inside his helmet and the pleasant scream of the engine down below. Alone. The spirit of freedom.

Set into the greenery a hundred yards further on, black and white chevrons pointed left. He slowed to sixty and leaned the bike.

1

And on. The curves seemed endless, rarely bending blind, always encouraging speed, speed, speed.

After a time, he slipped into a well-known sensation: it wasn't real any more; the road, the bike, his own presence. It was a game in a video arcade.

His tinted visor defined the screen. Drystone walls rushed by either side; hedges lined the route; trees formed a green tunnel above him; the occasional white or grey cottage whipped past; twin yellow lines streaked alongside in the gutters for a stretch. He wasn't moving – they were. It was all computer-generated, thrust towards him as he sat motionless on a stationary arcade motorbike.

He flipped open his visor and the illusion was blown from his mind. Too dangerous that feeling of invulnerability.

And he was pushing it now; bends beginning to tighten out of sight. The odds of a hazard at such an hour were slim, but it wasn't worth the risk. He had beaten the dark forces of death, depression and drink, and had toiled to create a future for himself where he had thought none could exist. He wanted to live.

He closed the visor, dropped a couple of gears, took a corner at forty-five. No obstacles in his path. But better safe than sorry. Rear-ending a milk float was not on his planned itinerary, and a head-on with one of the knee-down brigade wide on his side of the road would be more than upsetting. Their closing speed would disintegrate men and machinery into the island's hedgerows like so much tourist litter.

His body jerked as a red Ducati 916 with Isle of Man registration overtook on the bend, crackling by within three feet of him. He watched the rider in his flashy race leathers deftly shift his weight back onto his machine, flicking it upright for another fast stretch of tarmac. Then away.

He felt his safety had been threatened, recklessly violated. Instinctively, without thought, his left fingers grabbed clutch, left toe kicking down a gear, right wrist flicking to open the throttle.

He was giving chase.

The CBR responded crisply, surging forward. He piled on the revs, red-lining the tacho, but his adversary enjoyed an advantage: they were his roads, and the gap opened.

He began braking less going into corners, shifting his bum off the seat to pull the CBR round more quickly. Left-hander, right-hander, leaning lower and lower. Then tarmac chewed at the leather of his right knee.

Christ, it wasn't worth it. What was he thinking?

On the next straight he slowed and stopped at the roadside. He cut the ignition, kicked the sidestand down and rested the bike. In the calm air he could hear the Ducati's distinctive V-twin fading into the distance. He took stock of himself. Heart pounding, breath pumping, system rippling with adrenalin. He had so much anger inside. He was brimming with violence. It was all still there, waiting for a moment of weakness to reassert itself and destroy him. Was he really going to let some flash bastard on a 916 taunt him into a brick wall? After so much struggle?

He lifted his right knee and inspected the grazed leather. He vowed it would be his first and last brush with a hard surface. Feeling the fun had gone out of the day, he decided to go back to his Bed and Breakfast and sleep for a few hours. Later he would watch from the safe retreat of a pub garden as Mad Sunday got really mental, and listen as the wailing ambulances plied their sad trade across the island.

Very sedately, he got the machine off its lean, retracted the sidestand, started up, geared, checked behind and moved off.

He tootled along gently for a couple of miles, like a born-again biker rediscovering two wheels.

Until another 916 overtook, tearing past, horn blaring.

He caught the registration above the huge rear tyre. The same Manx plate. The same Ducati. The bastard must have pulled over to lie in wait.

The man on the 916 then stuck out his left arm, formed an 'O' with finger and thumb, and gave three brief shakes: *wanker*.

That did it. The will to hurt filled him. This time he was going to catch the Ducati and boot its rider into the gutter.

Fear took a pillion seat as he rode like a demon, displaying skills he had not known he possessed. He just had to follow the leader and echo his every move. The man in front was a local, knew the roads and could judge them perfectly. On the next straight he would accelerate alongside and stick a boot into some expensive leather. He was prepared to commit murder and was completely oblivious to the fact.

A village shot towards them as the green lanes petered out.

Arcade time again.

From the horizon, rows of cottages enlarged on his left, then his right, flowing past the peripheries of his screen. Buildings, stone and white and pastel, but too quickly gone to establish their purpose, whether garage or pub or shop or showroom. Black and white kerbstones bordered the rolling road under his immobile machine. Yellow lines streaked by either side; single, double, single, gone. He rode the broken centre line as though it was part of the game. Keep on track for maximum points.

The Ducati's rear tyre inched backwards. The village continued to zip by.

The road took a gentle curve and brought the low sun round, dead ahead. His visor filled with blinding yellow but he didn't slow. He dipped his head and cut the worst glare from view. The tarmac gleamed, the buildings glowed. He squinted to focus on his adversary.

Swift down-change, winding the tacho needle into the red, screaming the revs to the limiter, and the 916 moved backwards and came alongside.

He looked sideways, lifted his boot off the peg, and . . .

The Ducati disappeared. Behind him. Off screen.

Game over.

He whipped his head to the front. Where was the road? Eyes down. 120. Eyes front. Where was the road? He began to hit both brakes, but too late.

The Honda crested the rise and took off, and the ground dropped away beneath it.

And God hit the button marked slo-mo as lightning thoughts seemed to flow gently through his mind.

Ah, there's the road. Down there. Flash bastard knew. Sod it.

He released the brakes. Not good, a locked-wheel landing at a ton-twenty.

But the CBR had slewed off centre in the air, and the rear tyre landed off-true, causing the machine to whip sharply. The bars went light in his grasp, flicking wildly from lock to lock. Flapping left, right, left, right, the front rubber bit into tarmac and ripped the bars from his gloved hands.

His thoughts continued to drift by rather idly in the arrangement of brain-time God reserved for those horrific moments in the human experience.

4

Oh dear. The fabled tank-slapper. Bars out of control. At 120.
Oh dear.

He wrestled hopelessly. The machine was too far gone. He felt himself unseat slightly, his legs lift away from the bike as it bucked and twisted.

Richie Benaud's voice piped up in his head, delivering his calm cricketing verdict: *That's it. It's all over.*

And then he saw where the road was heading now: sharply to the right following that chevroned sign to avoid passing straight through that drystone wall in front of that quaint little cottage.

Bugger.

His mind even had time to register the understatement.

The CBR demolished the wall, and vice-versa.

Maintaining the bike's momentum, he shot through the air, across a front lawn, through a window, across a living room and partly through a brick dividing wall.

The elderly couple awoke with a nasty shock. At the foot of their bed, between two paintings of their fair island, was a new piece of decor, like a macabre hunting trophy. A chest of flapping black leather, and a head, mashed with black fibreglass, lolling on a broken neck and dripping on the carpet.

TWO

Tom Roker sat in his desk chair, swivelling it back and forth. Page 421 of his fifth novel was scrolled halfway out of his electric typewriter. For twenty minutes he had been toying mentally with the same sentence, unhappy with each permutation. As a result, and as usual, he had begun to question his ability, only reinforcing the block. Sadly, he was a past master at self-doubt, and for good reason. Of his previous four novels, only the first had been published. The three since had been rejected. He accepted he should have taken the hint by now, but the overwhelming success of his debut novel, *Hidden Blade*, eight years before, had kept him banging away at the keyboard.

He lit another cigarette. His small study was thick with stale smoke. He inhaled, rested his cigarette in the heavy glass ashtray, and re-fogged the atmosphere. Leaning back in his seat, he stared out of the window. The glass was filthy, yellowed inside by his habit, browned outside by layers of Fulham air. In contrast, the day was bright and clear. He turned back into the room, looked again at the familiar walls that boxed him in; the framed press cuttings, lauding the arrival of a new talent, anticipating a career to rival the greats. And in several spots he couldn't help but notice light squares in the nicotine-stained emulsion, another reminder of the pain he had suffered to follow up on his early promise, to fulfil expectations. Five years ago, they had been covered by photographs. Happy, smiling faces frozen in time. His then-wife Helen; Helen and four-year-old Charlotte; the three of them together; Charlotte on her own. He had left his daughter's picture hanging until just recently, but it had finally proved too distressing. Four years ago, Helen had remarried and emigrated to Colorado, taking his daughter to a new life. After voicing his objections he had let it happen. Selfishness aside, he guessed it was in all their best interests.

But losing them had somehow sealed his fate. Now, he could never give up writing. By shutting himself away in his study for days on end, nights without sleep, he had neglected his family. Even as they had packed and walked out, he had not been able to say the one thing that might have stopped them from leaving: *I did it for you.* Because he hadn't, and Helen knew it. He had done it for himself, for his own ego. After a while he had come to understand this, but by then it was too late. So now he had no choice; he had to write. He didn't want success, he needed it. It could never compensate for the loss of his family, but what else was left in his life?

The bottle of Rioja was nearly empty. He topped up his glass with the remaining liquid, and took a gulp. His stomach growled. Alcohol had never broken a block for him, but it did make it more tolerable. Again, he rearranged the problematic sentence in his head. If he could just get moving, he would have the novel tied up in another couple of hours.

He was too impatient. He began tapping at keys, committing his flawed thoughts to paper. He could always rewrite.

Tomorrow, Monday, he would have the final pages photocopied in the Fulham Road, then take the manuscript east under the city to his agent's apartment on the Thames in Rotherhithe.

THREE

———◆———

The Thames glittered like a diamond carpet, unrolled through the heart of a quiet London. The warehouses and wharfs were dark at its edge. Up river to the west, Tower Bridge was indistinct and grey through the rising smog of the mid-morning heat.

Carol Morgan enjoyed the view from the rooftop garden of her apartment building. It had been a derelict warehouse back in the early eighties, an empty, echoing reminder of a glorious Britain a century past. Then young London had gone Porsche and braces mad, and the guts of the great structures were suddenly alive again. Shares and the City had displaced the ghosts of Trade and the Colonies from their riverside coffins. But now the yuppies were gone, or at least they were older, less brash.

She leaned against the chest-high brick wall. Nine floors fell away beneath her chin, straight down into water or mud, depending on tide. She faced the sun and pushed her Ray-Bans up into her hair, then closed her eyes. Under her bare feet the concrete was blissfully cool. She felt her sarong riffling gently in the breeze. Warm rays beat at her skin. She wanted to discard her bikini top, but the thought of perverts and binoculars stopped her.

Besides, she wanted to get back to the latest manuscript. During her career as a literary agent she had been sent such compelling material only once before. That was eight years ago, when a new novelist had presented her with a thriller called *Hidden Blade*. She had signed him straightaway. Several publishers had joined a bidding war for the rights, and when she had milked the best deal from each one, she had taken her pick. The subsequent hardcover release had met with rave reviews, and five months later the paperback had climbed steadily to reach the number one slot of *The Sunday Times* Bestsellers.

And then . . . nothing. Talk about a one-hit wonder. Eight years down the line, Tom Roker had become the Kajagoogoo of the book world. But she kept reading the crap he brought her. Against all reason, she hoped he might still deliver the goods, because none of her other clients had even come close.

Which all made the manuscript delivered that morning very special. A seam of gold in a bed of worthless rock.

She smiled. At last she could give up on Tom Roker. Someone else had entered the frame. The irony was that her new prospect wrote in exactly the same style as the Tom Roker of old. In fact, had she not seen the name on the first page, she would have thought Tom had finally produced a worthwhile follow-up.

But there was no place for sentimentality in business. Tom Roker was a spent force. She decided that if his next submission was as tawdry as his last, she would sever their professional relationship, and not before time.

FOUR

———•———

Angie Kellett went to church that Sunday. She didn't know why.
She hadn't been in years. But here she was, kneeling in a pew with
her head bowed.

The parish vicar, Michael Shaw, approached from the vestry
in his cassock, shoes clicking in echoes around the small village church.

She looked up at the slim black form and the half-smiling,
half-frowning face.

'Hello,' she said.

'Hello, Angie.'

She pushed herself back onto the wooden bench. 'Sorry, I haven't
been in for a while.'

He smiled. 'I don't keep count. At least you haven't forgotten
about us.'

Angie returned a smile. She liked Michael. She remembered her
confirmation classes with him. She had been twelve years old. Each
hour-long session was never long enough. His soft voice and Latin
looks gave her the first big crush of her youth. She had always
imagined he knew; that God told him at night to watch out for the
one at the front with the blonde hair and dizzy eyes – she would
ruin him given the chance.

Twenty years had passed. He had to be knocking fifty now, but
he had changed little. A light brush of silver through the black hair,
skin made more interesting by the passage of time, but still the same
man who brought the village womenfolk to worship whether or not
they believed in the Lord.

'Would you like to talk?' Michael asked. 'I have time before the
next service.'

She didn't say no, just looked confused, so he sat down beside her.

10

'Is there a problem?' he asked.

'Not really.' She stared towards the altar. Her fingers played with a small prayer book.

'But something brought you here today,' he suggested.

She stroked a thumb absently against the gold pages. 'I feel very down. I feel awful inside. I don't know why.'

'Well, if I were a psychologist, I might call it free-floating anxiety. The ills of a sick world preying on a weary mind. No pun intended.'

She missed his meaning, too wrapped up in her strange condition. 'But it's something specific,' she told him. 'I just don't know what.'

Michael left a thoughtful gap. 'You know, it would feel like that. It's not logical to worry about nothing, so we tell ourselves there must be something very wrong. But when the evils of the world are brought into our homes every day by the television, the radio, newspapers, it's not unusual that sometimes we're infected by it. We don't see the good any more, and life seems very dark. It's not uncommon.'

She tried a smile. 'I'm sure you're right, but . . .'

He waited, but she had trailed off into a troubled silence.

'Are you happy generally?' he said.

'I'm okay.'

'And what about your brother Andrew?'

She shot him a suspicious glance. 'He's fine.'

'Forgive me,' Michael said. 'This is a small village. I know he's had his problems of late, and I know how you've supported him.'

She just shrugged.

Michael placed a hand on her fidgeting fingers and stilled them around the prayer book. 'It can take a toll, looking after a loved one in difficulties. You may be feeling the effects. That may be your current state.'

'It could be,' Angie conceded, 'but I haven't been worried about him for some time. It's two and a half years since it happened.' She looked at him. 'Do you know what happened?'

'His wife and daughter so tragically taken from him.'

'Killed,' Angie said coldly, against the religious euphemism.

'A drunk driver, wasn't it?'

'Scum,' she said. 'Sorry. Anyway, he's stopped drinking and he's not so angry all the time. I think he's over the worst.'

11

'Has he found work?'

'No. But he has been keeping busy.'

'At what?'

She gave a slight chuckle. 'I don't know. He said he'd surprise me soon; make me proud of my little bruv. Said he'd surprise the world, actually.'

'Sounds intriguing.'

'It does, but I'm already proud of him. He's pulled back from the brink.'

'And you've helped him.'

She said nothing, and a peaceful silence held between them for a minute until Michael spoke.

'You know, if he wants to talk about it, he's very welcome to drop by.'

Angie couldn't help but grimace. 'Well . . . thank you, but I don't think he's on speaking terms with God just yet.'

'Ah. Yes. I understand. He must be very confused. I don't expect he's very able to spot the Divine in his life at the moment.'

'No.'

'I could talk to him about that,' Michael said cheerfully. 'I'm free tonight after Evensong, even if he just wants to come and shout at me.'

'Perhaps, in time,' she said. 'He's not here now, anyway.'

'Oh?'

'He took himself off a couple of days ago for a little holiday.'

'That's good. Anywhere nice?'

'The Isle of Man. The TT.'

'Of course. He has a big motorcycle, doesn't he?'

'Yeah.'

Michael stood up. 'Well, I'll leave it up to you. When he gets back, if you think he might be amenable to an informal chat about things, do suggest he comes along. It doesn't do any good to hold on to anger and resentment. And don't you worry about things yourself. You're probably just tired and run-down.'

'Yes,' she said, 'I'm sure you're right.'

But as she watched him disappear back into the vestry she knew he was wrong. A terrible fear had struck her through the heart that morning, and it was getting worse by the second.

FIVE

Carol hated the way Tom Roker never thought to make an appointment, as though they were best buddies rather than business acquaintances. And he never failed to catch her in, which bugged her even more.

As she waited for him to come up in the lift, she told herself to be polite. There was always the remote chance that he might have brought her something worth reading. But, barring miracles, she felt she could still afford him a courteous five minutes. After all, he hadn't meant to betray her professional faith in him, and now she could finally let go of the last vestiges of hope which had lingered on for him. She would soon have a new bestselling author. After today, she would not have to deal with Tom Roker again.

She opened the door before he arrived, then nipped into the kitchen to get her handbag. She wanted to appear all set to leave the apartment. As she walked back into the living room there was a token tap at the door and in walked Tom, clutching a large manila envelope.

'Morning, Carol.'

She allowed him a lukewarm smile. 'Tom. Is that for me?'

'It is indeed.'

'Do you want to put it on the table? I'm just on my way out.'

'I'll have coffee if you're making.'

'Coffee . . .'

'Just a cup.'

She wondered if she could risk being rude. Probably, but perhaps he'd got himself laid or fallen in love since their last meeting, and his novel was filled with all that groinful inspiration.

'Right,' she said, and slipped her bag off her shoulder. 'Coffee.'

He followed her into the kitchen.

13

'So is this the one?' she asked, quarter filling the kettle so it would boil in less time.

'I'm sorry?'

'This novel, is it going to do the business?'

Tom beamed at her. 'Finally, belatedly, after many years . . . yes.'

'Good. I hope it is.'

Tom slapped his manuscript on a fitment. 'I'll put it here.'

Carol busied herself with the coffee. She resented him for his easy manner when she felt so awkward in her own home. Thankfully, the kettle began to warm up with a soft roar. Nothing to drown a conversation, but reason enough not to start one.

'So . . .' Tom said pointlessly.

'Mmm.' She smiled and searched the kitchen for a chore. The dishwasher was full. She went over, pulled down the door and began putting the crockery away in the cupboards.

The kettle climaxed and clicked off.

'What's new?' Tom persisted.

'You know . . . this and that.'

'Anything interesting?'

'Might be.' She poured the drinks, purposely adding too much milk to make them instantly drinkable.

He accepted his mug. 'Thanks, Carol. So when d'you think you might get round to reading it?'

Carol finished emptying the dishwasher. 'Reading what?'

'My novel.'

'Oh . . .' She paused, putting a knife in the drawer. 'Um . . . soon.'

'How soon?'

She put the knife in its slot and pushed the drawer hard so it banged in the fitment and shook the cutlery inside.

'I know you've got other things to do,' he said quickly.

But she didn't think he did know; it was just something he said. After all this time it seemed he still thought the publishing world revolved around him. Especially the career of Carol Morgan, literary agent.

'I do, as a matter of fact,' she told him. 'I have a real prospect for success. Funnily enough, he writes exactly like you used to.' She was aware how he might react to her use of the past tense, but she didn't care.

Tom put his mug down and stared into it. A difficult moment passed before he swilled down his coffee and rudely announced, 'Bit milky.'

Carol didn't reply. She emptied her own mug down the sink then upturned it in the dishwasher.

'So . . .' he said, 'what's it about, this book?'

'Thriller . . . horror . . . very dark humour in places.'

'When did you sign the author?'

'I haven't yet.'

Tom looked directly at her. 'You should. I mean it. If it's that good. You should get in there and snap it up before someone else does.'

She began wiping down surfaces with a J-cloth. 'There's no rush,' she said. 'He's only sent it to me. Says in his letter he doesn't want to waste stamps sending it to more than one agent. Cocky sod. Says he got my name from *The Writer's Handbook*, saw your name under my list of clients and decided I was the person to take him on.'

'So *he* thinks he writes like me as well.'

'Perhaps he does.'

'I hate him already,' Tom lamely joked, but Carol believed him.

'I'll show you the letter,' she said, taking the opportunity to get away from the pitiful atmosphere in the kitchen. She hurried out before he could stop her, heading for the desk drawer in her office. She returned with a red manuscript folder, opened the elasticated ties and offered him a handwritten letter from inside.

He didn't take it. 'Carol . . .' He indicated his own manila envelope. 'I'd rather you took an interest in *my* novel.'

She apologised and curtailed her excitement for her new literary discovery. The thought of yet another wad of words from Tom Roker kept it curtailed. She put the letter down, then faked some enthusiasm. 'Okay, what's it called?'

'*Dead End*.'

'Another thriller?'

'Yes.'

'And does it?'

'What?'

'Thrill?'

'You mean the others didn't.'

She shrugged. 'Publishers didn't think so.'

15

'Yeah, well this time it's going to be different.'

'Good. So what's changed?' she said.

'Carol, I don't know. I have no idea what *Hidden Blade* possessed that the others obviously didn't. I know they didn't thrill. I know that now. I think I even knew when I was writing them, but I didn't know how to change things and I didn't know how to stop.'

Carol didn't want to hear any more, but she felt duty bound to listen. She had been present at the birth of his career, so it seemed only right she should be present at the post-mortem.

'I had to make it happen again, Carol. I had to write another bestseller.'

'You know,' she said, without a clue what was coming next, 'perhaps you need to go back eight years. Even further, to before *Hidden Blade*. Forget the pressure to recreate, because there isn't any now. There hasn't been for years. Public expectation, critical acclaim . . . they don't last this long. And no one out there knows about the past eight years, the rejections. For all they know, you wrote one novel and didn't *want* to write another.'

Tom got annoyed. 'You talk as though my latest novel's already on the fire. I believe this one will sell. I really do. I've taken my time with it, over two years.'

'I know that. All I'm saying is, regardless of your current novel, if you could only find what you used to have, I know we'd have another bestseller.'

'So you still believe in me?'

'Of course,' she lied. 'If you just relaxed a bit, let it flow, I know you could do something like this new guy.'

'Fucking hell, Carol, you tell me to let it flow, then you tell me to imitate someone else.'

'No. I just want you to write like you used to. I only meant that this new guy happens to possess the exact same style you displayed in *your* first novel.'

'Okay, then, give me the sodding thing. You read mine, I'll read his.'

'Are you serious?'

'I wasn't. But maybe I should be.'

She considered the idea, then made a joke: 'Okay, but no plagiarism.'

'I'm not that fucking desperate.'

'Oh, Tom, lighten up, will you?'

16

'I'll lighten up when I get the advance for my new novel.'

'Right.'

'I want it before publishers within a week, Carol.'

'Tom, don't give me ultimatums. I promise I will start reading your novel the moment you leave.'

'But?'

'Yes, but. If I don't think it's, uh . . .'

'If you think it's crap.'

'Okay, yes, if I think it's crap, I can't involve any publishers. Not this time.'

Tom sat in silence as Carol continued.

'With the other novels, I hoped someone out there might like them. I didn't myself, but I still tried. Now, though . . .'

'Go on.'

'My reputation's on the line. I'll lose all credibility if I present anything else that really isn't fit for publication.'

Tom grunted and extended a hand towards her. For a moment, Carol took it to be a final plea for help. Then she understood; he wanted the red folder. She gave it to him.

In pretty much a monotone, he said, 'I'll get this back to you in a couple of days.'

SIX

———◆———

Unlike her brother's bike, Angie Kellett's had no engine, only pedals. She rode as a sort of therapy. During the worst months of Andrew's troubles, she had ridden every day, whatever the month, whatever the weather. She had heard somewhere that exercise released a natural anti-depressant in the brain. Andrew had his Prozac, she had her pedalling. Recently, her bike had stayed in the garden shed. It was a good sign. But this Monday morning, she had it out and rolling by five o'clock.

Her unnamed fear had built through the short summer hours of darkness, and she had not slept a wink. Latterly she had grown apprehensive at the thought of her brother hurtling around Manx roads.

She cycled out from the village and along the warm, green Cheshire lanes. Mile after mile, the countryside went unnoticed. The action was everything; pedalling. She needed her exercise high. But after two hours she was still no nearer to that better state of mind.

When her random route brought her up to Alderley Edge, she stopped. She wheeled her bike off the road and along a path which led to a stone outcrop, flanked by woods. She laid her bike on the ground and stepped up to the Edge. In front of her the world dropped away sharply hundreds of feet, then spread flatly towards the horizon to form the Cheshire Plain.

She sat down and let her eyes wander over the expanse of even land: the green fields, the hedgerows and trees that gave way in the distance to the silver and grey monoliths of Manchester. She guessed it should have brought her a sense of perspective, however momentarily, but it didn't. It merely represented a vista of possibilities to account for her present fear.

Out there, somewhere, something was awfully, tragically amiss.

She wanted to sit and contemplate for hours. It was a romantic notion for a romantic spot. Five minutes later she was heading back to the road. She mounted her bike and took the quickest route home. She had a vague feeling of being tugged back to the village, as though for an appointment.

The police Escort drew up as she wheeled her bicycle up the path. They had arrived in time to catch her before she left for work.

She knew: they had come to formally identify her fear, as she would have to formally identify her brother's ruined corpse.

SEVEN

———◆———

Tom Roker turned the final page. He shook his head in quiet disbelief.

'Bastard,' he muttered, though he couldn't help but smile. Carol had been absolutely right. The manuscript he had borrowed from her was a genuine bestseller. More than that, though, it was the perfect follow-up to *Hidden Blade*. It was just a shame he hadn't written it himself. The similarity in style to his work of eight years ago was uncanny. Occasionally, he thought he was reading work he had forgotten he'd written.

His study was stale and smoky again. Dark outside. The early hours of Tuesday morning.

'Incredible,' he whispered.

Kellett, the author, had created a character called Milton. He had introduced him as a sane, moderate, family man, and had then used the hand of fate to deliver him a damn good beating. He had removed from him his family, his job, his home, his savings. But as Milton struggled to find a reason for living, Kellett had removed a large part of his sanity, too, so as Milton's world warped with his new mind-set, he no longer needed a reason to carry on living because reason and sanity walked hand in hand. For Milton, life had merely started over. The light had been snuffed out for a time, and there had been blackness, and he had been faceless. But then his shadow soul had revolved out of the darkness like some alien moon, and soon it was the only face he knew. Soon he could remember, and wanted, no other. Now he could indulge himself. The whispering, vindictive, hateful part of him had come to the fore, and it didn't have to share its space with conscience and morality because those better things were gone. His evil was pure and true, for he possessed no opposite.

Tom neatly boxed off the pages. The top sheet read: *UNTITLED by Andrew Kellett*. He lit another cigarette, sucked in a lungful, picked up his third bottle of Cabernet Sauvignon and swigged from it. It went down the wrong way and he coughed, spluttering a spray of red spots across the title page, like an arterial spurt of blood.

'Fuck.' He opened a desk drawer and took out a sheet of paper which he rolled halfway into his typewriter. He tapped some letters into the liquid crystal display, then printed. He screwed up the old page and threw it in the waste basket, then pulled the new sheet out of the typewriter and studied it. *UNBTIRLEF ny Abfrew Lw;;ett*. He was becoming a cliché: a drunken, failed novelist. He binned the sheet and loaded another. This time he watched the letters which appeared in the liquid crystal display. *UNTITLEFD*, Cursor back and scrap the F. *UNTITLED by Andrew Ke;;ett*. Scrap the semi-colons, insert double *l*.

It was a different print type to Kellett's, but so what. He printed, added the page and replaced the manuscript in the red folder, closing it away in his desk for safe keeping. Before he returned it to Carol, he intended to give it a second reading. For the first time in years he felt truly inspired, and if he hadn't been so loaded he told himself he would have started a bestseller of his own. As it was, he stood up, wobbled for a moment, said, 'Daddy loves you,' to the lightest square in the emulsion, and went off to bed.

He was asleep in an instant and began to dream. Each page of Kellett's novel came vividly to life. Tom was too drunk to wake up from his horror show, so he just moaned and rolled around the bed, punching the air and kicking the duvet until it fell on the floor.

Milton wore black leathers with a black-visored black helmet. He rode a turbo-charged black motorcycle, which was stolen. But theft was a trifling misdemeanour. There were worse offences and Milton was trying his hand at all of them. He was having enormous fun. And when he eventually finished with the activities given to him by his literary creator, his blood-lust craved for more, and off he went again, streaking blackly through Tom's dreams, searching for new people to carve up, blow away, burn, beat and rob. Unfortunately for Tom, booze always led a nostalgic trail back in time to reunite him with his wife and daughter in a perfect coming together of hearts and tears. Such ultimate emotional bonding had never occurred in real life, but the loss on waking was quite genuine. This time, however, Milton was not about to let the delusion last even that long. The

21

nightmare met the wish-fulfilment head-on. Tom whimpered and thrashed. Milton did not have a family any more. Why should he be alone in his pain?

When Tom woke up at lunchtime he felt wrecked, as though all his running and fighting had been for real. The night before, Milton had crept out from the manuscript, followed Tom down the corridor, into the bedroom and into his head to haunt his sleep. No other fictitious character had ever done that. As a novelist himself, he was somehow immune to it. He could suspend his disbelief with the best of them, but when the book closed, its contents were confined within.

As he made himself a late fry-up breakfast, Tom felt something rather unpleasant happening to him. It was vague at first, difficult to identify, and then he pinned it down. Admiration for Kellett's work had turned sour on him. He was coveting another man's talent. He was soon filled with the lowest professional emotion.

Even before it had properly begun, Tom Roker's Tuesday was all but ruined.

EIGHT

In twenty-four hours, Angie Kellett had completed a round-trip to the Isle of Man. She had identified her brother and brought his corpse back home with her. It was now at a local undertaker's, and the undertaker had a task on his hands because Angie had requested to view the body again before cremation. Even professional beautification could little alter the final visage, but that she desired to see him in *some* better state spoke volumes about the extent of crash damage she had witnessed on the island.

Although she had shed a few quiet tears since learning of the tragedy, she had not properly broken down yet, and she did not believe she would. On the outward flight she had realised it was all morbidly predictable; a part of her had been secretly expecting news of this magnitude, and not only since her strange premonition. Andrew had been on borrowed time ever since the death of his wife and daughter. Something inside him had also died back then, and the rest of him was just waiting to go the same way, simply biding its time. His nature was never suicidal even at its depth. It was aggressive and outward-focused. Someone else had to show him the way off this earth. An eyewitness account had identified a Ducati rider as Andrew's mortal guide.

Angie dropped her overnight bag at the foot of the stairs and entered her small front living room where she collapsed on the settee. Around her were the possessions of her late parents. The cottage had been theirs and the place was still choked with their bits and pieces. She closed her eyes. In her head were memories, pictures of her dead brother. Her stomach churned. Too little food, too much emotion. She wanted to forget it all, to move out of her home and leave everything in it. To find another place, empty and soulless, and fill it with new things with no history, no past, no stories to tell. She was sick of people dying on her. In recent years, four grandparents, two parents, one maiden aunt, one sister-in-law and one niece had all shuffled off without warning. Andrew had been her only remaining family, and now he was gone.

But Andrew's death was different, because she believed she had sensed it psychically. She wondered whether the violence of the event had reached out to her. Or perhaps it was the sheer sense of futility, of seeing him struggle so hard to beat his demons, only to die anyway. Or maybe it was a heightened sibling bond, forged in that struggle. Whatever the reason, it suggested there was more to the world than her eyes would have her believe. Previously, person-to-person communication had meant the telephone or tele-gram. Telepathy was for oddballs. She had never wanted to entertain such mumbo-jumbo, and, before this, nothing in her experience had ever caused her to. It was hardly likely to lead her into the arms of Michael and the local God Squad, but it had certainly put a dent in the precepts of her rational world. To Angie's five sane senses, a sixth had been added, and it was a bit weird.

In a way, though, it was also strangely comforting, for if there was more to life, perhaps there was also more to death. Perhaps death was a misnomer, and there was only life and afterlife. It was dangerously theological talk, but it would help to dull the blow of a young life gone to waste.

Shamefully, she wondered how much of a waste it really was. Apart from her, there was no family to mourn him, and no friends. No career, so no pioneering work left unfinished and no professional contemporaries to sing his praises and grieve the loss to society. And though no one could have blamed him, he had been ill-tempered, foul-mouthed, drunk, depressed, violent, and generally not a lot of fun to be with. It was only his fightback in recent months that lent any genuine sadness to the event, but that was Sod's Law: when life's a chore, and death a distant haven, a person could stand in the middle of the M6 and be touched by nothing but fumes. Then when life picks up, the Grim Reaper comes as an old git in an Austin Metro who didn't see the light turn red.

With so much on her mind, Angie wanted to sleep and escape from it all. But she knew she might not wake up for hours if she did, and then she would not be able to sleep at night, and one hour of bleak nocturnal musing was like five spent in daylight.

She forced herself to get up. She went into the hallway and hefted her travelling case, then climbed the stairs. In her bedroom she emptied the holdall onto the floor. A clear plastic bag tumbled out, containing Andrew's personal belongings. Wallet, wedding ring, sunglasses, house keys and driving licence. The pink document had been in his leathers at the time of the accident. Now it was mostly red; torn and speared. She wondered why such a macabre memento had been included. Why not just go the whole hog and give her a piece of his skull?

Without warning she found herself boiling with anger, an emotion she had not expected. So much heartache was caused by the acquisition of that piece of paper. It was more than a driving licence, it was a licence to kill, and almost anyone could have one. Pissheads, smackheads, psychopaths, manic depressives with a death wish, kids with no common sense, geriatrics with tunnel vision, and all breeds of everyday, grinning moron. She wanted to take Andrew's possessions and throw them into his bedroom, then lock the door for good. Sadly, Andrew's door was already locked and his keys were in the plastic bag.

Thinking of the keys, a sudden question made her frown, and her temper eased. What had Andrew been working on these past months to make him so secretive?

She knelt down and clawed a hole through the plastic with her fingernails. Avoiding the driving licence, she extracted the keys.

She went to his room. At the door, she knocked as a superstitious mark of respect, then inserted the thin, rusting key and turned it. There was a releasing clunk. She twisted the knob and entered.

Andrew's room was stark white. His single bed was set beneath a window which overlooked a back garden dense with horse chestnuts. The room was always gloomy. A chest of drawers and a disorganised bookcase lined the left wall.

To the right, hidden behind the open door, was a cheap desk and sagging red director's chair. On the desk, under transparent dust covers, were items she had not seen before: a light grey word processor, the size of a portable television set, a keyboard and a printer.

She switched on a tall Anglepoise lamp. At the rear of the desk was a dictionary and a thesaurus, and on the wall Angie noticed a photograph of happier times: Andrew as a family man with a future. She averted her eyes. There were several pens scattered around, and a small blue plastic box.

She placed the keys on the desk, picked up the box and tipped the lid back. Inside was a set of compact floppy discs, a start-of-day and thirteen others numbered consecutively, each bearing the scribbled legend, *UNTITLED by AK*.

Her first thought was the obvious surmise that her brother had written a book, and she allowed herself a smile. Perhaps he had left a legacy to the world, after all. Then she wondered whether he had managed to finish it in time. She squatted down and looked under the desk for a manuscript, but there was nothing except unhoovered carpet. She pulled out the director's chair and sat in it, then checked the three drawers either side of the desk. None contained the manuscript.

Simple. She would have to read it straight off disc. She removed the dust covers, powered up the machine and popped the start-of-day into the single drive. Compared to the technology she tackled every day at the office, this stuff was prehistoric. Once the information had loaded, she removed the disc, inserted *UNTITLED by AK – 1*, and began to read.

NINE

Tom Roker was not a happy man. Carol had not called back about his latest novel. He told himself he was simply disgruntled by her discourtesy, but he was more afraid than annoyed; afraid that Carol was afraid; that she had read every word of it and that she didn't want to tell him what he didn't want to hear.

Sitting at his work desk in his small study at the front of the house, he found himself on the verge of tears. He felt his spirit had finally been broken.

His future turned black in his mind. He could not see his way ahead any more. As a small child he had felt the same depth of emptiness when he had tried to picture what death might be like. Lying in bed at night with his eyes tight shut in a silent house, he could only imagine that beyond life lay blackness, non-happening, never-ending. He had not shared this insight with his parents, though; they were obviously closer to death than he was and he didn't want to worry them. Those were strange moments for a little boy, trying to understand the nature of something so huge, and he wondered now, as he had at the time, whether he was alone in contemplating such matters at so tender an age. Then the years had passed and he had learnt about the diverse theories of the afterlife, and he had felt a little better knowing that no one else appeared to know anything for definite, either.

But this wasn't death as a black void, this was life. If he couldn't write, what else was he going to do?

He grabbed for the phone and dialled his agent's number.

'Carol Morgan.'

'Carol, it's me, Tom.'

A telling pause, which Tom tried hard to ignore, then, 'Yes?'

'I was just wondering . . .'

'Your novel.'

'Yes, if you need more time, that's fine. I know you're busy. Don't rush it. Really take it in, enjoy it. There's a lot of good stuff in there.'

'Tom,' she said, 'I've read it.'

He nodded to himself, fighting a growing panic. 'And?'

A telling pause, impossible to ignore.

'I see,' he said calmly, staring at the light squares in the emulsion.

'Listen, Tom, you know the manuscript I lent you? Could you bring it round? I want to get moving on it.'

Tom heard himself sigh. 'Tomorrow.'

'Why not today?'

'Because I'm about to get shit-faced today.'

'Oh.'

'It's the one thing I'm still pretty good at.'

'Tomorrow then,' Carol said, and cut the connection.

Tom decided whisky would be quickest.

An hour later, Tom picked up his *Times* from the desk. 'Let's have a look,' he said to himself. 'See if we can't find some poor bastard worse off than me.'

He had trouble with broadsheets even when he was sober. In his current state, they crumpled and dropped like a disastrous piece of origami. He let them fall on his lap and vaguely scanned the pages for reports of entertaining world events. It was the usual line-up: civil wars and border disputes born of godless religion; too much rain bringing floods, too little rain causing droughts; an earthquake; a threatening volcano; a forest fire out of control; war criminals left to prosper, decent folk struck by cancer; terrorists in suits, fluent in hypocrisy; food mountains and famines; pervert politicians and factious parties; violence, violence, and more violence.

And in two column inches at the foot of a page, a brief report headed *TT Crash Toll*. Tom read the names of the five dead, then went back to the second name and read it again.

He frowned, and sobriety began creeping in around the edge of his stupor.

Andrew Kellett. Now *there* was a name to conjure with. If only . . .

Wild, disgraceful, shameful thoughts shot as colourful possibilities across the blackness of his grieving mind. They were drunken thoughts, he knew as much, but they were coming *through* the drink, not from it. In its death throes, his ambition was pleading against all reason for one last chance.

The alcohol seemed to drizzle down from his brain into his stomach, leaving his head clear to think, but making his guts roll sickly.

He discarded the newspaper on the floor and reached to his desk for the red folder containing Kellett's manuscript. On the second page was a contact number for the author. He picked up the phone and dialled. One simple question followed by one sympathetic sentence, and Tom would know whether to dive back into the whisky or put a sinister plan into action.

After several rings, a young woman answered.

Tom said, 'Is that the home of Andrew Kellett?'

'Uh . . . Andrew?' said the bewildered voice. 'He's . . .'

'I'd like to offer my condolences.'

'Oh . . . thank you. Who is—?'

Tom hung up, and his future lit up, starkly brilliant, full of promise and ill-gotten gains.

TEN

Tom's headache reminded him that, by rights, he should still have been drunk. He sat nursing a coffee in the Pitcher and Piano Bar at the Putney Bridge end of Fulham Road. The interior was cool, airy and light, full of pine and prints. He had taken a window seat. The place was quiet. There were two businessmen at the bar, and a couple in their mid-thirties nuzzling each other at the rear of the room, next to a white grand piano.

He waited for Carol to arrive, and prepared himself for her foul mood. She had not liked being ordered all the way across London to meet a failed writer she no longer wanted to represent. But with what he had in mind he could not allow her the home advantage on top of the moral high ground she would most likely claim.

For nearly an hour he idly watched the mid-afternoon traffic creep by outside. His headache simmered gently as he plied it with orange juice and more coffee. The ashtray steadily piled up.

Then he saw her, marching down the pavement, visibly pissed off. Under one arm was a thick manila envelope: his manuscript. She was in T-shirt and jeans, with a bum bag; casual gear to reinforce the conclusion of their business relationship.

She stepped in from the street, saw him immediately and came over.

'Christ, you've got a nerve.' She slammed his manuscript down on the table.

'Take a seat,' he said.

'I'm not staying.'

The bartender arrived. 'What can I get you?'

'I'm not staying.'

'Two coffees,' Tom ordered.

'One coffee. I'm not staying.'

'Two coffees.'

'*One* coffee.'

The bartender dithered.

'*One* coffee,' Carol repeated, then noticed something. 'Tom, where's Kellett's manuscript?'

'We have a lot to talk about, Carol.'

'I'll bring a pot,' said the bartender, giving up.

Carol sat down. Perspiration glistened on her forehead. She shook her head slightly. 'I can't *believe* you're being so bloody obtuse. There's nothing left to say. I'm not your agent any more. Now where's Kellett's manuscript?'

'All in good time.'

'Typical. Tom Roker clichés to the bitter end.'

'All right, straight to the point. Kellett's dead.'

'What?'

'Don't worry. I didn't kill him.'

'What are you talking about?'

'He's dead.'

She squinted at him.

'True,' Tom said. 'Silly sod crashed at the TT.'

Carol followed a dismissive sneer with a considered opinion. 'Crap.'

Tom took his red disposable and lit a cigarette, angering the rabid anti-smoker across the table even more. The coffee arrived. Tom poured out two cups, sensing Carol was trying to assess him, hoping to size him up as a liar.

Eventually, she said, 'Go on.'

Tom took a sip, then placed his cup down on the table. He leaned back in his chair and dragged on his cigarette. 'It was in the paper. Two column inches. Five names. One was his.'

'How d'you know it's the same person?'

'It is. I checked.'

Carol stared out of the window. 'Damn,' she said to no one in particular.

'What are you going to do?'

'God knows.'

'You could contact the relatives, ask to publish posthumously,' Tom suggested.

'And look like a right mercenary cow.'

'Yeah, I suppose.'

31

'Shit. What did he want a bloody motorbike for?'

'Well, wait a while, then ask,' Tom said helpfully.

She looked at him. 'Have you read it?'

'Vaguely.'

'Then you'll know it's pretty sick stuff. It's not the greatest testament to a young life. People might say the warped bastard deserved to die. I don't think his family would *ever* want it to see the light of day.'

Tom appeared to consider this. 'Mmm,' he went. 'Yeah.'

Carol was almost spitting. 'Fuck, I've been searching for a talent like his since . . .'

'Since me.'

She nodded. 'Yes. For eight years.'

'Carol . . . ?'

'What?'

'Can I make a suggestion?'

Carol looked dumbstruck. 'Say that again.'

'Let me have Kellett's novel.'

'Publish Andrew Kellett's book as though you wrote it?'

'Yep. You said yourself the style's identical to *Hidden Blade*.'

Carol stood up. 'I don't want to continue this conversation.'

'Just listen.'

'No.' She pointed at the manila envelope on the table. 'There's your novel. Now I want Kellett's. Stand up, we're going to your place to get it.'

Tom could feel the blackness creeping over him again. He bowed his head. Then he heard Carol resume her seat.

She spoke with harsh pity. 'What happened to you? You had everything. Now look at you. You're washed-up, divorced, hitting the bottle, plagiarising other writers. Tom, you're a cliché. You belong in a novel yourself.'

'How would you know?' he said, looking up. 'Have you ever written a novel? Have you ever done anything more than live off the hard work of other people?'

Carol kept her cool. 'Eight years ago I took your hard work from you and gave you back a career. I believed in you. That's a lot.'

'You didn't make me.'

'No, and by the same token it's not me who's broken you. You've done that yourself.' She stood up. 'Let's go.'

He put his cigarette out in his coffee. 'Please believe again.'

'Believe in *what*?'

'Believe . . .' He didn't know. He had nothing to offer. She had no reason to listen. His future turned black. He grabbed her hand and squeezed it. 'Please.'

'No, Tom. It's over.'

Hearing those words as he held her hand, a memory sparked in his mind, and it dawned on him: there was a way to make her listen.

'Believe . . .' he said softly. 'Believe, Carol, that if you walk out of here without listening to what I have to say . . .'

'What?'

'Did you ever tell Pete about us?'

Tom felt her hand jolt, saw her body stiffen. She tugged free from his grasp. Her eyes blazed but she said nothing. Tom had pressed the razor blade of blackmail hard against her throat.

'Sit down,' he said, and she did. He put on a sunny face. 'Happy times. You'd been married to Pete for a year, if I remember. You couldn't believe you had your first best-selling author. And then you did have your first best-selling author. Celebrations went a little too far that night. And for several weeks after. Remember, Carol?'

Carol looked ripe to slap him. She fought visibly to calm herself. 'A few nights eight years ago,' she whispered furiously. 'That's all.'

'One night or a thousand nights. Technically, it's adultery.'

'You bloody hypocrite! What about your Helen? I bet you never told her.'

'No, but I'm not married any more. You are. And I've heard that nothing can restore perfect trust once its been violated.'

He waited for her retort, but she was quiet. Feeling more than a twinge of shame, he looked out of the window. 'Carol, I just want you to listen.'

'And what if I listen and I still think it's a crazy idea?'

Studying the table top, Tom ran his thumb through a spot of coffee. 'You won't.'

'But what if I do? Will you still tell Peter?'

'It won't come to that,' he reasoned. 'Don't worry.'

She surprised him then by laughing. But it contained no humour, only contempt for him. 'You've been a great disappointment to me for years, Tom. But today . . .' She shook her head. 'Oh, boy.'

Tom crumbled inside. He could cope with her anger, but not her disgust for his ignominy. He wanted to say sorry, but an apology without a complete withdrawal of his intentions would only make matters worse, and he couldn't backtrack now lest his future darken for ever.

His thumb smeared another drop of coffee across the table. He didn't look up as he said, 'Fifteen minutes, Carol. That's all I want.'

'All right, Tom. Not that I have much choice. But we play it my way. I ask a question, you answer it. I see an obstacle, you tell me how we'll overcome it.'

'Fine.' He took a cigarette from his pack and lit up. 'Go ahead.'

'No. Not now. Tomorrow. Bring Kellett's manuscript to my apartment at three o'clock. You're not having your blackmail *and* my novel.'

ELEVEN

———◆———

By the time Angie Kellett finished reading her brother's novel, it had turned four a.m. She had read through the dark, now it was light again. Her eyes were blurred and itchy.

She exited the final disc and shut down the word processor, then tried not to think of anything for a while. She closed her eyes and felt giddy from tiredness. Waves of birdsong drifted to her from the trees in the back garden – a calming sound. Lorries on the distant A-road – a reassuring sound: people were out there; life was moving on.

Thoughts on Andrew's novel did not stay away for long, but they were confused and contrary. She was glad he had managed to complete the book, and she liked his writing, but she was horrified that he should have put his skills to such poor use. Perhaps the whole experience had been cathartic for him, a release of emotions akin to a purging of bad blood. If that was so, she was pleased he had found a harmless focus for all his aggression. But to think he might have been writing with a view to publication actually made her feel angry towards him. She didn't want her surname attached to such a story; having people think she came from the same deranged stock.

She replaced the dust covers over the monitor and keyboard, and closed the discs away in their box.

When she left Andrew's bedroom and locked the door behind her, she vowed she would never go back inside.

Angie rose at noon. The first half-hour on her feet she felt drowsy, punch-drunk. She thought it was Wednesday, but she couldn't be sure. Andrew's novel weighed like a lingering bad dream. She had been too tired not to sleep soundly, but she had nevertheless woken with a sense that she had been riding a motorbike for the past eight hours.

She had a light lunch, then took a shower. Afterwards she experienced an intense desire to cut her hair. She had always kept it long. Now she wanted it short. She had changed so much recently, and she wanted to see this different person when she looked in the mirror.

She went downstairs to get the kitchen scissors then returned to the bathroom. As she was about to take the first snip, the front doorbell sounded. She slipped into a bathrobe and headed back down the stairs. No doubt it would be the first of the villagers, who would try to comfort her by talking in a monotone and looking depressed.

When she opened the door she was pleased to see Michael.

'I'm sorry,' he said, backing away. 'I'll come back later when you're properly up and dressed.'

'That's okay,' she said. 'Come in.'

'Are you quite sure?'

'Yeah. Come in.'

Michael approached and stepped inside. 'I just wanted to call by and express my deepest sympathies; see if there's anything I can do.'

'Thank you, uh . . .'

'You can call me Michael, I don't mind.'

She smiled. 'I meant to drop by, but . . .'

'I understand.'

'Make arrangements, you know.'

'I know. We can discuss all that.'

'Do you want tea?'

'Please, Angie. Why don't you show me where everything is and I'll make it while you find some clothes.'

Angie led him into the kitchen. 'It's okay, I'll make it,' she said, switching the kettle on.

'No, you get dressed.'

Angie took two mugs from a cupboard and felt her bathrobe gape across her breasts. She set the mugs down and pulled the white towelling together. In her present company, it made her feel nicely sinful.

'I can do that. You get dressed,' Michael said.

She popped a tea bag into each mug and turned to him. 'No. I wanted to cut my hair before I got dressed.'

Michael made a face. 'Oh, Angie, don't. Your hair's beautiful.'

36

'Thank you, but it's got to go.'

'Why?'

'Sugar?'

'Pardon?'

'How many sugars?'

'None. Thank you.'

She put a spoonful in her own mug. 'I need to start afresh.'

'Pardon?'

'The hair. I suppose it's symbolic.'

'I see,' Michael said. 'Well, on your own head be it.' He immediately apologised. 'Forgive me. I shouldn't be making jokes at a time like this. Especially not bad ones.'

'Don't worry about it. I'm probably going to have a stream of people through here soon who'll look so miserable on my account I'll feel obliged to cheer *them* up.'

Still ashamed, he looked down at his feet.

She watched him for a moment, then said, 'I don't know how you do it.'

'What?'

'Your job. You christen people, you marry them, bury them. You need so many different faces and they all have to be genuine. I mean, what if you're in a bad mood when you're about to conduct a marriage ceremony? Or what if you've woken up in a good mood and you've got a day full of funerals? And how d'you cope with christening a baby when the parents themselves are only kids and you know they can't teach it anything because they don't know anything themselves?'

'And what happens when people ask me questions I can't answer?' he said with a smile.

Angie saw the irony. The kettle boiled and she brewed up.

Michael took his mug. 'It's not easy, Angie. As I say, I don't have all the answers. Only God does. Sometimes all I can do is point people towards a relevant passage in the scriptures. As for me, I'm only human; of course my emotions rollercoaster from time to time, but I try to maintain a balance by always seeing things as a cycle. Birth, death, birth, death, and so on. Like Nature. Like the seasons. That way I have to accept that nothing lasts for ever, and at the same time nothing really dies. So in sorrow I can look ahead to a time of healing and further ahead to a time of joy.'

'And then to a time of sorrow again.'

37

'Yes. The way of the world. But if we can accept that, we won't be so surprised when bad things happen. We may fear them coming, but we won't be caught off guard. Half of suffering is shock.'

Angie thought about it. Michael was right. Andrew's death had not been the blow she might have expected precisely because it had come as no great surprise.

'So you've found the secret of life then, have you, Michael?'

He laughed. 'The secret of life is the afterlife.'

'You'll have to explain that,' she said, and was amazed that this man – that anyone – could have got her into a theological discussion inside ten minutes. She realised time had not diminished her crush on him.

He began, 'Well, if we gave due thought to the afterlife, we might all live blameless lives on earth. We would know only our souls abide so, ultimately, material pleasures are of no consequence. In the same way, we'd be afraid to sin because we'd know our sins return to judge us. We'd know our bodies are simply containers for the soul during our time on earth, and in the final equation we're all drops in one big ocean, indivisible from one another. So why would we want to fight each other when we only hurt ourselves in the process?' He took a gulp of tea. 'Seen that way, the only thing that makes any sense is love.'

'So the secret of life is love,' she said.

He shrugged. 'Why not?'

She smiled. 'Nice theory.'

'I think so.'

'And what about Andrew?'

'Now? He's at peace.'

'I hope he is. There was so much anger inside him when he was alive.'

Michael nodded. 'He's with his family again.'

Angie felt her eyes well up. Everyone else was dead and happily reunited. She was alone, alive and miserable. Michael put his mug down and came over. She needed a hug but he seemed unsure of whether to make any physical contact.

'Hold me,' she said.

He made an awkward face.

'Please.'

Half-heartedly, he opened his arms and she walked into them. When they closed around her she could barely feel them. For all his talk of love, he was scared to embrace another human being.

She began to cry, her forehead against his shoulder.

She stayed like that for five minutes. Michael never made a sound the whole time; not a single soothing tone. Twice her lower stomach had accidentally brushed his groin and she had felt he was hard. To think she could lead him into temptation made her feel achingly erotic. Inside her, grieving and lust had combined into something wickedly potent. Her heart banged beneath her breasts which were pressed against his torso.

Slowly she lifted her head off his shoulder and looked at him. She felt a moment pass between them, the kind of sexual frisson she had thought could only happen in the movies. He stepped away from her and stared at her. His features were impassive, but in his eyes was a glint she would not have normally attributed to a man of God. Then his gaze dropped from her face, but not to the floor. She glanced down and saw her bathrobe was gaping. She was exposed to the waist. When she looked back at him, he could not take his eyes off her breasts. He was in awe, or in shock. Her body, the simple container for her soul, had awoken and enflamed his earthly passions. He was like a small boy who had mistakenly stumbled into the teenage girls' locker room at shower time.

She raised her hands tentatively to the towelling belt cinched around her waist. All the time she was expecting Michael to scream for her to stop her evil seduction and run from the house. But as she loosened the knot she heard only an expectant change in his breathing. Then the sash unravelled and the robe parted all the way to her knees.

Michael's visible reaction was confined to minute facial changes, but with ultimate sexual relish, Angie spotted them. His eyes flared and blinked. He swallowed. His lips parted. The tip of his tongue pushed between them.

She sensed she would have to take the lead, keep it moving along; prevent a second's doubt from entering his head and replacing the deadly sin which was presently guiding his eyes from her pubic hair to her breasts and back again. She approached, and his Latin features broke into the slightest of smiles; more appreciative than lustful. Silent gratitude for the gift of her naked body. Gently she pressed her lips against his, but received nothing back. So she kissed him harder and flicked her tongue between his lips. This time he pouted

39

in response and returned the kiss. His hands slipped inside her robe, round her waist, and stroked up the curve of her spine. She shrugged the bathrobe onto the floor. Michael brought his hands to the front and reverently touched her breasts. After a few seconds she took his right hand and placed it between her legs, holding it there until his fingers began to move.

TWELVE

The red folder contained the power to stop his future turning black. But as Tom shot along the District Line through the dark tunnels towards Rotherhithe, his future flashed on and off, on and off, like a faulty bulb in his head.

He held Kellett's manuscript on his lap, gripping it preciously like a billion pound bearer bond.

When the train pulled into Temple Station, the seat opposite him became vacant. Moving through the dark again, he stared across at his reflection in the window. The double glass distorted his face, made him a stranger to himself. Which he was. The course of his life had veered and he had become a different person.

At Whitechapel he changed to the East London Line and travelled south three stops to Rotherhithe. From there, a five minute walk saw him to Carol's apartment building. He buzzed up.

'Yes?' she said coldly through the intercom.

'It's me,' he said, ashamed to say his own name.

She didn't reply, just buzzed down to let him in.

The apartment door was ajar. He went in. Carol was standing at the open balcony window. She was nothing more than a silhouette against the sun.

She approached and held out a hand. 'Manuscript,' she ordered.

He tapped the folder, debating.

'Manuscript or forget it,' she said.

'Later. When we've talked.'

'Now, or we won't talk.'

He gave in and surrendered the folder. She opened it to check he hadn't given her a stack of blank sheets, then she took it across the lounge to her office.

Tom sat on the settee and lit a cigarette.

She returned a minute later and sat in an armchair opposite him. 'Put it out,' she said.

'Pardon?'

'The cigarette. Kill yourself, not me.'

Tom drew a defiant lungful, savoured it, then blew a grey stream towards her. 'Ashtray?'

Carol was indignant. 'I don't smoke. Peter doesn't smoke. What would I want with a fucking ashtray?'

'Okay.' He took another drag then stubbed the butt in the soil of a Yucca plant beside him on a small table.

Carol seethed. 'All right, clever dick. It's illegal and immoral.'

'Smoking?'

'What you intend to do with Kellett's work. How do you get around that?'

Tom smiled. 'I see. Council for the prosecution has opened its case-in-chief.'

'Answer me. If you can.'

'I don't have to,' he said. 'The argument isn't a fair one.'

'Oh, and I suppose blackmail is.'

'Carol, if my proposal were legal and moral, there'd be nothing to discuss. We'd just get on with it.'

Carol was shaking her head. 'Don't say "we", Tom. It's you. You're the slimy shit in all of this. I don't want anything to do with it.'

'All right. Continue. Next question.' He began to absently retrieve a cigarette from his pack.

'*Oi* . . .'

He puzzled, then noticed the offending item in his hand. He put it away.

'Right,' Carol said, 'what if the identical manuscript is sitting on the desks of a dozen other agents in this town?'

'It isn't.'

'You hope.'

'I *know*. You told me it isn't.'

Carol hesitated. 'When?'

'Last time I was here, you said Kellett was so sure of his talent he'd only sent it to one agent: you.'

'I don't remember saying that.'

'Then go and get his letter. Remind yourself.'

Carol leaned forward meaningfully. 'You can't know his family haven't read it.'

42

'No, but I'm willing to wait a few weeks and see if anyone makes contact with you.'

'And what will it prove if no one does?'

'That no one's read it.'

Carol gave a scornful laugh. 'That's a huge assumption.'

'Not really. If he's included someone to the extent of allowing them to read it, he'll surely have told them his next move, *vis-à-vis* agents. Stands to reason.'

'Excuse me, Tom, but nothing you're saying stands to reason. Grief has a habit of putting things into perspective. The people close to him will not be thinking about getting a stupid novel published; not for a long, long time.'

'So we'll beat them to it, and if his wife or whoever does pick it off a bookshelf a year hence, she might not even twig that its familiar. And so what if she does? It's in my style, it's got my name on it; who's more likely to have written it? A complete unknown, or me, a previous bestselling author?'

'It's still too risky,' she said. 'They could sue.'

'Great. Think of the publicity. A bestselling author accused of plagiarism. Sales would go through the roof.'

'And if we lost?'

'How? Their star witness is dead. And what else have they got? Some computer discs with the story on it? A second manuscript? How could they prove he didn't copy it from me? Carol . . . Kellett's dead. He can't write another novel, so no one can ever prove he had what it took to write the first.'

'Okay . . . okay. You're right. Once we're published, we're safe. But what if someone contacts me after the publishers have seen the novel but before it's out in the shops?' She seemed suddenly close to giggling with the insanity of it all. 'How would you explain someone being able to plagiarise your work when your work isn't available to read yet?'

Tom struggled for a quick response. Beneath his jacket, his shirt was wringing wet.

'Tom, as long as there's another manuscript out there somewhere, or a set of discs, and someone reads it and decides to do something with it before we're published . . . we're fucked. So make me feel better. Reassure me. Tell me why it won't happen.'

He was stumped. There was only one way to make certain, and he was hardly going to—

But why not? It was a dire option, but his life was in dire straits already. He couldn't make it any worse.

'Can I see the letter that came with the manuscript?' he asked.

'Why?'

'Don't know. Curiosity.'

'What's the point?'

'No point. I'd just like to see it. Where's the harm in that?'

She debated, but got up and retrieved the letter from her office.

'There,' she said, handing it to him. 'Read, it, then leave.' She stood over him.

But Tom only feigned reading the letter. Instead, he stared at the top right-hand corner of the page, making certain both the address and telephone number were firmly committed to memory.

'Okay, give me twenty-four hours,' he said, handing it back.

'Pardon?'

Tom got to his feet. 'By this time tomorrow I'll have it all sorted out.'

'Oh, for God's sake, give up. Stop clutching at straws.' She moved to the door and opened it for him. 'You had your chance.'

Tom resumed his seat. Very deliberately he checked his wristwatch. 'I wonder,' he said innocently, 'what time does Pete normally get in from work?'

He watched Carol stiffen at the implied threat, her features pinched with fury.

Staring daggers, she said, 'Oh, *brother*, are you going to pay for this.'

THIRTEEN

━━━◆━━━

They lay naked next to each other on top of the duvet in her stifling bedroom. The window was open but the net curtains were motionless in the still air. His shyness had long since passed.

'How do you feel, Michael?'

He turned his head on the pillow to face her. 'Wonderful. Maybe a bit bad.'

'Am I bad?' she asked.

'No. It was me. I could have walked away. But seeing you like that, I didn't want to.'

'You were very good,' she said, then giggled. 'Even if you were a bit bad.'

Michael flushed. 'You're being kind.'

'I'm not. You were very gentle, very giving.'

'I think . . . I think I was perhaps too quick. Was I?'

Angie smiled. 'Only the first time.'

He stroked her cheek. 'You're so beautiful, Angie. You're an angel. All my years in the Church and nothing's made me feel closer to heaven than these past few hours with you.'

'Blasphemy,' she teased, throwing a leg across him to rub it gently against his groin. 'Was this your first time?'

He didn't answer.

'Was it?'

'No,' he whispered.

'When was the first time?'

'Angie . . .'

'Come on.'

He sighed and closed his eyes as he spoke. 'I was eighteen. I hardly knew the girl.'

Angie ran her fingers through the hairs on his chest. 'How did it happen?'

'It . . . just happened. I wanted to know what it was like. So I could rationalise any feelings of temptation in the future.'

'So you screwed someone to cure the itch before it needed scratching.'

'Oh, *Angie*.'

'Didn't work, did it?' she joshed.

He smiled. 'Apparently not.'

'And what about a loving relationship? The Church allows you to marry.'

'Yes, but you have to meet someone first.'

'I see.' She gently rolled on top of him, kneeling with her legs straddled across his chest. She leaned down and kissed him.

Out of the blue, he asked, 'What happens now?'

'Well, I think you'd better shower. You can't go around smelling of sex.'

'Us. What happens to us? I have feelings for you. I think this has set something free inside me. Something I've felt for you for a long time, but wouldn't acknowledge.'

She looked down between her breasts at his face, full of childish bewilderment. 'Michael . . . sex can cause some very heightened emotions. Lust can seem like love.'

'You think it's just lust?'

'I don't know.'

'Well, how do you feel? About me?'

'Right now, I'm not sure.'

'Do you feel *anything*?'

'I do feel strongly, yes. Then again, I know I'm vulnerable at the moment with everything that's happened.'

Instantly, Michael looked deeply ashamed. 'Can I get up?'

She got off him. He sat upright and swung his legs off the bed. He grabbed a pillow and placed it across his lap.

'I suddenly feel very bad,' he said.

She knelt behind him on the bed, but didn't touch him. 'Why?'

'I came to offer help, to ease your suffering if I could. And all I've done is betray your trust, then ask you to ease my own suffering which I've brought upon myself.'

Angie didn't know what to say. She was a party to his biggest life-crisis, and the answers, the forgiveness, were out of her domain.

'And I've betrayed my vocation. There's no excuse. If I lacked the strength to fight temptation, I should have asked for God's help. But I didn't. What's worse, I didn't want to.'

'It's okay,' Angie said quietly, without conviction. 'You're only human.'

'Angie, I gave in to lust. It's a sin for anyone. But for me it's . . .' He hung his head, and clawed his fingers into his protective pillow. 'Would you mind getting my clothes from the kitchen for me?'

At the front door, Michael kept his gaze downturned to the carpet. Angie watched him, this familiar figure from the village, now intimately familiar. It hardly seemed real their afternoon together. He shuffled about, clearing his throat, visibly soul-searching for answers he had never thought he would need; at least not for himself.

'About Andrew,' he said, releasing the latch. 'Mr Stapely asked if it's convenient for you to view the body tomorrow, after two o'clock.'

She watched him struggle with his vocational duties, and wanted to reach out to him. Never was a man more in need of a reassuring hug. But neither was a man more likely to run away if she so much as poked a finger to touch him. So she kept her arms folded across her chest. 'I'll be there,' she said.

He let himself out through the porch, then hovered on the doorstep but had nothing more to offer.

'Michael . . .' she said.

'Yes?'

'It's not so bad, you know.'

'Maybe.' He smiled but it seemed to pain him. He looked close to tears. Then he walked away.

FOURTEEN

———————◆———————

After Tom had skulked off, Carol found it difficult to rationalise her feelings. A quiet part of her had actually wanted him to clear all the hurdles she had set up for him. In truth, she wanted another bestseller as badly as he did, and when Andrew Kellett's manuscript had arrived by Registered Delivery, it had seemed she was destined to have it.

The news of his death, therefore, had sent the whole thing up in flames.

Until Tom, in his vile and crass way, had rescued it from the fire.

Unfortunately, this afternoon, he had failed to convince, and she could not imagine how the extra day he had demanded would make a difference.

No, she was going to lose Kellett's novel, she could feel it. Her only course of action was to contact his family, let them know she had his work, and ask their advice. But she still thought, as a final testament to his life, they would consider it too lurid, and quite unfit for publication.

With her mind in a fog she wandered into the kitchen. From the freezer she took a microwaveable chicken dinner and a packet of oven chips and put them on the side for later.

Shortly after seven o'clock, Peter arrived home. Another hectic day trading commodities in the City brought him through the front door in his usual state. His dark, slicked-back hair had worked loose and was dangling at the temples. With his garish braces and expensive suit he was Michael Douglas in *Wall Street*, but without the kudos. Forty-two and not likely to reach retirement. Too many heavy meals on the expense account, too stressed out and no time to relax, too much suppressed anger at too little reward. An Armani-clad heart attack waiting to happen.

'All right, love?' he said wearily. 'Good day? I had a stinker.'

She got up and checked on the chips. Nearly done. Inside the humming microwave, the salsa chicken was revolving through its final minute. She stepped through into the living room.

'Bastards,' he said, dropped his briefcase beside the settee, and sat down heavily. 'Jesus.'

It was the usual routine. She didn't know who the bastards were on this particular day. Buyers, fellow traders, London Underground, the government, the rest of the rat-race. She wouldn't ask and he wouldn't explain; not until they were opposite each other at the kitchen table. Then they would look at each other for the first time that evening, and she would obligingly ask the questions he wanted to answer. She would set him up to spill his hard-done-by guts.

Now, though, she had to fix him a drink. It was never the other way around. He would loosen his tie, kick off his shoes, switch on the television, enquire about dinner. And she would comply, playing the role of the stay-at-home housewife, because, in his eyes, her job was nothing more than a glorified hobby.

She poured a large Teachers and handed it to him. He grunted his thanks and took a swallow. Then he loosened his tie, kicked his shoes off underneath the coffee table, retrieved the TV remote from between the settee cushions, and switched on for the night. A holiday show lit up the screen. 'What are we eating?' he asked without interest, staring at a young female presenter in a bikini, swanning smugly through Fijian surf.

'Chicken and chips.'

She saw him nod, unmoved by news of the menu, and she returned to the kitchen.

Ten minutes later she called Peter through. His meal was on the table. He sat down with a replenished glass of whisky and immediately began to eat. Carol brought her own plate to the table. As ever, she was mildly and pointlessly miffed that he could not have waited thirty seconds for her to join him. But it summed up their marriage. They never quite got it together. It was a soulless communion they enjoyed, if enjoyed was the right word. Granted, even at the start it had never threatened to set the world alight, but she had been shocked by how quickly the flames had died. If she was honest, it was a sham. It still smouldered occasionally, but not with any conviction. It was like a small mound of burnt out garden refuse, that only smoked now from the cold drizzle falling on it.

As they ate, she could see Peter's eyes flick up to watch her between mouthfuls. She should have started by now to gently coax him into revealing the exact nature of his grumbles that day. This evening, however, she couldn't have cared less. In fact, she hadn't done for years. She might have, had he bothered to even cursorily reciprocate, but he hadn't.

All of this she might never have noticed had Tom not used his blackmail against her. His threats had forced her to think how to protect her precious alliance with that special man in her life. And it had brought to her notice that neither 'precious' nor 'special' were applicable adjectives in either case.

Now, as she listened to her husband chew on some meat, she felt their lack of connection like never before. She had always wondered whether she loved him, but in those few seconds, hearing his teeth work on their prey, she understood she had not been addressing the real problem. She didn't love him; that was suddenly very easy to admit. It wasn't a question of love, it was a question of hate: how much did she hate him?

Oddly, she wanted to smile. It was amazing how the most insignificant moment could carry such transformational power; just hearing him gnash on his food. It had sickened her. Not the sound; the sound was innocuous. It was that she had chosen to hear it, above her own chewing, above the ticking of the wall clock, above the television in the next room.

Peter's eyes bore into her; she wasn't playing the game. She could feel his annoyance, his impatience. It wafted across the table like a cheap cologne, pleading for attention it didn't deserve.

They finished their meals in an awkward silence. She cleared the plates.

'Do you want dessert?' she asked.

'What is there?'

She loaded the plates noisily into the dishwasher. 'Nothing.'

'Oh.'

She returned to the table and collected his empty whisky tumbler. He grunted, expecting a refill. Carol took the glass, placed it upside down in the dishwasher, and slammed the door on it.

'Ca—' he stuttered, then fell quiet.

She ignored him and left the kitchen. In the living room, she picked up the remote and switched the television off. She smiled at her further break with habit: the television always stayed on until after midnight. Then she went through to their bedroom, into their en suite bathroom and locked herself in. She turned on the shower, but did not undress and step inside yet. She sat on the loo seat, thinking her new thoughts.

Tom Roker, worm though he was, had unwittingly done her an immense favour. He had shaken up her world, woken her from the bland slumber of her marriage.

She wanted Andrew Kellett's novel. For herself. For her own reasons. Fuck Tom. Fuck Peter. Carol Morgan would have another bestseller, and no ten per cent this time. Fifty. She might even try for more, because she was the one holding all the cards. She had Kellett's manuscript, and if she no longer cared about her marriage, then Tom's blackmail no longer held any threat.

As for Peter, one evening, sometime soon, she would really break with tradition. She would be gone when he got home. She would be jetting Stateside, riding high and travelling far on the back of her latest blockbuster novel. She would see its US publication, then cash in on the movie interest, making new contacts so she could sever her redundant ties in Britain. Tom would no doubt trot along behind for a while, but only for a while. Just until he tried to legitimately write another bestseller by his own hand, at which point, eight years of history would repeat itself and he would fade away again. What a strange career, people would comment. Ah well, she would reply, *c'est la vie*.

The only problem was the one she had thrust in front of Tom that afternoon. How to be sure a second manuscript wouldn't surface before they were published. There had to be a way. She had to find a way. She wanted the new life she had envisioned for herself. She undressed with lazy, preoccupied moves, and left her clothes in a pile on the floor. She reached into the cubicle and turned the tap round to the blue marking; it had been a hot day.

With a cool head she stepped into a cool shower, and really began to think.

FIFTEEN

Tom Roker passed slowly by the twee, detached cottage. A little further down the road he pulled his silver BMW onto the grass verge and switched off the ignition. He twisted round in his seat and looked over his right shoulder at the home of Andrew Kellett, deceased.

Magenta ivy grew wildly across the dark grey stonework, cut back at the windows. His eyes searched for an alarm box among the leaves, but he couldn't see one. A timber porch surrounded the front door. The roof was slated in large, light grey tiles. To the left of the building was a copse of horse chestnuts, with several trees in the back garden which towered above the roof. To the right was the entrance to a field, a tubular metal gate giving straight onto the road. Tom assumed the land behind the cottage belonged to a farmer. For a few feet into the field he could see deep troughs moulded into the sun-baked earth: tractor tyres from the wetter months. The front garden was nothing more than a few sods of turf surrounded by an undug, weed-filled border, separated from the road by a low stone wall. There was no driveway, only a path down the wooded side of the cottage. A red Mini Cooper was parked on the verge. Tom wondered whether it belonged to Kellett's wife.

As for the location, it was more isolated than he had dared to hope. It was a hundred yards to the next cottage, then the same distance to the first of the red-brick houses that wound down the road into the village itself.

Now he just had to wait, and not lose his bottle through the remaining two hours of daylight. He calculated he could begin to make his move some time after ten p.m.

He took a final mental picture, then turned back to the steering wheel and keyed the ignition. The engine spluttered several times before complying with an unhealthy roar. He couldn't blame the car. It had gone two years without a service. Money had been extremely tight. With the initial advance from *Hidden Blade* he had bought the house in Fulham and the BMW. The royalties paid every six months thereafter had dwindled as badly as his talent. The dole had entered his life, and his wife and daughter had walked out of it. Occasionally he supplemented his income with a magazine article under a pen name, but he never amassed enough to justify servicing the BMW. Besides, it pained him that he still owned the same bloody car after eight years. His intention had been to update annually. Then again, another intention had been to write a second decent novel.

He gunned the engine, shifted into first and headed up the road, leaving Kellett's home and the village behind him.

He drove two miles until he found a lay-by off a quiet A-road. He pulled over, parked, and turned the radio on low. The countdown had begun. He reclined his seat and settled back to wait until darkness fell.

U2 were complaining that they still hadn't found what they were looking for.

Tom opened his eyes again and checked the car's digital clock. This time it announced 9:59. He yanked the lever by his right leg and the seatback urged him to sit up straight.

He reached for the dial to silence Bono, and realised he felt horribly sluggish. Fear of the forthcoming deed had acted like a subtle drain on his nervous system, sapping his energy. He leaned down to the holdall in the passenger footwell and lifted it onto his knees. He was about to unzip it and check the tools when he became aware that something was very wrong outside the car. He looked up at the sky, and the full face of the moon beamed back, mocking him for his lack of preparation. He had not considered what phase it might be in.

Great. As if seventeen hours of sunshine wasn't enough, God had decided to pop a few tokens and pull down the canopy of a celestial tanning machine, bathing blue light on a land that should have gone dark.

He sat with his jaw clenched, contemplating. There was not even a chance of intermittent cloud cover; it had been clear all day.

It was just the sort of excuse he needed to abandon everything.

But if he drove back to London now, what would happen when the nights *were* dark, and he was lying awake at three a.m., without a family, without a career, and with only blackness in his head?

He had no choice. Do or die.

He opened the holdall and dipped a hand inside. He touched the screwdriver, the chisel, the hammer, the crowbar, the torch. Going Equipped. He pulled out his knit cap and put it on, then dropped the bag back into the passenger footwell.

Repeating Kellett's number in his head, he got out of the car and jogged towards the phone box at the end of the lay-by.

On the TV, News at Ten was presenting its usual array of tragic tales. Angie listened, but thoughts of Michael were never far from her mind. He had walked out earlier with shame hanging over him like a storm cloud. She had used him for comfort, and now he was the one feeling guilty. There could be no hope for their relationship. She could not compete against God.

Next to her on the table, the telephone began to ring. She quietened Trevor McDonald and picked up the receiver.

'Hello.'

'Er, hi, uh . . . is that Mrs Kellett?' said the man's voice.

'Why, who's this?'

'Are you Andrew Kellett's wife?'

'Who is this?'

Silence.

'Who is this?'

'I saw him die.'

Angie tapped the mouthpiece against her chin, a moment away from hanging up. She had seen Andrew's wrecked corpse. She had been told by the police how it came to be that way. Even if the caller were genuine, how would she benefit from hearing it all over again?

'Hello?' said the man, uncertainly.

'What do you want?'

'I know who killed him.'

Angie pressed the receiver hard against her ear. 'Go on.'

'A group of bikers ran him off the road.'

'What?'

'Yeah. Four of them.'

'The police said there was only one other person involved.'

54

'Did they?'

'Yes.'

'Well, they weren't there, I was.'

'And have you told the police?'

'No. I was involved. Racing with them. I've already got points on my licence. I'd be banned.'

'Then tell me and I'll tell the police.'

'I can't.'

Angie's temper flared. 'Listen, whoever you are, if you've got nothing to say, put the phone down.'

'I took some pictures,' the man said quickly. 'I followed the gang to their campsite and photographed the bikes. I got the registrations.'

'And why the sudden concern?'

'Don't know. Conscience. Listen, if you're not interested—'

'No . . . I am.' Typical. Her brother was even proving to be a pain in the arse now he was dead. 'Where are you?'

'A pub on the A535, the other side of Holmes Chapel. The Rising Sun. Do you know it?'

'I'll find it. How will I recognise you?'

'I've got a crash helmet. I'll be at the bar.'

'Right.'

'Can I say . . . ?'

'What?'

'Sorry about your husband.'

'He was my brother.'

'Oh. Well, if there's family with you, pass on my condolences.'

'There's not. He didn't have anyone else. Give me half an hour.' She put the phone down and looked at the video clock. She would get to the pub at about ten-forty-five. She switched the news off remotely, just catching a glimpse of another motorway pile-up.

As she hunted for her car keys in the kitchen, she almost cracked up. Instead, she laughed; a confused, tormented sound.

'This is it, Andrew,' she said as she searched. 'I'll do this one last thing for you, and then I want a life.' She discovered her keys under the daily paper. 'And I want you to rest in peace.'

Ten minutes for her to leave the house. Twenty minutes to reach the pub. Five to park and check inside. Twenty to get back. No.

Better make that fifteen. Once she knew she had been tricked she would drive hell for leather on the return journey.

So he had roughly fifty minutes to play with.

Tom climbed back in the car and checked his watch. Ten-seventeen p.m. To be on the safe side, he decided he should be out and long gone by eleven o'clock.

He turned the key and the engine coughed and stalled.

'Come on, don't piss about.'

He tried again, with the same result.

'I bloody hate this car. *Come on.*'

He turned the key and stamped furiously on the pedal as the engine wheezed pathetically.

'Come on, you vindictive bastard, *start*!'

From under the bonnet, a very poorly engine signalled its reluctance to obey. Tom continued for a minute to no avail. He knew nothing about automotive engineering, except that there was a thing called flooding the engine, and he had probably just done it. He stopped trying.

'Shit shit shit! *Shit!*'

He pulled the sleeve of his black sweatshirt back at the cuff. Ten-nineteen p.m.

'All right, all right,' he said with forced calm. 'I'm about two miles away, and it's . . .' He got out of the car and calculated the direction as the crow flies from his present spot to Kellett's house. He stared over the hedgerow and across the moon-lit fields.

'Over there. Where those trees are.'

Actually, he wasn't at all sure he had managed to pinpoint the wood beside Kellett's house, but that was the spot he would head for. If he debated for too long, there would be no point in setting off at all.

He ducked his head into the car, grabbed the holdall, then stopped. The tools would clatter as he ran, making him visible *and* audible. He might as well insert a police tracking device up his backside. He stuck his hand in and pulled out the crowbar and his Mini Maglite. He pushed the bag into the shadow of the footwell, picked up his driving gloves from the dash, put them on and locked the door. Before setting off, he tucked the torch and his keys safely into his front pockets.

When the road was clear, and traffic sounds had fallen dormant in the air, he ran along the lay-by. Behind the phone box he found a hole in the hedge. He got on his hands and knees and crawled through. A twig hooked his hat and pulled it off. In the field he reached back and retrieved it.

Then he froze as a distant noise, like a momentary crack of thunder, split the night. Somewhere over the fields, sheep began to bleat. Tom ran down a check-list of possibilities and decided it was an automatic bird-scarer.

He focused himself and set off at a sprint across the field, maintaining a paranoid crouch. If he didn't stumble upon the cottage by ten-thirty-five he would have to abort. He ran through the shin-high grass, arms pumping, crowbar held like a baton in a race against the clock.

Two things he would have to do when he got back to London: service the BMW and join a gym. His heart raged and his breath heaved hoarsely as he stood bent double at the drystone wall that bordered Kellett's back garden. His forehead was hot and itchy under his knit cap, his hair damp. He wiped his face. Fingers of moonlight dabbed at him through the foliage of the horse chestnuts, which were already clustered with baby conkers. He moved his wrist into the light. Ten-thirty-two.

He had found the place with gratifying ease. He had moved in a straight line diagonally across several fields to arrive at the precise location. Pure SAS. Apart from the occasional bleating sheep, the night had been silent.

Looking down to the road, he could see that the Mini was gone. In the cottage, an upstairs light was on: a naive precaution against burglars.

He scrambled over the wall, clanging the crowbar as he went, and scurried across the lawn, keeping low. The back door was glass-paned and led directly into the kitchen. On a fitment he could see a microwave, its green clock digits glowing in the dark, reminding him to get a move on if he wanted another bestseller. He tried the door handle, just in case, but it was locked. Peering through, he could not see a key in the hole so there was no point in breaking the glass. He inserted the sharp, curved end of the crowbar between door and frame just above the lock. The wood creaked. He jemmied for a few seconds, easing the tip of the crowbar further in.

He swore under his breath. Time was short. The softly-softly approach could take for ever, and if the door had concealed bolts top and bottom it might never work. He stopped what he was doing and stood back. He decided he could probably get away with one conspicuous noise.

He lifted his right foot and placed the sole of his trainer against the door. It had to be an accurate kick or he would go through the glass. He lowered his leg and stood back on it slowly, like a rugby player lining up for a conversion.

One chance only. One firm kick. He couldn't worry about hurting himself. Anything less than a committed strike might not do it, and he couldn't risk having to try again.

Before he had time to reconsider he sent the flat of his foot hard against the wood. There was a splintery snap as the lock was smashed from the frame inside, and the door flew open. One pane of cracked glass fell out and tinkled on the tile floor.

Tom froze for the second time that evening, straining his ears for the unbolting of a back door by an inquisitive neighbour somewhere down the road. Thirty seconds later he had heard nothing, so he stepped inside, avoiding the broken glass, and twisted the end of his torch to send a beam through the murk. A cursory glance around the kitchen proved fruitless. He carried on down the hall. To his left, an open door led into a dining room. He darted the beam here and there and moved on. In the front living room he had to draw the curtains before searching around. The room was like an antique shop, cluttered with a hotch-potch of furniture and ornaments, but nothing of interest to him.

He turned and climbed the stairs. The landing light shone above him, failing dismally in its role as crime deterrent. The room at the rear of the house was shut. He tried the knob and found it locked. The door to the bathroom was ajar; nerves were getting the better of his bladder, but he was on too tight a schedule. The front bedroom curtains were already drawn. His Maglite led the way. There was a double bed with a crumpled duvet and unplumped pillows. A slim black dress hung on the wardrobe door. A compact dressing table was strewn with bottles, sprays and lotions.

Absorbing the feminine atmosphere, Tom experienced a painful longing. It caught him at odd times how much he missed his wife – ex-wife. It was the intimacy; the knowledge built up over years as secrets are divulged, one by one. Likes and dislikes, passions and pet hates. All the stuff so easily taken for granted. And the sex. The easy way of making love; knowing what, where and when.

58

He wondered if Kellett's sister was attractive. He felt he knew her by proxy. He knelt down and shone under the bed. No manuscript. He got up and checked on top of the wardrobe, then in the chest of drawers. Entranced, his eyes lingered over the neatly folded clothes. When he went to the dressing table, he knew he was not about to find a manuscript – the drawers were too small – but he opened them anyway. Tights, suspenders, bras and panties. He put his torch in his mouth to free his hands, and reverently inspected the underwear. He felt perverted, disgusted with himself, but also turned on; gripped by an intense yearning for sex with the woman who had worn each of these soft garments tight against her skin, He closed the drawers, turned his torch to the bed, and stared. Time was ticking away, but he had to know. He stepped up, yanked back the duvet and surveyed the sheet.

Kellett's sister was sexually active.

He looked at the stains for a moment longer, then quickly covered the bed and left the room.

At the locked rear bedroom he briefly considered using the crowbar, but instead launched a kick which bust the door wide open. He was really getting the hang of this.

He entered, closed the curtains and put the main light on. There were bike posters on the walls. Behind the door was a desk. On it, under dust covers, was a word processor, keyboard and printer. Beside them was a blue plastic box.

Grinning, he set the crowbar down, opened the lid and picked out the first disc. On the label was written *UNTITLED by AK – 1*, and a note of the pages contained on it. Tom picked out the last disc in the box and checked the final page number. It tallied with the printed manuscript in Carol's possession.

'Gotcha,' he said, replaced both discs and shut the box, but he wasn't finished. Kellett might have been fatally reckless in his hobby, but if he was a typical writer, he would have been paranoid about the safety of his work. If so, there would be a set of copy discs and a second manuscript.

He checked the desk drawers. As he pushed the bottom one to, a corner of something caught his eye. He tugged the drawer out again, moved some paper and stared at the sender's half of a Registered Delivery coupon. From Andrew Kellett to Carol Morgan. Stamped and dated.

Tom could not believe how close he had come to missing it.

He put it in with the discs and checked the time. Ten-forty-one.

On the bookcase at eye level was a spare crash helmet and a row of paperbacks. The lower shelves were filled with hardback novels and reference books. On the floor beneath the case, a pile of motorcycle magazines spilled onto the carpet. In among them Tom noticed a black folder. He knelt down and slid it out from between the glossies. His heart hammered as he released the elasticated ties, opened it, and found Kellett's personal manuscript. He sealed it and put it on the desk, then turned his attention to the chest of drawers. In the good old burgling tradition he proceeded to ransack the contents, but there were no hidden discs.

He squatted down at the bed and lifted the duvet from the floor. Underneath was a pair of old trainers and a sports rucksack. He brought the rucksack out. He could smell the dirty washing inside even before he tipped it onto the carpet. But the bulky side pockets were a sweeter proposition. He unclipped them . . . and there they were.

UNTITLED by AK, copies 1 through 13. Seven in one pocket, six in the other.

Time check: ten-forty-four. Status: all compromising information gathered and secured and ready for incineration at the earliest possible opportunity.

He scrambled to his feet, went to the desk and chucked the blue boxful of discs, the copies and the second manuscript into the rucksack. He tightened the drawstring, clipped the flap, and slung it over his right shoulder.

Looking up from the desk he came face to face with Andrew Kellett. At least, Tom assumed it was Andrew Kellett, beaming happily from a photograph on the wall. With Kellett was a young woman and a little girl. Tom didn't know the story and didn't trouble his mind to work it out.

'Sorry, pal,' he said to the smiling young man. 'But you don't need this stuff any more. I do.'

He picked up his crowbar and torch and left the room but stopped abruptly at the top of the stairs. Warm sweat trickled down his suddenly fraught face, and he felt his brain cooking inside his hat; if this was meant to look like a regular break-in, why had only one room been turned over? But the alternative was to needlessly trash the rest of the house, and he reckoned Kellett's sister had suffered enough.

He slipped his left arm through the other strap, tightened both around his shoulders and hurried down the stairs.

Treading over the smashed glass at the back door, Tom sensed a presence outside. In mid-stride his left foot hovered in the air, and he balanced on one leg for several seconds, listening. But he hadn't heard anything. His fear was irrational; for a fleeting moment he had simply felt stalked.

He strained his ears, and peered into the garden. The dense foliage allowed only a few blueish puddles to dot the overgrown lawn, offering scant comfort to a man afraid of the dark.

He shone his torch from tree to tree, then backtracked across the kitchen and reached for the light switch. The overhead fluorescent tube flickered and brightened. He slipped the torch into his pocket.

At the door again, he unconsciously whiteknuckled the crowbar. Artificial light spilled into the garden through the doorway and the kitchen window. Adrenalin pumped in his veins and made him shake. Still he neither saw nor heard anything to make him wary, and still he feared to venture out.

He trotted through the kitchen once more, down the hall to the front door, but it was locked from the outside, and no doubt the same would apply to the porch.

No choice. It was out through the back or wait around for Kellett's sister and the local constabulary.

He crept nervously towards the threshold, and put one foot out onto the paving stone. His head swung left and right, eyes scrutinising every tree trunk broad enough to shield a human body.

He stood there for a full minute, but all was quiet. He decided he was alone. Only then did he notice his iron grip on the crowbar. He relaxed and let a smile soften his face, and became aware how cool the air was against his fiercely hot skin. Taking off his hat and gloves was sheer bliss. He tucked them into his back pockets and ruffled the wet hair plastered to his forehead, then began walking briskly towards the rear wall.

'Stay where you are and don't move a muscle.'

The man's voice came from behind him, calm and well spoken. Tom stopped and the voice continued.

'I have a gun trained on your back. Drop the jemmy.'

61

Tom opened his palm and let the crowbar fall to the grass.

'Now turn around very slowly. *Very* slowly.'

Tom shuffled round on his feet. The man was standing beside the tree closest to the back door. He was a tall, thin-faced country gent. Flat cap, light check shirt under a shooting jerkin, dark trousers and hiking boots. Carrying an over-and-under shotgun.

The man said, 'Some dog's been killing my sheep. Half an hour ago I finally caught up with the damned thing and shot it. I was just checking on livestock when I heard you.'

Tom realised it was too dangerous to run for it. Maybe Mr Farmer was secretly itching to kill something bigger than a dog, with fewer legs. The black holes pointing at his chest gave him more pause for thought, because if the farmer did let rip, a lot would depend on what exactly issued from those black holes. Tom knew from firearms research that if the gun was loaded with buckshot rather than slugs, one blast would pepper an area roughly six feet square over a distance of just ten to fifteen yards. With that coverage, even Mister Magoo could chuck the odd ballbearing his way.

'Right, chum,' the farmer continued, 'you and I are going into the house to call the police. So . . . very slowly.'

With reluctant steps, Tom started to walk. The farmer retreated a couple of paces from the door as he approached.

Tom's bright future was fast suffering a terminal eclipse.

'It's not what you think,' he said stupidly, stopping to plead with the farmer.

'It's not what I think that matters, chum. It's what the police will think. And then the courts. Now inside.'

Tom entered the kitchen and stood on the broken glass, cracking it underfoot. The farmer kept his distance. Tom realised that if they reached the telephone, he was screwed.

As his panic grew, an idea struck him. He instinctively seized on it, using the first name that came to mind, and pitched a whisper into the hallway.

'*Milton!*' Hushed enough to sound covert, loud enough to be overheard.

'Stop,' said the farmer.

Tom did as he was told.

'Who else is here?' the farmer asked anxiously.

'No one.'

Tom heard steps behind. He could sense the farmer peering past him. He could also feel the presence of the dual muzzles an inch from his spine, but at least he had succeeded in drawing the man closer to him.

'Hmm,' went the farmer. 'Well, if someone is with you, don't think I haven't got a barrel for the both of you. I did reload after shooting the mutt. Now, carefully, inside.'

Tom moved forward. Glass shards on his soles scratched at the tile floor. The fingers of his left hand brushed the edge of the open door, beneath the broken lock.

Then he heard it: a hiking boot crunching glass.

Simultaneously, Tom dodged from the line of fire and slammed the door behind him. It struck its target with brutal force. As glass shattered and fell, the farmer began to scream. Tom cowered against the sink in the narrow kitchen and peeked outside at the damage.

The farmer had staggered backwards a couple of paces. His face was badly gashed, his flat cap knocked comically sideways. His eyes were squeezed tight shut against a dark stream pouring from a vertical wound in his forehead. Cuts to his chin and neck leaked blood down his shirt. His features were creased in shock. The barrels of the shotgun poked menacingly through a holed pane.

The next moment, the farmer lurched forward blindly in search of his assailant. The steel screeched thinly as it slid over the jagged glass and protruded further into the kitchen.

Then one of the barrels exploded. A wad of buckshot tore past Tom's face and embedded itself in the wall and ceiling above the kitchen door. A shower of plaster crumbled noisily onto the floor tiles.

Tom kicked wildly at the door and sent it crashing into the farmer again. The farmer howled and reeled into the garden. He dropped his gun, spun around, headbutting a tree trunk, and sank to his knees. For one eternal second, Tom stared through the back door at the shotgun on the grass. The disorientated farmer was already fumbling towards it, moaning, hampered by his bloody veil. Tom fleetingly wondered if the man truly had been blinded, but this was no time for sympathy. He pulled open the back door and leapt into the garden just as the farmer happened on his gun and stood up with it. But, luckily for Tom, his hapless opponent was facing the wrong way, and by the time he could react to the coming attack, Tom was already upon him. He shoved him in the back and sent him stumbling headlong into the tree.

What happened next was one of life's ghastly flukes.

The farmer hit the trunk and, with a deafening blast, his head exploded.

Tom watched in horror as the headless man slid down the trunk, slumped onto his haunches and toppled over onto his back, shotgun still resting on his chest, barrels pointing up to where his chin had been. Slowly, two lifeless hands released their grip on the gun. Pivoting at the elbows, the forearms traced graceful arcs in the air before settling palm-up on the grass.

Tom couldn't believe it. It was all a bit much for a humble writer of previously unblemished character. He stood transfixed, gormless with horror, morbidly intrigued by the gore and cranial matter drizzling from the lower branches.

After the longest moment of his life, he took to his heels and ran.

By the time Tom arrived at the lay-by hedge, the night air was undulating crazily with sirens. He had heard the first one a mere sixty seconds after fleeing the scene, and they had grown in number since. He imagined every vehicle in the county with a swirling blue light on its roof had been dispatched to the Kellett residence.

He was relatively young to suffer a heart attack, but he thought if he escaped one tonight, he could live to be a hundred. Never had he been so physically and mentally wired. So much for the sedentary lifestyle of a writer. His mouth was parched, his skin soaked. The breath in his throat was short and hot, pumped out of burning lungs. His vision was smeared with sweat. The muscles in his legs had turned to jelly and gone into spasm. His head spun as his brain suffered a massive overload, like a rookie telephonist alone at the switchboard of a hectic corporation with a thousand buzzing lines.

He sank to his knees by the hole in the hedge and fiddled with the rucksack straps to loosen them. He removed the bag from his shoulders, and the sodden material on his back felt suddenly icy. When the road was quiet, he pushed the sack through and crawled after it, emerging at the base of the telephone box. Hidden from view, he stood up and leaned against the sheet metal wall of the kiosk. He could hear the sirens converging at their destination across the fields, and cutting out one by one. He listened for approaching vehicles, heard nothing close, and scurried out. But before he could get to the BMW, a high-powered engine seemed to loom from nowhere. Tom froze for an instant, then crouched down and hustled towards his car, trying to conceal himself behind the front wheel. Peering beneath the bumper, he saw full-beam headlights sweep around the bend just up the road, accompanied by a roofload of silently revolving blue bubbles.

The police car sped past and on its way.

Tom delved into the front pocket of his jeans and clawed out his car keys. He hoped to God that the bastard thing would start this time, though he realised God had precious little reason to look kindly upon him tonight.

In his crouched position, he unlocked the driver's door and opened it, pushing the rucksack across to the passenger seat. His bag of tools lay in the driver's footwell. Seeing it, his heart nearly gave out. Where was the fucking crowbar?

'Shit.' Not only had he dropped it on Kellett's lawn, but he had left his prints all over it, having prematurely removed his gloves.

'*Shit.*' And the back door was dabbed.

Too late now. Beyond repair.

He shifted the bag into the passenger footwell and climbed in. He let his head fall against the hub of the steering wheel, and the horn sounded. He jerked upright and cursed. Belatedly, his stomach churned queasily and he felt his dinner rise. Just in time, he stuck his head out over the tarmac and vomited.

Afterwards, he wiped his mouth with a rag from the glovebox, closed the door and wound down the window for some fresh air.

'Christ, what a night. Now, please . . .' He put the key in the ignition, gave a twist and the engine stalled. In the silence that followed, a terrifying sound drifted down to him from the sky.

A distant helicopter.

His eyes searched the starry sky above the fields. After a moment he saw it. Red and white pinpricks of light moving slowly across the horizon from left to right. He estimated it to be about two and a half miles away, heading for Kellett's house. As he watched, a vertical tunnel of light shot towards the earth. He tried the engine. It almost caught. Panic twisted his guts and nearly made him throw up again. He had to get moving; the police chopper was starting off with a search radius which would include his BMW at its present location. He could not even hoof it, the thermal-imaging camera would seek him out.

'Please,' Tom begged of his car. 'Start now and I'll service you every fucking month.'

He turned the key and the engine stuttered then roared into life.

'I lied,' he said as he shifted into gear. 'Piece of crap. Soon as I get my advance you're going straight in the crusher.'

SIXTEEN

'So, just to recap, Miss Kellett . . .'

Angie heard herself utter a tiny moan. She sagged in her armchair in front of the two detectives.

'Miss Kellett . . .'

She gave a sullen look to the burly DCI then closed her eyes. The coffee mug in her lap warmed her fingertips. It seemed the only real sensation. Fatigue and caffeine had queered her mind.

'Miss Kellett . . .' urged the DCI in his depressing Mancunian accent.

Angie opened her eyes, took a swill of coffee and spoke with plain impatience. 'Detective Chief Inspector Nelson, I'm very tired. I've told you everything I know.'

The Detective Sergeant, a gangly individual called Ash, smiled sympathetically but repeated the same questions. 'You can't think of anyone your brother might have owed money to?'

'No.'

'You can't think what someone might have been searching for in his belongings?'

'No.'

'What about drugs?'

Angie wanted to snap an angry reply but didn't have the energy. 'I've already said: Prozac, yes. Smack, no.'

Nelson took the reins. 'And you didn't notice anything missing from your brother's room?'

'I really can't say.'

Ash was about to speak when he was silenced by the sound of footsteps descending the stairs. Angie turned to the doorway to face a man and a woman in white overalls, both carrying metal cases. Angie nearly laughed. All this time waiting for Andrew to go completely insane, and now she was the one suffering an invasion of whitecoats.

'All done, Karen?' asked Nelson.

'Guv.'

'Anything?'

'We'll see.'

'Keep me informed.'

'Guv.'

Angie watched as the scene-of-crime officers tramped out of her house. Then she stared at the two men settled on her living-room settee.

'It's past five o'clock,' she told them.

'Well, that'll be it for the time being,' said Nelson, finally taking the hint.

'Yes, thank you, Miss Kellett,' said Ash, standing up. 'Thanks for the coffee. We'll be in touch.'

'And if you think of anything . . .' said Nelson.

She nodded.

As she stood on the front step watching the detectives walk to their maroon Granada, Angie enjoyed the warmth of the early morning sun on her skin. It had been a long night.

Inside the porch she closed the outer door and peered through the glass at the road. The detectives were chatting over the roof of their car. Nelson had his thickset back to her. His shoulders shrugged at some comment from Ash. Then Nelson must have spoken because Ash raised his eyebrows and shook his head.

They hadn't a clue.

She watched them get in and drive away, then went in and shut the front door. She needed to sleep but her head was buzzing too much, so she sat at the foot of the stairs, put her face in her hands and let her mind wander haphazardly over the past few hours.

She had returned from her bogus rendezvous shortly after eleven p.m. It was obvious that someone had tricked her. She had hoped it was simply a sick joke, but she had feared a more sinister explanation, which had been confirmed fifty metres from her home when a police officer had waved her to a standstill and she had looked beyond the cordon to an unreal world of arc lamps, spinning blue lights, milling uniforms, white overalls and dark suits.

Unfortunately, it was worse than her worst fear. She had expected to come across the aftermath of a burglary, which she had, but nowhere in her imagined scenario had she pictured a headless corpse.

Her mind whirled and cartwheeled. When was life ever going to revert to its normal, plodding pace? How far off was that glorious day when she would be able to say, 'Shit, I'm so bored'?

And, to top it all, she had an appointment to view her brother's body that afternoon.

Carol Morgan hadn't slept a wink. Half the night she had lain awake, a valley of duvet between her and her husband, his every snore meeting with a muttered curse from her tense mouth. When the sun had thankfully dawned, she had dressed and gone up to the roof garden to sit quietly alone with her developing thoughts.

Now, approaching seven a.m., sitting in her deck chair, she had developed her thoughts as far as possible, and she had come up short. Both she and Tom had accepted that Kellett must have printed more than one copy of the manuscript, but even if no one else had read it, and even if she knew where to find it, how the hell could she get hold of it? Last night, her decision to upheave her staid existence had made hope feel like inspiration, and she had believed she would find an answer. This morning, she felt deluded; shamed and cheated by her own naivety.

Kellett's novel would never be hers. It was a hard fact – the hardest – for it consigned her to more of the same in a life she despised. Of course, she could always take that blind leap with Tom – he was desperate enough to be fool enough – but she was afraid to. She wasn't keen on more of the same, but at least she knew she could handle her dull and unsurprising existence. The imponderables of change, however, never knowing when the roof might fall in, would tax her temperament to the limit.

Behind her, the door to the roof squeaked open. She turned to see Peter step through.

'Yeah, here she is,' he said coldly, holding the door wide and avoiding Carol's questioning gaze.

'Thanks, Peter. Sorry to wake you,' said Tom Roker.

'No problem. I had to be up. Some of us work for a living.'

Tom smiled but Peter disappeared without reciprocating. The door squeaked shut.

Carol stared back over the Thames at the hazy cityscape. Tom

Roker was the last person she wanted to see. More fool ideas, no doubt.

'What do you want. Tom?'

'What's up with Peter?' Tom asked, coming to stand in front of her.

'You're blocking my sun.'

Tom shifted and sat on the edge of an empty concrete flower tub.

Carol gave him a scathing glance then looked away. 'What do you want? Do you know what bloody time it is?'

'I didn't wake you.'

'That's not the point. I don't want to see you. Not in office hours and certainly not out of them.'

'You're looking good, Carol. Nice shorts.'

An unwanted sexual pang made her frown. She didn't answer.

Tom took a small rucksack from his shoulder and dumped it at her feet. He tapped her knee and she flinched, her lips pursing for an unspoken expletive that could never match the hatred in her face.

'Take it easy,' Tom said. 'I was just wondering whether success second time around will make you just as horny as eight years ago.'

Carol lost her temper; it had been brewing all night. 'Oh, what the fuck are you on about now? What is it? You still think we can steal Kellett's novel? Or have you got something else of your own you're too stupid to realise is crap?'

Tom grinned smugly, pulling a packet of Silk Cut from his shirt pocket. 'I still think we can steal Kellett's novel.'

Suddenly, her sleepless, fretful state caught up with her and she felt a calming tiredness trawl through her. She even smiled. 'Bye-bye, Tom. Safe journey back to Cloud-Cuckooland.'

Tom took a cigarette from the pack. 'So you don't want to steal Kellett's novel?' He lit up.

Carol moved forward in her deck chair and rested her elbows on her knees. 'The only way we can steal Kellett's novel, Tom . . .' she sighed wearily '. . . is to steal Kellett's novel. I mean break into his house and actually steal it. Copies, discs, everything. So unless—'

Tom kicked the rucksack so it struck Carol's shin.

'What?'

He stretched, got to his feet and wandered to the corner of the building where he stood with his back to her. Carol noted the ease of his movement, the nonchalance. She eyed the rucksack and knew what was in it even before she opened it to delve inside.

She laid the blue box of floppy discs, the thirteen copies, the second manuscript and the Registered Delivery coupon on the concrete between her legs. She stared down at them for a very long time. If he had presented her with only the discs and the manuscript she might not have believed they were genuine, but the Registered Delivery coupon verified their authenticity. Stamped by a Cheshire post office with a date that tallied exactly with the arrival of the original package.

Tom turned to her and drew a lungful of nicotine. Carol studied the slight smirk, the twinkle in his eyes, and she knew her own silence would be taken as tacit approval of his actions.

After a while, Tom said, 'Well?'

'What about his family?'

'One sister. I'm pretty sure she hasn't read it.'

'Hmm . . .' She left a dramatic pause. 'I want fifty per cent.'

'*No way!*' Tom said. 'No effing way, lady. You don't know what I went through to get this stuff.'

'No, and I don't care. Fifty per cent. Take it or leave it.'

'Really? Shall we invite your Peter into this conversation? Talk about old times?'

Carol rose casually and strolled towards him. 'Tom, you could put me in a divorce court, I realise that. On the other hand, I could put you in a criminal court. Or did Andrew Kellett leave you these things in his will?'

'You're a party to all this, don't forget that,' Tom said, stamping out his half-smoked cigarette on the concrete.

Carol smiled coyly. 'Not yet I'm not. So far all I've done is allow you to view a manuscript of a potential client of mine. And now you've gone off and done God knows what. I understand, Tom. You were unbalanced. You wanted success. I'll speak up in mitigation. I'll tell the court all about it.'

'I'll wreck your marriage,' Tom said angrily.

'Go ahead. I don't care. I'll do it myself soon enough. My marriage is already dead.'

'You're bluffing.'

'Okay, let's go downstairs. You talk to Peter, I'll talk to the police. See which one of us sheds the most tears.'

'You're quite the little bitch, aren't you?'

Carol leaned her forearms on the wall and gazed out over a London just starting to hum. 'Then we're well suited to enter this partnership together, Tom, because you're proving to be the biggest bastard I've ever known.'

Sod's Law dictated that now he had the entire London transport system at his disposal, his BMW was choosing to behave impeccably. He made his way back to Fulham through the trickling beginnings of the morning rush-hour. He drove with all the windows down and the sunroof wound back. The circulating air helped him stay awake. He hadn't slept after returning from his trip up North; the night's events were not easy to push from his mind, and he had been going quietly crazy thinking that Carol might still refuse to collaborate.

He was only grateful she had not pressed him for the details. His cool façade had not been easy to maintain. The farmer's decapitation was like a grotesque jack-in-the-box, bursting into his mind when he least expected.

The next twenty-four hours would be critical. If the story found its way into a national newspaper and Carol saw it, he would lose his career at best and his liberty at worst. At the moment, his fingerprints at the scene were meaningless – the police had no record of them – but if Carol were to discover the truth of last night before fully embroiling herself, and inform on him as revenge for his blackmail, the police would take his prints and find a perfect match.

As for the trifling matter of his conscience, his new status in the criminal world somehow didn't belong to him. How could he reinvent himself in only one night, after forty years stuck in the same boring mould? It was impossible, and just as the crime was in getting caught, so, he hoped, was the guilt. Getting away with it was the ultimate acquittal.

Traffic lights on Kensington High Street went against him and he came to a halt. He patted the rucksack on his passenger seat as though it was a beloved pet. Included in it now was the original manuscript and Kellett's introductory letter which Carol had surrendered so that he might personally destroy all signs of its true authorship. He didn't trust her to do it herself. But that was okay; she didn't trust him, either. Until he had signed a binding contract dividing all spoils fifty-fifty, he had been warned that the police were only a phone call away. She had no idea how much of a threat that was.

He arrived back home ten minutes later. Feeling like a zombie, he decided he wasn't safe playing with matches, so he went straight to bed.

Later that day, however, he would have a small bonfire in the kitchen sink, and, if fate proved kind, from the ashes would arise a new life for Tom Roker.

SEVENTEEN

———————◆———————

Jesus stared down on him from an ornate golden cross on the altar. Sitting in the chancel, in the front row of the choir stalls, Michael reckoned the Son of God's expression was giving him a stern ticking off. Behind the crucifix, the stained glass of the east window was dull, its morning magnificence spent, abandoned by the midday sun.

Hours had passed in quiet solitude. Mental anguish had quickly turned to gentle contemplation and finally to wandering daydreams. He had tried to hold on to the mental anguish for longer; perhaps if he'd been a Catholic . . . What little guilt he had was mainly intellectual. He knew he should have felt bad, but his heart wasn't in it. He had not expected to wake up feeling this way. Then again, neither had he expected to wake up every hour of the night with a hard-on. Angie Kellett was constantly in his thoughts. Not the vulnerable, mourning, grief-stricken parishioner she should have been to him, but the recently showered temptress with the gaping bathrobe and fabulous body.

'Oh, dear,' he sighed, lamely struggling to wipe the vision from his mind. He shook his head. 'Lord, give me strength.' But he didn't really want any strength. Not to resist temptation. Giving in to it had been a lot of fun.

The real problem was the timing. He had never expected to question his vocation this late in life.

Had it all been a sham? Had he been hiding from feelings he was too scared to confront? Did he believe a single word he had preached from the pulpit over the years? It was easy to dispense wisdom about conducting harmonious relationships and attaining marital bliss when he himself wasn't prey to the vagaries of intimate human contact. And for all his talk of The

74

Other Side, he had never personally experienced the slightest paranormal event. Though a graveyard surrounded the church, ghosts had been conspicuous by their absence. Premonitions had failed to spark across his subconscious-conscious divide, though he had shaken hands with folk on a Sunday who would be dead on the Monday. Of course, true faith did not require proof. It was religion that demanded faith visibly manifest itself. Hence churches, man's attempt to turn the intangible into something literally concrete. True faith was an individual creed; belief in God housed in the soul. It needed nothing built or explained. It was simply the desire for good, felt within and expressed outwardly towards others. Secretly, he suspected that religion did not have to figure at all in living a good life. He knew some wonderful atheists in the village. Similarly, he knew that several of his regular flock were complete bastards whenever they set foot off hallowed ground. On a global scale, of course, religion was something of an embarrassment, both an excuse and a pseudonym for genocide and general unpleasantness.

Thinking this, he accepted he had been a fraud. The church had provided a retreat for him to look out at other people making the mistakes he had feared to make himself.

Now, though, he *had* made a mistake. He had become too deeply involved in a life outside his safe cocoon, and he couldn't just walk away as he knew he should.

He needed to know how Angie felt. Not her sympathetic opinion on why he might be suffering; no amateur psychology to explain his heightened state. He didn't need his state explaining. It was enough that it existed. She had to tell him how she felt herself. Did they have a chance together?

He stood up and hurried into the vestry. He tugged his cassock from his back with rough impatience, and felt like Houdini freeing himself from a chained sack in a grave of his own making. He left it in an unceremonious pile on the polished parquet, pulled the dog collar from his shirt and dropped it on top. Looking down, he smiled. It appeared vaguely supernatural, as though he had simply ceased to exist inside his clothes and they had collapsed on the floor in a heap.

He took his suit jacket from a peg and slipped it on. Without his dog collar he was now dressed entirely in black. His reflection in the vestry mirror surprised him. Rather swish. From Man of Cloth to Man of Mystery. If he'd been sporting a moustache he would have twiddled it.

After locking up, he walked out from the shadow of his church into the streaming sunshine. It was a magnificent day. The sort of day designed for new beginnings.

He set off briskly through the narrow streets of his picture-postcard village, in the direction of Angie's house. He contemplated how he might approach her. He was new to dating. He wondered whether he should feign some more higher-worldly concerns as his pretext for visiting. Then he realised, at least with Angie, he could never go back to playing the role of the comforting clergyman. There was only one thing to do: pour out his heart to her.

Something was wrong with Angie. Michael recognised this as soon as he crested a rise in the lane and saw her there. She was sitting on her porch doorstep, her blonde hair radiant with sunlight, but she wasn't sunbathing. Her knees were drawn up tight to her chest, her arms crossed on top of them, supporting her bowed head. A forlorn shape.

As he passed her Mini Cooper he stopped. Angie hadn't moved a muscle. After a moment he went in through the gate, heels clicking loudly on the concrete path, but still she didn't stir.

'Angie?' he said softly.

No response. Sleeping.

He gently laid a hand on her shoulder, gave a squeeze, then a little shake. Angie woke violently with a startled intake of breath. Her head snapped upright.

'Sorry,' said Michael. 'I, er . . .'

She didn't smile. She looked exhausted. 'Oh,' she said, then closed her eyes and rested her forehead back on her arms. 'It's you,' she whispered.

He waited for more, but her breathing quickly steadied, slowed and deepened. Fast asleep again. He could not have imagined a less enthusiastic reception.

'Angie.' He gave her another shake.

Through heavy, flickering eyelids, she looked up at him. 'Mmm?'

He squatted down in front of her. 'Are you all right?'

'Sorry.' She stretched out her legs and rubbed her eyes. 'Bad night.'

He wanted to take her hand, but he was afraid of rejection. As each second passed without the special contact he craved, a sense of impossibility began to overwhelm him. A fluttering panic in his chest told him he had been wrong before: he couldn't just pour out his heart. He didn't know how to.

All he could say was, 'Would you like to tell me about it?' and, with that, he knew he had made his cowardly retreat. All safely shackled up in his sackcloth again.

Angie nodded.

With the sun burning down on his back, he was struck by the ongoing inevitability of it all. Nothing would change for him. Not outwardly. Not in this life.

'Shall we go inside?' he asked.

'No.'

'It'll be cooler.'

'No.'

Michael wondered if he would ever again truly give a shit about his chosen career. If he ever had. Sweat was popping on his brow and upper lip. He removed his jacket and sat beside her on the doorstep.

'Angie . . . has something happened?'

In an emotionless, fatigued voice, Angie began to recount her tale. Michael listened but felt curiously unmoved. It was a shocking story, but what could he do about it? He wasn't a miracle-worker; that was his Boss. All the while his eyes kept wandering over her legs, those sweet denim contours.

'Awful,' he said when she finally finished. 'Just awful.' And if she could find comfort in that, good for her.

She gave a humourless chuckle. 'What's going on, Michael?'

'Life. Death.'

'But . . . all this. Why me?'

'Why not you?'

Angie twisted to face him. 'I beg your pardon?'

'We all have our problems, Angie. In Bosnia, I expect a corpse in the back garden is rather commonplace.'

'But this isn't Bosnia. And why are you being so nasty?'

'I'm . . .' He shook his head. Why was it so hard to tell her? Why couldn't she see it for herself? 'Sorry, Angie, I'm . . . I suppose I'm suffering a crisis of conscience.'

'Oh. I see.' She looked away from him. 'Sorry.'

'It's not your fault.' Beneath his shirt, warm rivulets of sweat trickled down his flanks.

There was a long silence between them.

'Friends?' Angie said, finally.

He smiled. 'Friends.'

'Good, because I did want to ask, if you're not too busy this afternoon, could you come with me?'

'This after– I'm sorry?'

'To the undertaker's. You don't mind, do you? I'd just rather you were with me.'

'No. No, I don't mind at all.'

'The first time I didn't say goodbye. There are things I want to say.'

'Mmm.'

'And things I want to take back.'

'I see.'

Angie stared at him. 'Do you know what I mean?'

Michael realised he hadn't been listening. 'I think so. Perhaps you'd better explain.'

She gave him a doubtful look, then gave him the benefit. 'Well, when Andrew was alive he drained me of energy. These past couple of years I've felt dead. I need my life back. It's like people say: there's always a trade-off. Someone dies in the world, someone's born. That's what it feels like.'

'And where do I fit in?' Michael said, knowing he would only receive the more mundane of the two answers she could give.

'I don't know.' She shrugged. 'You're a link, I suppose, because of what you do. Between life and death. You're a bridge. I need you to lead me away from all the bad stuff.'

Michael wanted to be more than a bridge. He took it inside as an insult to his reawakened manhood.

'We'll have something to drink and then go,' she said.

'All right.'

The meek shall inherit the earth, he thought to himself as he followed her indoors. Maybe, but they'll never get the girl.

EIGHTEEN

———◆———

Tom was in his study, writing a sequel to Kellett's novel, when little Charlotte walked in. Tom was puzzled. Why was she not in America? Before he could ask, she grabbed a box of floppy discs from his desk and scarpered, slamming the door behind her. As he rose to his feet, he could hear Charlotte giggling outside. He understood. It was a game. She wanted him to chase her. He opened the door and stepped out, but not into a corridor, into a dense wood. When he turned back, the door had disappeared. His daughter was nowhere to be seen, but her laughter kept moving around the trees. He called her name but there was no sound – he was dumb. He listened, trying to pinpoint her location, but she never stayed still for long enough. Then he heard another sound, a distant drone, getting nearer. After a while he was able to identify it. A motorbike. Something powerful. But he didn't know what it meant. Then an object fell on his head. He looked at the ground and saw a conker. He looked up and saw a canopy of horse chestnuts. Now the bike made sense.

He had returned to the scene of the crime and summary justice was about to be done. Milton was coming, and Tom knew he was about to die.

But as he listened, the blood drained from his face. Somewhere in the distance, Charlotte's laughter and Milton's motorbike were converging.

Milton had not come for him. Only for the discs.

Soundlessly, Tom screamed for his daughter, then began to run.

Still yelling his dumb warnings, he raged through the wood, dodging between the trees in a half-blind panic as he felt branches tear at his face, exposed roots trip him, and trunks punch at his shoulders.

Now only seconds away, he was fully resolved to accept the due punishment and sacrifice his life for his daughter's, but as he heard Charlotte's innocent laughter and Milton's evil exhaust note merge into one, his stride became hampered and he was forced to a standstill. He looked down.

He was up to his thighs in conkers.

Suddenly, the shells all split open. But there were no horse chestnuts inside, only eyeballs – brown like Charlotte's. As he struggled to move, he felt a thousand sorrowful stares boring into him, reproaching him.

Then he heard Milton's motorbike cut out, Charlotte's amusement die in her mouth. A gun-shot. The sound of red rain drizzling on the forest floor. Then silence.

At his feet, the shells sealed themselves and the eyes closed.

On the drive into the nearby market town, Angie and Michael hardly said a word to each other. Angie felt the silence between them to be far from comfortable. Their agreeing to be friends had obviously not eased his bad mood.

'Where now?' she asked as they approached the outskirts of the town.

'Keep going,' he said.

'You'll tell me when to turn.'

'No, I'll let you drive straight past.'

Angie would have smiled had it been said with any warmth, but he was being plainly facetious. She reached down to switch on the radio-cassette, and pushed a tape into the slot, wondering why she hadn't done so at the start of the journey.

Billy Joel piped up, singing one of his greatest hits, asserting that he would rather laugh with the sinners than cry with the saints, because sinners are much more fun, and only the good die young.

Angie turned it off.

After a few moments, Michael said, 'I have to admit, he does have a point.'

When Angie clicked to his meaning, she burst out laughing.

'Next left,' he said.

She slowed and turned.

'To the end, then right.'

Angie followed the directions, heading into the backstreet maze of terraced houses.

'Where now?' she asked.

'To the end, then pull over.'

Angie drove down the street. The final terrace on the left was not a residential property. Twin garage doors were built into the wall, shuttered by steel rollers. She assumed there were hearses inside. She parked the Mini in front of them and cut the engine.

'Feeling okay?' Michael asked.

She nodded. They both got out and walked round to the front of the building.

The undertaker's premises occupied the space of three standard houses on the corner of the two streets. Angie found it quite sick that the owners of the abutting homes had no qualms about living so close to a bunch of dead people. But she decided it was probably better than living in the same house as a major depressive.

Michael rang the bell. After a moment the door opened. Hugh Stapely, the undertaker, was in his mid-fifties, silver-haired, short in stature, and bespectacled in a black suit and tie.

'Hello, Hugh, this is Miss Kellett.'

Stapely looked at Angie and conjured a perfect expression of dour sympathy. 'My condolences, Miss Kellett. Please, do come in.' He stepped aside.

Angie found herself in a hall with plain white walls and a crimson carpet. There was a door to her left, one to her right, and one straight ahead. For some reason she knew she would be taken through the one at the end of the corridor, as though she could sense her brother's corpse lying beyond it.

Stapely closed the front door. 'Now, Miss Kellett, I should warn you, Andrew's injuries were rather extensive.'

'I know, I saw his body after the crash.'

'Of course. Now, I have done what I can, but you must realise that the damage is still quite visible.'

'Don't worry, I'm prepared.'

'This way, then,' he said, indicating the door at the end of the corridor.

If it were possible for a sane man to truly hate a fictional character, then Tom Roker hated Milton the Biker. He had woken from his nightmare not knowing where he was, or even when it was. He could have been a different person entirely, and the nightmare simply his subconscious trying to deal with an event that had genuinely taken place.

After a few moments, reality dawned, and it wasn't much better. Someone was dead. Not his daughter; a stranger. Nevertheless, he was responsible. A family was in mourning, irreparably damaged, so that he might have a second taste of worldly success.

Yet what was his overwhelming feeling now that he was fully awake? Not self-loathing, but a persistent and irrational hatred of a man who did not exist. Tom guessed that if he stretched out on a psychiatrist's couch for long enough, all that execration would eventually boomerang, but the nightmare was still vivid in his mind; Milton had visited his callousness too close to home.

Tom hoped that the threat of detection had been partly responsible for brightening his nightmare images. If so, perhaps he could look forward to a more peaceful night ahead, because he was just about to dispose of much of the physical evidence which might indict him.

He felt in his dressing-gown pocket to check for his cheapo lighter, then emptied the stolen rucksack onto the kitchen table. He placed the copy manuscript in the black folder safely to one side – bit ironic if he accidentally burned the whole bloody lot and left himself with nothing to plagiarise. The other manuscript, Kellett's introductory letter, the twenty-six floppy discs and the Registered Delivery coupon he dumped on the sink drainer. With the drying-up cloth he mopped around the sink, then opened the kitchen window and yanked the cord on the extractor fan. From a cupboard he retrieved a can of Swan lighter fuel and stood it on the sink side.

All set.

He took out his lighter and reminded himself he could do with a cigarette. He found a half-smoked emergency pack in a drawer, lit up and inhaled deeply. Weed in mouth, he dropped Kellett's letter into the sink and squirted a little petrol on it. From the red folder he peeled off the first ten or so pages, added them and doused them. He lit the post office coupon and threw it in. The fuel ignited and an orange flame leapt six inches then settled down to dance in gentle waves.

Tom watched. Like magic, Kellett's words were disappearing as black and white turned to brown. He tittered maniacally. Charred flakes spiralled upwards to float around the kitchen. Some caught the draft of the open window and were spirited away into the Fulham sky. He added more pages, squeezing a line of fuel across them to keep the fire alive.

A grisly thought struck him: he was cremating Andrew Kellett. By secretly burning his legacy to the world, Tom was in effect stealing the final months of Kellett's life, killing him even before his fatal bike smash by making his last labours on this earth a totally fruitless exercise, at least for the man himself.

But Tom smiled. He had to. Things were too far gone for remorse.

On the other side of the door, the scene was straight from Hammer Horror. It would have been less spooky had all the corpses been on show.

Angie was standing in a wide corridor roughly twenty feet long. At the end was a panelled wood door. The same crimson carpet covered the floor, but the blank white walls had become floor-to-ceiling crimson velvet curtains, three sets along either side. Between each was a sliver of white wall and a single mock candle, flickering unconvincingly. Angie thought Hugh Stapely's choice of light fitting was the ultimate in tacky. Either that or he had a rather theatrical sense of occasion. Quiet organ music floated eerily around like an unwelcome visitation from the ether.

'This way,' he said.

She was led to the last set of curtains on the left. Michael kept back a couple of paces: there if she needed him.

Hugh Stapely reached a finger behind the velvet and Angie heard a muffled click and noticed soft lighting spill under the hem of the curtains. Then he pulled a draw rope and the drapes swished apart, only adding to the overall theatricality.

A lidless white casket rested on trestles in the centre of the cubicle. The walls were white, the lighting suitably subdued, courtesy of those same imitation candles. She wondered if there weren't regulations governing how tasteless undertakers could be with their decor. In the rear corners were white columns, topped by simple arrangements of white carnations. Angie assumed they were plastic. There was certainly a sweet fragrance, but it smelt more like the product of an aerosol can. Still, what did it matter? Apart from the visiting bereaved and Stapely himself, no one else in the place was going to be sniffing the air.

Hugh Stapely stood back. She looked at Michael, who smiled kindly and gave a little nod.

She stepped up to the casket. The curtains closed behind her.

Only her brother's head was visible, resting on a white satin pillow. A taut sheet of the material extended from his feet to his neck, and the box itself was satin-lined.

It was hard to recognise him. His hair had been carefully combed in an unfamiliar style. But there were places where his hair was missing and nothing short of a wig could have disguised the trauma caused by brick or fibreglass on skull. Great dents and hollows. Jagged lines of sutures. Across his face as well. Funnily enough, his skin had a nice healthy colour, but she knew that was just the effects of the embalming.

She shook her head. She didn't know what to say to him. That business about reclaiming her energy was garbage. Looking at Andrew's sorry state, she saw he was utterly powerless. He couldn't hold onto anything that was rightfully hers. In fact, he had never stolen anything from her in the first place, because he had been equally powerless in life. One way or another, after losing his family, fate was always going to lead him to this. As his sister, she had chosen to stand by him of her own free will. Now, it would also be her decision if she developed a complex about his death.

It was simple. He was gone. She was still there. That was it. She wasn't going to screw herself up about it.

'Goodbye, Andrew,' she whispered. 'Rest in peace.'

She gently adjusted his hair more to the way he had worn it, then she turned, divided the curtains with the backs of her hands, walked through and rejoined the living.

The smoke alarm on the upstairs landing began beeping shrilly. Tom only had the last few pages of the manuscript to burn so he finished the job before toddling off to disconnect the battery. When he returned he noticed how dense the atmosphere was in the kitchen. Just like his study during a chain-smoking and futile late-night session at the keyboard.

The fire in the sink had died out apart from small pieces of browned paper still glowing orange at their edges. Tom watched the creeping heat nibble them down to nothingness.

On the table behind him, the discs were still intact. He had decided against burning them, not keen on the thought of noxious fumes from the plastic cases lingering in the house for days. He crossed the kitchen and bent down to the tool drawer for a hammer. One by one he placed a disc on the linoleum floor and gave it three or four shattering blows. Afterwards, he collected up the debris and chucked it into a black bin liner, along with any partially destroyed scraps of paper from the sink. The ashes he soaked under the tap, turning them into a black mush which swirled away down the plughole.

Now there was only one thing left to do: run off copies from the remaining manuscript, then destroy it. Whether it was strictly necessary was a moot point; he was paranoid, so it was essential. For all he knew, Kellett might have been partial to scoffing doughnuts as he edited his work, and every page could be invisibly marked by a greasy fingerprint.

Once he was dressed he would head off for Prontaprint on the Fulham Road, but first he wanted another cigarette. He took a seat at the kitchen table, lit up and leant back. After a moment he pulled the black folder towards him. If he was to pass off the novel as his own, he had to be totally familiar with it. He opened the cover to begin re-reading.

'Oh, fuck.'

The man at Prontaprint knew him well, so he might have raised an eyebrow had he seen the first page of Tom's new manuscript proclaiming itself to be: *Untitled by Andrew Kellett*. From printshop manager to Chief Witness for the Crown. He would instantly have become a liability, and Tom was keen to avoid bumping off any more third parties. Once was allowed – a genuine mistake – but he didn't want to get into a cycle of murdering people who got in his way.

He frowned. What was that? A cycle of murder? A murder cycle? He still hadn't settled on a title for the novel.

Murder cycle. Motorcycle, murdercycle. It had possibilities. He recalled from somewhere that the Americans had labelled the early Harley-Davidsons murder cycles. Keen to test the limits of this new mode of transport, young bucks had taken to racing them, which frequently involved falling off and dying.

'*Man on a Murder Cycle*.' He spoke it out loud several times. Yup. Sounded all right.

He put the title page to one side, and noticed something else. A dedication page. It had been left out of the copy sent to Carol.

For my darling wife and gorgeous girl, Nina and Sally. With all my love. I miss you so much.

Tom assumed Kellett must have been divorced. But the phrasing seemed a little incongruous with that scenario. Then he remembered the photograph he had seen in Andrew Kellett's bedroom, and the telephone conversation with Kellett's sister before he broke in. She had claimed to be his only family, but even if she was excluding his estranged wife, she would surely not have discounted his own daughter.

What the hell, it wasn't his problem, and as soon as Carol signed on the dotted line, making herself a willing accomplice and nullifying her threats, he could forget all about a man called Andrew Kellett.

Who? Andrew Who?

See? Forgotten already. Tom smiled. *Man on a Murder Cycle* was his, and with a healthy dose of self-delusion he would make himself justly proud of it.

Without shifting to the sink, he took his disposable and set light to the title page, discarding it in the ashtray as the flames reached his fingertips. It curled to a black crisp among the cigarette butts and mounds of ash. He picked up the second surplus page, touched the flame to a corner, and watched the fire leap up to wipe out Kellett's strange dedication.

Having finalised details of the funeral with Hugh Stapely, Angie and Michael were being shown out into the street when something heavy crashed to the floor in the Chapel of Rest. They froze in their tracks and stared in shocked bewilderment at each other, then at Hugh Stapely. They all turned to look back at the dividing door.

Angie felt a deathly chill go through her. Goosebumps had sprung, and her hackles were standing. Then a grief-stricken moan drifted through to them, and Angie knew she would never forget that sound as long as she lived.

In the silence that followed, she realised she was clutching Michael's arm. She gripped him tighter. Her eyes were fixed on the dividing door. No one spoke for what seemed an eternity. Angie guessed it was no more than ten seconds.

'Hugh, what was that?' Michael asked, his voice quivering.

Stapely didn't answer. His face was creased in frightened puzzlement.

'Is Arthur in today?' Michael asked.

Angie felt relieved at hearing another name brought into the frame. In an instant she had figured out a quite logical explanation for the whole thing: Arthur was a co-worker who had come through from the back and had somehow knocked over a coffin and hurt himself. She looked eagerly to the undertaker for confirmation.

Stapely briefly glanced at Michael then returned his gaze to the door. He shook his head: not Arthur.

A new wave of goosebumps made Angie shiver violently. 'Perhaps this Arthur fellah dropped by for something,' she suggested hopefully.

'I've been in my office all day,' Stapely said. 'I would have heard if he'd come in the front.'

'What about the back?' Angie asked.

'I'd certainly have heard.'

'You might not.'

'The garage shutters make a racket. I'd have heard.'

Panic suddenly ripped through her. 'Great. Is this some kind of sick joke?' She pinned Stapely with a fearsome, fearful glare. 'Well, I'm staying here. This is your place, Mr Stapely. Would you like to see what that was?'

Stapely dithered, but succumbed to the fire in her eyes, and began to creep along the corridor. Nearing the door, he invited Michael to join him. Michael silently asked Angie for permission to leave her side. She shooed him down the corridor. When he got to Stapely, she retreated outside onto the pavement, and the fresh air and sunshine greeted her like a sane old friend in a land of loons.

She would not have believed it possible, but life was getting even more screwy. What was happening here, God alone knew. As she saw the two men open the door and enter the Chapel of Rest, she wondered if they were all afraid of the same thing. Because, hearing that awful sound, she had regressed. She had become a petrified child, curled up tightly under cold sheets, unable to sleep for unwillingness to close her eyes, and sincerely rueing her decision to sneak into her parents' bedroom and watch that late-night horror film on their portable. After all these years, the Bogey Man was still alive and well in her.

The intrepid explorers disappeared from sight. She prayed for them to come back to her with a happy explanation, because if they couldn't do that, she felt perhaps they wouldn't be coming back at all.

She crossed to the far side of the street and walked several yards down the pavement to bring the garage doors into view. With her imagination running amok, blind corners seemed a bad idea.

For five minutes, no one appeared at the front door. The crash and moan she had heard echoed in her head, a perfect audio playback.

When the boys finally emerged, they were deep in discussion. She hurried across to them. Michael evidently heard the footsteps because he shot her a glance, but he never broke the flow of conversation with the undertaker. Rather, in the seconds before she reached them, she suspected their talk had degenerated into more of an argument.

They abruptly shut up as she drew to a halt. Their faces were ashen; even her brother had a better skin tone. Stapely inclined his head away from her. He was shaking like a leaf.

'Well?' she said.

Michael kept quiet.

'Up to you,' Stapely said to him, and went inside.

'What is it, Michael? What's happened?'

Michael inhaled deeply, and Angie could hear the rhythm of his heart in his breath. Something had spooked them, something that Stapely had no desire to share with her.

'Michael?'

'Hugh is of the opinion I shouldn't tell you.'

'Tell me what?'

He kicked his heels like a guilty schoolboy.

'*Michael?*'

'Come inside.'

They stepped in and closed the door. In an office to the left, Stapely was standing at a filing cabinet, pouring himself a large tumbler of Smirnoff.

Angie shook Michael by his lapels. 'What the hell is going on?'

'Michael can't tell you,' Stapely said, coming out of his office. He loosened his tie, removed his spectacles and pinched the bridge of his nose. 'And neither can I.' He gulped down a mouthful of vodka, making his eyes water. 'But if you'd like to hazard a guess yourself, feel free to take a stroll into my Chapel of Rest. Take a gander at your dear departed.' He laughed, but it sounded like the precursor to madness.

Angie turned her eyes to Michael, requesting his company on her journey into the unknown. But he turned to the undertaker. 'Have you got a spare glass, Hugh?' Stapely nodded, Michael joined him in his office, and Angie was left on her own.

Through the dividing door, the curtains to her brother's cubicle were open. Slowly, she walked along the crimson corridor and peered in.

The trestles were overturned. The casket lay on its side on the floor. Andrew's body had been spilled partly out, his legs still twisted in the white satin cover. He was face down to the carpet.

Angie assured herself that she didn't know what all the fuss was about. Obviously, a trestle had given way and the box had tipped over. She could even account for the moaning. She had heard of corpses being wheeled along mortuary corridors and gasping when they hit a bump as the last breath of fetid air was jolted from their lungs.

'Turn him over.'

Angie jumped.

Michael and Stapely, drinks in hand, had decided to join her.

'Go on,' said Stapely, 'turn him over.'

Angie hesitated.

'Okay, hold this.' Stapely gave her his glass. He knelt down and pushed her brother over onto his back.

Andrew's mouth was gaping, his eyes half open. It was not a particularly pleasant sight, but Angie considered it not out of keeping with the probable effects of his fall to the floor.

'So a trestle collapsed,' she said.

Stapely let out a bark of his hysterical laughter.

'Hugh . . .' Michael reprimanded him.

'Miss Kellett, the trestles are fine. Look. And let me tell you something about the embalming process. No, first of all let me ask you a question. Do you ever watch police dramas on the television?'

'Sometimes.'

'Then you'll have seen many a caring detective close the eyes of a corpse with the gentle downward stroke of two fingertips.'

Angie sensed some awful revelation was heading her way. 'So?'

'So it doesn't work that way. Try it. Close his eyes for him.'

Michael wrapped a protective arm around Angie's shoulders, and drank some vodka. 'Hugh, just make your point.'

89

Stapely pushed himself unsteadily to his feet, spilling his drink. His impromptu afternoon tipple had gone straight to his head.

'Shit,' he muttered, wiping his leg. 'My point, Miss Kellett, is that the eyelids of a dead person droop, but cannot be made to stay fully closed, and therefore what you have is a pair of vacant, glassy eyes peeping blindly under half-shut eyelids. This, of course, can be a tad upsetting for the bereaved relative, so as part of the embalming process, the eyelids are glued down. Which is exactly what I did with your brother.'

Angie winced. There was a suggestion inherent in Stapley's little lecture, but she didn't want to acknowledge what it was. She made a feeble attempt to refute it. 'Well, the fall must have—'

'No!' Stapely snapped, then calmed himself. 'No, Miss Kellett, the fall did nothing.'

'How do you know?'

'Because I use Superglue.'

'*Superglue?*'

'It works.'

'Jesus.'

'Now, if you want, I can squirt a dribble of the stuff into your eyes and then you can test if it comes unstuck when you bang your head on the floor.'

'Don't be stupid,' she said.

But Stapely wasn't cowed. He had only just begun to expound the secrets of his profession. 'And as for the open mouth, the jaw of a cadaver will naturally drop open slightly if it is not fixed shut.'

'Good old Superglue,' she said flatly.

Stapely swilled down the last of his drink. 'Surgical thread,' he informed her. 'If you insert your tongue right down between your lower lip and teeth and move it sideways back and forth, you'll feel a ridge.'

'So?'

'I take a curved needle and I sew through that ridge, Miss Kellett, then I come up between top lip and teeth, into the nasal cavity, through the septum, back down, pull tight, and tie off. It keeps the lips nicely together.'

'Okay, enough,' she said.

Stapely tipped his tumbler and drained a few last clear drops into his mouth. 'Good stuff,' he commented, and slouched off down the corridor, talking over his shoulder as he went. 'Do you understand what I'm saying, Miss Kellett?'

She heard the sound of a bottleneck clinking on glass, then Stapely wandered back to them and reappeared theatrically through the curtains with a full tumbler, like a sozzled old actor.

'You see,' he resumed, 'someone could well have medically neutralised the glue in your brother's eyes and also snipped the thread in his mouth. But neither of those things actually happened. If you look very closely, you'll notice skin and lashes from his eyelids still adhering to the lower rims of his eyes. And the loop of thread is still intact in his mouth, but it's been torn through the skin inside.'

'All right, shut up,' Angie said.

'Hugh, that's enough,' Michael agreed.

Stapley sat down on the end of the casket. A dejected, miserable man, he hung his head and spoke to the carpet. 'I'm sorry if I've overloaded on the details, Miss Kellett, I truly am. But at the end of the day, it doesn't really matter how my work came to be undone. What matters is that without interference from person or persons unknown, it simply can't have happened.'

Angie pounced on the fact. 'So someone came in, ripped his eyes and mouth apart, knocked over the coffin, made a moaning sound, and left. It was a sick joke. I'm happy with that.'

'Sorry, no,' Stapely said. 'We checked; Michael and I.' Without lifting his head, he pointed to the panelled wood door. 'Chapel of Rest to embalming room, locked. Embalming room to garage, locked. Garage, locked. So unless someone came past us at the front door—' He looked up at her with his bloodshot eyes. 'No one did come past us at the front door, did they, Miss Kellett?' When she didn't reply, he answered his own question. 'No.'

But Angie could not allow him to win. If she did, she would be agreeing to accept a set of circumstances absolutely beyond belief.

'What about this Arthur fellah, then?' she said. 'He could have done it. I mean, who is he? Has he got keys?'

Michael answered. 'Angie, Arthur's knocking eighty. He's Hugh's father. Practical jokes aren't really—'

'He's not renowned for his sense of humour, my old dad.'

Angie felt the parameters of accepted reality warp around her. She was being sucked into a dark fairy tale where corpses walked and talked. Or at least where corpses threw themselves on the floor and whinged at the impact.

'I can account for that moaning sound,' she said quickly, in desperation. She thought if she could get Stapely to concede that just one aspect fell outside the supernatural domain, then, given time, she might be able to convince herself that it all did.

But Stapely cut her off. 'I know what you're going to say—'

'No, you don't.'

'And, yes, the dead can burp and break wind, but, believe me, it sounds nothing like what we heard. Nothing like.'

Defeated, Angie slumped against Michael. She pinched his vodka from him and finished it. Then she regarded her brother's tortured, broken face.

And she had to admit: if souls did exist, then never had a person possessed one more liable to wreak havoc when released from the confines of its corporeal state.

NINETEEN

The green Cheshire lanes, dappled with shadow and sunlight, moved Angie almost to tears. How could a world that offered this much simple beauty contain such a level of sickness as she had been forced to witness? It wasn't just today; the events of that afternoon were not meant to be understood. They were merely bubbles rising into her world from an unseen dimension. What caused them, what they signified, were questions so potentially loaded that a person could never risk searching too deeply for the answers if they valued their sanity. Anyway, it was the nature of such bubbles that they always burst the moment they appeared. And Angie decided that was just as well.

'Angie? You okay?'

She looked sideways at Michael, then returned her eyes to the road. 'Yes,' she said. 'You?'

'I should be.'

'But you're not.'

'I should be able to cope with bizarre circumstances. To me, they shouldn't *be* bizarre. I should say, "Oh, yes, another restless spirit making a nuisance of itself". That's why you wanted me with you today. Because I'm supposed to understand death in terms beyond the physical. But up to now it's all been theory.'

'And you feel you've just failed the practical.'

He snorted. 'You might say.'

'I suppose it's like a soldier shooting at paper silhouettes for years, then he's sent to war and told to kill real people. No amount of training can prepare you for an experience like that.'

He patted her thigh. 'Thanks.' But his hand overstayed its welcome.

With a sharp kick, Angie needlessly engaged the clutch and

shifted down into third. Michael quickly got the message. His hand lifted, hovered for a second, then shot back to clasp its opposite number resting in his lap. The engine was racing at the unnecessary burden of revs. She accelerated and changed up again.

Michael cleared his throat and looked out of his window at the passing scenery. They didn't speak again until they were approaching the outskirts of the village.

'Where do you want dropping off?' Angie asked.

'Go back to yours. I'll walk from there.'

'Sure?'

'Yes.'

She couldn't argue without sounding as though she wanted some distance between them. Which was quite true.

'Unless you don't want me at your house for some reason,' he said.

'No-no. No.'

'Good.'

Angie felt a pang of conscience: she had used him for a second time. He had agreed to be with her during her moment of crisis, and now it was over he was excess baggage. What was worse, he seemed to know. But despite her guilt it was easy to resent him, because he had shown there were strings attached. Underneath the dog collar and cassock he had proved himself to be a man like any other, and, just like a man, having tasted forbidden fruits he was hungry for more.

They arrived back at the cottage. Angie pulled the Mini onto the verge and switched off the engine. A warm breeze of country murmurs floated in through the open windows.

'Strange day,' Michael said quietly.

Angie nodded. 'Weird.'

They looked at each other and smiled, but Angie quickly broke the moment. There was something else in his eyes – an unwholesome twinkle – and it angered her to see it. This afternoon she suspected they had shared an experience of profound spiritual significance, and now he was trying to gain sexual advantage from it.

She wanted the solitude of her own home. Peace and quiet. A break from sex and death.

'Bye, Michael.' She made to open the door but he spoke up and stopped her.

'I hope Hugh's all right.'

Angie imagined Hugh would be slugging back the last of his Smirnoff by now. 'Give him a buzz,' she said.

'Would you mind?' Michael asked.

'Why should I?'

Michael was out of the car and standing expectantly by her gate before she understood she had unwittingly agreed to let him use her telephone. She wound the windows up and got out. Michael smiled at her, and they went into the house.

He used the phone in the living room. From the doorway, she watched him dial. He stood with the receiver to his ear for over a minute. Angie wanted him to hang up and leave her alone.

'He'll be passed out somewhere,' she said.

He grunted in agreement but kept on listening.

'Try later,' she said. 'When you get home.'

He nodded, replaced the receiver and sat down on the settee. 'I'm worried about him, you know.'

Angie didn't reply. She really couldn't have cared less. She wanted to mope around the house feeling sorry for herself for a while. She deserved it.

Michael looked at her and slapped the cushion beside him. 'Sit down.'

She didn't respond, verbally or facially, but he wasn't deterred.

'You see,' he said, 'Hugh and I have discussed matters of the supernatural before now.'

'And he doesn't believe,' she stated disinterestedly.

'On the contrary. He's at ease with his work precisely because he does believe in the spirit world. He believes he's dealing with nothing more than empty containers. Now, though, I think he'll have a lot of trouble knowing he might be taking delivery of bodies that haven't completely emptied out. For want of a better expression.'

Angie yawned. 'Yeah.'

'Angie, come and sit down.'

'No.' She closed her eyes momentarily. 'Michael, I am so tired.'

'So sit down.'

'I need to lie down.'

He stood up and approached her. He cocked his head to one side and gave a sickly smile, although he was clearly trying to strike an expression of sympathy. 'I do understand. Could I lie down with you?'

She shook her head, more in exasperation than rejection. 'No. I need to sleep.'

'Sleep's perfect. I'm tired, too. I just want to be next to you.'

'Michael . . .'

'Please.'

'No.'

'Just sleep.'

'No!'

He stared down at his feet, and Angie heard the thud of emotional blackmail land on her doormat. He had the quivering chin of a hurt little kid. Angie had never felt more awkward in her entire life.

'Michael . . .' She sighed. 'You have to go. I can't cope with anything right now.'

'Just sleep,' he muttered.

'Pardon?'

His eyes were brimming with tears. 'I just want to be near you,' he said, and raised a hand to gently stroke her cheek. She flinched. 'What have I done wrong?' he moaned.

'Nothing. It's me. I've made the mistake.'

'I want you,' he said.

Before she could respond, his hand fell to her left breast and gave a squeeze. Angie yelped and backed out of the room to the foot of the stairs.

'Bloody hell, Michael.'

He moved in and grabbed again. This time his fingers dug through her T-shirt and slipped inside her bra.

'Michael! *No!*'

He pulled and Angie felt her breast pop out of its cup. She squealed, but he kept dragging on the T-shirt, ridiculously trying to expose her breast through the neck hole. His other hand went to the button of her jeans.

'Get lost! My neck! You're hurting!'

Michael's eyes were flared, his teeth bared. He was breathing harshly, panting stale vodka fumes in her face. Angie couldn't believe what was happening. Strangely, she felt absolutely furious that he was pulling her T-shirt out of shape. She began to pummel his temples with her knuckles but it only seemed to spur him on. He made to kiss her. She turned her head. Then the waistband of her jeans seemed to give and she realised he had managed to pop the button.

She raised her knee and sent it slamming into his balls. He groaned and creased up, his hands withdrawing to caress his own genitals. She took the opportunity to turn and scamper up the stairs.

'*Angie!*' he screeched.

She froze halfway up and looked back.

He no longer resembled the local vicar she had known since childhood. Yesterday had begun the transformation. The past few minutes had completed it. The demons in him had surfaced, and they were the ugliest.

Then he was coming for her.

She grabbed the nearest thing to hand. He lunged up the stairs and she swiped him across the face with it. There was a sound of cracking glass. He stopped dead and she hit him again. Blood began to ooze from his cheek. He didn't move. His expression was deeply puzzled, as though he had come to his senses, but Angie couldn't trust that this was the case. She struck him a third time. Glass fell to the stairs. More blood leaked from a fresh cut. He bent and picked up a long shard, inspecting it closely, but Angie didn't hit him again. She sensed the threat had passed. He lifted the jag to his forehead and carefully scored a cross deep into the skin between his eyes. Blood ran down the bridge of his nose and dripped on the carpet. It obviously tickled, because his nostrils twitched and he giggled for a moment. Then he quietened, turned and descended the stairs. He closed the front door softly behind him as he left the house.

A few minutes later, when it was clear he wasn't coming back. Angie sat down. She stared at the object in her hands, the enlarged photograph she had unhooked from the wall to use as a weapon. The pine frame was broken. One small triangular piece of glass remained, wedged into a corner. The photo had been badly scratched. To Angie, that seemed the saddest thing. She had taken the picture herself, outside the cottage: Andrew in full leathers, sitting proudly astride his new CBR 600; the start of his recovery. She had grown very fond of that picture.

She was still sitting there, staring at it, when night fell.

TWENTY

Hugh Stapely wheeled the casket through the embalming room and into the garage. He paused to switch on the fluorescents, then pushed the trolley round to the rear of one of his shiny black hearses. His head was pounding as he lifted the tailgate, lined up the casket and rolled it in.

'Not another peep,' he said, but he didn't smile. He closed the rear and locked it. Mentally, he felt a little better. Physically, he was a wreck. Besides the hangover, his neck was badly cricked. He had woken at teatime, slumped awkwardly in his office chair. Straightaway he had gone to the Chapel of Rest and foolishly over-exerted himself. How he had found the strength to manoeuvre the corpse into the casket, and the casket onto the trolley, he would never know. But he was paying for it now, and tomorrow promised even more pain and discomfort. His sciatica was screaming, he had strained his long-forgotten stomach muscles, and he thought he might well have slipped a disc. Still, he would have risked a coronary to get Kellett's body under lock and key.

Carefully, he rolled his head on its axis, trying to free the tension in his neck. He tipped his head back and looked above him. Through the barred skylight he could see dusk descending. He was glad he had managed to tidy up before nightfall. For the first time since childhood, he was scared of the dark. He realised there was a very fine line between belief in the spirit world and the onset of insanity. It was nice to have faith; a real comfort. Unless some bastard came along to cloud the issue with concrete evidence.

He wished his wife wasn't away at her sister's in Southport, but he wondered if he would tell her anyway. She wasn't the type to dumbly accept such a story, even from her husband, and he didn't relish having to plead for her understanding.

Before leaving the garage, he peered through the side window of the hearse. He knew he had screwed down the casket lid, but his mind kept cutting out on him. He didn't want to get upstairs and have any doubts. He unlocked the tailgate and checked inside. It was okay, the lid was secure. He locked up again, then tugged the front door handles. Locked. He switched off the lights, left the garage, turned the key and shot the bolts.

In his embalming room he stood for a moment. He looked at the slab in the centre of the room. On it, he had cut and sowed, pumped and drained Kellett's body like a carcass of meat; with respect, always with respect, but never thinking it was anything more than skin and bone, flesh and blood. Dead. Empty.

He surveyed the tools of his profession. He tried to imagine lying naked in the long well of the slab, feeling his thigh being cut open, the femoral artery being hooked out from deep between the muscles. What would it be like to feel the Formalin flowing in from the pressurised container? Hearing the vacuum pump drawing the blood from his veins back into his heart, then out through the steel trocar inserted into it? Hearing it splosh into the demi-john? Feeling the leakage of excess fluids from his thigh as the Formalin completed its circuit of his body? Hearing the waste trickle down the plughole at his feet?

No. He couldn't imagine such a thing. And yet, if somehow Kellett had not been strictly dead, he might have felt and heard every part of this procedure.

Stapely shivered. His outlook on life had changed. His job had become a complete mystery. He rushed out of the embalming room, wincing at his injured back. He locked the door behind him, then hurried through the Chapel of Rest. In the entrance hall, he turned and locked the dividing door and retired upstairs to the living accommodation, bolting the door behind him.

He had enough money put by. He could take early retirement.

TWENTY-ONE

———◆———

Yet another perfect morning in old London town.

Tom was sitting in the office of Simon Collins, junior partner at the Rotherhithe practice of Moody, Carter and Collins, Solicitors. He was gazing sideways out of the window at the dreamy blue sky. He was drumming his fingers on the top of the briefcase down by his side. Today, he felt dynamic. World at his feet. World his oyster. All that nonsense. Next to him, Carol Morgan was perched stiffly on her seat as though she had a broom handle for a spine. Collins was across the room, sifting through a stack of brown files on a shelf. A pale, chinless individual, pitifully bald at barely thirty, he wore a tasteless, shiny green suit which hung poorly from his weedy frame. He didn't look to possess a backside.

'Aha, got it,' he said cheerfully, and came to sit at his desk. He withdrew three identical contracts from the file and set them before his clients. 'If you'd like to read one and sign each at the bottom.'

Tom picked up a Bic and poised it above the dotted line as he checked the details.

'I must say, Mr Roker, I did enjoy *Hidden Blade*.'

'Thanks. Glad you remember it.' Tom squiggled his name. His hand was shaking. Carol pushed the other copies towards him and he signed again.

'Is your new novel similar to *Hidden Blade*?'

'Better,' Carol said. 'Much.'

Collins simpered. 'I look forward very much to reading it. If you'd like to sign as well, Ms Morgan.'

Tom offered the Bic, but Carol produced her own fountain pen.

'And I'll just witness them for you,' said Collins, smiling ingratiatingly. He made his mark with a series of meaningless loops and a final sweeping line back through the whole mess which appeared to cross it out.

Tom sniggered.

'I know,' Collins said, looking up. 'It's a terrible signature.'

'No, it's not that.' And it wasn't. Now Tom had a legal document, he was home free. Carol had made herself an accomplice. She couldn't spill the beans without incriminating herself.

'That's it, then,' said Collins. 'All monies from the sale of the as-yet-untitled novel will—'

'*Man on a Murder Cycle.*'

Carol frowned at Tom's interruption. 'Pardon?'

'It's called *Man on a Murder Cycle*. I meant to say.'

She considered briefly, then said, 'Okay.'

Tom was staggered. He had fully expected her to fight, if only for the sake of arguing.

She addressed the solicitor. 'Will you redraft the contracts, please?'

'We can amend and initial.'

Tom shrugged. 'Whatever.'

Carol collected the documents one on top of the other and tore them in half. 'You're charging enough, Mr Collins. You can re-do them.'

Collins blushed. 'Right, won't be a tick.' He grabbed the two halves of a contract. 'I'll have my secretary print up some new ones. *Man on a Motor Cycle*, you say?'

'Murder Cycle.'

'Murder?'

Tom nodded.

'Ah, nice. Murder Cycle one word? Two words? Hyphenated?'

'Two.'

'Two words it is.' Still scarlet, Collins left the office and shut the door behind him.

'That's a first,' said Carol. 'A lawyer easily shamed.'

Tom smiled. 'You haven't used him before?'

'No. I didn't want my regular man asking why I'm suddenly on fifty per cent.'

'Course.' Tom was glad they seemed to be getting along a bit better. Perhaps she had realised his blackmail had been a very last resort; nothing personal. 'So how come you like the title?' he enquired, amiably.

'*Man on a Murder Cycle*? It's good.'

'Oh, I see. Thanks.'

'Yeah, I'm not about to pooh-pooh the first decent idea you've had in years.'

So much for their rekindling. Tom sighed and shook his head. 'Is this how it's going to be? You sniping every time we meet?'

'Hopefully, after today, we won't *have* to meet.'

He hated her acting aloof, but a slanging match would only serve to lower his own status. He decided to smoke a cigarette instead.

'Do you have to?' she said with disgust as he pulled out the pack.

'Don't have to, no,' he replied casually, and lit up.

Carol rose haughtily to her feet and strode to the open window. With deep, audible breaths she began to inhale the street air.

Tom said, 'Mmm, smell that carbon monoxide.'

'Up yours.'

'So much better than those nasty cancer-sticks.'

'Up *yours*.'

'Oh, come on, Carol, make an effort,' he said with good humour. 'We're in this together. Partners in crime, as they say.'

She ignored him.

Collins returned to the office. His colour had faded only slightly. 'Here we are,' he said, placing the revised contracts side by side in front of Tom.

Tom drew on his cigarette and eyed the solicitor as he rounded his desk and sat down. Collins tried a conciliatory grin, but he had clearly sensed the atmosphere.

'She hates me smoking,' Tom explained, a little implausibly.

'Ahaaa.'

Cigarette in mouth, Tom scribbled on each copy. Carol came over and scrawled three angry signatures, and Collins witnessed them.

Sliding both of the interested parties a contract, Collins said, 'These are yours, and I'll keep the other one here.'

Tom folded his and put it in his breast pocket. Carol snatched hers and shoved it in her handbag. She brought out a wad of notes in a rubber band and slapped it down.

'Cash. Very kind,' Collins said as he scooped his fee towards him, pulled out a drawer and dropped it in. 'Receipt?'

'No.'

'Even better. Uh, before you go, Ms Morgan . . .' He chortled modestly. 'I've actually written a novel myself, and I was wondering if you wouldn't mind, uh . . .'

Tom tried not to laugh; Collins' imposition had made Carol even more visibly riled.

'What's it about?' she asked, perfunctorily.

'A legal thriller. Sort of John Grishamish.'

'God, I wish,' she muttered.

'Pardon?' said Collins.

'I said Grishamish, is it really? How fab.'

Tom felt sorry for the lawyer; the snub in Carol's voice was unmissable.

'I believe it is, yes,' Collins said, undaunted.

'Well, keep it away from Mr Roker here.'

Bemused, Collins' grey eyes flicked from Carol to Tom and back again.

With some difficulty, Tom maintained a cool façade. 'In-joke,' he said to the solicitor, then spoke incredibly nicely to his agent. 'Carol, why don't you offer to read it for Mr Collins?'

'Why don't you read it yourself, Tom? I know you can recognise a good thing when you see it. Goodbye, Mr Collins. Ish.'

Tom made an apologetic face at the insulted, sulking lawyer, before grabbing his briefcase and following his agent out of the office.

Clicking stilettos echoed ahead of him on the stone staircase. Tom took the steps in twos and caught up. He barged past and stopped her progress.

'That was bloody stupid, wasn't it? Are you *trying* to get us caught?'

'Not nice being put on the spot. *Is it?*' She carried on down the stairs.

He opened his mouth to yell at her, but she had stolen his thunder. He realised from now on she would always have the upper hand. One mention of his blackmail, even the slightest inference, and she could make him feel lower than whale shit.

On the street, Carol was waiting for him. 'When can I have Kellett's novel for the publishers?'

Tom heard himself squeak like a startled mouse – or rat. He urged her to the inside of the pavement, out from the flow of pedestrians.

'Christ, Carol, you have got to stop saying that.'

'What?'

He lowered his voice to a whisper. '*Kellett's* novel. You'll say it to the wrong person one of these days.'

'I'm not daft, Tom. When can I have it?'

Tom dragged the last nicotine from his dimp, then squatted down and opened his briefcase across one knee. He brought out a gaudy purple folder and handed it to her.

'Thank you,' she said.

He shut the case and straightened up. 'Who are you sending it to?'

'Neptune.'

'I see. Going for the big boys.'

'Going for the big money. And I know their list's a bit thin at the moment, so I'm going to push for a January publication.'

'January?'

'The sooner it's out under your name, the safer I'll feel.'

Tom's smile offered more confidence than he felt inside. 'We are safe, Carol. No one can touch us. We got away with it.'

'I hope you're right.' She lightly kicked his briefcase. 'Have you got a spare manuscript for me in there?'

'Why?'

'I want one.'

'Why?'

'Because, Thomas, I have this awful fear that you might have got yourself all deluded, convinced yourself you wrote the damned thing, and tinkered with it.'

He scoffed, and lit another cigarette from the butt of the old.

Carol stepped back from the poisonous cloud. 'Apart from the odd sentence. I don't expect an editor will want to change a thing. And I absolutely don't want you giving it the Roker kiss-of-death.'

Tom had not thought of rewriting Kellett's work, but this was an ideal opportunity to wind her up. 'I haven't had a go at very much,' he said. 'Promise.'

She flared viciously, swiping the cigarette from his mouth, catching his nose as she did so. 'If you've altered one fucking word of it, I swear to God I'll blow this whole deal wide open.'

Tom rubbed his injured snout. 'Temper. You'd screw yourself in the process.'

'If necessary.'

Tom struggled to hide a sudden panic. He had been a fool to bait her. It would be an unmitigated disaster for him should the truth be exposed.

'I wasn't being serious,' he said. 'The novel's perfect. I wouldn't dream of touching it.'

She stared hard at him for several seconds. 'Good. Well? Have you got a copy for me?'

''Fraid not.'

She tucked the folder under her arm. 'Not a problem. I'll get one run off on my way home.'

'Don't trust me, do you?'

'I'd sooner smother my tits in marrowbone jelly and trust a rabid pit-bull not to bite.'

'That's very good. I might use that sometime.'

'Not a single, solitary comma, Tom. I'm warning you.'

TWENTY-TWO

'Blood and sand, Adam. What the hell's that?'

'Oh, morning guv,' said Ash. 'What's what?'

DCI Nelson pointed towards the bed. 'That thing.'

'A trocar.'

Nelson turned and glanced at the door, which was hanging off its hinges. Then he surveyed the interior of the bedroom. A terrible struggle had taken place. Furniture was disturbed and fractured. Pictures were hanging at all angles. The curtains had been torn from their rails. The surface of the dressing table was bare; all the items had been swiped onto the carpet. The mirror was cracked. The bed clothes were strewn across the floor. Even the light fitting had been pulled out from the ceiling, as though someone had tried to climb up the wire to get away. The atmosphere was sickly pungent: spilt aftershave, perfume, blood and bowels. People in white overalls were lifting dabs and scraping samples. A photographer was recording all aspects of the scene.

'Busy few days, Karen.'

The chief forensics officer nodded to Nelson. 'Mad,' she said.

Nelson moved closer to the bed to inspect the body. The under-taker was lying on his back in his blue-white striped winceyette pyjamas. He was wearing his spectacles, but the lenses were smashed and the metal frame bent. His flesh tone was blending in nicely with the white sheet beneath him. Despite the evident struggle, there was only one facial injury: some bruising to the left temple, consisting of four small depressions in a row.

Ash flipped his notepad. 'Name's . . .'

'Hugh Stapely. It said on the door. Anyway, I knew him.'

'Oh. Sorry.'

'Didn't like him. So what's a trocar when it's at home.'

'Ironic terminology, guv, given that it's at home right now.'

'Explain.'

'It's used in embalming to drain blood from the body. It's stuck in the heart—'

'I can see that.'

'No, I mean that's its function.'

Nelson didn't look impressed. He peered at the trocar, a two-foot long steel needle which had pierced Stapely's pyjamas at an angle beneath the left-side ribs. 'Go on.'

'It's hollow. There are several holes in the sharp end.' Ash traced with his finger the route of the blood out of the heart. 'Blood is drawn up the trocar, along the rubber tube and into the container via the airtight bung.'

The container in question was Stapely's demi-john, three-quarters full of his own blood, cradled lovingly in the crook of his right arm.

'The other tube leaving the container is attached to the vacuum pump.' He indicated a small electrical unit on the bedside table, next to a telephone.

Nelson dug in his pocket and produced a Mars bar.

'You're hungry?' Ash asked incredulously.

'Missed breakfast,' Nelson replied, missing the point. 'Funny, I thought you did English at university.'

'I did.'

He tore off the wrapper and began chewing. 'So how come you know about embalming.'

'Just know.'

Nelson gave a look which said: graduate smartarse. 'Time of death?'

'The coroner's pretty vague about it. Lividity's been affected by the draining of the blood.'

'Vaguely?' Nelson asked around a mouthful of chocolate.

'Midnight.'

'Right. Come with me. Let's have a quiet think. Kitchen okay to use?' he asked Karen.

'Yes, guv, all done in there.'

They went from a crowded room into a deserted one. Nelson threw his Mars wrapper in a flip-top bin, and pushed the door to. He sat down at a table and elbowed a congealed dinner plate away from him. Ash leaned his tall frame against a fitment.

107

'Where's the wife?' Nelson asked.

'Lounge.'

'She a suspect?'

'No. She was away all night at her sister's in Southport.'

'Nice welcome home,' Nelson said, pushing a silver salt cellar around the table as though it were a miniature Dalek. 'Do we know Stapely's last movements?'

Ash nodded. 'Yes, and this is rather interesting. According to his appointments book, Stapely's final visitor was Angie Kellett.'

'You mean Angie what's-that-headless-man-doing-in-my-back-garden Kellett?'

'The very same.'

Nelson began absently tapping the salt cellar on the top of the pepper grinder. 'I'm beginning to like this case, Adam. So what else do we know?'

'All indications are that the killer . . . uh.' He lost track. 'Sorry, guv, could you stop doing that?'

'What?'

'Tapping the condiments. It's disturbing my train of thought.'

Nelson put the salt cellar down and began the Dalek thing again.

'Yeah, all indications are that, uh . . .' Ash shook his head. 'No, it's gone.'

'The killer came from the garage,' Nelson said.

Ash tutted. 'That's it. All the doors are smashed off their hinges in a direction consistent with the approach of the perpetrator from the garage.'

Nelson's baggy features seemed to sag even further. 'The killer came from the garage.'

'Yes.'

'Have forensics found any boot marks? I'm assuming the doors were kicked open.'

Ash smiled knowingly. 'No boot marks. But footprints, yes.'

Frustration made Nelson start tapping again. 'Don't split hairs, Adam.'

Ash reluctantly had to contradict his boss. 'No, I mean they were foot prints. Prints of a foot. Not a boot or a shoe or a trainer.'

Nelson put the salt cellar down and leaned forward. 'A *bare* foot?'

'The garage floor's dusty, the door to the embalming room is white. It's a clear print.'

'Big foot?'

'No, I'd say it was human.'

Nelson narrowed his eyes and tried to appear annoyed. He didn't like it when underlings made the jokes. 'Was it a big foot print?'

'Size 10 or thereabouts.'

'You're right, it wasn't the wife.'

Their banter was interrupted by a knock at the door. Karen popped her head in. 'Coroner's about to remove the body. All right?'

'Yeah, he can have him.'

The door closed.

Nelson suddenly cursed and called after her.

She poked back in. 'Guv?'

'What's happening in there with fingerprints?'

'We still need to take from the deceased and Mrs Stapely before we'll know what's what.'

Nelson rubbed his top lip with his finger, making the stubble rasp. 'Hmm. If you come up with a strange set, check them against those found at the Kellett residence the other night; the back door and the crowbar.'

'Will do. Anything else?'

'No, ta.'

'What are you thinking?' Ash asked when Karen had gone.

'Not sure yet.'

It was a joy for Ash to see someone so deeply suspicious of everything and everybody. He couldn't be like that himself. But true cynicism took years to cultivate. He'd learn.

'All right,' said Nelson. 'Questions.'

Ash produced his flip-pad and pen and listened intently, ready to scribble in his own special shorthand to get it all down.

'Why was the body arranged so precisely on the bed? Why was it arranged at all? Why was it drained of blood? Why not just stab him and leave it at that? What are the marks on Stapely's temple? Why, when Stapely's spectacles obviously came off in the struggle, did the killer later replace them on the victim's face? Why – and this is very strange – why when Stapely must have heard the first door being broken down – the first of five, remember, including his bedroom – did he not place an emergency call when there's a phone sitting by the bed?'

Ash continued writing frantically for a few seconds. When he'd finished, he flicked back over the pages, and came up with another question: Would he be able to decipher a single word of it? 'Answers please on a postcard,' he joked, closing the pad.

'No. Answers now. I want your immediate response to all these questions. Gut reaction. Instinctive feeling. We can sit down and think logically about them later on.'

'Oh.' Ash reopened his pad.

'See, Adam, this is like the other night at Kellett's. We can explain everything, but it doesn't make sense. We know what happened, but not why.'

Loosening his tie, Ash took a seat opposite his boss. 'You think there's a connection, don't you? Between what happened here and what happened at Kellett's.'

'I don't believe in coincidences. Everything has a reason. If it doesn't, there's a reason it doesn't have a reason.'

Ash made no effort to feign understanding. Nelson leaned heavily against the back of the wooden chair. There was a splintering sound. He didn't comment, but he sat up straight before the chair could collapse and began eyeing something behind Ash. He licked his lips very deliberately.

'Think those Cocopops are Stapely's? He wouldn't miss a bowlful, would he?'

Ash swivelled in his seat and looked at the box of cereals on the fitment. When he turned back, all set to reprimand his superior, Nelson had a Twix in his hand.

'Maybe not,' Nelson said, pulling apart the crimped seal and easing one finger of the snack out into the open. Before he could bite, his mobile phone began to cheep in his inside pocket. He retrieved it and put it to his ear.

'Nelson,' he announced, then bit into his snack. He received a piece of information and glared at Ash. 'No, I didn't know, go on,' he said, offering a rather horrible glimpse of masticated chocolate, biscuit and caramel. Then he huffed. 'Is it really?' He blew out his cheeks and shook his head at Ash with evident disappointment. 'Yes, I know it. All right. Twenty minutes.' He switched off the mobile and tucked it away. Ash was subjected to one of the DCI's infamous plant-wilting stares.

'What?' Ash said, on the defensive.

'Anything you'd like to share with me about the case?'

110

Ash racked his brains.

'Anything missing downstairs?'

'Downstairs? Oh, *shit*! The hearse.'

'Uh-huh. It's been found burnt out.'

'Where?' Ash asked, still cringing.

'North road, out of town. Have you done a head count downstairs?'

'No, why?'

'Because whoever killed Stapely and nicked his car also took a coffin with them.'

'What? You think there was a body inside?'

Nelson stood up. 'Let's have a look at Stapely's records. See if anyone's missing.'

Ash rose and trailed his boss out of the kitchen and down the stairs.

In the office they confirmed how many corpses should have been on the premises, and found they were one short. Kellett's cubicle was empty.

On the way out to their car, Ash felt compelled to say something. Oddly, he knew he was about to talk bollocks, but he couldn't stop himself. 'You know, guv, I saw a film once. *Psychomania* it was called. Sixties film with Nicky Henson, about a gang of bikers.'

Ash unlocked the Granada by remote and slipped in behind the wheel. He waited for Nelson to ease his bulk into the passenger seat before continuing.

'Anyway, this gang of bikers discovers how to return from the dead, and . . . well, that's not the point. The point is that the first to kill himself is Nicky Henson, the leader, and the rest of the gang want to bury him in his leathers, sitting upright on his bike. So they steal his body and that's what they do.' He chuckled. 'And it's great when he comes back because there's this bloke walking across the field and he hears the muffled sound of this motorbike and, er . . . he, er . . .' Ash tailed off; Nelson was drooping his eyelids on purpose. 'Anyway, I was thinking, if Kellett had any biking friends, might they have stolen his body to give him the same sort of send off?'

Nelson now appeared to be fully comatose.

'Guv? What do you think?'

After a dour pause, Nelson pretended to come to. 'Shall we go now, Adam?'

Ash nodded. 'Sure.'

The maroon Granada joined the stream of rush-hour traffic. The morning sun slanted in through the driver's side window, making Ash squint. As they moved slowly along, the glare was intermittently blocked by flanking houses. To Ash it felt like a harsh spotlight blinking on and off under the command of some Supreme Interrogator. He began to feel uncomfortable and his resentment towards Nelson surfaced.

'Guv, I'm confused.'

'Go on.'

'You say you want my gut reaction, answers off the top of my head.' He paused, debating whether to swear. 'Then you take the piss when I mention that film. I mean, this is a weird case, it might just have a weird explanation.'

'Of course, and the killer could be a biker.'

'So it wasn't such a stupid suggestion.'

'Which means the killer could be a solicitor. Or a garage mechanic. Or an accountant. Or a bus driver. Or he could be employed in any other trade or profession you care to mention.'

Ash slowed the Granada behind a line of traffic which was backing up at a red light. He turned to his boss. 'What d'you mean?'

'You know what I'm going to do this weekend if the weather holds?'

'No.'

'I'm going to join a group of people, including a solicitor, a garage mechanic, an accountant and a bus driver, and we're going to head off into Wales.'

'Hey?'

'We're a bike club. I ride a Triumph Trophy.'

Ash raised his eyebrows. He couldn't picture his boss on a motorbike. He couldn't imagine one big enough.

'It's not *what* you said about the film, Adam, it's why you said it.'

The traffic edged forward towards the lights.

'I'm not with you.'

'What I'm saying is, it doesn't help to lump people together. You're damning a biker simply because he rides a bike. It's a cliché.'

112

'Come on, guv, I've seen some pretty mental antics from bikers in the past.'

'And all car drivers are saints.'

Ash said nothing. Clearly, he had hit upon Nelson's pet subject. Here was another argument he wouldn't win.

'Bikers kill themselves,' Nelson said. 'And sometimes they kill other people. Agreed. But you know the biggest cause of bike deaths? Car drivers. You wouldn't believe the amount of times I've nearly been knocked off at a junction, and then when I catch the silly fucker—'

'You *chase* them?'

'Damn right. When I catch them, they always say, 'Sorry, mate, didn't see you.' Well, shite, they weren't bloody looking. Anyone sitting at a junction, I always clock their expression. If I didn't, I'd be dead by now. Bloody dormant, most of them. If they don't notice a big square block of metal descending on them out of the corner of their eye, they assume there's nothing coming.'

'Getting back to the case,' Ash said quickly, 'if this is to do with Andrew Kellett, do you think a biker might be responsible?'

'Did you know, bikers have to pass Compulsory Basic Training before they're even allowed out on the road? What do car drivers have to do? Turn seventeen. It's bloody stupid.'

'Guv?'

'What?'

'About Kellett.'

'Adam, I'm not ruling anything out at this stage. But if it is a biker, it'll be a nutter who happens to ride a bike, not someone who's mental by dint of the their chosen hobby. I mean, I ride a bike, am I deranged?'

Ash considered it prudent to lie. 'No, guv.'

'Well then.'

The Granada slipped through the traffic lights at amber. In his rear-view mirror, Ash saw the car behind follow on.

'I'm going to give this bloke a tug,' Ash said, itching to take his mood out on someone who couldn't answer back.

'Why?'

'He just ran a red.'

'Leave it.'

'But, guv—'

'Keep going.'

'Then let's shift this lot.' He nodded towards the vehicles in front and his hand reached for the siren switch.

'Don't. Five minutes won't make any difference, and we can use the time to discuss one or two things. Where are those questions you wrote down?'

Ash dug in his shirt pocket and handed Nelson the flip-pad. After a few seconds, Nelson said, 'Adam, what the bloody hell does this say?'

Ash remembered his alien alphabet. 'Ah.'

'Here, you read it,' Nelson said, offering the pad.

'I'm driving.'

'We're not going fast.'

Ash wanted to mention something about double standards, and wondered if he'd get any sympathy from Nelson if he killed a motorcyclist whilst deciphering his notes on the move. He took the pad and held it at the top of the steering wheel. Shifting his attention between it and the road, he tried to make sense of his notes.

'All right. First few questions ask essentially the same thing: why was the murder ritualised, what with the draining of the blood, etcetera?'

'Well?'

'Okay, perhaps the killer specifically wanted to do to Stapely what Stapely does to his dead bodies.'

'Why?'

Ash shrugged. 'Revenge? A message from an angry relative? But that doesn't make much sense. It's not as if Stapely's a doctor who accidentally lost a patient. How can you mistreat someone who's already dead?'

Nelson didn't respond.

'Well, I think we're dealing with a psychotic,' Ash ventured.

'Why?'

'Because his mind was totally focused.'

'And why does that make him psychotic?'

'Because of what his mind was totally focused *on*. It was midnight and he kicked down five doors to reach his victim. You don't do that in a quiet neighbourhood unless your sole aim is committing the crime. If I wanted to kill someone. I could think of easier, quieter, less suspicious ways of doing so.'

'You think anyone intent on killing is legally insane?' Nelson asked obtusely. 'Christ, if that was the case, defence barristers would have a bloody field-day.'

'No, I'm not saying that at all. At the very least he's a psychopath, mentally disturbed to some extent, but I think the facts suggest more. A psychopath will carefully choose his target, location and timing. He's sick, but he knows right from wrong, and consciously decides on a path of evil because he likes killing; it gives him the ultimate high, usually sexual. It's a power thing. Which means if he's caught, he's going to lose the chance to kill again, and therefore his power and his biggest turn-on.'

'Is this leading anywhere?'

'Yes. Why would a psychopath choose a window of opportunity with so much risk involved? He wouldn't. But to a psychotic, someone legally insane, acting on voices in his head, for example, such considerations wouldn't apply. He'd be driven to kill by forces beyond his control. Killing would be his only intent. And killing *now*. An immediate response to the impulse. That's what I'm saying: a psychopath would have been more concerned with getting away with it, and, given the existing circumstances, I can't see that was the case.'

'So you're saying we've got a genuine sicko on our hands.'

'Definitely. Which gives us somewhere to go with it. We need to check out anyone who's been receiving treatment on either an in-patient or out-patient basis at psychiatric departments in the area.'

Nelson grunted an acknowledgement. 'Good. I'll get someone onto it. How come no one reported the disturbance last night?'

'The neighbours either say they didn't hear anything—'

'Bull.'

'Yeah. Or they say they thought Stapely was working late.'

'Bull. Don't want to get involved.'

'One couple even said they did hear but thought Stapely had started making his own coffins.'

Nelson's laughter bellowed out of him. 'At midnight?'

Ash smiled. 'I know. What can you do?'

'So what else is scribbled in that book of yours?'

For safety, Ash pulled back from the car in front as he looked at his pad.

'Spectacles. Why were the spectacles replaced after the struggle?'

'What d'you think?'

'I think this goes back to the ritual nature of the murder. Stapely was laid out very carefully. Apart from the trocar in his chest, he looked as though he could have just fallen asleep. Which is the impression any undertaker would want to give when presenting a body to a relative.'

'So it does smack of revenge,' Nelson said. 'It is a message.'

'I'd say.'

'Okay. Next question.'

They were through the centre of town now and the traffic was thinning out. Ash had picked up speed and was even less confident about reading and driving at the same time.

'Next question,' Nelson prompted.

Ash glanced down quickly three times, then popped the pad onto the dash, having taken in the gist of the remaining questions.

'The killer gave Stapely a punch to the temple. The bruises are knuckle indentations. It was a single knockout blow, delivered at will. Highly clinical. Which means the damage to the bedroom was probably caused by the killer simply teasing his victim, stalking him for a while. As for Stapely not dialling 999, the only possible explanation I can think of is that he knew there was no point: that help would arrive too late. Not just help from us, but, more significantly, medical help. He knew he was going to die. So I'd say he knew who was coming for him, which reinforces our suspicions about revenge being the motive.'

Ash realised he had nothing more to say. He shut up, and suddenly feared he might have been somewhat overambitious. If the salient fact of a stolen hearse could escape his attention, how confident could he be about offering an overview of the entire case?

There was a rustling then a snap, and Ash had a chunk of Yorkie thrust under his nose.

'Want a bit?' Nelson asked.

'Uh, no thanks.'

Nelson ate it himself, then quickly devoured the rest of the bar. When Ash considered his boss might be able to speak, he asked a question.

'Where exactly are we going?'

'Weeliz.'

'Pardon?'

116

'It's a motorcycle showroom owned by a petite Scottish lady named Elizabeth.'

Ash grinned. 'Wee Liz? You're joking.'

'No, and she's a pal of mine so don't take the piss. Anyway, the hearse is on some wasteground behind the building, and the place has been broken into.'

'Bikes,' Ash mused. 'Funny, eh?'

'Yeah, we'll have to arrest that Nicky Henson.'

'Guv, if I say something, promise you won't take offence.'

'Go on.'

'You're a facetious bastard.'

'Thanks.'

After a couple of minutes spent in silence, they arrived at the next crime scene.

TWENTY-THREE

It had started out as an interesting exercise, nothing more. To pluck Milton from the end of *Man on a Murder Cycle* and let him loose at the beginning of a second novel. Tom had not intended to spend more than fifteen minutes on it.

That was at lunchtime. Now, the last light was seeping out of the sky, and he was still going strong. Twenty pages so far. Twice as much as he usually managed in a day, whether the day was good, bad or indifferent, and for years the days had rarely been better than awful. It seemed like some kind of miracle, as though by coveting Kellett's words he had stolen the man's talent, or perhaps rediscovered his own. And it wasn't like all those times before. He wasn't kidding himself. It was good work. Really good. Flowing.

He didn't want to stop writing. He was paranoid that if he went to bed, the magic would not be there in the morning. But he needed to sleep. After the signing of the contract that morning, the stress of recent events had dissolved through his system and now he felt weak with tiredness.

The nightmare had come to an end. The gathering blackness he so dreaded had finally lifted.

He didn't *want* to stop writing, but he did. He ended the paragraph and switched off the typewriter.

From now on, Tom Roker was in command. In control of his writing, in charge of his career. He didn't need the booze. Fear and paranoia were things of the past. If he wanted to sleep, he would sleep, and when he wanted to write, it would all be on tap for him. He had never been more certain of anything.

He boxed off the completed pages, then reached and turned off the desk lamp. It was an effort to rise from his chair. He put out the main light but didn't leave the room. He went to the window,

118

opened the curtains and lit a cigarette. For a long while he gazed out above the rooftops opposite, enjoying his smoke, watching the stars brighten against the deepening blue. He was alone in the dark in silence, and it didn't scare him any more. He felt serene.

When the telephone rang, Tom was miles away. He jolted with the sudden intrusion. His cigarette had burnt out. He dropped it in the ashtray on his desk and picked up the receiver. 'Hello.'

'*You stupid arsehole!*'

Tom pulled his ear away from the source of the insult. The abuse carried on.

'*Shit-for-brains!* You did it, didn't you? I told you. I told you not to.'

'Carol?'

'I can't believe you did it. After everything I said. You fucking *moron*!'

'Carol?'

'You . . . you . . . *twat-and-a-half*!'

'Carol, what the hell are you on about?'

Maniacal laughter screeched down the line. 'Act the innocent, why don't you?'

Tom sat down at his desk; it looked like being a long call.

'Christ, Roker, you are so dumb. You are so fucking deluded. It was perfect. Perfect. *Why?*'

'Why what?'

'*Dickhead!*'

Tom let out an involuntary snigger. He wasn't used to Carol cursing with such gusto. 'Carol—'

'Don't you laugh. Don't you dare laugh at me. You of all people are not in any position to laugh.'

'Carol, just talk to me. What have I done?'

'You changed it. You changed Kellett's novel.'

A shiver went through him. He knew he hadn't altered a word of it, but he was in the deepest trouble if he couldn't convince Carol of this.

'I gave you the novel as you gave it to me,' he assured her.

'Sure you did, *prick.*'

Tom wondered whether Carol had a thesaurus in front of her, open at *Idiot* (*slang for*). He grabbed his cigarettes and lit up.

'I don't know what to say, Carol. I swear to God I didn't touch it.'

119

Quietly, she said, 'Well, something's missing.'

'Missing?'

'That scene in the bank. You know?'

'It's gone?'

'Part of it. Where Milton does that thing with the baseball cap. It's not there.'

'That's impossible.'

Carol began shouting again. 'I'm not making this up, you know!'

'Okay, okay,' Tom calmed her. 'But, Carol, why would I delete it? I liked it.'

'Then why's it gone? *How's* it gone?'

'Carol, I don't know. All I did when you gave me those manuscripts was burn one and copy the other.'

The line fell silent.

'Carol?'

'Which one did you burn, Tom?'

'Which one? What's it matter?'

'Which one?'

'Hold on.' Tom had a think. 'The red one. Yeah. Then I photocopied the black one and burnt that as well.'

'Fuck.'

Tom had already cottoned on to his mistake, but he played it dumb. 'What's it matter?'

'You burnt the one he sent to me.'

'So?'

Carol's voice rose in pitch. 'Well, obviously they were *different*.'

Tom decided to play it down. 'Not much. Is it just that one thing?' He drew on his cigarette. 'I could always write it in.'

'No. Let's exercise some damage limitation, shall we?'

'Are you sure? Because I can do it. I've just started a new novel. A sequel. I've got the style down pat.'

Before hanging up, Carol tittered humourlessly, then affected a miserable monotone. 'A new novel by Tom Roker. Yippee.'

TWENTY-FOUR

———◆———

Fierce warmth blasted out against her calves from under the seat. Angie turned away from her fellow commuters, squashed together in the carriage, unsmiling in their isolation. With her glove she wiped a clear patch in the steamed up, grubby window. The countryside rolled by, shrouded in a freezing mist. She could feel the cold touch her face through the glass. Night was finally lifting, only to reveal a grey and burdened sky.

Eight months had passed. Against all her worst expectations, Angie's life had proceeded in a blissfully uneventful fashion. Only two things had changed, and they were her choice. She had a new job as a travel agent in Manchester, and her hair was cut short.

The routine of travel, work, eat and sleep was humdrum, and she loved it. There were no surprises. Of her remaining, distant relatives, none was ill, dying or dead, peacefully or otherwise. The police stayed away. No one broke in. In her immediate circle of acquaintances, not a single person had been brutally murdered. Life was boring, and, for the time being, that was just fine.

On a final visit, Nelson and Ash had informed her of the business at Stapely's, of the burnt-out hearse and the empty coffin, and the break-in at Weeliz the bike shop. Considering the only items stolen were one set of racing leathers, a full-face helmet and a special fuel-injected, turbo-charged motorcycle, Ash had seemed tremendously excited about the theory of a lunatic biker at large in the area. Nelson had told him to shut up, several times. Both of them, however, had been convinced there would be further bloodshed, and that it would happen soon. In return for this information, Angie had told them zip. She had kept quiet about the strange occurrence at the undertaker's; had made no mention of the fact that Michael had been with her; had not let on that he had attempted to rape her back at the cottage. All were serious omissions, and all would have prolonged a period in her life she wanted to end. So she had said nothing. Their suspicions were clearly aroused, not least because she had absorbed all the ghastly details with apparent indifference. She wasn't unmoved, of course – she realised it was terrible – but she was just too sick and tired to register the news with much more than a shrug. On that particular day, the Second Coming would not have fazed her.

As for the local Man of God, he had returned to the village only a few weeks ago. Angie had bumped into him twice since then. Both times, he had flushed scarlet and looked away and hurried by. She gathered that his self-inflicted cross had left a scar on his forehead, because he had grown his fringe unusually long. According to a notice outside the church during his absence, the Reverend Michael Shaw had been taking a six-month sabbatical. His temporary replacement had been one of the new breed of women clergy. Female attendance had waned dramatically.

Angie had decided against a church service for her departed brother, mainly because he really had departed. She had not been keen on the prospect anyway, worrying what his next party piece might be, especially with a larger audience to impress. The planned cremation was cancelled. At least his casket had gone up in flames.

Ash and Nelson had not disturbed her again. The feared murder spree had not materialised. The fingerprints were never traced. Psychiatric records had drawn a blank. The culprit was still at large. The stolen bike was never recovered. And neither was the missing body.

Angie had spent Christmas alone, in quiet remembrance of happier times. It was a sad and lonely few days, but she didn't cry. On New Year's Eve she had joined some colleagues from work for a night on the town. The atmosphere was happy and loud, and she had bawled her eyes out all the way through Auld Lang Syne.

She concluded she was better off on her own.

Overall she was proud of her progress thus far, particularly that she had not repeated her mistake of seeking solace from sex. It was the easiest route in the world to take, and often the most attractive, but it always led to more heartache. She was glad she had learned the lesson early.

Nevertheless, the episode at the undertaker's had left its mark on her. Death she could understand. Life she could cope with. But that afternoon at Stapely's, she had caught a glimpse of something else. Something outside those black and white categories. Most of the time it didn't bother her, but in more contemplative moments she felt unsettled. The problem would not slot itself away in her mind. It was a shape that had no corresponding hole.

The hulking businessman next to her decided to read his *Financial Times*. The huge pink pages opened out like stork wings, invading her already limited space. She tensed, her head filling with a torrent of justified abuse, but her mouth, as always, stayed shut. On the train, there was no equivalent to road rage. Without the protection of a steel cage, folk seemed a little more wary of confrontation. If track temper and carriage choler did exist, they were not visibly manifested. They just turned inside and loused up the day within the first hour.

Angie, however, was able to let it go very quickly. She was only human – she couldn't help reacting – but the insignificance of everyday situations was more apparent to her than to most people, and she didn't stay angry for long. Some time in the not too distant future, Mr Bigshot Businessman would come to realise the emptiness of his current preoccupations. Nose-tubes and chest monitors were great levellers.

The train continued on its ponderous journey to Manchester. Angie closed her eyes and let the rhythms of noise and movement and the artificial fug of warmth take her to sleep.

She was startled awake by a mass slamming of doors: the Piccadilly exodus. Still half-asleep, she collected herself and joined the droves. As she walked briskly down the platform she was passed by a multitude of hurrying figures. Everyone always rushed. It was odd – they couldn't all be late for work. But she understood. It was just modern life, the fear of being left behind. When a person physically slowed down, pulled out from the crowd, dangerous mental processes began. Questions popped. Cruel questions that begged answers you knew but didn't want to hear. Answers that made you want to turn and walk in the opposite direction, away from the crowd. Of course, everyone had times like that, at night, lying in bed, contemplating the universe. But those soul-searches rarely brought the momentous changes they threatened, because sleep came swiftly. Like some devious vicious circle, the stress of the working day caught up and closed down the mind, snuffing out both question and answer, ensuring that the next working day would happen just like the last.

But sometimes she wondered whether she really resented her fellow commuters' ignorance because she so longed to return to a similar state of unknowing.

In the cold air, under the high domes of the station roof, Angie trotted on towards the barrier, hurrying to keep up.

At lunchtime Angie took a wander around the shops on Deansgate. She didn't want to buy anything, but she often enjoyed the feeling of separateness found only in a streetful of strangers. She munched a pastie as she gazed in the windows, fascinated by the huge array of goods people hankered after and believed they couldn't live without.

Further down the road she came to a large bookshop, each window arranged with promotional stacks of new releases. She thought of her brother and his truncated literary career, but these days the memory made her weary more than sad.

The window next to the main entrance was devoted entirely to one novel. A free-standing poster in the centre of the display explained the fuss: *From TOM ROKER, bestselling author of* Hidden Blade, *comes a new thriller* . . . MAN ON A MURDER CYCLE. There was an accompanying image of a biker in black leathers on a black motorcycle against a hellish red background. It put her in mind of her brother's story.

Above her, on the inside of the glass, was another announcement. She stepped back and looked up. Strung high up across the width of the window was a banner: *TOM ROKER will be here on Monday, 13th January, from 12 till 2 p.m., signing copies of his new novel.*

Angie checked her watch. One-fifteen. She cupped her hands to the glass and peered in. There were two lines of people. One led up to the cash register, whilst the other, much longer, proceeded slowly towards a table just inside the entrance. Many customers were paying at the till only to develop nervous smiles as they joined the second queue for book-signing.

Angie couldn't see Tom Roker; his public surrounded him. She wondered who the hell he was; she had never heard of him. Mildly inquisitive, she moved to the entrance and pushed the door open to go inside.

She was stopped in her tracks. Still holding the door wide, she turned to look up the street.

A bone-shaking, goose-bumping noise was heading her way.

Tom's hand halted mid-signature. He had not suffered any Miltonian nightmares since last summer, and his conscience had troubled him very rarely, but the sound outside nevertheless sent an icy shiver through him.

He inclined his head to see round the man who was blocking his view of the street. In the doorway, a young woman was allowing the January air to sweep inside and chill him even more. She had her back to him, her blonde head cocked to one side, like a dog hearing a sound inaudible to human ears. But this sound was not inaudible, and out on the pavement, as in the store, people were turning to stare.

Tom stood up, then absently excused himself and walked towards the street, leaving the half-signed book on the table. The blonde woman at the door gave him a friendly but frowning sideways glance, which he returned, then they both stepped outside.

Twenty yards away, a large black motorcycle had mounted the kerb and was now stationary in the middle of the pavement. Its single oblong headlight was beaming towards them. Below it to either side, faired-in orange lenses were blinking simultaneously, warning of some impending hazard. The rider was clad in black racing leathers, wearing a gleaming black helmet with the black visor pulled down. He was on and off the throttle. The exhaust can was emitting a raucous din which crackled and whined as the revs eased. Tom guessed it was a thoroughly illegal pipe. That and the position of the bike on the pavement were attracting a mixture of scowls and smirks, depending on age. But no one had the guts or foolhardiness to tell him off. And he would not have heard anyway.

Tom mused whether the biker was a fan paying bizarre homage, or if he might have been hired in an irresponsible publicity stunt arranged by Neptune Publishing. Or indeed whether the whole thing was entirely unrelated, just some nutter.

In that moment, Milton came to mind, but although Tom had ventured a little way towards it, he had not yet crossed that divide beyond which he might believe fictional characters were out to get him.

Suddenly, the biker wound the revs to a crescendo and maintained full throttle. He clawed the fingers of his revving right hand around the front brake lever and pulled it tight in, then let the clutch out with his left hand. The front of the bike dived on its forks as the rear wheel began spinning furiously, hissing and squealing on the concrete flags and snaking from side to side. Burning rubber sent blue-white smoke billowing into the air, obliterating everything behind the bike. Then the spinning rear began creeping in a circle around the static front.

Tom knew exactly what he was seeing. Milton performed countless identical manoeuvres in *Man on a Murder Cycle*, normally before or after an episode of violence.

The bike continued with the donut, completing three hundred and sixty degrees, before the rider pulled a wheelie out from the dense cloud and tore along the pavement towards the bookshop.

Tom froze, but a hand grabbed his arm and yanked him into the doorway. He turned to his saviour, the blonde woman, and mouthed 'Thanks.'

Man and machine shot a few yards past, then stopped so abruptly that the rear of the bike lifted three feet off the ground, before thumping down again. Armoured boots clunked on the concrete to balance the machine.

Tom was impressed: a donut, a wheelie and a stoppie. Decals told him the bike was a Kawasaki ZZ-R1100, and an insignificant marking above the back light read 'Turbo'. Seeing the massive rear tyre, Tom couldn't help but smile. It was shredded by the burn-out, the tread pattern essentially erased from the centre section. When Tom noticed the number plate, his smile broke into laughter. The biker's parting message to all he overtook: P155 OFF.

The revs settled to a wicked burble, then the biker looked over his shoulder. A bunch of people were now crowded in the doorway, many clutching Tom's novel, but, strangely, Tom felt he was the one being singled out by the glaring black visor. In fact, he sensed an unfathomed menace was lurking behind that impenetrable plastic shield, and it was all meant for him. His amusement vanished.

A distant siren came as a great comfort, but the biker kept his hidden gaze focused, in defiance of the approaching powers of law and order. After ten seconds the indicators winked off, the revs rose and the exhaust can burst into life, once again shattering the crisp January air with its mighty, jagged-edged tones.

Further up Deansgate, the cops were on their way. The siren was whipping madly, parting the traffic. Tom could see the strobing blue rooflights weaving between cars.

The biker gave a little nod in Tom's direction, then hurtled into the road and roared off down the centre line, between the lanes of slow-moving, rubbernecking drivers, towards the oncoming police.

'Thanks,' Tom said to the blonde woman by his side.

'You're welcome.'

'You saved my life.'

She smiled. 'I doubt it.'

The exhaust and the siren were now barely audible in the distance. By comparison, the normal city hubbub seemed tranquil. The pavement had resumed its flow. Shoppers were disappearing back into the stores.

'Were you coming in?' Tom asked, gesturing through the open door.

Angie shook her head.

Tom patted her arm. 'Wait a minute.' He went inside and took a novel from a pile by the till, then retrieved his pen from the table. He came back out and opened the front cover, nib poised.

'What's your name?' he asked.

'Angie.'

Tom wrote something then handed her the book.

She read the message. *For Angie, my guardian angel. Ever in your debt, Tom Roker.*

'I see,' she said. 'You're the author.'

'For my sins.'

'Was that . . . ?' Angie pointed towards the black circular scorch mark twenty yards along the pavement.

'Publicity? Beats me.'

Angie stared at the cover design, the image of the biker from hell.

'Well, better get scribbling again,' Tom said reluctantly, cocking a thumb over his shoulder at his signing table.

Angie nodded vaguely, still absorbed by the picture.

'Are you all right?' Tom asked.

After a moment, she looked up at him. 'Fine. Miles away. Thanks for the book.'

'Pleasure. Hope you enjoy it.'

'I'm sure I will.' Angie tucked the hardback novel into her handbag.

'Bye then,' said Tom Roker, and returned to his duties.

The chase took them east, out of the city centre, through Salford and onto the M602.

Once on the motorway, the lead was taken by a Jaguar pursuit car. Two Vauxhall Senators and a Range Rover brought up the rear. The outside lane cleared as the sirens reached ahead.

Sergeant Wellings, driving the Jaguar, knew that the bike in front could outpace him, but only if traffic conditions allowed. Eventually, they would close him down and run him onto the hard shoulder. If he didn't crash first. A police helicopter had been requested in case the target vehicle managed to open a gap and slip quietly off the motorway. Not that this particular suspect vehicle could slip any place very quietly whilst sporting such a deafening race exhaust.

They were across the Eccles by-pass in no time. The Jag's tacho needle varied between 100 and 130. Several members of the public attempted to get in the way of the biker, but he skilfully manoeuvred past them, and even travelling at a ton-plus the front wheel was seen to lift with the next spurt of acceleration.

At junction 12 the 602 turned into the 62 and headed south-west for a few miles, before continuing eastwards.

Wellings had never wanted to nick someone so badly. It was the number plate. P155 OFF. It really pissed him off. He felt the biker was toying with him. A machine that size could do over 170, but even when the road ahead was clear, the rider wouldn't push it past 130.

North-east of Warrington, the ZZ-R joined the M6 going south. One by one, four vehicles from the Cheshire Constabulary joined the chase, making eight. Further on, two of the Greater Manchester units pulled off down slip roads to return to their regular stretch of tarmac.

Wellings kept the lead. He was going to follow this little bleeder to the end of the line; Land's End if necessary. P155 OFF indeed.

As confirmation crackled over the radio that the police chopper was finally on its way, it seemed that it was no longer needed. The bike began to slow, moving across the three lanes to coast along the

128

hard shoulder at around 50 mph. Either some mechanical problem, or giving up in the face of overwhelming odds.

Rooflights swirling, headlights flashing, Wellings overtook, followed by the remaining Manchester Senator. A Cheshire Omega edged over onto the inside lane to flank the ZZ-R whilst, behind, the three other Cheshire vehicles crept into formation. The 4 X 4 Discovery moved onto the hard shoulder and eased closer to the bike's rear wheel as the Carlton and Rover staggered themselves in the slow and middle lanes respectively.

Wellings coordinated the final seconds. The Senator was to block the inside lane ahead of the bike, and the Jag itself would plug the hole directly in front of it on the hard shoulder with a diagonal swerve.

Each vehicle drifted further into position, closing the gaps, cutting down the options.

Then Wellings barked the order to commence a rapid slow-down and squeeze.

In that last moment before the box sealed completely, the ZZ-R rocketed forward, escaping between Senator bonnet and Jaguar boot, tearing straight across into the outside lane.

Wellings cursed. He shifted down and stamped on the gas, but he had already resigned himself to the fact that catching up was a forlorn hope. Never had he seen anything accelerate so swiftly, and, unfortunately, there was no traffic in the outside lane to impede its ballistic progress. He estimated the bike had shot from 50 to 130 in around 200 yards, and, even now, he could see the bike shrinking into the distance. Using his years of experience, he was able to gauge the speed of the target vehicle. But nothing in his experience had ever caused him to calculate a velocity well in excess of 200 mph.

The aerial support had arrived too late. Ground units alerted up the motorway had also failed to locate the black Kawasaki. Wellings had travelled as far as the Sandbach Services before giving up. He was miles out of his territory.

Sitting in the Roadchef restaurant, he sipped his coffee. The motorway hum infiltrated the room. Every so often, thinking he could hear a familiar exhaust note, he perked up, but it was only his imagination. No doubt the ZZ-R would be long gone by now.

He smiled, then shook his head. The speed of the thing. He

couldn't get over it. They were fast enough when standard. Fastest production bike in the world. But this one had to be nitrous or turbo.

He drained his coffee and picked up his car keys. Faces stared as he stood up, then quickly looked away, as though he might psychically read their motoring misdemeanours if he caught their eyes for too long.

Wellings could see his driver's side window was smashed the moment he left the restaurant. As he approached his car, he noticed a piece of paper stuck to the dash.

He stopped and surveyed the service area. The scene was unremarkable. The usual comings and goings. But his instincts told him something was very amiss. He shivered. It was a cold day, but it was more a symptom of the alarm bells jangling in his head.

Slowly, eyes peeled, he walked to the Jag.

Then he stopped again and his head whipped right; a sudden noise from the petrol station forecourt. Adrenalin dumped into his system. He began trembling.

From behind the BP Shop, the source of the noise emerged onto the exit road.

The ZZ-R rider pointed to his number plate, then gave the thumbs up.

Wellings reached in through the smashed window and unlocked his door from the inside. He yanked it open, tore off his jacket, threw it in to cover the glass on his seat, jumped in and fired up the Jag. Tyres squealing, he sped out of the car park to join the exit road. The ZZ-R was burbling placidly along to join the motorway. Wellings radioed in, then tugged his seat belt across him and clicked it home. Hitting the lights and siren, he put his foot down.

Ahead of him, the ZZ-R responded in kind.

They joined the motorway and veered straight across into the outside lane, picking up speed all the time.

Wellings' eyes were increasingly drawn to the note stuck to his dash by a silver piece of gaffer tape. There had been no time to read it. It was folded in half, the message contained within. Eventually, curiosity got the better of him. He peeled it off and opened it, and, against his better judgment, read it whilst maintaining breakneck speed.

Oi, wanker, it said. *Don't touch any knobs.*

He glanced at the console of switches and frowned. His eyes returned to the biker; weird fucker. He balled the note and chucked it on the passenger seat.

The miles passed. A second unit joined the pursuit. Then a third.

The biker was toying again. He had already demonstrated the power within his grasp – he could twist the throttle and be gone – but he stayed below 130 for the thrill of the chase.

Wellings kept looking at the switches.

The motorway zipped underneath.

The switches. Wellings wanted to press them all. Why not? The siren was blaring; the rooflights were swirling; the blue spots in the grille were strobing; the headlights were in flash mode; he had keyed the mike on his radio; the rear-window heater had been on all day. There was nothing wrong. The electrical circuits were fine. Besides, he didn't take kindly to scumbags giving him orders.

He activated the hazard warning button. The indicators flashed. He put them off.

He poked a finger at the buttons on his VASCAR computer. It responded normally.

He tried his fog lights.

And at the back of the car, the mischief sparked.

Seated in its small bayonet socket, the bulb lit up. But its strange liquid environment caused the glass to instantly smash. The exposed high intensity filament did not agree with its new surroundings either.

Wellings first suspected he might have done something silly when his car exploded.

TWENTY-FIVE

———◆———

For the life of her, she didn't know why she had agreed to read it. Another novel from Tom Roker. Actually written by him. Oh, whoop-de-fucking-do.

But Carol was extremely glad she had agreed to read it. It was brilliant. A worthy sequel to Kellett's original. Eight months ago, when he had first told her it was under way, she had not believed his claims, but Tom had been right: he had rediscovered his old style. Or he had managed to copy Kellett's. Either way, it amounted to the same thing. As a novelist, Tom Roker was reborn.

She set the five-hundred-page manuscript on the coffee table, leaned back on the sofa and gazed across the lounge, out through the balcony windows. Beyond the Thames, the cityscape was grey and bleak, reflecting the sombre clouds. In her head, the sky was a bright Californian blue.

Man on a Murder Cycle had been sold around the world, including to the lucrative US market. Doors were opening up to her all the time. She believed she had already made enough contacts to facilitate her move to America whenever she chose, and now she had the unexpected bonus of this sequel to further bolster her reputation.

Poor Peter, dutiful spouse, slogging his guts out in the City, trying to make ends meet to support his little wifey in her daft hobby. He had no idea. He had no inkling of her earnings to date, nor the fortune that lay in store for her. The only cloud on the horizon was the prospect of him suing for a share in any divorce settlement. But he'd probably work himself to death before that happened.

When the telephone rang, she realised she was half asleep in her daydream. It took three rings for the sound to register.

She went to the sideboard and picked up the receiver. 'Carol Morgan.'

'Carol, Roger. Pyramid Pictures Stateside are offering a million for rights.'

It was Roger Mercer, Carol's film agent. He wasn't big on small-talk.

'Hello, Roger.' She feigned nonchalance: 'Dollars or sterling?'

'Sterling. Well?'

'Leave it a while,' she said coolly. 'They'll wait. They could have gone for the option and offered a pittance, but they went for the rights. They're keen. We can afford to see who else bites.'

'My thoughts exactly.'

'And, Roger?'

'What?'

'There's a sequel.'

'Ah. Is there? Right. That'll up the ante. I'll get back to you.'

The line went dead.

'Yes, bye-bye, Roger. Nice talking to you.' She put the phone down and couldn't keep the imbecile grin off her face.

After Roger had sliced off his agreed ten per cent, half of the remaining ninety per cent would be hers. Assuming Pyramid stood firm and no bidding war ensued, she would make four hundred and fifty thousand pounds.

However, she was confident that a bidding war *would* ensue.

And now she had the sequel, which would really quicken their pulses and have them scrabbling about in their coffers for their last spare cent.

TWENTY-SIX

The following day, Tom had another book-signing, this time in Leeds.

Late on in the session, he checked his watch. It was well after two p.m., but he had clearly not outstayed his welcome. They were still queuing. Tom's hand ached from the constant signing. His cheeks ached from the perpetual smile. The folk who continued to thrust open books in front of him had long since become faceless. After the terrible years of failure he was grateful for the renewed attention, but he just wanted to go home. Every so often, as he scrawled his increasingly ragged signature, he was overwhelmed by the emptiness of his perceived triumph. He didn't deserve it, any of it.

'Who's it for?' he asked the next individual at his table.

'Sandra.'

Tom squiggled his best wishes to the faceless Sandra and thanked her. She gently touched his hand as she gave her own thanks, and suddenly her face came into focus. She was beautiful. Then she was gone.

What the hell, of course he didn't deserve it, but a moment like that put it all in perspective. He had stolen from a dead man; he had deprived no one. But for Tom Roker, *Man on a Murder Cycle* would never have reached the streets. Albeit posthumously, he was giving Andrew Kellett his day, even if it wasn't Kellett's name on the cover. Besides, it was now clear that the whole episode had proved a catalyst for Tom's rediscovery of his own talent. His new novel, though still incorporating Kellett's nemesis, was one hundred per cent his own work. He could be proud of that, at least.

The next thing to be thrust under his nose put the fear of God into him.

'Detective Chief Inspector Nelson, Cheshire Police; this is Detective Sergeant Ash.'

Tom's heart skipped a beat as he took in the indisputable fact of the warrant card, then he swallowed and looked up at the two plain-clothed detectives.

'Can we have a word?' said Nelson, snapping shut his ID.

Tom felt his head drain of blood. He went dizzy.

Damn. They had finally caught up with him for the business at Kellett's house. Why else would he be collared in Leeds by Cheshire detectives?

'Uh . . .' Tom gestured towards the waiting line. 'I'm in the middle of—'

'It's important.'

Tom tried to appear innocent, if only for his fans.

'This way,' said Nelson, tipping his head towards the interior of the store.

Tom stood up and apologised to his disappointed public. He was led to the rear of the building and through a fire exit. Ash cleared a couple of workers from a smoky staff room, and Nelson closed the door.

'What's this about?' Tom asked, lighting up to calm his nerves.

'We were hoping you could tell us,' Ash said.

Tom offered a clueless, friendly smile, and a shrug for good measure. His eyes quickly checked for a possible escape route, but the windows were barred and the door was blocked by the immovable bulk of the senior detective. Tom inhaled deeply on what felt like his final cigarette before sentence was carried out.

'You were witness to an incident yesterday afternoon,' Ash said. 'Around one-fifteen. Involving a motorcycle outside a bookshop on Deansgate in Manchester.'

'Oh, *yeah*,' Tom said with far too much enthusiasm. He was grinning and didn't care if it looked odd. He sank into a chair before his legs could give way with the relief.

'Amused you, did it?' Nelson said gravely.

'No, not at all. No, I was just . . . um . . . go on, what did you want to ask?'

'Well, what do you know about it?'

'Nothing. Why would I?'

'Considering the subject of your novel,' Ash said helpfully.

135

'Oh, I see.' Tom dragged on his cigarette, shot the smoke with a hiss and said, 'No, nothing.'

'No connection?' Nelson said.

'No.'

'No one you might know?'

'No.'

'It wasn't publicity for your novel? Nothing like that?'

'Not as far as I'm aware.'

'What was your impression at the time?'

Tom shrugged. 'What a nutter, I suppose.'

'Nothing else?'

'No.' Tom gave a laugh. 'Bikers, eh? They're all nutters.'

Ash visibly winced.

Nelson narrowed his eyes. 'I ride a motorbike.'

Tom nodded sagely. 'Well, not all of them, obviously.'

The dour scrutiny continued.

Tom rose to his feet. 'Anything else? I'm losing sales out there.'

Meaningfully, Nelson leaned back against the door and pulled a bag of Maltesers from his overcoat pocket. He opened the packet with his teeth.

Tom's initial fear surfaced again. There was more to this little chat than they were letting on. Nelson in particular was acting very oddly. Not that Tom knew what normal might look like, but there was certainly some great question mark waiting to loop itself around Tom's neck and drag him deeper into the mire. Cheshire detectives in Leeds. It didn't figure.

'You know why I like Maltesers, Mister Roker?'

'No.'

'Because they remind me of certain cases I've worked on.' He rolled a chocolate out of the bag into the palm of his hand, then put the rest back in his pocket. He pinched the choc between two fingers and held it up. 'On the surface it's brown. Let's say it resembles a coating of shit. Better still, *bull*shit. But . . .' He bit it in half and showed Tom the inside of the piece in his fingers. 'Inside, it's actually a honeycomb. A very complicated structure. Do you understand what I'm getting at?'

'No,' Tom said, suddenly sick of the bullshit himself. 'Do you?'

Nelson grinned and popped the half Malteser into his mouth.

136

'Not really. I was making it up as I went along. Pretty bloody mystical, though, you must admit.'

Tom sucked his cigarette down to the butt, dropped it and ground the dimp into the carpet. 'Have you finished?'

'I don't like coincidences,' Nelson said. 'Coincidences are bullshit.'

'What's this got to do with me?' Tom asked.

'Don't know.' Nelson paused. 'Yet.' He went over to the staff coffee percolator and poured himself a cup, then returned to the door, barring the exit. 'This might be a long shot, Mr Roker, but does the name Kellett mean anything to you?'

'No,' Tom said instantly, deadpanning for all his worth to submerge his true feelings.

'Kellett,' Nelson repeated. 'Have a think.'

Tom was grateful to be given another chance; his first reaction must have appeared too glib. He affected a thoughtful attitude.

'Kellett,' Ash said.

Slowly, Tom shook his head. 'No. Can't say it rings any bells. Why?'

With great eagerness, Ash took the reins. 'Well, my theory is—'

'Doesn't matter,' Nelson interrupted forcefully. 'It's just some tenuous link we were working on the last time.'

Tom frowned. 'I'm sorry . . . last time? What last time?'

Nelson appeared to debate. Eventually he nodded to Ash. 'Tell him.'

Ash was ready for his moment. 'Well, about eight months ago something happened in our neck of the woods. The ritualised murder of an undertaker. Very nasty. Anyway, whoever did it then went off and stole a motorcycle.'

'Kawasaki ZZ-R1100,' Nelson said. 'Turbo, fuel injection. Very special. Fast? You wouldn't believe how fast.'

'Anyway,' Ash resumed, 'after that, nothing happened. The trail went cold.'

'Until yesterday,' Nelson said, snatching the best line for himself.

Ash glowered at Nelson, who sipped at his coffee.

'The bike outside the bookshop?' Tom said.

Nelson smiled. 'Yup.'

'How d'you know it's the same bike? That had to be a false plate.'

'Correct,' Nelson said. 'But a bike like that is a definite one-off.'

Tom didn't know what to say, so he lit another cigarette. Nelson put his coffee down, took out his Maltesers, chucked five into his mouth and crunched for a few moments. 'What clinches it for me, though,' he went on, 'is that even if there are two such bikes around, I doubt both riders would posses the same homicidal tendencies.'

It took a moment for the implications of the comment to click. 'Hold on,' Tom said, 'he didn't kill anyone yesterday.'

'That's where you're wrong,' Ash dived in.

'We initially lost him on the M6,' Nelson said.

'Then we found him again,' Ash said.

'Then we found him again,' Nelson said, trying to ignore his precognitive parrot of an underling. 'But this time as the chase got under way—'

'He blew up a pursuit vehicle and from the wreckage we've been able to piece together what happened. Whilst the car was unattended at a motorway services, the biker rigged one of its rear fog lamps. Using lengths of electrical wire he extended the bulb directly into the petrol tank, so when the driver hit the relevant button on the dash, the bulb blew and the tank exploded.'

Tom blinked and swallowed hard. He stared down at his shoes.

'So you understand why we're keen to find this maniac,' Ash said.

Tom didn't answer.

Staring at Ash, Nelson crumpled the empty Malteser bag in his fist. He hurled it at a waste basket, missing by several feet. 'So if there is anything . . .'

Face still hidden, Tom shook his head. Now he had heard the details of the motorway murder he certainly did have something to tell them, but he just wanted them to go away. They had already skirted too close for comfort. If they stuck around, he felt he couldn't trust himself not to let something slip, and he gathered he might already have done so by his snap response to the name Kellett.

'Is it good, then?' Nelson asked suddenly.

Tom blanked his expression before looking up. 'What?'

'This novel of yours?'

138

Tom managed a smile. 'That's probably not for me to say.'

'Find out for myself then, should I?' Nelson said, opening the door for them all to leave.

'Pardon?'

'I'll take a copy. You can sign it for me. Come on.'

Walking back through the store, Tom searched for a plausible reason why Nelson should not buy the book. His mouth twitched but nothing came out.

They reached the signing table. The queue had disappeared.

'It's expensive,' Tom blurted. It was all he could think of.

Nelson raised an eyebrow. 'I might not be on your money, Mister Roker, but I can afford to buy a hardback every so often.'

'I know, it's just . . . it's a lot of money when you might not like it.'

'I'm a biker. I'd be keen to find out what you think about us. Nutters, wasn't it?' He picked up a copy from the pile beside the table and held it out. 'Can you put *To Kenny*?'

Reluctantly, Tom took a pen and wrote the required message inside the cover.

'Ta,' Nelson said, taking some banknotes from his trouser pocket.

'Forget it,' Tom said quietly. 'On the house.'

Nelson didn't argue. 'Much obliged.' He received the open book and smiled at the message, then turned the first few pages and looked puzzled. 'Where's your dedication? You haven't dedicated it to anyone.'

Tom dismissed it with a shrug. 'I haven't got anyone.' Which was the truth but not the reason. He had decided it would have been terribly inappropriate.

'No one? Ah, well,' said Nelson, handing Tom a card. 'In case you think of anything . . . Come on, Adam. Home time.'

Ash nodded at Tom and trooped after his boss.

From behind his table, Tom watched them disappear into the street. For several minutes, he remained there, unmoving, his mind in a daze, unable to focus. He was vaguely aware that someone spoke to him, something about his book, but by the time he thought to respond, they had given up and gone away.

He collected his overcoat from the staff cloakroom, then meandered between the browsers towards the exit.

Nelson and Ash had delivered a simple message: a policeman

dead; blown up in his car. But, for Tom, that information had struck home like an immense hammer blow to his skull, and his brain couldn't quite compute what it meant.

One thing was for certain, though. As soon as Nelson got part-way into *Man on a Murder Cycle*, he would receive his very own hammer blow to the skull, and, soon after that, he would be paying a second visit to that less than forthcoming author, Tom Roker.

At the door, Tom turned up the collar of his overcoat, hunched his shoulders and walked out into the cold grey streets.

TWENTY-SEVEN

———◆———

Night-time was the worst. That period between switching off the television and the onset of sleep. Darkening the downstairs and trudging up to a cold bed. The radio didn't help. It was company, but the wrong sort. The late-night play-list of mellow tunes for lovers and melancholic songs for the lonesome. Celebrating both extremes of the human condition with the same tearful sounds. Mocking the afflicted: those in fear of losing and those already suffering the loss.

Angie preferred the silence of an empty house.

She tucked herself under the winter duvet, reached and put out the lamp, turned on her side and closed her eyes.

It took five minutes for her to realise: she was tired, but it was about to be one of those nights. Sleep would be a distant shore for ages yet. Then shortly before her wake-up alarm, it would rush upon her and beach her for all of two hours. She would sleep like the dead and wake up feeling barely alive.

It happened every so often. She was resigned to it these days. Bouts of insomnia for no apparent reason. She would lie awake, thoughtless for a while, but gradually the insoluble problems of life would begin to circle, and sleep would slip out of sight, beyond the horizon. Then she would submit, put the light on and read. Market-stall paperbacks of no real interest, but anything to divert her mind. In the summer she would have had her bicycle rolling, even in the wee hours.

Now she understood how Andrew must have felt. All those nights he had claimed he simply couldn't sleep. She had sympathised, but she hadn't believed him. Obviously, he wasn't counting his sheep in the correct manner. It had seemed ridiculous to her that anyone could look so shattered and still not be able to sleep. It was simple: you closed your eyes, you fell asleep.

But the flipside was just as simple. You closed your eyes and stayed awake. Sleep felt like a skill, and she had forgotten how to use it.

Tonight, Angie decided to pre-empt the usual attack of free-floating anxieties. She put the lamp on and sat up in bed. For several minutes she stared blankly at the wall opposite. It was stupid. There was nothing wrong. Not any more. She was happy enough in her work; fair salary. Okay, she was lonely, a little miserable in the evenings perhaps, but winter's miserly gift of daylight had always made her feel blue.

She wondered if she might need psychiatric help. Was she hoarding a shitload of angst? Possibly. But after coping with Andrew on her own, she was damned if she was going to crumble on a couch in front of a complete stranger.

No, she was okay. It was a phase. It would pass. In the meantime, she would have to cope. Story of her life.

She picked up a paperback from her bedside cabinet. The marker indicated she had finished reading it. She couldn't remember doing so. She put it down again.

On her dressing table was the hardback Tom Roker had presented her with the day before. Given the probable cause of her current state, its title was hardly a recommendation, but she had read everything else in the house. And she might be surprised; perhaps the story would prove some kind of exorcism for the lingering ghosts of last summer.

She jumped out of bed and grabbed the book, and dived back in before the chill could catch her.

Pillows propped behind her, she turned to the first chapter and began to read.

TWENTY-EIGHT

Henry Kent, Solicitor of considerable mediocrity, was hardly about to walk home; it was bloody freezing out there. Besides, he had driven plenty of times. It was only a couple of miles to his house. Along quiet roads. What harm was he doing? What harm had he done to date? None. And he worked hard. He deserved to relax of an evening.

He felt fine. He didn't weave to his wife's old Volvo. He got his key in the door first try. He had single vision. Basically. It certainly wasn't double. He was very strict about that. He always stopped short of double vision. Then he knew he was safe. It was the youngsters who caused the problems. No common sense. No idea when to call it a night. The older generation knew how to handle it. They were used to it. They weren't reckless. They didn't go tear-arsing around. They tootled home very gently, obeying speed limits and reading road signs with their basically single vision. Henry Kent wasn't a danger to anyone.

The dark brown Volvo saloon pulled out of the pub car park into the deserted country lane. Couple of miles. Straight home. No problem.

He had travelled half a mile when he had cause to check his rear-view mirror. A motorcycle was coming up fast. He heard its exhaust before he saw its headlight round the bend behind him.

No doubt it would be some youngster, tanked up, tempting fate.

Henry eased off the accelerator and moved closer to the hedgerow; as close as his basically single vision would allow without mishap. His car was full of white light. He squinted. His rear-view mirror was blinding. He flipped it upwards to the night setting. The motorcycle slowed and maintained its distance.

'Go on,' Henry whispered. 'Piss off. Pass.'

It occurred to him that it might be a police motorcyclist, but he dismissed the thought before it had a chance to raise the slightest alarm in him. The police had their hands full with the local town. They wouldn't waste resources patrolling empty back roads, certainly not with a motorcycle. Not at night. Bikes were for chasing bad guys down motorways, or for hiding behind bushes and radar-zapping the lead-foot brigade.

He lifted his left arm into the glare and waved at the motorcyclist to pass. Despite the clear road ahead and the Volvo's creeping 20 mph, the biker declined the invitation.

Ah, well. Stuff him. Henry picked up speed. He'd be home soon. Another mile. If the biker wanted to sit behind until then, that was his business.

As the speedo needle passed thirty, the light in the Volvo seemed to gain an extra flash of colour. Henry's heart skipped a beat as his eyes shot to the mirror. He tipped it back to day-view, but all he could see was the same oblong headlamp. He blinked, flared his eyes and blinked some more. Perhaps he didn't have double vision, but he was definitely seeing things.

When it happened again Henry knew it was real, because this time the blue light kept on flashing. There was no siren, but it wasn't needed. Only a blind man could have missed the invasion of colour which completely filled the car.

Henry squeezed the steering wheel. 'Fuck.' His luck had run out. How could he have thought it wouldn't? Why had he been so blasé? He swore again, slowed and stopped beneath the first streetlamp of his village. So near and yet . . .

'Fuck.'

He switched off the ignition, blew a breath against his cupped palm. Beer came back at him. He shook his head, swore again, and watched the end of his career loom in his mirror. The Law stopped ten feet behind him. Fleetingly, Henry wondered whether the exhaust wasn't a little loud for a police bike, but then the engine fell silent and his fear of the breathalyser took precedence again. The rider leaned the bike over onto its sidestand. The headlight and the blue flashers went dark. A black form swung one leg off the machine. For a few seconds he just stood there, legs apart, like some comic-book avenging angel.

'That's right,' Henry muttered. 'Enjoy yourself. Take your time. Bastard.'

With a cool and menacing strut, the policeman approached.

Henry sat still, eyes front, until he heard a tapping. He looked to his right. Black leather filled the glass frame of his side window. He wound it down.

'Volvo, eh?'

Henry tried not to breathe on the officer. 'Mmm?'

'Could you get out of the car, please, sir?'

It wasn't a request. Henry obeyed.

The overhead streetlamp gave an eerie orange glow to the figure in black. He was around six feet tall. His armoured leathers appeared to only accentuate an underlying solid physique. He was wearing his helmet with the visor up, but the section of visible face was in shadow. For some weird reason, Henry felt extremely glad about that.

'Didn't see me, did you, sir?'

'Mmm?'

'I was parked opposite the pub. Didn't see me, did you?'

Henry shook his head.

'I saw you.'

'Mmm.'

There was a pause. Henry couldn't hold his breath any longer. He exhaled and beery fumes billowed visibly from his mouth. He half wanted to break down and plead pathetically for his licence.

'Do you know why I've stopped you?'

Henry frowned – the policeman's breath made no clouds in the chill night air. He shook his head.

'Are you sure?'

'Mmm?'

'Speeding?'

'No.'

'Light out? At the back?'

'No.'

Henry shook his head. 'Don't know then.' He supposed there was no harm in them both playing games. If he kept calm, acted innocent, wasn't cheeky, perhaps he could front it out.

'You really don't know why I stopped you?'

'No.'

The policeman sighed. 'Come to the front of the car, would you, sir?'

Henry obediently followed.

'What's that?' asked the policeman.

'What?'

'That.' He indicated the grille.

'Hey?'

'Sir, what is that thing in the middle of your grille?'

Henry smiled crookedly as he answered. 'It's a red nose.'

'And why is it there?'

Henry let out a brief laugh. 'Red Nose Day.'

'But this red nose is actually now pink. Hence I deduce it has been attached to your vehicle for a good five years.'

Henry smiled broadly. 'Are you winding me up?'

'You have had a red nose on the front of your car – your cak-brown Volvo – for five years.'

Henry felt his smile fade. The policeman sounded not only serious, but quietly mental. Suddenly, Henry was frightened for rather more than his driving licence.

'I'm sorry, officer, but it's not an offence, is it?'

'I find it very offensive, yes.'

'No, I mean . . .' Then Henry smiled again. 'Did the lads put you up to this? Are you some sort of, I don't know . . . cop-o-gram?'

'Do I look like some-sort-of-I-don't-know-cop-o-gram?'

Henry stepped back a pace. 'Listen, pal, I don't know what this is, but if the lads did send you, then very funny, ha-ha, but the joke's over. And if you really are a police officer, then I want your name and number. I'm reporting you. This is a gross misuse of your powers.'

In a low, grating whisper came the reply: 'Milton. Six six six.'

Henry sneered at the man in black leathers. 'I've had enough of this. I'm going home.' He barged past and grabbed for the doorhandle.

'Henry . . .'

Henry froze. 'How d'you know my name?'

'I'll do a deal with you, Henry. You give me a good reason why that red nose is still on your car a full five years after the event, and I won't punish you for drink-driving. Because you should be punished for drink-driving. You know that, don't you, Henry?'

Not a cop-o-gram. Not a policeman. A psycho. Henry nodded and felt nauseous. His wife was down the road, waiting for him. His sweet, darling wife. Mother of his children. He wanted to be with her. In that moment, his life fell into place. No more mistresses.

No more drink-driving. A simple existence. It would suffice. If he survived tonight, he would make amends.

'The red nose . . . I'm waiting,' Milton said.

'It's not my car.'

'*Strike one!*'

'It's not! It's my wife's.'

Milton looked disgusted. 'You're a filthy rich solicitor and you bought your wife this piece of old shit? You tight *bastard*. I bet you own a Porsche. I think this deserves a . . . *Strike two!*'

'Please! What's this all about?' Henry pleaded to know, practically peeing himself.

'The red nose. Explain.'

'I can't! We just haven't taken it off!'

'*Strike three!* You're *outta* here!'

Henry was freezing cold, pissed and scared. A poor combination. He felt anger blossom inside and he snapped. Not since his youth had he experienced such instant rage. He lashed out. His fist torpedoed through the face-hole in Milton's helmet and caught him square on the nose. But once the punch had been thrown, he knew his aggression was spent.

'That's more like it,' said Milton, touching his fingers to the blood trickling from his nostrils. 'That redundant piece of plastic on the front of your car now has significance.'

'Can I go then?' Henry squeaked.

Milton began stalking him around the Volvo. 'No, I don't think so. You did rather stumble upon the answer, didn't you? And drink-driving is a very, very, very, very . . . very very very serious offence.'

'Please.'

'So let the punishment fit the crime.'

'Plea—'

Henry's request for leniency was interrupted by an uppercut to his nose.

He dropped like a dead weight. Which was apt. The force of the blow had driven the bone into his brain.

TWENTY-NINE

———◆———

Had it been a normal novel. Angie would have ruined it for herself. She had read the first page, then the last, then about twenty random pages in between.

This, however, was not a normal novel, because before she had even finished the first paragraph on page one, she knew precisely how the story would unfold.

At least the break-in last summer was no longer a mystery. That was one nag less in her subconscious.

She slipped out of bed and went to her brother's room. The door was ajar; the frame and lock had not been mended. She put the light on and peered around the door at the desk. Sure enough, the box of floppy discs was gone. At the time she had not known what, if anything, had been stolen. Andrew's novel had not been high on her list of most-coveted items.

She rested her forehead against the door and sighed heavily. Dead eight months, and Andrew was still being the same disruptive influence. She lightly head-butted the wood, then wandered to his single bed and sat down to think.

What was she going to do? Ignore it? She certainly wanted to. She had fought too many battles on her brother's behalf, and suffered enough already. She was entitled to some peace.

She chuckled humourlessly; she could no more ignore this than she could an alien landing in the back field. It would be against all the unwritten laws of human nature. Besides, forgetting Andrew, she had been a victim herself that fateful night. She had been tricked over the telephone; false hope offered for the apprehension of a guilty party. Then her home had been violated, and a man decapitated in her garden.

Whether she liked it or not, she was involved.

The sensible route was straight to the police. The crimes were unsolved. It was their job.

Maybe, but to Angie it was personal.

Anyway, what proof did she have? The discs were gone, and the state of the room after the break-in suggested that any duplicates would also have been discovered. She was not about to invite the police into her life all over again if they were still unlikely to make any progress. If she found anything herself, she could always pass it on.

She let her eyes wander around the bedroom. She did not expect to see anything important. She was waiting for inspiration, a starting point for her private investigation.

Certain things were plain: Tom Roker had stolen her brother's novel, and from the pages she had read, from what she could remember, stolen it word for word. Of course, he would not have done the physical breaking in; some low-life would have been specially hired for that. Some *vicious* low-life from the condition of her interfering neighbour. As for the publishing house responsible for *Man on a Murder Cycle*, she knew that Neptune was highly reputable. She doubted they had the slightest inkling of the true origin of their latest bestseller. Which meant there had to be a missing link. Something to have brought Tom Roker into contact with her brother's manuscript. A middle-man.

She realised she had been staring for several seconds. Like a magpie drawn to a glittering object, her eyes, surveying the shelves, had come to rest on the brightest spine among the books. It was a thick volume in lemon yellow, with electric blue writing that clashed so strongly the letters appeared to be jiggling. She had to get up to read the title.

The Writer's Handbook 1997.

She pinched it out from its slot and sat down on the bed. When she opened it, the pages wanted to naturally part at the section marked *UK Agents*. She allowed it to guide her. She flicked through page after page, each one pristine. Until she came to an entry which was circled in red Biro.

Carol Morgan Literary Agency Ltd.

So, not a middle-man, a middle-woman.

The blurb beneath included the address, phone and fax, when the company was founded, how writers should approach, prominent clients, and levels of commission.

'Of course,' she whispered; Tom Roker was listed as a prominent client. And to think she had saved him from being knocked down outside the bookshop. She shook her head, even managed a smile. Then she laughed bitterly, briefly. The coincidence was incredible. Had she not been standing next to him, been able to grab him and pull him clear, Tom Roker would have learned that what goes around, comes around. Jeez, of all the people to have saved him from that lesson, it had to be the one person who knew he needed to be damn well taught.

Unconsciously grinding her teeth, Angie looked down at the entry circled in red.

Morgan. Carol Morgan. Roker's co-conspirator.

She jabbed her fingertip hard at the name.

'Woman, you have got some serious explaining to do.'

THIRTY

———◆———

Tom Roker was about to receive some very interesting phone calls.

He was enjoying a lie-in, a mug of tea beside him, nestling in a hollow in the duvet. The radiator was pumping wondrous heat. It was past eleven a.m. The weather looked foul. Lumps of sleet slapped the window and slid melting down the glass. Snug in bed, Tom felt safe and content, cosseted from the cruel world outside.

Man on a Murder Cycle was sitting closed on his lap. His own name shone up at him in silver capitals. TOM ROKER. It was total justification. It meant everything. Without it, he had been nothing. His existence had become a futile passing of empty days, dwelling on losses – personal, financial, creative.

He was happy.

So what if DCI Nelson made further contact? It was inevitable now he had the novel, but so what? The events of the previous summer were ancient history. If he called again, it would be concerning a more recent occurrence which simply *had* to be a coincidence, whether Nelson liked it or not.

For the next five minutes Tom just stared at the front cover, a slight smile making dimples.

TOM ROKER. TOM ROKER. TOM ROKER. TOM . . . ROKER. ROKER. TOM ROKER.

It had all been worth it.

The phone rang. He picked up the novel, leaned over the side of the bed, and exchanged it for the receiver on the floor. 'Hello.'

'It's Carol. Thought you should know: there's been an offer for film rights.'

'Oh?'

'A million sterling.'

Tom's mouth fell open. 'A million? Jeepers.'

'But I suggest we hold out for more. See who else bites.'

'And Roger agrees?'

'Yes.'

Grinning insanely, Tom shrugged to himself. 'Right. Fine. Anything else?'

'Your new book . . . I like it.'

'Good.'

'You dedicated this one.'

'I wrote this one.'

'Mmm. Think they'd appreciate it? Helen and Charlotte?'

Tom picked up a cruel glee in her tone, as though she was overjoyed that they'd left him. 'Not the content of the book. But hopefully that I still think of them, yes.'

Carol grunted rudely. 'Get on with another.'

Click, burrrrr . . . End of conversation. A fairly standard exchange given the flavour of their relationship these days.

He put the phone down and pushed himself back into bed. His mug of tea was on its side.

'Bugger.'

He quickly got out of bed, put the mug on the carpet and dragged the duvet across to the radiator. The cover was patterned with swirls of greens and browns. A tea stain would make no difference. As he tucked an edge of duvet behind the radiator, the telephone rang again.

More good news, he could feel it. He hurried over and answered. 'Hello.'

Silence.

'Hello.'

Nothing.

'Hello.'

Dead.

'Bye-bye.'

He returned to the duvet and pressed the damp patch against the heat.

The phone rang again.

He turned and went to the bed, picked up the unit and sat on the bare sheet. He let it ring twice more, then lifted the receiver.

'Hello.'

A faint murmur of breath.

'Who's there?'

No response.

'Prat.'

He pressed the cut off, but kept the receiver to his ear. A moment later, it rang again. He instantly released his finger, opening the line, and shouted, *'What?'*

Breath, loud, rasping.

'God, I'm so frightened,' Tom said with childish sarcasm.

'You will be, Tommy.'

Tom jumped. 'Wha—?'

'They all get frightened, Tommy. As the final seconds tick away.'

Tom could feel his pulse thudding in his neck. He wanted to hang up, but something in the man's voice would not be dismissed so easily.

'What are you on about? Who are you?'

A long pause.

'You'll find out.' And the connection broke.

Eventually, Tom's ear began to hurt. He realised he had been holding the handset too tightly to his head. He pulled it away and his ear started throbbing. Gently, he set it back on the cradle.

Sleet battered the window and drummed on the roof. Despite the radiator, the pyjamas and the dressing gown, Tom shivered.

When the phone rang again, he swiped it furiously up to his mouth. *'Fuck off, you fucking weirdo!'* he screamed down the line.

After several seconds, a gruff Mancunian voice said, 'DCI Nelson. And a very good morning to you, too.'

Tom scrunched up his face. 'Sorry.'

'Expecting someone else?'

'Uh . . . I just had a nuisance call. It happens.'

'Hmm.'

'Well?'

'What?' said Nelson.

'What do you want?'

'Did I call you?'

Tom sighed. 'Yes.'

'Right. I got confused. I thought you might have called me. You know, to tell me what you forgot to mention the other day. Or didn't you want to spoil the story? Is it raining where you are?'

153

Tom ran a scratching hand through his hair, closed his fingers at the crown and pulled. He inspected the damage: nine hairs. He was losing it. In more ways than one. 'What are you saying?' he asked irritably.

'I can hear rain.'

'It's sleet.'

'Ah. I suppose we'll get it later. Looks that way. Why didn't you tell me?'

'What?'

'About . . . let's see . . . chapter nine. Milton and the exploding police car.'

Tom hung his head, closed his eyes. 'I didn't think it was important.'

'What, you thought it was—?'

'A coincidence,' Tom finished for him. 'Yes.'

'Bull—'

'Shit, I know. I know what you think.'

Tom stared at the icy onslaught against his window. Splat, slide and melt.

Nelson was quiet.

'I can't help you,' Tom said. 'You think it's some sort of copy-cat . . .' He shrugged to himself. 'I don't know. Time will tell.'

'Time, Mister Roker, has already told.'

'Pardon?'

'Do you want to explain your little outburst when you picked up the phone? You weren't expecting our friend, the biker, were you?'

'How the hell should I know who it was?'

'It's just . . . he's been at it again.'

Tom paused to allow a shudder to pass before speaking. 'What d'you mean?'

'Well, if I said that a biker killed a drink-driving solicitor called Henry with a red nose on his Volvo by shoving Henry's nose into his brain then propping him up against the front bumper with the plastic nose strapped to his face before leaving a circle of burnt rubber on the road, would you know what I was talking about?'

'Milton's second kill.'

Nelson made a fake gasp. 'Bugger me! What a coincidence! Because that also exactly describes a real event that happened last night, a few miles down the road.'

Tom looked at his novel on the carpet.

'Mr Roker? You still there? So what's next on the agenda? Got your book handy? Page . . . I've marked all the violent bits . . . page one-sixty-four. Think our boy'll go for it?'

'I have no idea,' Tom said flatly, reaching down to pick up his copy. 'You do, though.'

'Think he'll kill again? Absolutely. And you've provided a blueprint for him to work with.'

Flicking through from the back of the book, Tom stopped to defend himself. 'I've done nothing. It's not my fault if some loony decides to act out scenes from a novel.'

'No, just don't write a sequel,' Nelson joked, and chortled.

Tom kept quiet.

'You found it yet? One-six-four. The bank job.'

'Yeah.' It was the chapter Carol had suspected him of tampering with. 'I can't get my head round this,' he said softly, and continued on towards the front of the book to the scenes already made fact.

'Any idea where it might take place?' Nelson enquired.

Tom stopped a few pages shy of the Red Nose murder. He rolled his eyes before indulging Nelson's persistence. 'No.'

'What town's it supposed to be in?'

'I didn't name it.'

'Come on, you must have had somewhere in mind; based it on a real town. A town someone might recognise if they were looking for a fitting venue?'

'I didn't.'

'Wait a sec . . . why did you set it up here, anyway? What's your connection with the North-West?'

'I lived there for a while,' Tom lied fluently.

'Oh, whereabouts?'

Tom gave an incredulous laugh to cover his momentary blankness. 'What's it matter?'

'Doesn't. Just asking.'

Resuming his page-search, Tom found the relevant scene.

Well, he did and he didn't.

His jaw dropped. He gawped at the pages and spoke in a quiet monotone. 'Someone's at the door. I've got to go.' As he missed the cradle with the handset, he vaguely heard Nelson protest at their foreshortened conversation, then managed to seat it properly. He

155

put the phone to one side and grasped *Man on a Murder Cycle* with two hands.

For a very long while, he scrutinised the same pages with eyes wide and clueless. He was waiting for his brain or the paper to stop lying, but they never did.

THIRTY-ONE

The sky was dumping its winter cargo like an act of vengeance. From the tarmac came a blinding mix of muck and sleet. Angie kept to seventy, too fast for the conditions, slower than most, but at least it kept her out of the inside lane, domain of the thundering juggernauts.

She felt trapped, intimidated. Wheels as big as her Mini to one side, suits in side windows to the other. Looked down on literally from the left, metaphorically from the right; a woman in a small car, daring to encroach on male territory. She was pipped, honked and barped. She was a menace. Mobiles glued to their ears, they drew alongside, slowed to glare, gesticulated, made sure she knew that bloody women drivers caused accidents, allowed her to get all jealous about the wank-worthy trim level on their Mondeos, then forged back up to a steady ninety, looking more like speed boats with the spray they left in their wake.

She let them get on with it. It was their funeral.

By the time she came off the M1 in north London, the sleet had turned to rain. Angie felt thoroughly jaded. She had not slept all night, waiting for the weather to improve, which it hadn't. Eventually, at eight o'clock, she had made a move. It was now past midday. She had stopped at services twice on the way, but had not thought to phone work to explain her absence. It seemed a trivial oversight considering her present mission.

Following her A–Z, she headed south-east across the city to Rotherhithe. What a nightmare. She hated London. Prior to leaving, she had done all she could to ensure her journey would not be wasted, that Carol Morgan would be in. She had telephoned her apartment in the early hours. An answering machine had picked up, but there had been only one beep before the tape was ready to accept her message, which meant messages were not backed up; they were being regularly checked. Naturally, Angie had opted to hang up without announcing her intentions. She hoped Carol Morgan liked surprises.

The renovated warehouse loomed nine floors above her. Angie stared up at the windows, blinking as the rain spotted her face. She locked her Mini and walked to the main entrance, clutching *The Writer's Handbook 1997*. The doors were metal, with wired security glass. Inside, an atrium rose up the full nine floors, domed at the roof in glass. A small fountain spouted its pretensions in the centre of the foyer. Red-painted tubular guardrails, hung with creeping plants, ran round the four sides of each floor. Set back, the apartment walls were a mosaic of pink, mauve and yellow brick. It was the type of place people thought they should aspire to, but didn't quite know why.

Beside the door was a polished steel console with an array of buttons and a speaker. Angie found the name she wanted and pressed for apartment 904, presumably the fourth unit on the top floor.

A very businesslike voice answered. 'Who is it?'

'Carol Morgan?'

'Yes.'

'The literary agent?'

'Yes. If you're a writer, I'm afraid I don't take personal callers. You need to mail a couple of sample chapters, a synopsis and a little bit about yourself. It's all in *The Writer's Handbook*.'

'I know, I'm holding a copy. And I'm not a writer.'

'Oh. Then what do you want?'

'Well, *I'm* not a writer, but my brother was.'

'I'm sorry?'

'You stole his novel. You gave it to Tom Roker.'

The intercom went dead. Angie waited. The rain was beginning to flatten her hair. Her shoulders felt damp. After fifteen seconds, the speaker clicked back on.

'I don't know what you're talking about.'

'Yes, you do.'

'No, I don't.'

The intercom went dead again. Angie pressed, and kept pressing.

158

Carol Morgan resumed contact. 'If you don't go away, I'll call the police.'

Angie tilted her head back, looked to the top of the building, then focused on a single raindrop as it fell to earth. 'I'm getting wet,' she said. 'If you don't let me up, *I'll* call the police.'

A pause, then, 'Fine. Come up. But I really have no idea what you're talking about.'

The door released with a buzz, and Angie went through into the foyer. Above her, a drum-roll of rain battered the atrium glass. Apart from that, and the patter in the fountain, the place was utterly quiet. It felt strangely uninhabited. It was spartan, over-clean and soulless.

Angie turned to her right and took the lift to the ninth floor.

They were all affected. Every copy. Each one of Tom's twelve complimentary hardcovers told the same story. And it wasn't the full story Andrew Kellett had written.

Two of the copies were open on the bed, their spines broken to keep them from closing, one at the exploding police car, the other at the Red Nose murder.

Tom stared gormlessly at the blank white pages. Chunks of the narrative had simply disappeared. Specifically, the violent bits. Gone. Vanished. *Poof!*

Madness was pushing to come in. Tom could sense it forcing that invisible divide.

Perhaps guilt had caught up with him. Perhaps it was manifesting itself as some form of selective blindness. He felt certain he had caused the farmer at Kellett's to lose his sight, at least for the short time the man still had a head to see out of. Perhaps this was symptomatic of a burdened subconscious which had finally cracked.

To remedy it, he had tried holding the pages in front of a mirror, a reversal of spot-the-vampire; trying to trick his eyes into registering what he knew had to be right there in front of them. But still blank.

He tried to tell himself he must have received the books in this state, that it was a printing error he had overlooked. After all, he hadn't bothered to read the entire novel since its publication. But he couldn't kid himself. There were too many built-in fail-safes, just too many intermediate checks which would have spotted a cock-up of such proportions. Besides, if all the shop copies were similarly affected, how would Nelson have known to make the call he had made earlier? If the pertinent details were missing from the story, Nelson couldn't possibly have compared real-life and fictional events, as he clearly had.

Tom moaned with the sheer magnitude of his incomprehension.

Carol couldn't settle on a suitable expression as she waited for her visitor to rap on the door. She was guilty as hell, of a terrible crime, of an awful breach of agent etiquette, to say the very least, and she had never imagined this moment would happen. She had feared it so greatly, she had put it entirely from her mind, so had not spent any time in front of the mirror practising angelic smiles and blameless little shrugs.

Instead, she raced to the booze table, unscrewed the gin and slugged back cheek-blowing gobfuls of the stuff. If she couldn't get her face to feign innocence, best she lost control of it completely.

Features twisting with the sudden punch of alcohol, she rushed with the bottle into the kitchen and filled a tall glass. If it looked like water, fine. If the contents were sussed, and she was seen as an old soak, so be it. As long as she got sozzled swiftly enough to mask her guilty conscience.

The knock came. Carol glugged back some more, then put the living-room lights out to further mask her guilt. In the dullness, the rain seemed to chatter more loudly on the balcony windows.

She opened the door to an unsmiling young woman with short blonde hair clinging wetly to her scalp. Carol tried shaking her head and grimacing as Andrew Kellett's sister entered her living room, as she guessed she might have done to any stray nutter she had been forced to let into her home.

But this woman was neither stray nor nutty. She had known precisely where to come, and the exact accusation to level.

Carol closed the door and continued to shake her head.

Kellett walked right into the room like she owned the place, then turned, and, not without some levity, said, 'What? You're still going to tell me you don't know why I'm here?'

Carol nodded, distorting her face into what she hoped was a passable façade of painful ignorance. By way of response, she was hit in the stomach by a flying yellow object. It fell to the carpet, landing open, spine up, like a tiny tent.

'*The Writer's Handbook*,' Carol said. 'So?'

'Find your name,' she was told.

A wave of nausea rolled through her, courtesy of the gin. It hadn't helped at all. It had simply fuzzed her mind, and increased her fear of discovery. She put her glass down and picked up the book. Ominously, it had fallen open at her entry, which, more ominously, was circled in red.

'Uuum . . . ?'

'That belonged to my brother,' said Kellett. 'He marked your name. He sent you his novel. You gave it to Tom Roker. He liked it. You both had it stolen.'

Carol tried a head-shaking titter interspersed with forehead frowns and flapping hands. Her repertoire was nearly exhausted.

Kellett continued: 'Doesn't it bother you that a man had to die so you could have what you wanted?'

Carol stilled. She felt her expression go slack with another nauseous swell inside. 'I'm not responsible for your brother's death,' she stated.

There was a dangerous, loaded beat before Kellett replied: 'I didn't tell you my brother was dead.'

'Well, how else could we have stolen his book?' Carol retorted, and felt pleased with herself for returning the ball so swiftly.

Kellett raised her eyebrows.

'Hypothetically,' Carol said quickly. 'I mean hypothetically, if someone did steal a book, the original author would have to be dead, or it wouldn't work. Would it?'

Kellett squinted across at her. Through the dribbling glass of the balcony windows, the teeming winter sky provided the unlit room with an almost monochrome murk. Carol prayed it would hide the growing panic in her eyes.

Slowly, Kellett began to nod. 'Hypothetically,' she agreed.

Carol couldn't help but smile.

'But I wasn't referring to my brother.'

Time dug its heel in and Carol nearly fell over as her world slowed around her. Now she really was in the dark. She was expressionless, and she realised she was finally wearing the true mask of ignorance. Closing her eyes, she heard her interrogator approach.

'You didn't know, did you?' Kellett said, a touch of amusement in her voice. 'Whoever you got to break into my house didn't tell you, did they? They didn't tell you they had to kill someone. You didn't know a neighbour got his head blown off with a shotgun. Did you? And it wasn't one little pellet in the brain. To all intents and purposes, the man was decapitated. On my back lawn. *My back lawn!* Christ, bits of his brain are still up my bloody tree! So how about taking a load off your mind? Tell me about it.'

After a moment, when Carol had recovered her equilibrium, she spoke very calmly. 'You can think what you fucking well like, dear. If you thought you had a case, you wouldn't have come to me, you'd have gone to the police.' It suddenly struck her that Kellett might be taping the conversation. 'But you don't have a case because I've done nothing wrong. I'm sorry about your brother, but don't take your grief out on me. He might have circled my name, but that does not mean he sent me his work. Now, Miss Kellett, sod off back up north, and if you want to contact me again, do it through a solicitor, but if I were you, I wouldn't waste my time.'

As she spoke her last words, the telephone started ringing. Kellett made no effort to leave, but Carol decided she would end the intrusion by getting back to her everyday business, as though nothing had happened. She reached to the coffee table and picked up. 'Carol Morgan.'

'Yes, hello there, you're advertising a Penis Enlarger in the classified section of this month's *Rumpy-Pumpy*.'

'I *beg* your pardon?'

'Is that a machine or a personal service?'

'Who is this?'

'It's me.'

'. . . Tom?'

'No. Me. Milton.'

'Mil—' Carol stared at Kellett. Shit. A set-up. She pulled a face at the woman, then returned to the caller. 'Listen, I don't know who you are, but—'

'I told you, Caz, Milton's the name, murder's the game.'

'Fine. Whatever you say.'

'Two so far. Well, okay, three, but the first doesn't count. He wasn't in the plot. I've come to think of him as a sort of little prologue of my own.'

'Sure,' Carol said, unimpressed. 'I suppose you'd like to talk to my visitor, then she can tell you herself: this hasn't worked and it's not going to.' She offered the receiver to Kellett. 'For you.'

162

Kellett appeared confused. Carol shook the handset impatiently. 'Stop acting and speak to your boyfriend, or whoever it is.'

Tentatively, Kellett took the receiver. She put it to her ear, waited a moment, then said, 'Yes?'

Carol could faintly hear the caller's voice, but not the words. She watched Kellett's expression as she listened. It remained puzzled. She was one damn fine actress.

Then, just before Carol heard the caller hang up, she saw Kellett's face change dramatically. Real Oscar material. Seemingly in slow-motion, Kellett replaced the receiver. She seemed to be miles away.

'Oh, quit it,' Carol told her, getting up and heading for the kitchen. At the sink she poured herself a mug of cold water and gulped it down.

When she returned to the living room, Kellett hadn't moved, either bodily or facially. Carol switched on the lights and inspected the woman more closely. Something had fazed her, seriously, genuinely.

'What?' Carol asked.

'He told me . . .' She shook her head slightly. 'He said he'd make it right.'

'Who?'

'I don't know. He called himself Milton. I don't understand. But then . . . he called me Angel.' She was whispering now. 'I was a kid . . . only one person ever called me . . .' She trailed off into a private reverie.

Carol had listened to quite enough. She didn't want to know. 'Out, please,' she ordered, taking advantage of Kellett's distant state to usher her towards the front door.

At the door, Kellett swivelled on her heels so their faces were mere inches apart. She had come back to herself, at least partly.

'Before I go,' she said, 'I am Miss Kellett, and, as you suggested, I will sod off back up north . . .' She left a pause.

Carol felt compelled to speak. 'Good. Then go.'

'The thing is, if you're really not involved, then how do you know my name and where I come from when I didn't mention either?'

THIRTY-TWO

In his rush to get in from the rain, Tom didn't notice the red Mini parked outside Carol's apartment building, nor the figure inside, face in hands, rocking with emotion.

He hurried through the puddles, head down. Behind him, the engine of his put-upon BMW was having terrible trouble obeying the removal of the ignition key. The revs rolled in splutters, threatening to conk out, only to revive, like some amateur actor milking a death scene. Tom had reached the front entrance before he heard it give up the ghost and quieten.

'Twatting car.'

He hunched his shoulders and squeezed the package under his right arm against his ribs. His grey mac was darkening with the merging spots it absorbed from the heavens.

He didn't relish buzzing up. He didn't want to give Carol any opportunity to snub him, like leaving him standing out in the rain. But he had to see her. She needed to witness the empty pages in his novel. He had to know if hers were the same.

And he wanted his new manuscript back. Nelson had made a joke of it, but his point was sound: if another set of violent events was on offer, the biker would keep on killing. Of course, the bastard would probably be caught long before publication of the follow-up, but Tom needed to know he retained the option of destroying it if the unthinkable happened, and the biker somehow did elude capture.

He flicked some droplets from the end of his nose, then steeled himself. He lifted his left arm to the console, but before he could press the button a kid in a red cagoule darted between him and the door. Tom stepped back as the kid produced a key and let himself into the building. The door swung to, but Tom stopped it with a palm and slipped inside.

164

The kid was around twelve years old with wild hair and a cheeky face. He unzipped his dripping coat and scowled up at the strange man who had followed him into the foyer.

'I'm visiting Carol Morgan,' Tom explained with a smile, not expecting the boy to know who she was.

'Oh, right. Yeah, snooty cow, top floor.'

Tom grinned.

'She's fucking fit, you know. For her age.'

In spite of himself, Tom howled with laughter. 'And how old are you?' he asked, shocked by such forthright views in one so young.

'Fifteen,' came the defiant response, with a sneer that said no one had better argue.

Tom took the oblong package from under his arm. 'Good age,' he humoured, shaking the fresh rain from his coat. Then he unwrapped *Man on a Murder Cycle* from the plastic bag.

'Oh, *wicked book*!' the kid squealed. 'You read it yet?'

Tom thought to boast, but decided he wasn't in the mood. 'No,' he said.

The kid grabbed the novel. 'God, there are some great bits.' He opened it and thumbed through from the back, soon stopping. 'That bit there.' He showed it to Tom. 'Fucking great.' He folded the page corner so Tom would not forget to enjoy it, and continued searching.

Tom wanted to seize it back before the kid happened on the blanks, but an overprotective mum might have had him in court for such politically incorrect behaviour. *Bestselling novelist sued for beating young admirer.*

'And *this*.' The kid turned the book towards Tom, and Tom got an eyeful of white paper, unmarred by a single speck of black print. 'Cool, listen,' said the kid, putting the book back under his nose and starting to read.

From a page devoid of words, Tom received a perfect recital of the moment Milton murdered Henry. When he'd finished, the kid folded the page corner, returned the book, and grinned up at Tom. 'You want to read it.'

Tom forced a smile. 'I'd really like to.'

Just for the ride, the kid travelled all the way up to the top floor with Tom. In that short time, Tom found the blank pages where the exploding police car should have been, and showed them to his new friend.

'What d'you think of this bit?' he asked, handing over the book for scrutiny.

The kid took a moment, his head making an exaggerated motion, right, left, right, left, as his eyes followed the invisible text; invisible to Tom, at any rate.

The kid nodded. 'Yeah, cool. Thought you hadn't read it.'

'I skim-read it.'

'What's that then?'

'It's . . . lazy reading.'

'Oh.'

The lift slowed swiftly, then inched up to a full halt before the door slid open onto the ninth floor. Tom stepped out.

'See you, mate,' said the kid. 'Give her one for me.'

Carol's door was ajar. Tom put his ear to the gap. All he could hear was the rain above him on the atrium roof. He knocked lightly, pushed the door and looked into the living room. The lights were on. Framed by the balcony windows, the moody skies and dark edifices on the opposite bank of the Thames resembled a huge drab painting.

'Hello?' he called. There was no reply, so he wandered in.

On the coffee table was a *Writer's Handbook*. He poked his head in the kitchen. On the sideboard was a bottle of Gordon's and an empty glass. He walked across the lounge and looked in Carol's office, but she wasn't there. He hesitated before venturing down the hall into the bedroom.

The door was open. Lying sprawled, face down on the bed, was his agent. Her body twitched and her breathing was erratic, as though she was currently entering deep sleep. She was in an orange satin kimono. The contours of her backside shone seductively. Tom traced his eyes from her feet up to her calves. Above that, her flesh was covered, but a fond recollection filled in the blanks for him.

And another memory came to mind; of standing in Angie Kellett's bedroom, fingering her underwear – an intruder with pervert thoughts, soiling her property by his touch, and his conscience by the enjoyment.

'Carol?' he said softly. She stirred but didn't wake. He called again, louder.

166

She groaned. 'Peter?' she muttered into the pillow.

He opened his mouth but said nothing more. Slowly, she rolled over on the bed, lifted her head and opened her eyes. He expected a torrent of abuse – how dare he barge in like that. The quiet derision he actually received was somehow even worse.

'Oh, look,' she said. 'The Man Who would be King.' She noticed the novel in his hand. 'Come to read me a story? How nice.'

Tom shifted his weight from one leg to the other. Carol moved to sit on the edge of the bed, exposing her legs in the process. She stared at the floor. Tom stared at her thighs, ready to glance away if she glanced at him.

'I've been drinking,' she announced. 'Stupid, really. You shouldn't drink on an empty head.'

'Pardon?'

She looked at him. 'I must have been brainless. Totally brainless to go along with it.' Eyes back to the floor again. 'I should have known. Experience should have taught me. You screw everything. You screwed your career, your marriage. And still I let you back in. I'm stupid. Brainless.' She got up and wobbled past him, down the hall into the lounge.

After a moment, Tom followed to find her at the windows, surveying a dirty, swollen Thames, sliding through a gloomy metropolis. Her head was tilted slightly to one side. Even from behind, in silence, she appeared thoroughly fed up.

'Carol?'

'It's ironic. The only time you didn't fuck up is when you fucked me. You were good in bed, Tom. I don't know why I'm telling you this. Maybe to convince myself our acquaintance hasn't been completely wasted; to salvage *something* from the wreckage. But you even screwed that, didn't you?'

Tom sensed she was watching him in the reflection. He stayed quiet; he knew what was coming next.

'Blackmail. Shit, Tom . . . sexual blackmail. D'you know how low that is?'

Tom nodded to himself, and to Carol if her focus was on the glass and not through it.

'A real man wouldn't have done it. Not that. Anything else. *Everything* else. But not that.'

Tom cast his eyes around the room, as though capturing an

167

image for posterity. There was something final in her voice. It worried him.

'Why are you talking like this?' he asked.

'But I doubt you are a real man any more, are you, Tom? Fucked in that department as well, I expect. Can't get it up. It's the only explanation. Bitter. Bitter enough for blackmail. Keep the sex alive in your head, if not in your prick.'

Tom was getting riled. Not five minutes ago he had reluctantly labelled himself a pervert. Now Carol had him down as impotent. What a sad combination. And perhaps it was true. He had not made love to a woman in over six months. Perhaps these days it would only stand when he was alone.

'Don't push it,' he warned, though he knew she had every right to.

She turned to face him. 'Or what? You'll slap my legs with Mr Floppy?'

He studied the shape of her breasts beneath the satin, lingering on her nipples. He prayed to God it wasn't true; prayed he could still satisfy a woman. Lust erupted in him like a fever. And desire; desire to prove a point, to her and to himself.

He turned his back on her and headed for the door. He was almost out of the apartment when she said it.

'Talentless, blackmailing, slimy, impotent little shit.'

He stopped. He knew he ought to leave. There was a challenge in her words he could not reply to without breaking the law and what few moral codes he still maintained.

He spoke to the white wood of the front door. 'I don't mind *blackmailing*, or *slimy*, or even *little shit*. I admit those. But *talentless*? No. And you have my latest manuscript to prove I'm not. And as for *impotent*. Well, there's only one way to prove that wrong, so you'd better let me get out before you learn the hard way.'

She didn't respond, so he reached for the handle and pulled the door open.

'You wouldn't dare,' she said as he crossed the threshold.

He halted. Debated. Then stepped back inside the apartment, closed the door and locked it. His hard-on throbbed in his pants as he faced her. She had moved away from the windows and she was leaning against the back of the settee, showing him a sickly, drunken smile. Her arms were folded. He shook his head, and approached.

'Get lost,' she said.

He dropped the novel he was holding and came for her, unbuckling his belt. She uncrossed her arms to fend him off. He grabbed and made to turn her. The satin slipped in his hand. She struggled free and swiped him across the cheek, squeaking at the impact. He stilled, then launched himself at her, fingers digging through the satin into her flesh. He swung her round and bent her over the settee. Giddy with alcohol, she fell forward easily. All the while, a part of him was trying to gauge her true level of resistance, ready to give it up if he thought she was sincerely objecting. But another part of him guessed that all rapists thought the same, and went ahead anyway.

She was telling him not to, but his penis was out now, in his hand, and far from impotent. He drew her kimono up over her back to reveal a bare arse. He had one hand on her spine, keeping her bent over, but the pressure he exerted seemed very light. She wriggled, but her arms didn't fight, and her legs were apart, feet planted firm, not a single kick of a heel to his shins.

No, she was saying, stop it. Then he was inside her with her wetness around him, hearing her gasp, and he knew she was eager. It wasn't rape, and Tom felt disappointed.

He banged away, grunting, making believe she didn't want it.

'I hate you,' she growled, and thrust onto him, taking him deeper inside.

Rain pelted the glass outside, like applause.

Bringing both hands to her hips, he tensed his abdominals, pulling in his stomach as flat as possible to view every stroke.

Carol orgasmed quickly, juddering, squealing, then settled into the rhythm again.

He couldn't believe it was happening. Their relationship was shot. She really did hate him, she wasn't lying about that. But she had taunted him into screwing her. Why?

Something must have happened – the way she'd been talking, as though it was all over. He imagined a suicide might talk like that the moment before they jumped.

All of a sudden, he felt himself going soft. She would not have sensed it yet, but he knew that the blood was draining from his penis. And in a few seconds she would feel it too. She would complain, then push him away. She would turn and mock his glistening, shrinking manhood, laughing, ridiculing, saying she'd told him so, perhaps until he felt compelled to strangle her just to end the insults.

It was all wrong, what he was doing. Not because she was married, but because she should not have wanted it, unless she had completely lost control of her reason, except she didn't seem anywhere near drunk enough for that.

Something had happened to change her. He didn't know what it was, but it scared him.

He concentrated, spread her buttocks with his palms, looked down at her vagina offered up to him. It was a wonderful sight – his brain accepted as much – but the communication lines to his prick appeared to have been cut, because the message wasn't getting through.

'What?' she said breathlessly, somewhat startled.

She had felt it.

Tom closed his eyes, seeking images from his mind-files to regorge himself. Women he had known, women he had wanted to know. Desperately searching for the horn.

Kellett's sister.

She popped into his head. He didn't know her name and, as far as he was aware, they had never met.

But the black dress on the wardrobe door, the stains on the bedsheets, her underwear: bras and panties; black, white, coloured, flowered, patterned. Textures of cotton, lace, silk. Stockings, sheer and gossamer. Suspenders, dangling, frills, hooks and eyes. G-strings, minuscule, garrotting.

Yep, what a perv.

Carol moaned almost in pain, and he could feel her muscles tight around him, gripping, a ribbed sensation as he slid in and out. He was huge. Bigger than before. Bigger than ever. Almost in pain himself.

He wanted to finish it, go out on a high. He began pumping harder, using his full length. His balls slapped on her inner thighs, and Carol's sounds rose to a crescendo.

Tom kept his eyes shut.

Bras and panties, G-strings, stockings and suspenders. Kellett's sister, the unknown quantity, but his fingers in her underwear, touching the places that had touched the most intimate parts of her body.

170

Tom exploded with semen. Carol rippled and screamed and came. The rain teemed against the windows.

Draped over her back, Tom breathed heavily. Carol had gone limp beneath him. Slowly, he went soft as well and fell out of her. He pushed himself off and pulled up his pants and trousers.

Taking the less strenuous route, Carol crawled over the back of the settee and flopped on the cushions. She rearranged her kimono, making herself respectable – after a fashion.

He waited for her to speak, to explain. She lay there, chest heaving, eyes glazed.

'Why?' he said after a minute.

She didn't look at him. 'Why not?'

'*Why not?*' he echoed incredulously. 'Plenty of reasons, and you know it.'

She tightened the satin across her breasts. 'I wanted a good shag to keep me going on the inside. Peter doesn't . . . well, he would but I won't let him any more.'

'I'm not with you.'

'You'll get sex, but not the sort you want.'

'What?'

'They'll do to you what you just did to me. But I expect there'll be more than one, and they'll get you in the shower, or the laundry.'

Fearful of her strange riddles, puzzled still by her sexual surrender, Tom hurried around the settee and sat down at Carol's feet.

'Talk sense!' he half shouted.

She smiled sadly at him. 'This time, Tom, you've really screwed me.'

Tom frowned.

'She was here.'

'Who?'

'Andrew Kellett's sister.'

The name went straight to his heart, and, improbably, to his groin again.

She gave him a little nod. 'True.'

He didn't want to believe, but his instincts told him she wasn't lying. Only something so shocking could have provoked what had just taken place.

'When?'

'Half an hour ago. You must've just missed her.'

Tom's eyes settled on *The Writer's Handbook* on the table.

'She left it,' Carol said. 'He'd circled my name.'

'She can't know for sure.'

Carol hesitated before answering. 'Go straight to jail. Do not pass Go; do not collect one million pounds from Pyramid Pictures.'

Tom glared at her, his fist clenching. 'Shit, you didn't tell her, did you?'

'No. And you didn't tell me.'

'What?'

'Ba-boom,' she said simply.

In his mind's eye, Tom saw the farmer's head come off, the corpse sink and topple, the dark drizzle from the branches. He leaned back in the settee and made a disturbed sound in his throat.

Carol brought her knees up to her chest and hugged them. 'So in the scheme of things, you'll see an illicit fuck with you isn't such a big deal.'

Tom said nothing. For a long time neither of them spoke. They both gazed at the filthy weather outside, the low scudding clouds, and listened to the comforting splatter against the glass as the wind drove the rain in silver curtains.

'So you think the police are on their way?' Tom asked eventually.

She considered. 'I don't know.' She sighed. 'But I'd say not. Not yet, anyway.'

'No,' Tom agreed, attempting to bolster his nerve. 'No, or she wouldn't have come on her own. She knows, but she also knows she can't prove anything.' A second later, Tom realised he was very wrong. He turned his head away so Carol would not catch the dull horror in his eyes.

The crowbar. The back door. His fingerprints.

He swallowed, then asked: 'Did she mention anything else?'

'Like what?'

'Like . . . if she's going to ask the police about anything . . . you know . . . specific?'

She extended a leg and lightly kicked his ribs, making him face her. She studied his shifty eyes for several seconds before concluding, 'She can prove it, can't she? She thought a freelance had broken in, but it was you, and, as usual, you screwed up. You're incriminated, aren't you? Aren't you, Tom?'

Tom made a casual face and shook his head.

The flush of sex had nearly left her skin. She was growing paler. 'Oh, yes. Yes, I can feel it. You did something stupid, and the only reason you're not in prison already is because she doesn't know to send the police in your direction.'

'Crap. She's got nothing. She won't bother us again.'

Carol burned her eyes into him, until he felt inclined to get up and head for some gin from the kitchen. He swigged a couple of mouthfuls from the bottle and swore as it flowed scorching down his throat, then returned to the living room.

'I tried that,' Carol told him. 'Drinking to cover the lies. It doesn't work. And you're wrong: Kellett *will* keep on at us. Any way she can. Even whilst she was here, she got some man to phone up and pretend he was Milton.'

'Pardon?'

'Personally, I think she's warped.'

Tom squatted down in front of his agent, and was hit by a sweet waft of mingled juices. 'What did he sound like?'

Carol shrugged. 'Hoarse. Scary. Well, meant to be, I suppose. Why?'

Tom shot quickly to his feet and went to the windows. He had almost forgotten about Milton and the disappearing text.

Down in the Thames, a barge chugged upstream.

He weighed it up, but decided she would find out about it sooner or later.

'Carol, you won't like this, but I'm afraid I'm going to have to tell you a story.'

Carol sat dumbstruck. Three murders. Holy shit.

Tom had secretly taken great pleasure in causing her distress. He had also been looking forward to showing her the blank pages in his novel, but he had refrained from doing so because his suspicions had clearly been correct. The kid downstairs had proved it was some form of selective blindness. The words were there, only Tom couldn't see them. It would not serve any purpose for Carol to know he was experiencing mental problems on top of everything else.

Tom was sitting on the coffee table in front of her. 'Anyway,' he finished, 'the reason I came by was to get my latest manuscript back from you.'

Carol snapped out of her distracted state. She narrowed her eyes suspiciously. 'Oh?'

'Obviously it can't be published if it might lead to more deaths.'

She raised her eyebrows. 'This from the man who shoots people in the head. You'll be telling me next you have a conscience.'

'It was an accident. It just went off. I wasn't even touching the bloody thing.'

'Tell it to the judge.'

He leaned forward, elbows on knees. 'I want it back.'

'So you can take it to another agent and cut me out?'

'No.'

'I'm on fifty per cent, Tom. In perpetuity.'

'Fine. Whatever. But if the biker isn't caught, this particular novel doesn't see the light of day.' He opened his palms in supplication. 'Yes?'

Carol tucked her legs underneath her. 'Yes, okay.'

'Good. Can you get it for me?'

She slowly got up, then squirmed and rubbed the satin between her legs.

'I'm dribbling. You were full to bursting, weren't you, Tom?'

Tom felt himself blush. 'Carol, the manuscript.'

She started for her office, then stopped. 'Ah, damn. Sorry, forgot. I gave it to your editor.'

He regarded her doubtfully.

'Honestly. But it's not a problem. He said he wouldn't get round to it for a few days. I'll get it back this afternoon. Tell him you want to rewrite. Okay? You can pick it up tomorrow. Okay?'

'You don't have it here?'

'I just said.' She sat down.

He snorted a laugh. 'And I'm meant to trust you?'

'From now on, Thomas, we're going to *have* to trust each other. Distasteful as that may sound.'

Tom offered a grunt and stood up. 'It sounds more impossible than distasteful.'

'And whose fault's that?'

He didn't grace her with a reply. He went behind the settee and picked up his hardback which he'd dropped to concentrate on matters in hand.

'Tomorrow, first thing,' he told her, straightening up. He wanted to say, *or else*, but his bargaining powers were nil with all that she now had on him.

'Tomorrow. Trust me.'

He got to the door, then came out with it. 'I'd rather smother my knob in marrowbone jelly and trust a rabid pit-bull not to bite.'

If the police couldn't do their job and apprehend a serial killer in the year it took to bring Tom's sequel to publication, that was their lookout. She, Carol Morgan, was not about to lose possibly millions in sales across the board in deference to official incompetence.

Once Tom had gone, she showered, handwashed her kimono in the bathroom basin, and dressed. She collected Tom's latest manuscript from her desk drawer and slipped it into a briefcase. Raincoat on, collar up, umbrella and briefcase in hand, she left the apartment.

First port of call, the local print shop. After that, Simon Collins, at Moody, Carter and Collins, Solicitors.

Collins had a safe in his office. Which meant he could do a little safe keeping. An insurance policy should the biker remain at large, and Tom wimp out on publication of the sequel to *Man on a Murder Cycle*.

THIRTY-THREE

———————◆———————

The offside tyres of the Mini bumped up onto the sodden grass verge. Angie switched off the engine. The rain thundered on the roof, crashing down from a depressing black sky. Two tunnels of slashed light shone ahead of her. She peered along them into the darkness and wondered what other perils were charging her way, as yet out of sight, cloaked by time and night.

She shivered and felt another bout of sobbing rise in her chest. She fought it down. It was okay; she was home now.

Home. Sure. Immense comfort that was. Bricks and mortar, empty and violated.

The journey back had been terrifying. Rain outside the car, tears inside. Two veils to obscure the road. The tears were worse. The rain she had been able to count on – it had never looked like letting up – but the tears had come upon her on several occasions out of the blue; for a multitude of reasons, but without warning, flowing down her cheeks at no invitation from any particularly maudlin thoughts.

In between these mini-breakdowns, there had been plenty to occupy her mind.

For example: What was she going to do about Carol Morgan? Should she call the police now or let the matter lie? Was meeting Tom Roker coincidence or fate or cosmic tomfoolery? Who had phoned whilst she was at Morgan's apartment? Who else knew to call her Angel? How had he known she was even there? Was it the biker from outside the bookshop? Who was he? What did he want? Bloody hell, was he the same person who had murdered Hugh Stapely last summer? It had almost slipped her mind. A murder, then a stolen motorbike. A turbo, like the Manchester bike.

She didn't know the answers. How could she? What had she done to deserve the questions? Bad karma? A past life of evil catching up with her?

Angie turned the headlights off and climbed out of the car. She pulled her jacket over her head, locked up and dashed towards the cottage.

Halfway up the path, she saw the package. At the doorstep, she hunched down and picked it up. It felt like a book, a hardcover. It was wrapped in a black plastic bag, sealed underneath to keep the contents dry.

She let herself into the porch and into the house. In the lounge she put the light on, drew the curtains, shed her wet jacket and sat down.

Somehow she knew exactly what she was holding in her hands: inside the black plastic was a copy of *Man on a Murder Cycle*. She tore the bag apart and confirmed it.

But why should anyone have sent her the book? Who else knew of her connection with it?

She opened the cover. On the second title page, *MAN ON A MURDER CYCLE* was ticked in black Biro. Beside it was the comment, *Like it*. The handwriting seemed eerily familiar. Under that, where Tom Roker's name should have been, was a ragged, shredded slit in the paper. At its edges, black Biro loops were scored deep. Roker's claim to authorship had been annihilated.

Next to it was written:

For Angel,
        Making it right . . .
                Milton.

Now it was impossible to deny: she did recognise the handwriting. It was her brother's.

She tutted to herself. What on earth was she suggesting? Andrew was dead. She had seen his body at the under—

Ah. Yes. The undertaker's. What exactly *had* she seen there?

She inspected the page again. Roker's name had been completely obliterated. The pages directly beneath were holed and scrawled black, progressively less so, to a depth of seven pages. But she had to flick through another eight to arrive at the first pristine sheet, unmarked by the slightest imprint of Biro.

Someone out there was very angry.

But that same someone was also a potential ally. Because that someone appeared to share in her knowledge that Tom Roker was not the true author of the novel he had put his name to.

Only, who else *could* know? She had been closer to Andrew than anyone. If he had not told *her* what he was doing all that time, locked away in his bedroom, she could not imagine who else he might have shared it with. Besides, there *wasn't* anyone else. It had been just the two of them in their own private nut-house, and visitors weren't interested and weren't invited.

Which brought her back to . . .

Crazy.

But the handwriting, and the childhood name only Andrew had called her, and the bizarre business at Stapely's, and now this, the knowledge that no one else could possess.

And here was the real brain-ache: although even to momentarily entertain the notion was preposterous, it seemed to Angie that, given the evidence to date, it was the most logical explanation.

Surprising herself, she suddenly threw the book across the lounge and took a porcelain dancing lady off the top of the television. It hit the wall behind and fell to the floor in pieces. Angie cringed and felt tears well; the ornament had been a favourite of her mother's.

Instead of crying, she became livid with confusion. Because what was she telling herself? That her dead brother was making contact from beyond the grave? That he hadn't even *got* to the grave? That he was still in this world, riding around on a motorbike, claiming to be a fictional character he had created in a novel, which had subsequently been stolen?

Best she check in now. Pack a bag, drive to the local psychiatric ward and check in. They would find a bed for her, even if they had a full complement. Shit, if she told them what was currently in her head, they would *build* a bed for her. On the spot.

She breathed deeply, a groaning sigh. She could bat between belief and denial all day, but it would solve nothing. Something was happening out there, and, whatever it was, she did not want to handle it on her own. She couldn't. No one could.

She decided. The police. Give them the headache. Considering the circumstances surrounding Stapely's death, she could at least offer them a tenuous link to recent events: the turbo-charged motorcycle. How rare were they? She didn't know, but the police would have to listen. And perhaps that was all she wanted: someone to listen to her for a change.

The phone was in her hand when the sound of slamming car doors made her jump. Heart racing, she replaced the receiver and went to the window. She pulled back the curtain. A large, dark-coloured car was parked behind her Mini. Its interior light winked out as she watched. A moment later there was a knock at the front door.

She let the curtain fall shut, hesitated, and decided to ignore it. It wasn't late, but it was dark outside and she was alone.

Another knock. She ducked down; if someone came to the window, her silhouette might be seen against the ceiling light.

Fifteen seconds and another knock, then a long pause. Angie assumed her visitor was walking back to their car. She was inquisitive to see who it was, even if she could only distinguish the sex and vague shape.

She peered over the window ledge and inched the curtains apart, and a fat white face peered back at her. She eeked and fell on her bum. There was a tap at the window and a muffled voice.

'Miss Kellett! DCI Nelson! Miss Kellett?'

Angie gained her feet and opened the curtains. Heart pounding, she glared at his dripping face. 'What?'

'Some questions.'

'Fire away,' she said, not seriously intending to keep him out in the rain.

Nelson made a face and held his hands up to the deluge.

'Oh, right,' she said, and pointed towards the front door.

She let Nelson in, followed by a hunch-shouldered Ash, who politely said hello and apologised. They removed their coats and hung them over the newel post, then squelched into the lounge after her.

'Sorry about that,' Nelson said. 'But I knew you had to be in. I mean, your car's outside and I couldn't see you walking anywhere in this weather.'

Angie sat down and nodded to the settee for her guests, who settled themselves.

'Have you been out?' Nelson asked.

'No.'

'Well, that's strange, because the bonnet of your Mini is very warm.'

'Nowhere special,' she clarified, on the defensive. Now they were here, she wasn't sure she wanted to tell them anything.

'I wasn't nosing,' Nelson said. 'The bonnet was steaming, that's all.'

'I was visiting a friend.'

They had caught her in a lie already. She felt they had *made* her lie. She was in a quandary. She wanted them to listen, but it would not end there. If they did decide there was a case to pursue, they would want to hear it all. She would no longer be the judge of what was important or trivial in her life. The police would decide on such matters. What were TV detectives always saying? *Tell us, however insignificant it may seem to you.* Because that was their job: to detect; to sift through a pile of garbage and tweezer out a clue, minuscule but vital. If she opened up to them now, how many more times would they need to invade her space, and her head, over the coming months? She could imagine herself lying to them simply to maintain the façade of a personal life.

Suddenly it dawned on her that she had not called them to her home; they had arrived uninvited.

'What d'you want?' she said.

'Adam . . .' Nelson invited.

Ash smiled. 'We're at a bit of an impasse, Miss Kellett. You recall our last visit some months back? We told you about the murder of Hugh Stapely, the undertaker?'

Angie nodded.

'You may also recall mention of a break-in at a motorcycle showroom? A burnt-out hearse belonging to the deceased found behind it? The theft of a motorcycle from that showroom?'

'Yes.'

'A turbo?'

'I wouldn't know. I was more concerned with the theft of my brother's body.'

Ash bowed his head. 'Of course. Well, it was a Kawasaki ZZ-R1100. Turbocharged, fuel-injected. A beautiful machine.'

Nelson's forehead creased up as he looked sideways at his cohort.

Ash smiled happily. 'I'm learning to ride,' he explained to Nelson. 'I've found out what all the fuss is about.'

Nelson beamed. 'Good lad, Adam. Good lad.'

Angie stood up. 'If you two want to talk bikes, do it somewhere else. I'm not a great fan.' She went into the kitchen. From under the sink she retrieved a bottle of Bailey's, unopened since Christmas.

She took it to the sink and grabbed a glass. She hated when people forced her to seek escape in alcohol. She poured, but before she drank any she happened to look outside at the featureless shape of the garden shed. Inside it was her bicycle. Her eyes went from the cream liquid to the shed and back again.

'I didn't mean to upset you,' Ash piped up from the doorway. 'Unthinking. Sorry.'

Angie placed the bottle and glass in the sink. She gave a tiny nod to the shed. If she needed help, she would not seek it from the same futile source as her brother. She turned around. 'It's okay,' she said.

She couldn't help liking Ash. It was a shame he had to carry the bulbous appendage that was Nelson. Alone with him, she experienced a compulsion to speak freely. The words welled up inside her like tears, and she realised her sobbing today had been just that – emotions waiting for ordered expression.

'I went to Lon—'

Nelson appeared in the hallway behind Ash.

'You went to . . .' Ash prompted. 'What, Miss Kellett?'

'Lunch. Today. With my friend. In case you were wondering.' She strode out of the kitchen.

'I wasn't,' he said, nonplussed, stepping out of her way.

She brushed Nelson aside as she entered the lounge.

'So what about this motorbike?' she called into the hallway. Nelson and Ash came in and sat down again. Ash seemed reluctant to resume his spokesman's mantle.

'Rolo?' Nelson said, extending half a brown tube towards her with crinkled gold foil at the end.

'No, thank you.'

'Sure?' he said, taking one for himself.

'Positive.'

'All right.' Nelson began chewing and talking. 'For eight months, nothing. Not a murmur. No one else killed, no sign of the bike. Then, couple of days ago, it shows up outside a bookshop in Manchester. The author Tom Roker's inside, signing copies of his latest novel, *Man on a Murder Cycle*. Coincidence? Crap. Apparently, bloke riding does a few tricks, draws a crowd, nearly knocks Roker on his arse but for some woman who pulls him clear, then shoots off, our boys following.'

'How d'you know it's the same bike?' Angie asked coolly.

181

'That's what Tom Roker said. And I said we don't for sure, but I'd bet my pension on it.'

'Why?'

'Because I've checked, and I can't find another bike like it the length and breadth of this country.'

Angie shook her head. 'And you've come to me . . . for what? I don't know who killed Stapely. I don't know who nicked the bike. Why bother me after all this time?'

Nelson regarded her sternly. 'You're too quick to dismiss, young lady. I haven't come to ask the same questions I asked eight months ago. There have been several developments since then.'

Angie watched him expose another Rolo and throw it into his mouth. A flake of gold foil fell to the carpet.

Chomping, he said, 'You see, Miss Kellett, Hugh Stapely was just an appetiser. And now it seems we're getting the main course.'

'He's killed two more,' Ash put in. 'One of them a police officer.'

Angie was stunned into silence. Today, on the telephone, she had spoken to a serial killer. Now she had to tell them. She knew too much that might help. She was about to speak when Nelson chirped up again. And, once he had finished, she knew her chance to tell her own story had vanished for ever.

'And what's really disturbing is that he's using Tom Roker's novel as a blueprint, acting out the murder scenes.'

Angie leaned back abruptly in her chair, as though she had been slammed in the chest. She bit her bottom lip. 'Are you sure?' she said weakly.

'Positive.'

'The similarities are too striking, Miss Kellett,' Ash added.

'Uncanny,' Nelson said. 'So, we've got a problem, because I've read Roker's book and there are plenty of nasty scenes left.'

'Why haven't I heard about this on the news?' Angie asked.

'We're keeping a lid on it. We've asked the media to cooperate. We don't want any more unstable elements jumping on the bandwagon to confuse matters.'

Ash attempted a smile, then seemed to realise it was inappropriate. 'So that's why we're here. We're starting from scratch, Miss Kellett. Going back to square one, you might say. You're connected to the first murder by dint of the unfortunate Mister Stapely. So we need to know if there's anything you might have overlooked. Or if anything unusual has occurred recently that now makes sense in the light of this new information.'

'Clues,' Nelson said.

Angie appeared to think calmly. Her brain was fit to explode. As far as she was concerned, these two detectives had just confirmed the mad conclusion she had earlier tried to deny. So, what could she say to them? *Well, in the light of this new information, I am now certain my brother did not in fact pass away. I think he is out there in a rather vengeful frame of mind, hurting Tom Roker for pinching his novel by killing in accordance with the storyline of said pinched novel. And I offer this evidence: a rather lively dead body, followed by no dead body at all; a fortuitous meeting of the three main players outside a bookshop in Manchester; a phone call from a man claiming to be Milton, and addressing me as only my brother used to; and a novel delivered to my door, inscribed in my brother's handwriting, with a hitherto nonsensical message that, in the light of this new information, is now totally understandable. I hereby conclude that the serial killer you are after is none other than my pissed-off, undead brother, Andrew Kellett.*

Simple, concise . . .

Now would you like to strap these extra-long sleeves around me because I can't do it on my own.

. . . and completely out to lunch.

She could not give voice to a single word of it. They would never believe her. If they did believe her, they would not know how to help – unless they covered the paranormal at Hendon. And what if some tabloid did decide to break the story? Forget the UFO cranks. She would be in a league of her own: *SISTER CLAIMS DEAD BROTHER IS KILLER BIKER*.

She tittered crazily at the thought.

Nelson flared. 'Oh, fucking funny, isn't it? I expect Sergeant Wellings' widow is just killing herself.'

Angie guessed who Sergeant Wellings had been, but she didn't apologise. She could not change a thing. She could not explain anything. Nelson was so far out of the picture, his ignorance was hysterical. She laughed louder.

Nelson tore angrily at his chocolates, stuffing three into his mouth at once.

'Can I have your last Rolo?' she said, insanely.

'Fuck off!' Nelson pushed to his feet. 'Sick bitch!'

'You don't know the half of it.'

Ash was twiddling his thumbs and staring at the blank grey television screen.

'Ash! Shift yourself!' Nelson ordered. 'We're wasting our time.' He stormed out of the lounge and snatched his coat from the newel post.

Angie looked at Ash and noticed his eyeline drop and his eyes narrow. He tentatively began to point beneath the TV set.

'*Ash!*' Nelson bellowed from the porch.

Ash shot to standing, but before he left, he questioned Angie with his soft blue eyes. Hers pleaded with him not to linger, not to bring Nelson back into the room. Saying nothing, he moved to the door, holding eye contact, acknowledging the secret they now shared, but puzzling as to what it meant.

Ash collected his coat and closed the porch door behind him, and Angie heard Nelson yell for him to catch up, because Ash had the car keys and Nelson was getting soaked.

Just as she had done when Andrew was alive, Angie pedalled like a woman possessed. Away from the village, into the countryside. Her waterproofs wrapped themselves soddenly around her limbs. Her feet went cold as the rain permeated her trainers. Her New York baseball cap kept the worst from her head, but not for long. Gradually her hair dampened, her brow became icy, and a headache set in. Her eyes developed a squint, against the pain and the rain. She entered a long tunnel of trees and the wind brought freezing droplets down from the bare branches. As she moved further off the beaten track, cars troubled her less, until she felt totally isolated.

After a few miles, her speed slowed. With not sleeping last night, and the journey today, and the emotional bombardment both in London and back home, she felt faint with exhaustion. It could have been three a.m., and she had to remind herself it was still only teatime. That was another thing: she had not eaten all day.

She was not consciously aware of the direction she took, and she didn't need to be, she had travelled these roads so often in the past.

Two problems battled for supremacy in her aching skull.

Number one: if she was right about Andrew, and she sure as hell didn't want to be, then the police were going to find themselves vastly more clueless as each murder occurred. Which was not of direct concern to her, but it did mean there was only one person who might even begin to believe her, let alone understand or somehow help, and the last time they had met, that person had tried to rape her.

Number two: neither Nelson nor Ash had asked whether she had read Tom Roker's novel, and there had been no reason for them to suspect there was even that spurious connection. But since Ash had evidently spied *Man on a Murder Cycle* lying behind her television set, surrounded by the broken figurine, he now had to be wondering why she had not innocently volunteered the information. Which meant they would very soon be back to grill her, and, given Nelson's mood on departure, he would grill her to a frazzled crisp. And Angie knew, under pressure, she would talk. She would tell him what she believed if only to silence him for a moment. Naturally thinking she was winding him up, he would really give her a hard time. Then she definitely would crack. The strain of recent years would be released, hurt and fury gushing up through invisible fissures like bad blood purging itself. After that she would be of no use to anyone any more. A private room, pills at regular intervals throughout the day, and sleep, lots and lots of sleep.

A headache, a muddled mind, a bend, a dung-smeared road, and Angie lost control. Her front wheel slipped sideways and she sprawled onto the tarmac. Knee, shoulder, head. Bump, boof, crack. Her baseball cap came off. She skidded and tumbled into the verge, into a wet and weedy embrace. In those few seconds as she heard her mountain bike clatter to a standstill, she truly believed the decision was hers, that she could remain conscious if she so desired. But the closing eyes and the drifting thoughts felt so nice, and what was a little hypothermia between friends?

Her body leadened, her head lolled, and she blacked out.

THIRTY-FOUR

———◆———

The bank opened its doors to customers at nine-thirty a.m. It was a busy branch in the city centre of Manchester. The counter staff began their day with the fixed smiles that were as obligatory as the uniforms they wore. The smile was all the way from the US of A. It was meant to say, *Have a Nice Day*, but an essential part of it had been lost overboard somewhere in the Atlantic. In windswept, pissed-on Blighty, it translated all wrong. *I'm stuck on this face*, it said, *because my owner has been told to simper at you, the public, no matter how moronic you may be, and the instant you're gone, rest assured, so am I.*

It started off as a standard morning. Cheques in, transfer requests, cash in, cash out, complaints and queries.

On the streets, the weather had finally dried up, but the ground was still dark and puddled. A chilling wind sent tall white cumulus billowing across the sky, revealing momentary patches of pure blue. Every so often, for no more than five seconds, the sun flashed yellow at the city's cheerless citizens.

The pavements bustled. Trams whined along their tracks to the next raised platform of commuters. The rails buzzed in their wake. Cars and buses gave way. Dormant pedestrians were tooted. In the shops, January sales made a mockery of the pounds spent at Christmas. The prudent and the stingy were out in force, buying eleven months ahead of time.

In a concrete multistorey monstrosity two streets away, in the shadows of level four, Milton sat astride his black ZZ-R.

He sensed it was nearly time. An internal clock was counting down the minutes.

From the stairwell door, a young mum emerged, holding the

186

delicate hand of her daughter. Milton guessed four years old. The mum click-clacked briskly his way, making the toddler run to keep up. Milton understood: these places could give people the willies. When she drew closer, she noticed the all-black figure slotted between the cars, motionless and menacing. Before she swept her offspring into her arms and quickened her pace, the little girl smiled at him and waved. Milton lifted a black gauntlet in return and waggled his fingers.

Ten minutes later, he hit the electronic start. The engine turned over and broke into a promising burble, idling at 2,500 revs. He blipped the throttle to 5,000. The needle of the turbo boost dial swung off zero, and beneath the tank the Rayjay turbocharger gave an evil induction hiss, whilst the carbon fibre Renegade race exhaust sent shock-waves bouncing off every surface, threatening to smash glass, dent metal and split concrete.

He pulled in the clutch, tapped down into first and eased out of hiding.

Angie came to. She was lying on her left side, wearing knickers and a baggy T-shirt. Her place of rest was comfortable and dry. She was warm and snug. Her eyes opened a crack and she saw her wardrobe, then her dressing table. The duvet was heaped upon her.

It didn't figure. She thought hard. Last night . . .

It must have been a dream. High on physical and mental fatigue, she had gone to bed early and fallen into a world of make-believe. She tried to divide reality from fantasy. Where had the dream begun? As much as it would have pleased her to, she was not able to label Nelson and Ash as figments of her imagination. Their visit had happened. After that, however, she had obviously gone to bed. That she couldn't remember doing so did not alter the fact that it must be true. The bicycle ride, the accident – those things were false. Otherwise, how had she wound up in bed this morning?

Strange, though; never had a dream felt so real, seemed so vivid. Perhaps she was closer to cracking than she realised.

She rolled onto her back, then onto her right side to view the alarm clock on the bedside cabinet. The movement made her wince and squeal. She reached down to her knee and touched the painful swelling. She wriggled her shoulder and felt the bruising against the mattress. Carefully, she rolled onto her back and lay there staring at the ceiling. Her hand went gingerly to her head, fingers searching for the third phantom injury. In her hairline she found it. A sore bump.

She threw the duvet back, got out of bed and looked around the room. Where were the waterproofs? She ran to the bathroom doorway and saw them on the floor, rainwater still pooled in orange valleys and crevices. The rest of her soaking clothes were on top of the wicker linen basket. Above the basin, her reflection in the cabinet mirror showed her a gravel-grazed forehead.

In Andrew's bedroom, through his window, she checked the back garden. The shed door was open. She could see it was empty inside. Bicycle tyre tracks and her own footprints were visible on the shiny lawn where she had evidently wheeled her mountain bike across the grass and down to the road.

She shook her head and sat on the edge of the bed and suddenly realised: wearing only knickers and shirt, she was nevertheless warm. The heating was on full blast. But she never had the heating on full blast, she was too bothered about the bills. She preferred to wrap up in thermals, multiple jumpers and thick socks.

Andrew had always complained about the cold. She had often returned from work to find the house like a furnace.

She touched his radiator. It was burning hot.

She mentally kicked herself. She was going to have to quit this: convincing herself that the supernatural was afoot in her life. It was not at all healthy.

She padded down the hall and stopped at the bathroom door again. She stared at her waterproofs, at her pile of clothes. She closed her eyes, waiting for an image to flash on the black screen, hoping for some spark of recollection. But she could not remember a single thing after the accident. Not waking up, getting home, discarding her clothes, or going to bed.

She entered the bathroom, closed the loo seat and perched on it. The plastic was cold against her buttocks. She mused for a while. Brief bursts of sunshine broke through the window, making the washbasin taps sparkle.

There was only one conclusion to draw: last night she had suffered amnesia. Why not? She had suffered every other insult to her brain.

Satisfied, in a manner of speaking, with the explanation, she got up and transferred her waterproofs into the bathtub, then collected her bundle of clothes from the top of the linen basket. She lifted the lid and dropped them in. As they landed, her baseball cap was revealed among them. She reached inside and plucked it out.

But it wasn't her baseball cap. Hers had been navy blue with a white *NY* logo on the front. This one was black, bearing a logo in red: *ZZ-R*.

Ten yards from the bank, Milton mounted the kerb on his bike. Shoppers parted like the Red Sea. At the entrance he performed a smoking donut before parking up in the drifting blue-white fog. He killed the engine and lowered the sidestand. Passers-by were now standing by, gawping at his blatant disregard of pavement etiquette.

He got off his machine. The dull day looked like night through his black visor. Riding at night was a fucking scream.

At the door, he read the notice on the glass. *CRASH HELMETS MUST BE REMOVED BEFORE ENTERING.*

'Quite right,' he said to himself. 'Don't want to frighten the bankers inside.' He stepped over to his bike, unclipped the chin strap, clasped both hands around the black fibreglass and pulled it off his head, setting it on the petrol tank. Lingering onlookers, seeing his face, hurried away down the street, muttering gravely to themselves.

Back to business. He placed a black glove against the bank door and pushed it wide open. Behind him, he heard a car draw up to the kerb. He checked over his shoulder. A Kermit-green Vauxhall Nova GTE full of seventeen-year-old boys. Four speakers booming incessantly. A large KENWOOD transfer in the rear window. Lowered suspension and alloy wheels. Exhaust fumes barping through an end-can the diameter of a cake tin.

He returned his attention to the interior of the bank. A shuffling old biddy was coming towards him, her spine so bent that her eyeline was barely two feet ahead of her own two feet. Milton kept the door open for her; it was unwieldy and he liked to think he wasn't completely heartless, even though he knew he was.

The biddy shuffled level, stopped, and with the greatest difficulty inclined her face as high as it would go. Luckily for her, it was still too low to catch a glimpse of Milton's.

'Thank you, young man.'

'You're welcome, old woman.'

Before he could move into the bank, one of the Nova knobs

slouched through in front of him, ignoring his charitable gesture with the door.

'Don't mention it,' Milton growled.

The boy halted and swung round. 'I didn't,' he retorted before he had a chance to register the features glaring down at him. He cringed. 'Sorry.'

Milton let it pass – for now. He released the door and noted with distaste the current youth fashion. Trainers like inflatable boats; enough denim in the jeans to clothe the cast of *Dallas*, most of it in folds at the ankles; a vertically striped top, hanging outside the hanging arse of his jeans; a bright yellow, puffed-up jacket, like that of a colour-blind Michelin Man; and a red and blue *Nike* baseball cap, on backwards over a close-shorn head.

'Pathetic,' Milton decreed, and clumped over to the nearest closed-circuit camera, pointing down from the wall. He stared defiantly up at it for ten seconds, smirking. In the back office, a video tape recorded the moment for future police reference.

He joined the queue behind the boy.

'You know what they say: big exhaust, small penis.'

The boy clearly heard because he moved uneasily on his feet, but he said nothing and kept his eyes straight ahead.

'Nice car. Kenwood. Fantastic. Powered by a food mixer. Prototype, huh?'

The boy turned and made a face, but did not verbally rise to the bait.

'You've got your hat on back to front.'

The queue edged forward.

'I said you've got your hat on back to front.'

The boy turned round again. 'I know,' he said carefully. 'It's meant to be.'

'Oh, I see. I might try that with my crash helmet.'

The boy smiled doubtfully, then looked plain puzzled when he noticed two bumps inside Milton's jacket, like small breasts. Common sense made him turn away.

Another customer went to a vacant counter position. Milton was now fourth in line.

'You've got your hat on back to front,' he informed the person third in line.

The boy ignored him.

'Your hat's on back to front.'

190

Swivelling bodily to confront Milton, the boy's temper got the better of him. 'Leave it, will you?'

Milton saw the boy's eyes struggle to find the least disturbing part of his face. Three seconds and he gave up trying and turned his back.

'It's just, you look like a dickhead,' Milton offered quietly.

The boy spun. 'Oh, fuck off, man!'

Milton raised his hairless eyebrows, affecting a hurt expression. The boy kept sideways on to him, for safety.

The queue shortened, losing two, making the boy next in line. Milton watched him dip into his pocket and bring out a ten-pound note and a paying-in book. His movements were sharp, nervous, impatient.

'Good job I'm here,' Milton suddenly announced, jumping forward with both feet across the boy's toes.

The boy shouted. Customers stared and staff smiles vanished.

'Because I can fix that hat problem for you.'

There was no time for the boy to defend himself. Milton wrapped one leather-clad arm around the boy's head, squeezing it in the crook of his elbow, his gloved palm smothering his face. Milton's other arm rotated little finger up and clasped the back of the boy's skull, above the peak of the cap. It appeared as though he was about to unscrew a particularly stubborn, giant bottle-top.

The boy gave a muffled scream, and Milton ripped his hands round in a circle. Rooted to the spot by size twelve biker boots, the boy could not follow the twist of his head with a similar twist of his body.

A series of sickening snaps came from his neck. With the strength of the damned, Milton was able to alter the aspect of the boy's face by over one hundred and eighty degrees.

The bank was filled with screams and gasps and the scuttling feet of those with the presence of mind to flee whilst they still could.

The boy had gone flaccid, but Milton held him upright.

'There we go,' he said happily to the corpse. 'Problem solved.' Then he gave a mock frown. 'Ah. But now . . . damn it, your head's on back to front.' He sighed deeply, then became instantly gleeful again. 'Hey-ho, such is death.' He let the body drop to the floor and approached the counter. Only one cashier remained at her post, rigid with shock. He smiled broadly. 'Now, I'd like to withdraw some money if I may.'

No response.

'Yes, you may have guessed my dilemma. I do not have an account at this branch. Indeed at any branch, of any bank, anywhere. I trust that won't be a problem?'

The cashier's questioning eyes had fallen to Milton's chest.

'Nice tits, huh? Pert,' said Milton, admiring the small lumps beneath his leather jacket. He unzipped and produced two hand grenades. 'Now, about that cash withdrawal.'

A siren wailed in the distance.

'Alas, no time. I'll have to make a deposit instead.'

He pulled the pin and released the handle, rolling the grenade into the transaction drawer.

Nothing happened until he reached the street. The boys in the Nova were still waiting for their mate. *Boom, boom, boom, boom, boom, boom, boom*, went the speakers.

The explosion blew glass and shrapnel over the passing public.

A deathly lull followed, broken only by converging sirens and the continuing *boom, boom, boom, boom, boom, boom, boom*.

As people began to scream, Milton pulled the second pin, held it for a couple of seconds then chucked the grenade through the wound-down car window.

Boom, boom, boom, boom . . .

The shell-shocked boys scrabbled frantically, vainly, to be rid of it.

. . . *boom, boom, BOOM!*

THIRTY-FIVE

Manchester and Cheshire had joined forces in the biggest murder inquiry anyone could remember. Every constabulary in the country had been alerted. After this last incident, the media blackout had been lifted. It was too big to keep quiet, and the investigation had barely moved out of its starting blocks; it needed public input.

Nelson was in charge. It was his case. He knew it would either make him or break him. He could retire and never buy another round for the rest of his life if he cracked it, and he would retire and drink himself to death if he didn't.

The Joint Ops briefing had just broken up. Nelson was sitting with Ash in the station canteen. The rest of the team had gone to their designated tasks, replete with individual copies of *Man on a Murder Cycle*, for all the good it would do them.

Nelson's signed copy was open in front of him. He was poring over the author's fictional version of events. Ash was doing the same, his forefinger underlining each word as he read it.

'This bastard's going to kill again,' Nelson said, 'and it's all down in here how it's going to happen.' He stuck his fork into a chip, but pushed his plate away. 'To all intents and purposes anyone who reads this shit becomes clairvoyant. But it doesn't bloody help.'

'I think we ought to bring Tom Roker up here,' Ash said.

'What for?'

'Because he's responsible. He's caused all of this. He must know more than he's telling.'

'Yeah, I get the feeling he does.'

'So why don't we bring him in?'

Nelson searched for the best way to say it.

'Guv?'

Nelson took a slurp of coffee. 'Because I want him exposed. I want him to feel vulnerable. See, right now, I think he feels guilty that someone's turning the product of his warped imagination into real life. But guilt's not enough. He needs to feel vulnerable. He needs to feel so shit-scared that he'll come running to us, snivelling, ready to spew his life story from beginning to end.'

'But how do you know he'll ever feel like that?'

'Because whoever's acting out these scenes I think knows him.' Ash leaned forward on the table.

Nelson expounded. 'If I've got a screw loose and I'm potentially homicidal, any day something could push me over the edge, and I accept it could be the smallest thing, the tiniest thing. But it would have to happen to me. Directly to me. I can't see how a book's going to do it. It's too removed.' Nelson decided he did want a chip after all.

'People go nuts after seeing films at the cinema,' Ash said.

'Yuk.' Nelson dribbled the chewed chip back onto his plate. 'Cold. But are they ever more than isolated incidents? No. They're spur of the moment. A moment of madness. Most of us feel them. Few of us actually give vent. Even if we do, we instantly regret it. I mean, have you seen *Death Wish*? When I saw that film for the first time, I was working on a case. Local toe-rag, mugging, house-breaking, car theft, you name it. Everyone knew the score with this shyster, but no one dared speak up against him, and we didn't have enough evidence. But I swear to God, Adam, if I'd had a gun to hand that night, knowing the misery he'd caused so many decent folk round here, I'd have done a Charlie Bronson on the little fucker. For an hour after seeing that film, I'd have felt fully justified.'

Ash checked to see if anyone was eavesdropping on Nelson's confession.

'But only for an hour,' Nelson said. 'And that's the point. Films and books don't set serial killers on the rampage. Anyone who has the mind to commit multiple murder would not have the patience to wait and see if a novel's going to be written for them to act it out.'

'No,' Ash agreed, cringing as he watched Nelson absently stab at another chip. 'Don't eat that.'

'Oh, yeah.' He set the fork down again. 'From the tricks he gets up to, our boy's been riding bikes for years. He hasn't just learnt to fit the storyline. He could have waited a lifetime for the right book to come along. I just don't believe it.'

'Neither do I.'

'No,' Nelson reflected, 'this is personal.'

'And I don't believe he's psychotic any more, at least not in the sense I first thought.'

'Why's that?'

'Because these recent murders have been too clinical. He's waited for exactly the right circumstances, or he's sought them out, before acting. From what I can gather, that behaviour's more psychopathic in profile. But he's still taking huge risks, which again can be viewed as a psychopathic tendency, trying to accentuate his feelings of power by proving he can get away with almost anything, but it's just *too* blasé. Notorious serial killers in past decades have taunted the police with letters and clues, but that's once they're safely clear of the crime scene. This fellah's allowed himself to be filmed on video, he's killed in broad daylight in a busy street, risking intervention by both the police and the public. In fact, he's actively encouraged us to chase him. It doesn't make sense. He loves killing, a classic psychopathic trait, and yet he doesn't hide from us, when psychopaths traditionally do just that for two reasons: it gives them another kick knowing they can blend into society again until the next murder, and it obviously allows them to remain at liberty to *commit* the next murder.' Ash shook his head. 'No, this is weird. He doesn't really fit any given profile. Even taking into account the complexities of the criminally insane mind, it just doesn't make any sense.'

Nelson smiled crookedly, but not without a trace of admiration. 'You read a lot in your spare time, don't you, Adam?'

'I like to understand.'

'Fine. Just don't lose sight of the fact he's a murdering bastard. He can tell the prison shrink how his dad got him to wank him off at bedtime. I'm not interested. I just want him locked up. Or, better still, dead.'

Ash did a double-take, but ignored it. 'Okay, but it's not his father he's pissed off at. If, as you say, and I agree, he has been triggered by something personal, then that something must be Tom Roker, and/or his novel. But why would someone that deranged, with that obvious hatred of Tom Roker, not direct their violence specifically at him?'

Nelson pointed a finger at Ash. 'Exactly. So if Tom Roker does know who it is, he must be thinking the same thing. And sooner or later he'll come running to us for protection.'

'But why not pre-empt that? Frighten him. Make him tell us.'

'No. I can read people. He's not ready. The fact that he hasn't told us already proves he must have a lot to lose himself. I get the impression Tom Roker's been a bad lad. He's upset someone and now they're getting their own back.'

'By making him rich?' Ash asked in amazement. 'When this story breaks tomorrow, sales of his book'll go through the roof.'

'Which makes it even worse for him in the long run if he believes he'll never get his hands on all that money. Bit of an empty victory if he's dead or in jail.'

'Hold on,' Ash said. 'If this is some sort of payback, could we be dealing with a hired hitman?'

Nelson considered the idea for a moment. 'No. He's too good at the killing, which means he'd be a pro, and no amount of dosh would get a professional to even contemplate conspicuous crap like this. It's begging to be caught.'

'Yeah.' Ash drained his tea from the styrofoam cup.

Nelson made a futile stab at one last tepid chip as he stood up. He burped, then produced a Mars bar from his pocket before blundering away through the maze of canteen tables and chairs.

THIRTY-SIX

When Angie opened her front door to Adam Ash late that evening, she knew her face reflected her lack of surprise. She had been expecting him for twenty-four hours.

'I'm on my own,' he said straightaway. 'I'm off duty.'

'And off record, Sergeant Ash?'

He nodded. 'Call me Adam. What happened to your forehead?'

'Fell off my bike. Wait. I'll get my coat. We'll go to the pub.'

They walked down the hill in silence, their breath clouding in the crisp air.

Passing the village post office, Angie accidentally brushed past a black-clothed man who was slipping a letter into the box. She turned and apologised, and found she had just said sorry to Michael. Caught unawares, he appeared momentarily to forget their history. He smiled and opened his mouth to greet her. Then he seemed to remember, and the memory shone as pain in his startled eyes, which looked away and then settled on her companion. Then Michael really looked hurt. His mouth slowly closed and his gaze dropped to the pavement.

'Who was that?' Ash asked as the dog collarless vicar hurried off down the road.

'It's a long story,' Angie said. 'And not the one I want to tell.'

The low-ceilinged pub was dim and warm. Horse brasses hung on wooden beams, glimmering in the dull orange light. The landlord greeted Angie like a long-lost daughter. Ash ordered a pint of bitter and a brandy, then they found a quiet corner in one of the snug-rooms, out of sight from the bar. They removed their coats and sat down.

Angie took a mouthful.

'I like a woman who likes her beer,' Ash said.

Angie set her pint on the table. 'How's your brandy?'

'Gone.' Ash chucked it down, then went for another.

Settling himself again, he gave an awkward smile. 'Before you say anything, I need to tell you something. To up the stakes. So you know you really shouldn't keep anything back.'

Angie swallowed hard. 'What?'

'The biker's killed again. A bank in Manchester.'

'Hand grenades,' she said.

'You've read the book.'

'I've read the story, not the book. I've got the book, as you well know, but I haven't read it.'

Ash tried not to appear gormless. 'Pardon? You've got the book, you've read the story, but you haven't read the book?'

Angie nodded. 'If you shut up I'll tell you.' Strangely, she felt she could trust Ash, at least not to dismiss her out of hand. She lifted one leg onto the padded bench, slipping her ankle beneath her opposite thigh. 'Do you consider yourself open-minded, Adam?'

Sniffing his brandy, he nodded. 'Yes.'

'Good. You'll need to be.'

So she told him. What she knew, what she believed, what she suspected. Normal and paranormal.

Afterwards, Ash stared into his empty glass, swilling an amber drop around the base.

'I think I need another,' he said, getting up. 'A large one.'

Whilst he was at the bar, Angie prayed she had done the right thing. But, whatever the outcome, she felt a weight had lifted. A problem shared, etcetera.

He returned and sat stiffly. Angie watched him closely, assessing him. The silence persisted, and she was about to say something, anything, when he spoke, making brief eye contact every so often.

'When I was a kid, seven or eight, my grandad died. My father's side. I was named after him. He was fun, spoilt me, so I liked him. It's a simple exchange at that age. He smoked a lot. Menthol cigarettes. That's what got him in the end. Anyway, for a week following his death, I kept smelling menthol smoke in my bedroom. I couldn't see it, just smelt it. No one else in the house smoked, and when I called my parents in they said they couldn't smell a thing. Then one day I was playing in the drive, kicking a ball about. It rolled onto the street and I chased it, and kids' priorities being what they are, I was more intent on catching the ball than checking the road. I ran out between parked cars, and, too late, saw a van bearing down on me. I was running full pelt. I couldn't have stopped. But something did stop me. I can still feel it now. A hand grabbing my collar, yanking me back, literally lifting me off my feet. The van missed me, but only just. I turned round to thank whoever it was, but there was no one there. There wasn't anyone within a hundred yards of me. Then I caught it, a whiff of menthol. And that was the last time. After that, the smell disappeared from my room.'

Angie smiled to herself. Thank God: a believer.

'There'd been nothing before that,' Ash said, 'and there's been nothing since. I grew up, matured, became all sensible, joined the police, started dealing with hard evidence, and . . . well, it's funny how incidents like that simply file themselves away without a fuss. You know it happened, you know it's not within our natural realm of understanding, you feel it should somehow transform your life for ever . . . but it doesn't.'

'No. A million hard facts come between it and you. At the time, I thought I'd never recover from what happened at the undertaker's. The moan, the eyes, the mouth. But you're right, it gets lost, until you can't imagine it meant anything at all.'

She drank deeply from her pint. Ash downed his short. Then he shocked her by taking her hand.

'But this isn't going away, is it, Angie? And the problem is, I don't know what I can do. I'm not even sure I can believe it, despite what I know happened to me.'

She tugged her hand free and glared at him, but she realised she was asking a great deal to expect his total and instant faith.

He spoke quickly. 'I mean, it would explain certain incongruities in the murderer's profile, but . . .' He shrugged himself silent.

She patted his hand gently. 'Don't fret, Adam. It's not your concern.'

'But it is,' he said, twisting his body to face her. 'I want to help. As a police officer and a friend.'

She held his hands plaintively. 'Then get your pal Nelson to see Tom Roker again. Arrest him. Jail him. Kill him. Anything to appease my brother.'

Ash squirmed. 'Angie, I can't tell Nelson what you've just told me. None of it. He'd have me referred to psychiatric services.'

'Can't you even tell him that my brother wrote *Man on a Murder Cycle*?'

'There's no evidence. You said so yourself. No discs, no manuscripts, nothing.'

'Can't you tie Carol Morgan to the break-in?'

'How?'

Angie lost her temper. 'You're the detective, Adam. Detect, for Christ's sake.'

Clearly desperate to help, Ash pondered for a while. Then a bulb seemed to light in his head. 'The fingerprints we found on the crowbar,' he said almost to himself. 'And on the back door.'

'What about them? They'll hardly belong to Carol Morgan.'

The orange wall lamps flicked on and off, on and off. Last orders was called at the bar.

'Another?' Ash asked.

'What about the fingerprints?'

He seemed noncommittal. 'I don't know. It's unlikely. I can't see he'd have done it himself, but . . . I could always try a match against Tom Roker. You've got the novel he gave you. I should be able to lift a print from the cover.'

She gave him a sceptical look.

'Angie, I know, but have you got any other suggestions?' She didn't answer so he helped himself to her bitter. 'Don't worry, I'll keep it hush-hush. No need for anyone else to be brought into our whacky world of ghouls and ghosties.'

'Unless the prints match,' she said hopefully.

'Yes, there is always that outside chance. Tom Roker may yet turn out to be a complete cretin. But I'd give better odds on my being plucked from certain death by a dead grandad.'

It was well after midnight when they left the pub. The landlord had a rather liberal interpretation of drinking-up time. Ash did not reach for his warrant card.

On the stroll back up the hill, it occurred to Angie that Ash was vastly over the drink-drive limit. He tried to engage her in light conversation as they walked, but she could summon nothing more than one-word answers to his questions. All of a sudden she had become fuming mad at him.

'What's the matter?' he asked as they neared the cottage.

'Nothing.'

'Have I done something wrong?'

'No.' But he was about to, she could feel it.

He stopped her as they reached the front gate. 'Listen, I don't know how I've upset you but—'

She huffed with harsh prejudgment. He peered down at her, but she kept her eyes to the grass.

He cleared his throat. 'But if I have, I'm sorry. Unfortunately, I need to ask you a favour.'

She stamped her feet against the cold. 'What? You want one for the road?'

'Well, that would be nice, but I need to call a cab first.'

She looked up at him. 'Pardon?'

'That's the favour: I need to use your phone. Sorry, I should have called from the pub.'

Angie's frosty demeanour cracked into smiles. 'God, Adam, I'm so sorry, I thought you were about to drive home.'

He was aghast. 'I wouldn't *dream* of it.'

Laughing, she linked her arm through his and led him up to the porch.

'Oh, of course,' he said as she inserted her key in the door, 'your brother's wife and daughter.'

She paused to look at him – an acknowledgment – then let him into the house. He went to the living-room phone, picked up and dialled. Angie smiled afresh; he knew the firm's number off by heart. Having made his request, he followed her into the kitchen to be presented with a glass of Bailey's.

'Thank you for being one of the good guys,' she said, clinking glasses with him. 'Let's go in the lounge.'

In the front room, they sat opposite each other. Angie felt miffed that he hadn't chosen to sit beside her, but she guessed that mixing business with pleasure was not on the cards. Things were complicated enough already. And seducing him was out; the memory of Michael put paid to that.

Ash leaned back in the armchair and crossed his long legs. His eyes were pink with booze, his skin flushed with the recent chill.

'Don't buy a motorbike,' she blurted.

'Eh?'

'They're death-traps, Adam. Stop learning. You've survived this long without riding.'

'Aha, but I never knew how much fun it was.'

'Please.'

He grinned. 'I'm touched.'

'I'd say it to anyone.'

His cheeks reddened even more.

She sipped her cream liqueur. 'Don't let Nelson influence you.'

'I don't, thank you very much. It's my choice.'

She was shocked when she found herself in a minor sulk. But she gathered she was terrified, paranoid even; she seemed to jinx anyone who came close. Not that Ash was particularly close, but the death-curse which had swathed through her family like a sickle seemed now to be extending outwards, and she didn't want Ash dumbly offering himself up to it.

'Don't,' she said.

'Listen, I've got my bike test tomorrow. No one else knows, so no one'll know if I fail, but I promise I'll take a view after that. Okay? I mean, once I'm able to ride, I might not want to. It might be just a challenge I've set for myself.'

She wasn't happy, but he wasn't six and she wasn't his mother.

'So is that the hat?' he asked, changing the subject, pointing towards the black baseball cap on the coffee table.

She picked it up and threw it to him. He stared at the logo with a fascination only intoxicated eyes can have for something so straightforward. But Angie could see there was more going on behind the scenes.

'And you got this last night?' he asked.

'Went out with mine on my head, came back with that.'

'You know, the fat man wouldn't like this at all. Not one little bit.'

'You mean Nelson?'

'He hates coincidences. Doesn't believe in them.' Ash plopped the cap onto his head, then whizzed the peak round to the back. 'And right now, neither do I.'

'You mean the hats getting swapped last night, and Milton rearranging the kid's baseball cap in the bank today?'

Ash whipped the hat from his head and raised his voice. 'How the hell do you know about the kid in the bank?'

She gave him a startled, puzzled look.

'How?'

'Adam . . .' she appealed.

'*How?*'

She met his tone of voice with the same. 'Because it's in the bloody book, and you told me—'

'You said you haven't read the bloody book!'

'—you told me the scenes so far have been acted out to the letter.'

'You said you haven't read it!'

'I haven't, but I have read it on disc, I told you so in the pub.'

Ash's aggressive posture instantly collapsed. He seemed to shrink physically in his chair. Confusion ran amok across his face.

'Adam, what's the problem?'

He didn't answer and remained perfectly still.

'Adam?'

'Killing the kid isn't in the book,' he said finally. 'We all assumed Milton was just straying from the plot for the hell of it.'

'But I read it on disc,' Angie said lamely.

Ash nodded very deliberately. 'Therein lies the problem.'

But Angie knew that wasn't the problem, because that problem was easily solved: between disc and publication, the incident with the baseball cap had been edited out. No, the true problem for Ash was the implication of that omission, considering Milton had known *not* to omit it.

Gently, Angie said, 'D'you realise that a moment ago, for the first time this evening, you referred to the killer as Milton?'

'Did I?'

The sound of a diesel engine arrived outside, followed shortly by a sharp knock at the front door.

Standing up, Ash made a last-ditch attempt to deny the obvious, and the obviously crazy. 'Who else read the story on disc?'

'Apart from me? No one.'

'Think.'

'No one, Adam.'

'Hmm. Damn. That's what I thought.'

She went upstairs and brought down the hardback novel Tom Roker had given her, for Ash to lift a print. She gave it to him, then opened the front door. Freezing air swept in like an invisible alien invader. 'See you in the morning,' she said, feeling goosebumps rise.

'What?'

'When you get your car.'

There was a beat before it sunk in. 'Right.'

'And try to sleep well.'

His expression was comical. 'Oh yeah, don't have nightmares, do sleep well.' He smiled forlornly. 'Sure. Maybe next year.'

THIRTY-SEVEN

A solitary candle had almost burnt out on the altar. Its weak flame, barely alive, danced in one of the building's many drafts. A shadow of the crucified Jesus flickered against the stone wall. The angelic scenes in the east window, by day colourful and joyous, seemed satanic by night. Good made evil by the shroud of darkness.

Michael sat limply in the choir stalls with his face in his hands. As he had done daily since his lapse with Angie, he contemplated his career. He no longer thought of it as a vocation. He had only continued with his duties through lack of an alternative. It was too late to start over. Morbidly, he had imagined he would die in his pulpit, struck down by a God who was tired of listening to a dishonest employee.

The whole of his adult life he had clung by his fingernails to that rock called Faith. Then he had taken a risk. He had let go to reach for Angie Kellett, and for a few blissful hours she had held him.

Then she had dropped him, and how he had fallen from grace. Attempted rape. It was inconceivable. He shook with shame at the memory.

He had struggled every day since then to rediscover a spark of faith. Tonight, he could no longer fake it. Seeing Angie with her new boyfriend, something inside him had finally snapped. He could not stomach the thought of another Sunday spouting advice he had never followed to folk who never would. Wisdoms trite and glib for a bunch of nodding hypocrites. Watching their upturned faces as they smilingly tried to suck hope from his empty soul.

He had come to the end. Forget faith. If God was up there, Michael needed to see some proof. He did not want to spend the rest of his earthly life in self-denial, preparing himself for an afterlife that might not exist. There were pleasures to be had. Here. Now.

A vision of Angie, naked and beautiful, burned in his mind.

Then a less welcome image displaced it: her new boyfriend, also naked, in bed with her, making the beast with two backs.

'I wish he was dead,' he whispered suddenly, then uttered a small gasp because he had shocked himself. What a perfectly wicked sentiment.

Yet it was a relief to let go; to allow himself the luxury of hatred, of jealousy, for once. It felt liberating. Why should he be the only one in the village to keep a lid on his emotions? He had every right to feel resentment. He had spent thirty years canvassing for the Almighty, and his spirit still failed to rejoice in The Word. Why had he not been given a sign? Something to say his path was true? The stigmata of Christ on his body perhaps, or a heavenly visitation.

Or a thunderbolt to strike down Angie's new boyfriend.

He chuckled softly, bitterly. There was no way back from this. To be wishing harm on another human being, and to be wishing it sincerely.

A hundred feet away, the west door squeaked shut.

Michael froze, then turned slowly and peered into the murky depths.

'Who's there?' he said. Had someone come in or gone out? But how? He clearly remembered locking up. 'Who's there?' He rose to his feet, left the choir stalls, and crept along the nave.

In the shadows, at the big west door, he tried the handle. The door opened and the cold night air poured in.

His eyes searched among the gravestones, left to right. Nothing. Then beyond them, along the railings and trees that bordered the church property. No . . . noth—

He whipped his head back to a clump of leafless bushes.

Mouth agape, eyes wide with wonder, he fell to his knees in the doorway and quickly poked a fingertip beneath his fringe to trace a cross above the scar.

Out there, in the gloom of the undergrowth, was a face. It was indistinct, too far away to make out any features, and the body beneath it was either completely hidden or dressed in black.

But above that face, hovering in the air, Michael could quite clearly see a white circle that could only be one thing.

THIRTY-EIGHT

Sleep was becoming a difficult state to achieve, and when eventually Tom had been able to slip under, Milton was waiting for him, a carving knife to his daughter's throat.

Tom sat in his dressing gown at the kitchen table, a mug of coffee before him. He drew deeply from his first cigarette of the day, and left it dangling from his lips, surrounded by three days' stubble. The bags beneath his eyes felt as though someone had packed them for a round-the-world trip. The first flush of proper daylight was beginning to make the overhead fluorescent redundant. He briefly removed his cigarette before yawning cavernously and closing his eyes. He could sleep now, of course, now it was time to get up.

Along the hallway, at the front door, his letter-box snapped shut and his copy of *The Times* fell to the mat.

He went to retrieve it, shuffled back to the kitchen, sat down and perused the headlines. Domestic scandals and world atrocities. He couldn't have cared less. He turned the page, disinterested as to what he might find.

BIKER CLAIMS SEVEN VICTIMS IN A WEEK. A half-page article.

The cigarette fell from his gaping mouth. After a blank moment, he snatched it from his lap and stubbed it in the ashtray. Now he felt wide awake.

He didn't mind that the newspapers were belatedly on the case – he had expected it, and he couldn't have wished for better publicity – it was the figure *seven* that bothered him.

He shot upstairs. In his bedroom he feverishly checked his copy of *Man on a Murder Cycle*. Where the bank job should have been, there were blank spaces instead.

The killer was moving on apace with the plot. Seven victims. Tom totted up: the undertaker, the policeman, the Volvo driver – three. So four yesterday, exactly as written. A cashier inside from the first blast, and three kids in their car from the second.

Horrific.

But he jolted in his seat. Because he was wrong. The headline told of seven victims *in a week*, which meant that the undertaker was not included.

Which made five yesterday, which didn't figure at all.

He rushed downstairs again to examine the article. As he went, he wondered how the less restrained newspapers were headlining it, and what about the Gutter Press with their delicate, sensitive approach to such matters?

Sitting at the kitchen table again, he began to read. Shortly, he came across the explanation for victim number five.

His whisper would have been inaudible even to someone sitting opposite. 'Oh . . . my . . . God.'

The baseball cap. Back to front. The head. Back to front. The scene that made the difference between the manuscript in the red folder and the one in the black. Lost for ever when he burnt the red, much to Carol's chagrin. But, one way or another, apparently destined to appear in print.

He struggled for a handle on the situation. Logically, who else could have known about this unpublished gem but Kellett's sister? Unfortunately, logic did not warrant further suspicions in that direction. If she was exacting revenge on such a grand scale, why bother visiting Carol? That was like nuking Iraq, then faxing a stern warning to Saddam. And where did one hire a homicidal maniac these days? The *Thompson Local*?

But who did that leave? What did that leave? A man claiming to be Milton, with knowledge he shouldn't possess, and vanishing words, invisible only to Tom Roker.

Tom shoved the newspaper to the far side of the table. His imagination was running wild, fuelled by his recent nightmares. A deceased novelist, a headless farmer – vengeful spirits both, Chunks of text peeling off the page, transmitted through an unseen dimension into genuine acts of violence.

Damn. Payback time for Tom Roker.

Then he screeched with laughter. Vengeful spirits . . . it was a ridiculous proposition. He was simply feeling guilty, and that, coupled with his fear of being caught, had made his head all skew-whiff.

Just like the kid's.

He screeched again. It *was* payback time, but only by his own conscience.

Before his death, Andrew Kellett had obviously let a biking friend read his novel, and that friend, lacking the concrete evidence for a conviction, had now taken on the persona of Milton to exact retribution by other means, namely scaring poor old Tom to death.

'And you're doing a fucking good job!' Tom yelled at a fridge magnet in the shape of a motorbike, before screeching some more. 'Nutters! All of them! I said!'

An impulse to call Carol was savagely beaten down by a cruel streak. She could read it herself, or hear it on the news; take the full force of the blow, as he had done, unsoftened by a familiar voice.

He thought of his latest manuscript, surrendered by Carol the day before as agreed. A businesslike handover, the threat of sex heavy in the air, but not realised; the power-game was not theirs to play any more.

The manuscript was upstairs in his safe. Over five hundred pages of grisly goings-on. How many deaths in there? Thirty? Forty? More? Maybe. He hadn't counted. It had not seemed important. They were fictional lives and he had played God, blotting them out as and when it suited. But now, knowing the situation, it was inconceivable that he should willingly be a party to a further transfer of that much bloodshed into the real world.

Until the mad biker was safely behind bars, Milton's sequel would remain locked away.

Down the hallway, in the front living room, his telephone began to ring.

Ash was not due in work until two p.m. He had a full morning. Over to the greyhound stadium car park at Belle Vue, Manchester, for ten o'clock, where the motorcycle training centre was located. An hour on the roads with an instructor, covering the possible test routes he would be taken on. Then to the test centre for eleven-thirty, and the real thing.

Given the repertoire of weather for that time of year, he had struck lucky. A night-blanket of high cirrus had kept the frost at bay. Now the cover was gradually tearing and blue sky was peeping through. The air was perfectly still, not a murmur of breeze.

He picked up his car from Angie's house at eight-thirty a.m. He wanted to see her again, but her curtains were drawn so he decided to wait. He drove towards Belle Vue with a bootful of leathers and his crash helmet beside him on the passenger seat.

After a hopefully successful result, he planned to go in early to headquarters and drop in on Karen for a little unofficial forensics. Given the nod, she would leave him to it; ever thirsty for knowledge, he had made it his business to know how to lift a fingerprint, and how many matching whorls and whatnots were required to secure a conviction in a court of law.

The likelihood that Tom Roker had been involved hands-on at the crime scene still seemed ridiculously far-fetched. But then so was Angie's theory about her dead brother, and he believed that.

The telephone was a whingeing brat, crying for attention. Tom had not bothered answering. He guessed some journalist had got his number and was seeking an exclusive. Well, Tom had a prepared statement for the Press – No Comment – and he could deliver it just as pointedly by not picking up the receiver.

Tom covered his ears. The ringing was almost incessant.

In the next lull he raced upstairs and switched on his answering machine. A moment later, it rang again.

Hello, this is Tom Roker. Sorry I can't get to the phone but if you leave a message I'll call you back. Thanks.

Beep.

'*Boo!* Hiya, Tommy! I know you're there. Pick up. Come on You're standing by the phone, I can feel you. Pick it up pick it up pick it up!'

Tom rippled with fear; he recognised the voice.

'Tommy? Tommy? No? Never mind. I just wanted you to know I loved your first novel. I'm fairly ripping through the chapters. But I'm not a happy chappy, because what am I going to do when it's finished? You couldn't write another, could you? A sequel? Just for me? Or is my sneaking suspicion correct? Have you already written one? Have you? I think so, Tommy. Tommy, why won't you talk to me? I'm your biggest fan. No? Well, gotta go, but I'll leave you with this thought: I want more, and you're going to give it me, or I might just have to make my own entertainment. I know

210

where you live, capice? I've always wanted to say that. So publish and be damned, Tommy. But don't have me picking flowers; they'll only end up in another wreath.'

The line clicked dead. Tom stared at the machine for a very long time.

His first death-threat. He supposed he ought to be flattered; not every novelist provoked such intense reactions in their readers. But who was he kidding? He knew what was going on and it was no fan-worship, regular or otherwise.

He sat down at his desk and sifted through the contents of his wallet, but when he found DCI Nelson's card he immediately knew he wasn't going to call. It was best he kept his mouth shut where the police were concerned, at least for the time being. Tom could do nothing to prevent the remaining deaths in *Man on a Murder Cycle* from happening, and until they had happened, he was safe. He could reserve judgment until then. Anyway, surely the killer would be behind bars long before that.

As he lit another cigarette with trembling hands, the telephone rang again, and the machine picked up the caller.

'Bollocks,' said a dejected Mancunian on hearing Tom's message. 'Okay, this is DCI Nelson, Mr Roker. You may or may not know what I'm calling about – just read a newspaper if you don't – but I need you to call me soon as you get in. You've got my card; if you've lost it the number's—'

Tom lifted the receiver and stopped the recording. He sucked in a lungful of calming nicotine, and exhaled as he spoke. 'I've read my newspaper this morning, thank you very much.'

'Mr Roker!' Nelson chirped. 'Vetting calls are we? Why's that?'

'No reason.'

'No more nuisance calls?'

'Apart from yours?'

There was a slight pause. 'What d'you think, Mr Roker?'

'About what?'

'Whether Man City'll drop another division this season. Doesn't look good at the minute.'

Tom gathered his stupid question had deserved a stupid answer. He decided to stop being awkward; Nelson would take it for what it was: the sign of a guilty conscience.

'I can't tell you anything more than the last time we spoke.'

'Can't or won't?'

'Why don't you believe me?' Tom said.

'It's not my job to believe people, Mr Roker. Criminals tend to lie, it's a proven fact.'

'Is that so.'

'It is. Anyway, I called because I'm sending a car for you. I've got something I want you to have a look at.'

'And what if I'm busy today?'

'Cancel busy.'

Tom's heart was pounding. 'Am I under arrest?'

'Not yet. Do you want to be? I can arrange it.'

Tom leaned on his desk and absently wiped some dust from beneath his typewriter. He said nothing.

'I can issue a warrant, Mr Roker. Suspicion.'

Tom flicked the accumulated grey particles from the ends of his fingers. 'All right, come and get me.'

'Super,' Nelson mocked, and broke contact.

Tom replaced the receiver, knelt down, reached under the desk and disconnected the line from the wall box. He went downstairs and did the same in the living room, then peeked through the curtains. At least there was no one on the pavement, no cameras pointing at his front door.

His eyes settled on his old, silver BMW. He had finally opted to service it rather than buy new. Treating himself would have swallowed the majority of his initial advance, but it wasn't the money; he felt naïve for ever thinking a new car might make a difference. It was nothing more than a carrot he had caught up with. He was beginning to understand: his recent pursuit of a second bestseller had been a poor substitute for his true, and impossible, wish in life, to return to the time of his first bestseller, when he hadn't made the mistakes which had cost him his family. For an already contented heart, success was the icing on the cake. For Tom Roker, it was the booby prize.

THIRTY-NINE

———◆———

Engine noise crackled electronically in Ash's right ear. The inter-com system was one-way, voice-activated by the examiner, but the 125cc motor humming between Ash's legs was somehow transmitting its revs in a harsh undulating whistle directly through his earpiece. The earpiece itself was uncomfortable and painful, Velcroed inside his helmet where no gap had been allowed for such a device. An antennae was attached to a Velcro pad on the front of his reflective yellow waistcoat. On the back was the cautionary note to other road-users: RIDER UNDER INSTRUCTION. The radio set was inside his leather jacket, a garment designed to fit snugly without the insertion of any such bulky item. The box dug annoyingly into his ribs. He felt claustrophobic, trussed up. Despite his thick gauntlets, after the hour's training his hands were practically numb with cold. The sun offered brightness but scant warmth. He shook in waves, more so when his speed picked up and the air blasted his body. Working the indicators was a feat in itself. Remembering to cancel them was a separate achievement.

However, five minutes off completion of his twenty-minute test, Ash believed he had not made a single mistake, certainly nothing to fail him. He had used his mirrors, performed the life-saver glance over his shoulder where appropriate, observed speed limits and traffic conditions, executed a perfect emergency stop and feet-up U-turn, noted the unmarked crossroads and responded accordingly, demonstrated a faultless hill start, positioned himself correctly in the road, leaving plenty of room between himself and the vehicle in front, especially when stationary, and shown proper conduct at a roundabout. Barring disasters, a full motorcycle licence was his, and so was a pat on the back from Nelson.

In the course of his training, Ash had discovered that Nelson's gripe about car drivers was well-founded. They didn't know enough because they weren't taught enough. Why was there no Compulsory Basic Training for them? Surrounded by metal, with a heater and a stereo, they felt invulnerable, so drove as though their car was indestructible and they were immortal. Since taking to two wheels, Ash had begun to notice perilous situations where he would previously have been blind to them, despite his police training. He now realised that a slow-speed bump for a car driver meant a little dent, but for a biker the result was never so predictable. Nudge a bike and the rider invariably came off. Then it all depended on what had hit you, how it had hit you, at what speed, how you landed, what you then collided with, and what collided with you. Car drivers had it easy, and that was completely the wrong way around.

'At the next set of lights I want you to make a left turn. Turn left at the next set of lights.'

The examiner's robotic voice crashed into his ear. Static interference made it difficult to decipher what he was being asked to do. The volume had to be set louder than ideal for the commands to be at all comprehensible. Anyone prone to panic might have decided they hadn't heard right and pulled over to await face-to-face instructions.

Ahead of him, the lights turned red. He checked his mirrors, slowed and changed down, indicating as he drew up to the stop line. Coming to a standstill, the worst of the chill disappeared. Fifteen feet behind, the examiner pulled up on his grey BMW.

Waiting for the lights, Ash mentally retraced his route: through the busy town, eyes peeled for dormant behaviour in both pedestrian and motorist, then into the quiet back streets, lined with nose to tail double-parked cars. Ash knew the dangers of those all two well, it was only a dead grandad who had saved him from learning too late.

They were in a warehouse district now and the roads were almost deserted but for the odd container lorry lumbering by. There was no challenge here. Effectively, the test was over; they were heading back to the Centre.

Ash breathed a sigh of relief, misting up his visor in the process. He opened it and the January air bit into his nose and cheeks.

The lights changed to green. Ash clunked down into first, gave a life-saver over his left shoulder, checking for cyclists in the gutter and turned. Tall warehouses either side cut the sunshine, and the temperature seemed to drop ten degrees in an instant.

'At the next lights I want you to keep straight ahead. Straight ahead at the next set of lights.'

Ash couldn't wait to get rid of his torturous earpiece and the noisy intrusions it allowed from the man trailing him.

The light was green as Ash passed through, and in his mirror he saw the examiner follow on. In the middle of the junction a flash of sunlight struck him, then the shadow persisted as more bland and grubby buildings loomed to flank him.

'At the next set of lights I want you to make a right turn. Turn right at the next lights.'

Ash checked behind, indicated, manoeuvred and positioned himself.

As he turned into another empty street, the traffic light changed to amber and he knew his examiner would be caught at the red.

'Pull over when it is convenient to do so, and wait for me,' came the instruction in his earpiece.

The street was bright, with the sun at his back. Ash motored along a hundred yards, then indicated and pulled into the kerb. He checked over his shoulder but the BMW was obscured by the corner of a building. He returned to the view in his mirror, eyeing the signal behind him to anticipate the arrival of his examiner from the adjoining street. But for the sound of his own engine, translated by the radio into a gentle whistling buzz, all was quiet.

A moment later, a sudden ear-splitting screech erupted in his helmet. He reacted as though he'd been stung. His head flew round and overbalanced him. The bike began to fall, but as the sound abruptly died, Ash stuck out a usefully long leg and propped it upright.

He swore and settled himself, and stared back over his shoulder. The lights on his street had changed to red, but the BMW did not appear. Ash's professional instincts took over, and he felt duty-bound to investigate. He couldn't be sure, but the screech had sounded human rather than electronic. At the same time, he didn't want to jeopardise his test result by abandoning his bike if nothing was wrong. After all, he had seen his examiner slow at the lights without mishap, so what *could* be wrong?

'Radio trouble,' came an emotionless voice.

Ash nodded to himself and realised how jumpy he was; all sorts of crazy thoughts had begun to infest his mind. He stared into his mirror and indicated, ready to rejoin the road. The lights behind were on green again. When they ascended to red, Ash started to rev, deafening himself with his own engine.

A few seconds passed and still no examiner. Ash glanced over his shoulder and saw a cloud of smoke drift idly into view from the side street. His brain had just popped a question mark when a voice answered him.

'Mechanical trouble. Following now. Continue when safe to do so.'

Radio trouble *and* bike trouble. Ash laughed at his hapless examiner. It really wasn't his day.

Ash moved off as he glimpsed in his mirror a motorbike easing into the junction.

Ahead of him, two hundred yards away, a juggernaut took a wide sweep into the street and came his way, picking up speed.

Tom had made a legitimate excuse and nodded off within a mile of leaving the house. Thankfully, neither Nelson nor Ash had made the journey to fetch him. The unmarked, dark blue Mondeo was being driven by a young detective constable. Tom had not listened to his name and had climbed straight into the back seat; he had not been chauffeur-driven since the days of *Hidden Blade*.

His dreams were deep and vivid, the natural spawn of exhausted sleep. And they were unfortunately all too believable:

He was in an unmarked, dark blue Mondeo, being driven up North by a young detective constable whose name escaped him because he hadn't bothered noting it in the first place. They had just joined a motorway, bizarrely deserted considering it was mid-day. After a mile they did happen across other vehicles – overturned, crushed, crashed, mangled, smoking, blazing. Bodies were hanging out of windows, slumped in seats, strewn over the carriageway, damaged and gory.

Beside each scene of carnage was a familiar calling card: a black circle of burnt rubber on the tarmac.

Ash had barely shifted into fourth when he received his next direction.

'Turn right, next right.'

It seemed very hurried, but perhaps his examiner wanted to see how he reacted under pressure.

Ash stayed calm. He couldn't turn yet because the juggernaut was coming, but he perfectly executed the first part of the procedure. He checked his mirrors, gave a lifesaver, signalled, manoeuvred, and drew up opposite a narrow alley, leading all the way back to the main road from which they had first turned. Positioned just left of the centre line, he waited for the juggernaut to pass.

'Excellent,' came the verdict, and Ash smiled.

The juggernaut thundered relentlessly towards him. Ash could see the driver with a CB mike to his mouth, and he wondered vaguely if the reception could be all that clear with these high buildings.

A sudden query focused his mind. Until now, the examiner had not made any comment on his progress. They weren't meant to. Not until the end. So why—?

An irrational fear seized his heart. He checked over his right shoulder, but the BMW was nowhere.

Fast enough to cause a crick, he swivelled his head round to the left.

Parallel to him was another stationary motorbike, and it was not a BMW.

Time moved very slowly from that point on. Ash knew very well who was staring back at him through that impenetrable black visor. He knew the rider was sitting astride a Kawasaki ZZ-R1100 Turbo. He would have known that whether or not Nelson had furnished the whole team with identifying photographs from the listings of *What Bike?* magazine.

And, more than anything, he knew his time, however slowly it was presently passing, was up.

Milton booted the petrol tank of the blue Honda CG125, and Ash toppled with his bike.

On this occasion, his dead grandad was tragically conspicuous by his absence.

The juggernaut took man and machine before they hit the ground.

Ash did not feel anything, see anything, hear anything. A magical and merciful blankness was elapsing as he peeled out of the mould he had put into the lorry's radiator grille, but the velocity of the impact kept him splatted in place until the driver stamped on the brakes, causing the inoffensive little Honda to disappear beneath the bumper to be crunched under one, three, five, seven, nine huge rolling tyres. But Ash did not know this. Nor did he register his own dark journey under the lorry and beneath the wheels. And when he emerged, flopping, tumbling and cartwheeling from the rear, he still knew nothing about it. Even when he came to a halt, and the lorry screeched and skidded to a standstill just ahead of him, and a sliver of conscious awareness returned, it still wasn't happening to him. Because the Adam Ash he had known all his life had arms and legs, and a head that felt quite different in shape to the one he had now.

The lorry's brakes wheezed and sighed.

There was no pain. Staring out of a helmet that felt merged with his own skull, his eyes gazed up at a set of traffic lights, just turning to red. He was back at the junction. The examiner and his BMW were sprawled on the road, both defunct. He guessed he wasn't lying too far away from the black donut Milton had scorched on the tarmac; he knew what the smoke meant now. But he couldn't see it. The ground lost focus a few inches from his face. He supposed he might see it if he stood up, but no part of him responded, and he imagined there wasn't an awful lot left of him which *could* respond. And now all three lights of the traffic signal had turned shimmering red. And the buildings. And the sky. Why him? This wasn't in the novel. He heard a door slam, but the lorry driver did not appear in the fixed and bloody window which passed for his vision. Too scared, too revolted. Probably running off frantically down the road. Ash couldn't blame him. A smaller window now. Losing clarity. Still no pain. But sad now. Cold and dark. Lorry blocking the sun.

Then light again, wondrously bright, warm and supremely happy. Hello, grandad.

Time . . .

FORTY

The police headquarters was located in a market town on the edge of the hills, twenty miles south of Manchester. The town had recently been by-passed, but years of heavy traffic through its centre had already taken its toll: surfaces were caked in grime, most noticeably the original sandstone edifices which were now a less than glorious mottled fume-brown.

More damaging to its character had been the effect of late-twentieth-century consumerism. A historical town with a proud heritage, it had suffered the usual array of modern architectural insults. Beneath the grand upper storeys of the old structures, the sorry tale of the plate-glass window had snuck in. Ground floors had been gutted to accommodate another branch, outlet or franchise. There was an 'Arcade', but it was nothing more than a spruced-up shopping precinct; a wannabe mall.

Things clashed. Each decade of architects apparently paid no attention to what had gone before, nor did they realise the irony of their contempt for those previous styles – in another ten years, the same derision would be visited upon their own designs. They were simply creating the perceived monstrosities of tomorrow.

Thus the pretensions of new red brick sat alongside no-nonsense ancient brownstone blocks, among white-washed walls, next to black-timbered exteriors, beside vomit-inducing paint schemes over pebble-dashed façades, interspersed with the odd bland expanse of steel and glass, so futuristic, yet somehow more out of date than the market cross in the mercifully preserved town square. There were pavements of grey, and pedestrian walkways of trendy multi-coloured brick parquet. Of the two, the pavements were undeniably more dull, but at least they didn't show up a thousand blobs of discarded chewing gum. And, in the streets, where there were still cobblestones, they had been left not for posterity but for their traffic-calming effects. It seemed unless the past could serve the future, it was tarmacked over. The whole place was an insensitive melding of times, textures and chromatic incompetence.

But Tom guessed there were worse places to live, like within the perimeter walls of Her Majesty's Prison at Strangeways.

It was four p.m. when they finally reached headquarters. The light was fading fast. The stars had already claimed their place in the heavens, as though hurrying the day from the sky.

Tom yawned as he climbed from the back of the Mondeo, and the chilly influx made him cough. Two hundred miles north and the air was distinctly cooler. The engine ticked and pinked. He looked around. Frost was beginning to glisten on the car roofs, most of which bore large black numbers. It was an Official Vehicles Only car park. He didn't like being in the midst of all this law enforcement symbolism. POLICE emblazoned everywhere; blue lights; fluorescent orange stripes; constabulary crests. And he was being brought in the rear entrance, like a common criminal. Paranoia suggested Nelson had made the order to freak him out, but he tried to be rational; the Mondeo was an official vehicle and it probably belonged there.

As the nameless DC got out and locked up, Tom thought it odd that there was no activity, no comings and goings, as he imagined there should be at a large police station.

'This way, Mr Roker,' called the DC, heading towards some steps leading up to a steel grille door.

Tom followed, clutching his bulging holdall, filled with enough clothes to last a week. He assumed Nelson had a gruelling few days in store for him, and if Nelson had cause to delay him any longer than that, it would most likely mean an outfit was to be provided for him. Something plain, in blue, with a number over the shirt pocket.

The DC input a code, opened the security grille and the inside door, and ushered Tom down a short corridor.

Inside the building, the eerie quiet persisted. Strip lighting bounced off pale green walls. The place felt like an institution, but more sanatorium than police station. This sense was enhanced as Tom entered the suspect reception area, because now he *could* make out a sound. Someone was moaning, sobbing. The desk was deserted. The DC turned to him and offered a puzzled expression,

220

then pushed a couple of doors and frowned when he found no one in the rooms.

'Wait a minute,' he said, and scuttled off through swing doors into another corridor to disappear round a corner.

Tom stood alone. The sobbing unnerved him. Nearly everything did lately. He moved gingerly towards a set of steps descending into the basement. Peering down, he could see dark green cell doors with small blackboards beside them. He held his breath and listened. Whoever was in distress, it wasn't a prisoner. Downstairs was perfectly hushed.

He dropped his bag and pulled a packet of cigarettes from his coat pocket. He found his disposable and lit up as he stared at a No Smoking sign on the wall.

The DC returned. With him was the uniformed desk sergeant who resumed his position, then averted his eyes when Tom looked at him. As for the DC, he had gone off with a confused expression and come back grey and gutted. His struggle to keep back the tears was plain.

Tom sensed tragedy in the air. He had sensed it the moment he walked in.

In a faraway voice, the DC said, 'Take a seat, Mr Roker, DCI Nelson will see you shortly.' He didn't mention Tom's infringement of the No Smoking policy. Tom sat down. For some seconds the DC stood in his own personal fog, unsure of his next move, before walking one way a couple of paces, checking himself, and going off in another direction with equally uncertain steps.

Five minutes passed. The desk sergeant finally met his eyes. Tom was chain-smoking now.

The officer nodded towards the cigarette in Tom's mouth. 'Got one spare?' he asked.

Tom smiled politely and went over and proffered his pack.

'Ta.'

Tom gave him a light and sat down again. 'What's going on?' he enquired.

The sergeant inhaled the biggest lungful of nicotine. He exhaled on a sigh. 'One of our lads. He was murdered earlier today.'

'God, I'm sorry.'

'You're Tom Roker,' the sergeant suddenly accused.

Tom nodded slowly.

221

'Then you're going to hear all about it.'

Tom leaned back and put a hand to his face, hiding. The sergeant screeched his chair backwards, making Tom jump, then stood up and went downstairs supposedly to check on the prisoners. But Tom got the impression he simply didn't want to share the same space any longer.

Tom wasn't the Brain of Britain, and he didn't need to be to know the identity of the cop-killer. The impulse to clear off before Nelson arrived was as pointless as it was intense. So he sat and waited and tried to figure out why the plot of *Man on a Murder Cycle* had today been abandoned.

Eventually, the fat man burst through the swing doors and glowered at him. The pain in his eyes was white hot. The whites of his eyes were red with sorrow. 'Come,' was all he said.

Tom collected his bag and followed, trailing him down one corridor and then another. Through open doors, he saw police officers gathered in huddles, silent, occasionally sobbing, with blank, downcast faces.

He had never felt more of an outsider in his entire life. He felt like a man in a clown suit at a stranger's funeral.

Nelson stopped at a closed door and pushed it wide. He pointed. 'In.'

Tom obeyed.

Nelson slammed the door behind him. 'Tom Roker, meet Angie Kellett.'

Those few seconds lasted for ever. These two people could send him to jail. Ruin his career. End his life.

Tom gawped in shock at the blonde woman seated at the table, the woman who had saved his neck outside the Manchester bookshop. The odds on that coincidence were astronomical. Even Nelson would have bowed to the Fates if he'd known. But then, perhaps he did know.

Strangely, Angie Kellett registered minimal surprise, and certainly no neon sign that flashed up their previous acquaintance.

Nelson, the sod, standing behind, left a long pause. Tom pictured him with an evil grin on his face, anticipating a flood of incriminating facts from one or both parties.

'Well?' Nelson whispered hopefully in Tom's ear.

But Tom was not giving way that easily. If Angie Kellett had

222

said anything already, he would have been cuffed by the DC at his own front door.

'Well?' Nelson said again, his tone edged now with impatience.

I'll take the Fifth Amendment, Tom thought.

'Well what?' Angie Kellett asked.

Tom could not believe his ears. Or his luck.

'Sit!' Nelson barked at Tom.

Tom sat opposite Angie. The grey walls were bare. In the corner was a television and a video.

'Mister Roker?' Nelson growled.

The Fifth.

'Miss Kellett?'

'What?'

Nelson leaned down to her. 'You two know each other, don't you?'

'No.'

Tom could have kissed her. For some reason he couldn't possibly comprehend, she was lying. That she was protecting him in the process was nothing more than a happy bonus, but it didn't matter. She was saving him for the second time. Unhelpfully, he couldn't help but wonder what knickers she was wearing, whether he had fingered that particular pair, or whether his little root through her drawers had been detected and she had discarded the lot and bought fresh.

'Mr Roker?' Nelson pressed, swinging his face towards Tom.

I think I'm going to plead the Fifth, thanks anyway.

Fuming, Nelson started shouting. 'I don't believe you! Either of you! Something's going on! You two know each other! You're connected!' He glared back at Angie. 'And you, *missy*, you say you don't know the face on the tape? Bullshit. It's right there.' He forked two fingers an inch away from her eyes. 'Oh, you fucking know him all right. And you say you don't know our big-shot novelist here? Bullshit again.' In his impotence, Nelson appeared to suffer a momentary brainstorm before he grabbed Tom's holdall and lifted it onto the table.

'Oi!' Tom protested.

Nelson unzipped the bag and yanked it apart.

'Oi!'

With a pair of Tom's boxers in his hand, Nelson said, 'Roker . . . fucking shut up.'

'What are you looking for?'

'Anything,' Nelson answered honestly, and began pulling more clothes out, throwing them on the floor. He emptied Tom's sponge bag onto the table and sifted through the contents, grunting when he found nothing of interest.

From the bottom of the bag, he brought out Tom's copy of *Man on a Murder Cycle*. He fanned through the pages. Tom noticed the blanks flick by, but Nelson showed no sign of confusion. He then held the book by its covers with the pages hanging down, and shook it to see what might drop out. When nothing did, he discarded it and delved inside the bag again. This time he brought out three A4 writing pads and a bulky manuscript folder. He slapped them on the table.

'What's this?' he said, tapping the folder meaningfully.

'New novel.'

Nelson opened it. He silently read the dedication to Tom's wife and daughter. Although there was no title page, he only had to read the first couple of lines of the first chapter to get the gist.

'I don't believe it. A bloody sequel.'

'I'd finished it before all this started,' Tom assured him.

'And what d'you plan to do with it?'

'Nothing.'

'So why are carrying it around with you?'

'Uh . . .' Tom felt a blush of embarrassment. 'Writer's paranoia.'

Nelson came around the table and towered above him. 'Explain.'

'Well, I've got a copy at home and one here. So if the house burns down I've got this one safe, and if I lose my bag I've got the one back home.'

Pointedly, Angie said, 'But why do you care, if you're not going to publish?'

Tom squirmed. 'Well . . . I might publish, providing DCI Nelson here can catch the biker.'

Nelson reacted with a crazy expression. 'Then for fuck's sake, *help me*!'

Tom could only shrug, which made Nelson yell something livid and incomprehensible at the ceiling.

Angie rose to her feet. Tom pored over the curves of her arse, and the denim which hugged and delved between her legs at her crotch, and the swell of her breasts beneath her cream polo neck.

224

He tore his eyes away. It was mad. In his imagination, Angie Kellett had become a fantasy figure, a virtual goddess of feminine sexuality, symbolised by a simple black dress on a wardrobe door and literally a handful of assorted underwear. He hated feeling this way. He had never been fixated on any woman before this, not even his wife. But he supposed it was all symptomatic of his moral descent; yet more ugliness rising to the surface.

'And where d'you think *you're* going, missy?' said Nelson.

Serenely, she told him, 'I'm sorry about Ash, I really am. I liked him. He had a heart, unlike some. But nothing I can tell you is going to help your inquiries. You can't begin to conceive of what it is you're actually up against.'

'Try me.'

'Ash?' Tom muttered to himself, then asked out loud: 'DS Ash was killed by the biker?'

Nelson turned on him. 'Oh, bravo, fuckwit.'

Tom was stumped; why had Ash become a victim?

Angie removed her ski jacket from the back of the chair. 'I'm going home.'

Nelson retreated to block her exit. There was an uneasy impasse, two wills battling it out, but Nelson's move had been born of sheer desperation, and he stepped aside very quickly.

'Thank you,' Angie said flatly, donning her jacket in a leisurely fashion which only accentuated Nelson's mood. Tom suspected it was her ruse to leave Nelson in the foulest temper, so that he would bear the brunt of it.

When she had gone, Nelson gently closed the door. He picked up a remote control off the TV, zapped the screen into life and set the video to play. 'Watch,' he ordered.

Tom shifted his chair and concentrated. For twenty seconds he saw four different views of the interior of a bank, filmed by security cameras. Customers came and went. There was a queue for the counter. An old woman shuffled out at a snail's pace. As the sequence continued, a young lad with his baseball cap on back to front joined the queue. Coming round to the door camera again, a ghastly apparition in black leather was standing beneath it, grinning into the lens. The face was indistinct, but the skin looked sort of creased. His black hair was extremely short, except for a long white mane from his widow's peak over the top of his head, in the style of a skunk. Three seconds later, the view changed, giving an elevated side view of the biker, who appeared to be oddly well endowed in the chest department. The view flicked round the bank and returned a fraction before the biker turned away to join the queue behind the youth.

Nelson froze the image. 'Want to see the rest?'

'Not really.'

So Nelson let it off pause and Tom was forced to see the rest.

After the first grenade had exploded, Nelson stopped the video and darkened the TV.

'Thanks,' Tom said. 'When's it in the shops?'

Nelson laughed but didn't sound the slightest bit amused. He took a brown foolscap envelope from on top of the video and emptied a photograph onto the table in front of Tom. It was a grainy enlargement of the biker's grinning face.

'Who is he?' Nelson wanted to know.

Tom spun the picture so it was upright. The eyes were close together, large and dark under a heavy brow. There were no discernible eyebrows. Close up, the creases in the biker's skin were actually jagged, healed scars. He looked like Frankenstein's first botch-job.

'Pretty,' Tom remarked, juddering involuntarily.

It was one facetious comment too many.

Nelson grabbed him by the throat and hoisted him against the wall so only the very tips of his shoes were touching the floor. 'You're going to tell me what you know, you shite-arse!'

Tom could hardly breathe, let alone talk.

'You're protecting that cocksucker, but no more! You're going to give him to me!'

'I don't kn—' Tom managed, before Nelson slammed his head against the wall.

'I swear to God, Roker, if you don't start talking, I'm going to take you down those cells and you're going to have an unfortunate fucking accident. Understand? You're going to be leaving in the morning in a fucking *bodybag*!'

But Tom refused to cooperate, keeping his lips tightly sealed, because the eternal blackness Nelson was threatening still sounded better than the life-long mental blackness a confession of his crimes would bring. Writing was crap, but, considering the alternatives, he had to remind himself that at least it was something. It was better than prison, better than stewing in his own guilt and regret, counting the days away, and crying the nights. Nothing could be worse than that. Not even the whizzing of a zipper from toe to head.

Nelson threw him across the room in frustration. *'Cunt!'*

Tom crashed into a black plastic chair, tangling in it and overturning it. He landed with his full weight on his hip, and cracked the side of his head on the skirting. Silvery shards of light exploded behind his closed eyelids and his brain went fuzzy, but he remained conscious, and so able to worry what else Nelson had in store for him.

But the rage in Nelson's face visibly subsided. His shoulders sagged, then he trudged over to a chair and wilted into it. 'I lost a valued colleague today. A fine detective. A friend.'

Tom doubted the truth of Nelson's third claim, but kept it to himself. He merely crawled into a corner and sat there, rubbing his bumped head. 'Detective Chief Inspector Nelson, I don't kn—'

'Piss off, Roker. Just piss off back to The Smoke.'

Tom clambered to his feet, collected his belongings together and stuffed them into his holdall. 'I won't be making any complaints,' he said benevolently.

'Big of you.'

'I understand your grief.'

Nelson shot him a glare of barely contained fury. He let it go and shook his head.

'How can I get home?' Tom asked, thinking of the DC with the car keys.

Nelson stood up and came over to deliver his response nose-to-nose, snarling as he spoke. 'Call your pal. Go pillion. And I hope you fucking freeze to death.'

FORTY-ONE

———◆———

Tom plodded down the front steps and halted on the pavement. A lonely man in a strange town on an icy cold night, he felt like blubbing. He regretted that he hadn't physically retaliated against Nelson. Not to hurt him, just to provoke the fatal 'accident' the fat man had promised.

He was so tired. He didn't want the life he had struggled to attain, nor the spoils he had stolen, cheated, lied and killed for. Perhaps if his plan had run smoothly, perhaps if he still had someone special to share it with, perhaps if the view from his bedroom window had been different – perhaps golden sands, blue skies and turquoise ocean – perhaps if he could get sex from someone who at least didn't hate him, perhaps, then, he would not have felt so desperate. Perhaps. But 'perhaps' was just another word for 'if', and every wrecked dream since the dawn of time had been foundered on 'if'.

Without checking the road, he wandered across and into the public car park opposite. He found a quiet spot against the rear of a shop and squeezed between two industrial steel garbage drums. He was not unaware that dogs did the same, retreating to lick their wounds. Hidden away, he dropped his holdall and sat on it; death was okay, piles he could do without.

Cars were leaving from their slots, emptying out as the working day ticked down. Someone hurried by but didn't glance into the shadows. After a while, Tom had to clamp his teeth to keep them from chattering, and only with difficulty did he manage to light a cigarette, the one comfort left to him. Then the rhythm of a train clattered telegraphically into the clear sky, and Tom was able to locate the railway station as the train slowed, squealing through the points.

It made him think: he could be home in under three hours.

But home to what? To whom? Home to a space aching with memories, alive only with the ghosts of a family fled from him. Better he sat where he was, where nothing had any right to mean anything, until Jack Frost coated his skin and finally touched his heart to stop it.

Tom clapped his hands, stamped his feet, stood up and wimped out. Freezing to death had one major drawback: you got bloody cold in the process.

He chucked his smoke, picked up his bag and set off briskly towards the railway station. Pubs along the way attracted him with their warmth and light, not to mention their stock-in-trade, his only route to forgetting, but he kept on walking. What excuse for a life he had was down in London.

Besides, this was Skunk Territory. The scarred biker with the weird hair-do had claimed this area as his personal killing ground, and after the unforeseen demise of Detective Sergeant Ash, it seemed anyone was fair game.

Tom still could not understand it. This most recent murder was pure improvisation. He knew nothing of the details, but after the traffic cop in the Jaguar, no more policemen had been scripted to die in *Man on a Murder Cycle*.

'Did you break into my house?'

Tom turned sharply to the road, his thoughts an instant jumble, his heart working like a jack-hammer. Angie Kellett was kerb-crawling with the passenger window of her Mini wound down, and with her body leaned across to the opening.

'No,' he said, before walking straight into a lamppost. He reeled on the spot and collapsed on his haunches, supporting himself with one hand on the icy pavement.

'Did you?'

'*Yes!*' he answered testily, shocking himself by his admission. He straightened up and checked around for witnesses but there was no one near enough to have heard. Angie stopped the engine, and in the same second that Tom opted to deny his own words, he realised how good it was to tell the truth for once. Colliding with the lamppost had nothing to do with it; his senses were intact. He would have told her anyway. Being honest had allowed him to feel partially human again, fractionally decent.

He squatted down by the Mini. 'But I didn't kill that man. It was an accident. I'm not like that. I'm not violent.'

Angie straightened up in her seat and looked ahead. 'Well, I'm sure his widow will be very relieved to know it was a non-violent decapitation.' She faced him and smiled facetiously, then turned to the front again.

Cars were passing in the build-up to rush-hour. Tom watched several go by before looking in at her, something he could only do when she wasn't looking back at him.

He said, 'So what are you going to do? Tell Nelson?'

She huffed. 'No, and you know it, or I'd have said something earlier.'

Another brief illusion shattered. She was right: he had only confessed because he believed there would be no consequences. Which meant there was no improvement in his lack of nobility. It had been a selfish act, done to ease a burdened mind. He was offloading his guilt, sharing a commodity no one wanted. How very decent of him. Here – anyone for a piece of Tom Roker's suffering?

'So what, then?' he asked.

'Get in.'

'What?'

'Get in the car.'

'Why?'

'Because I'm probably the only person on this earth who can help you.'

Tom gave a disbelieving smile. 'You want to help me?'

'New concept in human thinking, eh? Don't worry, I have ulterior motives.' She started the engine. 'You recognise that concept, don't you?'

Sadly, Tom did. He opened the car door and climbed in with his holdall on his lap. 'Where are we going?' he said, his eyes flicking uncontrollably to her thighs.

'The place where all your troubles began,' she replied, and slipped the Mini into the traffic.

Five minutes passed, but not a single word between them. A Mini was the worst car to be confined in when much of the limited space was taken up by the hulking forms of Guilt, Awkwardness and Lust. Tom felt as though he were holding his breath. He wanted to gush his life story. If she knew the whole miserable tale she might view his misdeeds less harshly.

230

Eventually, he had to release. 'I know there's no excuse—'

'No, so don't make any,' she said, then switched the heater on. The vent began to rattle crisply, and Tom imagined a couple of autumn leaves were trapped inside.

Ten minutes later, they were snaking through the dark countryside. Tom watched the skeletal trees etched black against the night blue. They were complex, frightening patterns, stark and spiky; Nature in limbo, stripped of its soft edges.

Seemingly unbidden, Tom pictured The Skunk. 'Who is he?' he asked.

'Someone very angry at the world,' Angie answered immediately, as though, these days, she thought of no one else.

'Do you know him?'

'In a way.'

'What way?'

She turned off the annoying heater. 'I'm not the one who should be answering questions.'

'Well, you won't let me tell *you* anything.'

'When I want answers I'll ask for them. In the meantime, I don't want your weedy excuses.'

That made two women in his life with the upper hand.

'Just one question,' Tom tried. He waited a few seconds but her silence allowed him to continue. 'How did you know I was the one who broke in?'

'Why do you think Ash was killed?'

'Oh, I see, I've had my one question, have I?'

'No, I'm answering your question by asking one: why do you think Ash was killed?'

Tom needed to devote very little brain-time to that puzzle. He had no idea. 'No idea,' he said.

She kept her counsel, and Tom realised it was his job to figure it out.

Another winding mile passed before he received the revelation. 'Shit.' He looked at her. 'Are you saying Ash had proof it was me?'

She didn't lower herself to meet his eyes. 'Why? Did you leave any behind?'

'Uuh . . . mmm. Fingerprints.'

'I know. He was about to check them for a match.'

'How? He doesn't have my prints on file.'

231

'I gave him the novel you gave me in Manchester.'

'He was *about* to check for a match. You mean he didn't?'

'He never made it in to work.' She glanced sideways. 'Aren't you lucky?'

Tom didn't think so.

Streetlamps welcomed them into the village. In silence, they drove through the narrow streets with their twee, Christmas card shop fronts.

Tom was frowning. He felt there was something mentally just out of his reach. 'Hold on . . . you're saying . . . what? Ash was killed because he was about to prove my guilt?'

She nodded, and Tom understood it was well within his reach, he just didn't want to grasp it.

'You're saying the biker killed Ash to . . . what, to *protect* me?'

'Why else?'

Tom burst out laughing. 'The fellah wants to murder me, not marry me.'

'How d'you know?'

'Besides, how the hell could he have known what you and Ash were up to?'

'You're right,' Angie said carefully. 'Of course he couldn't.'

They headed out of the village and drove up a lane which Tom recognised. Seconds later, they arrived at the cottage and Angie bumped the Mini onto the sparkling grass verge, then cut the engine.

'How did he die?' Tom said quietly.

'Oh, now you ask. He went under a lorry.'

Her stare forced Tom to leave the car. When she got out herself, he followed her up the path and into the cottage, then dumbly up the stairs like some lodger at a B & B.

Angie pointed to her brother's broken door. 'You can sleep in there.'

Tom didn't move. 'I'll sleep on your settee.'

'You'll sleep in here,' she said, pushing the damaged door open and hitting the light switch.

'I'll sleep downstairs,' Tom said, retreating to the top of the stairs.

'You're in here.'

Tom started down the stairs and shouted up to her. 'I'll go home then.'

She raised her voice, but without anger or panic, just so he could hear what she had to tell him. 'That's not an option. It's either this room or a cell in town.'

Tom stopped in his tracks. 'All right,' he surrendered, but it had been a close contest, Andrew Kellett's bedroom only marginally winning in the Least Awful stakes. He turned and ascended.

'Yeah, that reminds me,' he said as he reached the landing, 'why *didn't* you drop me in it back at the station? What am I doing here?'

Angie smiled knowingly. 'At the moment, that's not important. All you need to know is that you really shouldn't refuse my hospitality.'

Tom walked sulkily past her and entered the second most detestable box in the world.

'Make yourself comfortable,' she said in a contrary voice. 'Have a bath if you want. Relax. My home is your home. Again.'

'What makes you think I won't kill you during the night?' Tom asked, trying to sound menacing.

She smiled condescendingly. 'If you killed me, you'd be hunted down inside an hour.'

'Oh, yeah?' Tom taunted. 'Nelson's useless.'

She left an expansive pause as her smile faded. 'I wasn't meaning the police.'

Life was strange. Once, he had broken the law to get inside the cottage, and now he was threatened with the law if he walked out. Tom took it as a punishment that he was being barred from the settee. Of course, for anyone else, a bed would have been a luxury.

Before he took his coat off, he unhooked the framed snapshot from above the desk. He studied the happy faces: Andrew Kellett's, the woman's, the little girl's. He hadn't known the story last summer. He could have ventured a guess, but he hadn't. His dip into Andrew Kellett's life had been highly selective. Even the original dedication in the 'Untitled' manuscript had sparked little thought for the author's true circumstances. Tom could remember it exactly: *For my darling wife and gorgeous girl, Nina and Sally. With all my love. I miss you so much.* Divorce had seemed improbable given the wording, but Tom had burnt the page before any other scenario could suggest itself. He had believed it was irrelevant to his own existence.

Now his education had begun, and the word for today was *repercussions*.

He had invaded another life. Briefly in and out. But, however short-lived, invasions were never benign. They disrupted, set shock waves in motion, and Tom was currently being swamped by one.

In the palm of his hand, three joyful faces grinned at him.

He pulled out the top drawer, apologised, and respectfully lay the picture glass down, then pushed it into the darkness.

Eight months after the event, Tom finally felt able to hazard a guess: Andrew Kellett had followed his wife and daughter to the grave. They were all dead. The dedication said so, every devil-may-care word in the actual novel said so, and Angie Kellett had said as much over the phone on that fateful evening. If Tom was honest with himself, deep down, he had known all along. He had simply chosen to turn his gaze to his own future rather than to the likely truth of Kellett's past. It had been easier on his conscience.

Now, though, if he didn't face up to it himself, there was someone downstairs who could make him. Angie Kellett had the power to seize him by the scruff of the neck and rub his nose in the shitty evidence.

He picked up his holdall and hefted it onto the bed. He unzipped. He wasn't going to unpack – he might be there a year and never presume that much – he just wriggled a hand between his clothes until he touched the cold surface of *Man on a Murder Cycle*, and felt the cardboard folder containing the manuscript of the sequel.

Total paranoia.

But it was the pads of A4 which completely revealed his state of mind. He pulled them out and stared at them. A total of four hundred and fifty pages, simultaneously virgin and pregnant, loaded with potential, for they signified that Tom was catering for all contingencies. In his heart, he wasn't certain how selfless he could be. He had told Carol that the sequel should be destroyed if the biker was still around come time for its publication, but that was before the biker had made this morning's telephone call, threatening Tom's life should a sequel not appear. For all his good intentions, Tom was not keen on martyring himself for a bunch of strangers. At present he maintained a safe gap. There was half the first novel and the entire sequel between him and a predictably sticky comeuppance. But should that margin be drastically diminished, he had the means to re-expand it; he could put pen to paper and create a Miltonian Trilogy.

Downstairs, the television was on. It had a ring of sanity, an ordinary, everyday sound, and Tom was drawn to it. He slung his coat on top of his bag and switched the light off. Passing Angie's room he had to make a conscious effort not to peek inside.

Quarter way down the stairs, he stopped. On the wall was another shot of Andrew Kellett, this time on his motorbike outside the cottage. It was under the protection of a glass clip-frame, but it was already damaged, defaced by white marks where the photographic film had been scratched off.

Tom sat down. Between ceiling and stairs, through the banister posts, he could see Angie curled up on the settee, watching telly, unaware of his scrutiny. He felt like a small child fresh from a nightmare, reluctant to disturb his parents' quiet time, but wishing one of them would turn and notice him there, cowering in the shadows, afraid and alone and in need of a hug.

Fat chance. There was no reason for Angie Kellett to feel the slightest spark of sympathy for his sad plight. She most likely had nightmares of her own, with Tom Roker the resident bogey-man, removing heads and breaking down doors to defile her home.

Tom was on his own. He had made his bed, and now he had to lie in Andrew Kellett's.

Shame overwhelmed him. To witness the cottage being lived in, the precious home of another human being – he was thoroughly ashamed of himself. Criminal was not the word for his actions last summer; it could never do justice to his present emotion. A court and its damning verdict was a slap on the wrist compared to the judgment he thought he deserved.

He had broken more than a door, more than a law.

Thou shalt not steal.

He had broken the Commandment. And, for that, he was more than criminal, reckless or misguided, he was wicked, heinous and evil.

With not a recognisable ounce of religion in his whole body his entire life, Tom Roker was making up for lost time and crucifying himself for his sins. He had an uneasy inkling that he might be losing his mind. And Angie Kellett wasn't helping, with the ulterior motives she professed to have regarding his stay at the cottage. Christ, maybe *she* was planning to kill *him* during the night. He hadn't thought of that. Bloody hell.

He stood up and descended the rest of the way. Angie looked at him as he hovered in the hall.

'If you're hungry, help yourself,' she said indifferently.

'I'm not,' he lied.

'Come in.'

Tom moved sheepishly into the room and stood awkwardly beside an armchair.

'Sit down,' she said frigidly.

He mumbled, 'Thanks,' but declined the armchair, which was next to the telly and therefore pretty much opposite her. Instead, he circled behind the settee to a wooden chair backed up to a glass-fronted display cabinet. He parked his rear on the very edge of the seat pad. Her coolness made him physically react with a shiver.

'I can put the heat up,' she said with apparent psychic talent, having not turned round to see him.

'That's kind, but I'm fine,' he said.

She looked over the back of the settee at him. 'I like the heat, but it costs. I don't mind, though, just for a while.'

'No, really, thank you.'

'Suit yourself.' She returned her attention to the TV.

Tom found her bland way of speaking disheartened him. Of course, he couldn't have expected any warmth from her, but at least she could have despised him. He wondered if she had managed to rationalise her feelings because she knew that hatred would only supersede her ulterior motives. What was the saying? Keep your friends close, and your enemies closer still? If she hated him, wouldn't she have found it impossible to keep him close? Sharing her space with someone she couldn't stand the sight of? Then again, perhaps he was so pathetic he didn't warrant the strength of emotion needed to hate him.

Immediately, tension started to ache in his back, but he didn't try to relax his posture.

'D'you watch this?' she asked, not bothering to address him directly.

'Sometimes.'

Tom dutifully concentrated on the screen, on a video recording of *The X-Files*, but his thoughts were crashing around in his head like hyperactive brats.

Fox Mulder was ranting about some unearthly force which was

236

rampaging through a local town, showing a lethal dislike of its inhabitants. Dana Scully appeared typically unimpressed by his theories.

'What do you think about the stories?' Angie wanted to know.

'Good.'

She inclined her head some way round, but not enough to meet his eyes, just to bring him into her peripheral vision. 'I mean, do you believe in that sort of thing?'

Tom found it difficult to engage in this meaningless small-talk, but he guessed weightier conversation would be steamrollering his way in due course. 'I suppose I've got an open mind,' he said.

'That's useful.' She swivelled further and gave him a twisted smile, straight to his face. 'Because the truth *is* out there.'

Fifteen minutes passed. *The X-Files* finished and Angie stopped the tape. As usual, Mulder and Scully had both seen enough to fry their brains, and, as usual, there was not a jot of evidence to support it. Next week, as usual, Mulder would bounce back into action, oblivious to the past hundred episodes in which he had failed to prove a single thing, and Scully would be the same doubting Thomas, despite having witnessed a thousand modern-day miracles during their implausibly eventful partnership.

'Miss Kellett,' Tom said softly, not really wanting to be heard.

There was a beat before she said, 'Call me Angie. I feel we know each other. Don't you?'

'Yes,' Tom replied feebly.

'Well?'

Tom didn't like talking to the back of her head – he needed to assess her facial nuances when she spoke, in case they contradicted her words – but locking eyes with her made him too acutely aware of the arsehole he had been.

Angie decided for him. 'Come round here,' she said and lowered the volume on the TV.

Grudgingly, Tom swapped his uncomfortable wooden seat for a plush armchair. He settled back into it as far as he could go, hoping the cushions might envelop him, and crossed his legs.

'What are you doing here?' she asked rhetorically, pre-empting him.

'Uh . . . yes.' He was talking to the carpet. 'Sorry. I know I don't deserve any answers, but . . .' He shrugged helplessly. 'Whatever you think of me, I do want to make amends.'

'But not by going to prison.'

'Not if I can avoid it,' Tom said, trying a laugh for size, and discovering it was a terrible fit. He coughed. 'But if I don't know why I'm here . . .' he shrugged again '. . . how *can* I help?'

Angie switched the TV set off, unfortunately for Tom, who had been grateful for the way it blunted the edge between them. The silence which leapt up in its place made Tom's muscles tense like stone.

'I've been threatened,' Angie announced. 'I don't know who the biker is, but I know he wants to hurt me.'

'How?'

'A telephone call.'

Tom looked askance, but decided it wasn't his job to appear sceptical of her.

'Why d'you look like that?' she asked.

'Well . . .' He recrossed his legs, wondering whether to tell her what he knew.

'Go on,' she said.

And Tom realised he was actually bursting to tell her. 'He called me, too. That's why I don't understand him threatening you.'

'Perhaps he thinks I'm in on it. You know, stealing the novel.'

Perplexed, Tom said, 'But why would you be? And who would be annoyed if you were?'

'Andrew knew some flaky characters. He was into drugs for a while with some bike gang. I reckon he must have shown the novel to one of them who's now doing the big revenge bit.'

That answered one query for Tom: how the biker had known about the baseball cap in the bank scene. Tom found himself leaning further forward in his chair. 'But why would he think you're involved?'

'Well, if I wanted to sell a novel by an unknown author, I'd have trouble. But if I gave it to an established writer to publish as his own work . . .'

Tom nodded but maintained his puzzled look. 'Okay, but you're Andrew's sister. You have every right to want to see his work in print.'

'Yeah, but with Andrew's name on it.'

'Oh . . . I get it. I've broken some sort of bizarre code of morality these bikers have.'

238

'That's all I can think.'

'God, talk about double standards.'

'No,' Angie said, 'I wouldn't if I were you.'

Tom hung his head for a moment. 'But his threatening you still doesn't make much sense considering what he said to me only this morning.'

'Which was?'

'That he'd kill me, but only if I failed to write a sequel.'

Angie's face lit up with comprehension and relief. 'Ah, well that's what he must have meant. He probably wanted me to tell you to keep on writing. But that's okay, isn't it? Because you've already written a sequel. I saw it in the police station, didn't I? That was a sequel, wasn't it, not just another book?'

'Yes.' Tom was sitting on the tip of the cushion now, knees out past his toes. He felt a blip of power return to him: okay, so he was indebted to Angie Kellett for keeping him out of jail, but she was equally relying on him to keep her alive. With a magnanimous smirk, he offered a vow of protection. 'As long as I'm writing, Angie, you'll be safe. I'll even start a third book if it'll make you feel better.'

She smiled, and with almost a flicker of warmth.

'Why haven't you told Nelson all this?' Tom asked.

'I have. He doesn't believe me.'

Tom made a comical scoffing sound. 'Yeah, tell me about it.' But Angie's smile had evaporated, and Tom sank slowly back into his chair.

Several seconds passed, during which time they both stared off into space. Tom was already plotting the first chapter of *The New Adventures of Super Psycho*. As for Angie, he hoped she might be contemplating sexual favours as payment for saving her life, but this particular hope was not destined to spring eternal. Even Tom's generous naivety could only stretch so far.

'Will you get writing then?' Angie said suddenly.

'I will. Don't worry.'

'Now.'

After a gormless interlude, Tom shut his mouth. 'Now?'

'Yes, please.'

With vigour he didn't feel, Tom shot forward in his chair and stood up. He was glad to be excused from her presence, but wasn't at all sure he was ready to embark on another book so soon; certainly

239

not that very evening. He managed two seconds' eye contact with her, felt unable to argue his point, so left the room.

As he started up the stairs to begin his set task, the television blared into life again. By the time he reached the landing, Angie had let out a burst of laughter, as though their little chat had been concerned with nothing more than tomorrow's shopping. Granted, her own amusement was echoed by that of a studio audience, but how could she laugh so easily, so quickly? Hadn't they just been discussing matters of life and death?

Tom didn't like it. He could almost believe she was laughing at him, and had he been a tad more paranoid, he might have believed the audience was as well.

FORTY-TWO

The red director's chair sagged under his weight, bending both wooden arm-rests inwards like some medieval torture contraption, ready to spring shut and squish his insides. Tom reached to the head of the Anglepoise and switched it on. The desk had a surface of reddish, wood-grain Formica. Before sitting down that second, he would have had no conscious recollection of its colour; he could picture every detail of the farmer's grisly death, he could close his eyes and be back in Angie's room, rooting through her underwear, but much of the remainder was fogged out. Thinking about it, he could not even remember the colour of her lounge carpet, and he had only just finished staring at that.

Strange thing, the mind.

He looked at the word processor, the keyboard, the printer, all under covers. He tried to imagine Andrew Kellett with the identical view, just before the covers came off and the words went in. But he couldn't. Perhaps his mind wouldn't let him. He snapped his eyes away.

He had to forget. The tragic sequence of events which had led him to this place, this time, had to be wiped from his mind. He needed only an ounce of inspiration to begin a new story – writing beget writing – but a burdened mind was like a ton weight planted over that one ounce. There had been occasions in the past when his need to create had been so desperate it had killed the muse stone dead, and he had sat at his desk in a non-productive stupor for days, with a blank sheet scrolled out of his Canon like a mocking flag of surrender.

He uncapped his blue Bic, and set his A4 pad at an angle, ready to receive the sloping scrawl of his handwriting. He started with

MILTON – THREE, and underlined it twice, as though he meant business.

But what stopped him continuing was far more recent than eight months ago. It was four things Angie Kellett had said that afternoon; things that had lodged in his brain like shrapnel rather than memory.

Firstly: *I wasn't meaning the police*. Her retort to his assertion that, should he kill her, Nelson would not be able to bring him to justice. *Hunted down* were her words. It had sounded like more than a hope or a threat or a promise, it had sounded like a premonition, as though she had peeked into the future and seen it happen. Of course, he knew who she meant, because the biker had already told him the score, but she had meant it in an odd context. Like if he killed her, he would be killed *in revenge* for her death.

Tom sought an explanation through the same convoluted process he used to sift and discard possible storylines. After much deliberation, all he could think was that if he killed Angie, he would be cheating the biker, who clearly needed no more of an excuse to add another victorious notch to his fairing. But would his desire to murder on this pretext be greater than his desire to see Tom produce a sequel? Tom couldn't say.

Secondly: *Just for a while*. If he had wanted, she would have put the heat up just for a while. Naturally, that could have meant for a short period during the whole time he would be there. But Tom had not heard it that way. To his mind, she was stating that the length of his stay would be limited. But how could that be when she wanted him to write a third novel to keep the biker at bay? She didn't appear to be daft; she couldn't think it was possible to knock up a few hundred pages in just a couple of weeks.

Perhaps she believed Nelson would have the biker in custody before very long. Or maybe she *was* going to stab Tom to death on that first night. But that was so straightforward it seemed almost trivial, and anyway, he didn't believe it.

Thirdly: *The truth* is *out there*. Cryptic crap of the first order, which Tom did not appreciate. This was practically a boast, as though the truth was out there but only she could see it. She had sounded too pleased with herself, too self-assured. If she was truly in the same precarious boat as Tom, she could *never* sound that smug.

Fourthly: *You can't conceive of what it is you're actually up against*. This had been her comment to Nelson, her reason why she was refusing to tell him what she knew. But if, as she claimed, she had already tried to convince Nelson of her theory about the aggrieved biker, then why was he asking to hear something he had already heard, and had already dismissed?

Tom wanted to lie down. There were too many questions, and no easy answer to any of them.

Instead, he surprised himself by starting to write. The ton weight had lifted. It was still there, but some force from beneath had raised it up and released the muse. Maybe this time the necessity to create had worked in his favour. With death looming on the horizon, hidden reserves of talent were trooping to his aid, scared to wait too long for the bugle of inspiration.

So Tom wrote. Fast and flowing. By comparison, the easy way he had completed the sequel seemed like sludge. One page . . . two, three, four. Not a single crossing out, hardly a stutter of ballpoint against paper. Five pages . . . six, seven, eight. Andrew Kellett's room was alive with literary genius, though Tom was not convinced he had brought it with him from London.

By eleven p.m. he had completed twenty-five pages. He took a break and read it back. It was flawless.

Afterwards, he closed the pad and smiled, amazed but also disconsolate. Why couldn't he have done this a year ago? A mad biker – it wasn't such a great idea. Surely he could have come up with something similar.

Of course he could, and he had. His ideas were fine, he had just failed to translate them onto paper with any power. Basically, after *Hidden Blade*, his narrative had stunk.

Now, though . . . what a transformation. If he could only put this recent nightmare behind him, his life would finally be back on track. A rejuvenated career, and perhaps new love, perhaps with Angie Kellett. Right now, that seemed unlikely, but no one could say they weren't already inseparably bound together, and when all this was over maybe she would allow him to reveal the more endearing side to his nature. It had to be in there somewhere. Given a safe interim, he could even make this entire mess work for him in literary terms. Why rack his brains for fresh ideas when he was currently living his next storyline?

Deprived of food since breakfast, his stomach groaned its displeasure. He had been vaguely aware whilst writing that he

243

was hungry, but then a dazzling new sentence would loop from his Biro, and thoughts of food would be swept away with the flow. With his mind now in neutral, he recognised he was absolutely famished.

Angie had offered him free run of the house, but could he really help himself to the contents of her fridge? He wondered if there was a packet of crisps he might liberate, some flavour she didn't much like from a multipack. Or some half-stale biscuits. He could not eat her food unless he felt he was providing a service for her, disposing of her unwanted provisions. He even found the thought of simply venturing downstairs and walking past her a second time awoke a self-loathing that made starvation seem the cushy option. But, like freezing to death, or sacrificing himself by refusing to write any more, Tom Roker had to confess to a lack of spirit where martyrdom was concerned. So he trod on the heels of his shoes and removed them under the desk to make for a quieter descent.

Quarter way down the stairs, he ducked his head beneath ceiling level to see if Angie was still in the lounge. He had been so engrossed in writing, for all he knew she might have gone to bed hours ago. But she was still there, only now she was slumped in the corner of the settee, arms folded, head nestled and eyes closed. The TV was on, the volume low. He tore his eyes away from her contours and crept the rest of the way, tiptoeing down the stairs, then moon-walking in giant steps along the hallway into the kitchen.

The fluorescent had been left on. He gently closed the door behind him. At the far end of the narrow room, the door to the back garden had been replaced. Once glass-paned – how could he forget? – it was now solid wood, oak-stained.

Apart from one banana and two apples on the sideboard, nothing edible was on show, and he had mentally placed a restricted entry on her cupboards, fridge and freezer. If she didn't open them for him, they would have to stay shut. He looked at the electric stove, and could not even imagine using one of her hobs to heat a can of beans, even if he bought it himself.

He was not a guest, he was a prisoner.

He turned to leave the kitchen and noticed another reminder of his previous visit. Above the door, in the wall and ceiling, sand-coloured filler was crammed unprofessionally into the holed and cratered plaster where the farmer's buckshot had impacted.

It was eerie. Last summer seemed unreal, like the stilted recollection of a movie; something he now regretted paying to see because it had stuck so nightmarishly in his mind's eye.

He hurriedly exited the kitchen, leaving the room in darkness. From now on, however long he was there, that space would be Out of Bounds for meals. He could eat out at the pub or the chippy, and stock his room with snacks and drinks for the nibbles he always felt when he wrote into the wee hours.

Chips, in fact, seemed the answer to his present pangs, and there was a chippy in the village; he had noticed on the drive in.

He managed to get upstairs for his coat and shoes and back down again without waking Angie. Before leaving, he peered round the door jamb at her sleeping form. He watched her for five minutes, although 'watched' was something of a euphemism. Ogled was closer.

He skulked backwards down the hallway and left the house.

Outside, the cold seeped beneath his clothes like water in a freshly submerged wetsuit. The frost had set hard on the tarmac and he had to watch his step. The soles of his sensible shoes were essentially gripless, which actually made them bloody stupid shoes for this time of year. He developed a skidding walk, like a mime-skater. It seemed safer if he slid of his own accord so he could control it. Above him, a half-moon hung in the clear, star-strewn sky, making his route sparkle silvery-blue ahead of him. The first streetlamp was still out of sight, but he could see its glow round the next bend, a diffuse orange hovering in the icy air.

On the village outskirts, Tom suddenly groaned out loud and cursed. It had to be past eleven-thirty. Would a sleepy village chippy be open at this hour? All depended what day it was. Hmm. What day *was* it? Thursday? Yes. No. Yes. No, Friday. Friday? He nodded and his stomach seemed to tumble over itself in greedy anticipation. There was a good chance the chippy would be late-opening on a Friday to catch the turf-outs from the village pubs.

He needn't have worried. The chip shop was bright; the pubs were not its only source of custom. Groups of bored youths were dotted in cosy huddles along the main street, scoffing their feasts, loitering harmlessly in the shadows of dead shop fronts, or crammed ten to a wooden bench, like survivors on a life-raft. These were the local rich kids, playing at street gangs in their designer gear, only it wasn't drug money that had paid for their outfits, it was Mummy and Daddy. No doubt half of them would have trashed their fathers' Mercs within a week of passing their tests.

Tom secretly eyed them as he walked. Girls and boys hugging and kissing, boys karate-kicking each other, girls gossiping and bitching. Gloved hands snatched at precious plastic bottles of cider. Warm, boozy breath floated above their freezing heads, mingling with illicit cigarette smoke.

And visions of his own little Charlotte flooded into his head. Gone. Lost. Thousands of miles away in Colorado. Of course, she would not be so little any more. She had been gone four years, and that would make her nine now. Her last letter had arrived a month ago, with a photograph enclosed: Charlotte the budding cheerleader. He could see how she had matured from the picture, but in his mind she would always be five years old, and thoroughly English. It was a defence mechanism, to ignore the awful chasm of years he had missed of her growing up. She had never got round to visiting, and neither had he. She always made the suggestion, but he guessed her mother had a hand in it never coming to fruition. Honestly, he preferred it that way. Some wounds never healed, but at least they weren't annually ripped apart for the sake of a fortnight which would be more pain than pleasure. His letters to her were very matter-of-fact: went here, went there, saw this, saw that. He could have said more, much more, but it was a dam he was keeping the sluice gate shut on. It all came out once he was asleep, anyway. Sometimes, in his more optimistic dreams, he would pass a schoolyard and Charlotte would break from a game of hopscotch and burst through the gates towards him. 'Oh, hi, Dad,' she'd say. 'Me and Mum moved back to England. How about making a family again?' *Mum and I*, he would mentally correct before the hugging and crying began.

Tom rubbed his eyes; the cold was making them water.

Passing the next huddle, he was greeted by a whiff of tobacco, and he realised he hadn't had a cigarette that whole evening. Writing had dulled the craving. He stopped, dug in his pocket and brought out his pack, stuffed a weed into his mouth and lit up. He carried on, without the sliding this time, as the village pavements had been thoughtfully gritted. He inhaled nicotine and a stream of air that felt like dry ice, and the combination made him hack his guts up. It was unpleasantly productive.

The kids ignored him. One more middle-aged fart, fresh from the pub, fit for the grave.

Several of the youngsters wore baseball caps, some back to front, and Tom was reminded of the biker. He shivered, a double-judder of cold and fear.

A few steps from the chippy, the illuminated sign above the door suddenly winked out, swiftly followed by the interior fluorescents. He ran to the window, just in time to see an elderly couple disappear through a curtain of hanging multicoloured ribbons into the rear of the shop. Only the low-wattage bulbs in the hot shelves were still lit, but the shelves themselves were bare. The bulbs produced yellow gleams against the stainless steel fryers and fitments. Perversely, the place looked infinitely more enticing in its darkened state. It looked, of all things, homely, and Tom felt a rush of emotion he could hardly contain. Ludicrously, tears brimmed, and he found himself tapping forlornly at the plate-glass, feeling it tremble in its frame.

He was ignored for a while, then a white-haired old gent broke through the tassled divide. His face was initially stern, as though he had expected to shoo away some inebriated youngster. When he saw Tom, he became puzzled, then a frowning smile brought him around the counter to the door. He unlocked and opened a head-sized gap.

'Sorry, I know you've just closed,' Tom said pitifully, 'but have you got anything left?'

'No, sorry.'

'Anything?'

The owner's wife stuck her kindly, enquiring face through the ribbons. 'There's a few chips,' she said, overriding her husband. 'They won't be very warm, though.'

'I don't mind,' Tom said, and the door was opened wide to him. The old fellah disappeared through the back and left his wife to it.

'Miss dinner, did you, love?' she asked, scraping noisily around the bottom of the chip well, collecting the remains.

'And lunch,' Tom said.

'Ooh, dear,' she sympathised, tipping the last few chips from her metal spade into a polystyrene tray. It looked just less than a small portion, and Tom found the price on the wall list: sixty pence. His fingers searched for a fifty and a ten at the pit of his trouser pocket. 'No, love,' she said, hearing the coins jingle. 'You can have them. They'd only go to waste.'

He beamed gratefully at her. 'Thank you. Thanks very much.'

'Salt and vinegar?'

'Please.'

She sprinkled them over the food, stuck a plastic fork in the top and handed them across the counter.

'Thanks,' Tom said again, but the polystyrene in his hand had not been even slightly warmed by the contents, and his disgust at the thought of cold chips made his smile fade as he turned and pulled open the door.

'Bye,' she called cheerily.

He stepped into the street. 'Bye,' he said over his shoulder, and didn't care if she hadn't heard. After a stutter of feet, he decided to head away from the kids, and further away from his bed for the night. He shovelled handfuls of tepid chips into his mouth, finally discarding his empty tray in a hedge.

He passed more shops, a pub, and a row of tiny alms-houses before he arrived in front of a small church. It was set back from the road, surrounded by a graveyard. Railings and lifeless, clawing bushes defined its perimeter, every bit as unwelcoming as barbed wire. He stopped at the gate and peered up at the spire, like a great arrow pointing up to heaven.

Thou shalt not steal, thou shalt not kill thundered in his head, sounding more like pronouncements on him than commandments for all. Oh, and *thou shalt not commit adultery*, don't forget that. Or was he being overly harsh on himself? Carol was the married one, not him. Or were they both adulterers in a situation like that?

Tom terminated his internal debate before it became any more pointless. He'd been a bastard, and he knew it. It was silly to suppose any different on the basis of a mere technicality.

Whoever the minister was of this small village church, Tom envied him. No doubt a simple man, uncomplicated and blameless. A man with good in his heart, who had renounced the works of the devil, who strove to enlighten the dark times of his loyal parishioners. A selfless man, tireless in his faith. Everything Tom wasn't.

How could anyone be like that? So . . . *nice*?

Completely out of character, Tom leaned on the gate, closed his eyes and put his hands together to pray.

Fifteen seconds and not a single silent word had been directed to The Man Upstairs. It was another dam he dared not breach.

He straightened up and shoved his prayerless hands deep into his pockets. 'Ah, bollocks to it,' he tried to convince himself, and set off back through the village towards Angie's house.

Grit crunched underfoot as he marched with arms rigid and shoulders hunched. He kept catching himself giving unconscious little shakes of the head, sort of wordless apologies for his ignoble inability to ask for forgiveness.

The village kids had all retired for the night in a Brigadoon-like disappearing act. Tom guessed a parental midnight curfew had scattered them back to their homes. Some rules it was evidently best not to flout. It was no use being one of the Home Boys if Dad grounded you for the weekend so you really did have to stay at home.

Tom left the shops and the main street behind, turned off and started slide-walking up Angie's road. Still beneath the orange glow of streetlamps, he suddenly stopped dead and cocked his head to one side. Somewhere behind him a motorcycle was approaching. One name sprang to mind: Skunk. Instinctively, Tom sought the nearest hiding place and ran for it, skidding and nearly going his length. That he would be trespassing on someone else's driveway was of no importance.

The parked car seemed like decent cover. He could cower behind it if the Skunk passed by, and if he halted right there, Tom could scurry up the drive, batter down the front door and seek asylum. It never occurred to him that there might be someone else out there with a motorcycle.

Tom estimated the bike was now on the main street, maybe level with the chip shop. It didn't sound anywhere near as loud as he remembered from the incident at the Manchester bookshop, but he supposed a noisy exhaust could always be swapped for a quieter one, which seemed logical. Old Skunkhead would not want to attract unnecessary attention; not any more, not with every cop in the country on the lookout for him. But that was always assuming the Skunk thought logically, and given that the guy was an utter psycho . . .

Tom flapped his hands in front of his mouth to dispel the visible

clouds of his panting breath. He gripped the plastic bumper of the
. . . what was it? He looked at the marque on the bonnet. Oh, a
BMW, like his. Only newer. A lot newer. P-reg. Sod.

The motorbike droned past the foot of the road and away, but
Tom didn't move until he heard it fade into silence in the distance.
He wondered if his reaction had been slightly over-cautious, then
he questioned whether it was possible to be too careful when a
homicidal maniac was out for your blood.

His eyes went to the bonnet badge again. He'd been missing the
one on his own car for several years. Some low-life had prised it
off, leaving a scratchy mess in its place.

Tom dipped into his pocket and tumbled his house keys around
in the palm of his hand. Then they were out, and a thin brass Yale
was levering at the rim of the circular badge. But it didn't want
to come, and when he really began to force it, a high-pitched
whooping erupted from under the bonnet.

He scarpered into the road and fell on the icy surface. He picked
himself up, and his chips rose in his gorge. He tried to run but his
gripless shoes made him feel as though he was in a nightmare,
where distance covered was in no correlation to energy expended.
Then he lost his footing again and cracked down on his elbows to
save his face. Pain flared up his arms as he struggled to escape,
hugging the hedgerow now where the tarmac gave way to frozen
ridges of mud.

Behind him, two soothing beeps ended the BM's tantrum, and
Tom gathered the owner had simply quietened his car through
the window by remote, probably doubting it was anything more
sinister than temperamental circuitry upset by the extreme cold.

Tom slowed to a quick walk with the occasional glance over
his shoulder, and soon he was passing beneath the last of the
streetlamps and into the beckoning darkness. His panic, his breath
and his pain all subsided, and he was left with a question he
couldn't answer: why had a forty-year-old man just tried to steal
a BMW bonnet badge when he had enough in the bank to buy
the whole car?

When he reached the cottage, he knocked and Angie Kellett
opened the door for him. He explained where he'd been, like a
prisoner returned from day-release, and she gave him a spare set
of house keys so he could come and go as he pleased.

Andrew Kellett's bedroom seemed even colder. Angie had made

up the bed for him, but Tom slept on top of the duvet that night, curled up tightly, fully clothed, with his overcoat as a blanket and a sweater rolled into a pillow.

He did not sleep well.

FORTY-THREE

The route through the village was the quickest way up to the new by-pass. Nelson steered his blue Triumph carefully. The streets had been gritted, but taking a spill in his present mood would launch him right into orbit, and this ride was meant to cool him down, not aggravate him even further.

Passing the end of Angie Kellett's road, he had toyed with the idea of dropping by to see her, but common sense had prevailed. She had been a brick wall for his questions earlier, and he didn't think he could stand any more of the woman's crap that day.

He rode with his visor up. His face was numb with the rush of air, and his eyes watered. No one had yet seen him cry over Ash, and probably no one would, so if the tears sneaked out now under the guise of watering eyes, it was as good a release as any. The icy trickles flowed back towards his ears and dampened his greying temples. He was half-blinded, blinking repeatedly to clear his vision, but at least he felt awake, alive, and on this particular evening he needed that.

He tried not to think about Ash. He wanted to blank his mind, but he felt a loss he could not ignore. He had liked Ash more than he had shown. It was in his character. No one had ever witnessed the extent of his finer emotions. It was only his anger he allowed himself to vent fully.

The by-pass would blow off some of the cobwebs. A good blast for a few miles, visor down, gut on tank and head dipped behind the screen. Really open her up.

He joined the by-pass at the second of the four roundabouts which made up its length. Grit crackled on the bike's belly pan, but the Triumph felt sure-footed. Dark embankments rose either side of him, dotted with saplings for a future generation to enjoy. A solitary car passed him on the opposite carriageway. He rolled open the throttle, shifted up, rolled open, shifted up, rolled open, shifted into sixth, and watched the speedo creep past 120, 130, 140.

There were no Gatsos along the dual-carriageway, no white Vascar blocks on the road surface, and no gaps in the roadside barrier for patrol vehicles to lie in wait. So if he kept a check in his mirrors after each roundabout, he assessed he should be safe. Of course, he believed he should have been immune from prosecution anyway, with him being a DCI, but times had changed. Loyalty was a rare quality these days, and he was as liable to get nicked as the next man.

He slowed to negotiate the third roundabout, taking the racing line through the curve, then roared off down the next straight, streaking past a lorry. The snazzy two-piece leathers he wore were expensive, but the night was too cold and his speeds too high for them to keep him warm for very long. He clenched his teeth and let the shivers ripple through his blubber.

At the final roundabout, he did a full circle and headed back along the dual-carriageway. This time, as he picked up speed, he began to yell inside his helmet, screaming madly to release some of the pain and impotence he felt over Ash and the case in general. He screamed to the first roundabout, to the second, and to the third, and then he had to stop screaming because his throat had lost its power and it hurt like hell. And did he feel any better? No.

But at the last roundabout, something was about to happen which would open the channels for a great deal of his aggression.

The approach of the left-hand feed-road was shielded by the grass embankment. Nelson only clocked the car as he was about to enter the roundabout. It wasn't travelling fast, and Nelson assumed the driver would have registered the Triumph's headlight looming on his right.

But Nelson was wrong.

Despite moving slowly enough to comfortably obey the Give Way sign, the car just kept on going, straight into the path of the oncoming motorcycle.

Nelson grabbed at brake and clutch, diving the forks. His bulk slid forward in his seat so his balls crunched agonisingly against the petrol tank. His front tyre halted less than a foot away from the side of the offending car which passed casually in front of him.

With a voice already hoarse from screaming, Nelson wheezed

useless profanities into his helmet whilst shaking his gloved fist at the car driver. Foolishly, the car driver turned his face and laughed as he circled 270 degrees to cruise off down the by-pass in the direction from which Nelson had just come.

Later on, Nelson would remember only snippets of what occurred next; a fury had seized control of his senses.

He pursued the car – a large, dark-coloured Peugeot – almost to the end of the by-pass. Speeds touched the ton, reducing only for the roundabouts. Nelson stuck to its rear bumper, sounding his horn, full beam glaring through the car's interior. Had the driver braked suddenly, Nelson would have been history.

Unexpectedly, the car veered onto the hard shoulder and stopped. Nelson overtook and pulled in just ahead. His whole body was trembling helplessly from cold and adrenalin. He quickly parked up, got off and lumbered like a raging bull towards the car driver, who was now standing on the tarmac wielding a grey and yellow Stoplock with violent intent.

But Nelson intended some violence of his own, and when the Stoplock swung at his helmeted head, he merely lifted one arm and quite painlessly took the impact against some armoured leather. Then he relieved the man of his weapon and battered him to the ground as he tried to climb back in his car.

When it was over, Nelson had a corpse at his feet. He could only recall landing the first blow, but the the man's head had been caved through to the brain by a flurry of vicious swipes. In one place where the underlying bone was still intact, the skin had split in a crescent, and the skull shone through like a macabre white smile.

With the Stoplock dangling limply from his hands, and his body heaving from the aftermath, Nelson attempted to picture the man's face prior to the attack. But he couldn't do it; his mind was a white-out. He certainly couldn't tell what the man had looked like from his present condition. If the car driver had been faceless before, he was now literally so. A bloody, distorted blob, with darkness pooling all around.

Nelson dropped the Stoplock and bolted for his bike. On the opposite side of the carriageway, a car passed by, slowing to take in the scene before accelerating away in a squeal of rubber.

Within ten minutes, Nelson was home and garaging the Triumph. When he had cut the engine, pulled down the up-and-over door and removed his helmet, he was able to hear the sirens across town.

He was shaking like a young Elvis, and felt about as healthy as an old one. In the unlit warmth of his garage, with only a pinking engine for company, he collapsed onto a gardening stool and began to sob.

Sometime later, he roused himself. There was vital business to attend to.

In the back garden he hosed down his boots and leather pants to remove the worst splatters. Then he wheeled his bike through and turned the hose on that. Every so often he would check the bedroom window, but the light stayed off and the curtains closed. His wife liked her sleeping pills, and for once he was extremely pleased she did. He hosed the concrete for ten minutes, directing the puddles along to the drain.

After locking up the bike, he went in the back door and straight upstairs.

In the bathroom, he turned the key. Carrying his crash helmet, he stepped into the shower cubicle without undressing. He switched on the jet and the hot water pattered noisily on his leathers. Gradually, it permeated through to his freezing skin and stung with a pleasurable pain. Fifteen minutes beneath the steaming downpour and he adjudged himself to be free from incriminating evidence. He switched off the unit. Waterlogged, he felt like a ton weight. But once he had removed his leathers, he noticed the feeling did not go away.

He hung the leathers over the shower door, placed his helmet in the airing cupboard and hurried naked to the bedroom for his pyjamas.

Before climbing into bed beside his dead-to-the-world wife, he helped himself to a double dose of her sleeping pills. If he could get through tonight, he assured himself that everything would be fine in the morning. People would assume the mad biker had chalked up another kill, and the real murderer would just have to convince his conscience that, in light of the reckless roundabout manoeuvre, Mister Peugeot would undoubtedly have killed someone else had he not been killed himself. Basically, it had served him right.

Yes indeedy. Tomorrow was another day. DCI Nelson had a psycho to catch, and he would devote his energies to that goal. If he did find he was lapsing into self-recrimination, he would simply marvel at the fact that he had not beaten to death some cretinous car driver years ago.

Mister Peugeot. Cutting him up. Laughing at him like that. Well, that'd teach the silly cunt to *Think Bike*.

FORTY-FOUR

◆

Tom's weekend flew past in a blur of scribbling. He shopped on Saturday morning, stocking his room with ready-to-eat snacks and cartons of juice, then wrote and wrote and wrote. He avoided any bad dreams by not sleeping again. Coffee and Pro-Plus kept him wired until Monday morning when he finally zonked out at his desk, forehead on writing pad.

He saw Angie several times that weekend as he waited for the kettle to boil in the kitchen, or when he ran, bladder screaming, for the upstairs loo, his unprecedented spew of words having kept him too long at the desk. She said hello with unconvincing pleasantness, or maybe quite genuinely but he couldn't believe it, and he simply looked away and nodded at the wall like a friendless soul in a halfway house.

He was terrified. In his current writing, he felt he had been granted a final lease of life. The very thing he had always believed he wanted was now his: dazzling narrative, sparkling dialogue, a literary mind in overdrive. But the more he wrote, the more he realised he was only carrying on because he was too afraid to stop. Admittedly, there was a dim sense of satisfaction in such startling creativity, but the enjoyment was purely cerebral. Though his brain acknowledged the achievement, his spirit could not remember where it had stored the bunting.

Not once did Carol Morgan or Pyramid Pictures enter his head. That was financial business, and he wasn't writing for money any more, he was writing for his life. His world had closed down to this one room. Beyond that, the ground fell away.

He did not even think to check his copy of *Man on a Murder Cycle*. If he had, he would have received an added spur to keep on producing the goods, because whilst he had been busy extending the gap, Milton had been busy reducing it.

The murder inquiry was a shambles. The bodies were piling up and the team did not have a single decent lead to follow. Since the death of Ash on Friday morning, two more homicides had occurred, only one of which was as described in Tom Roker's novel. This copy-cat murder happened on Sunday.

A known motorcycle thief had been found trussed up in the back of his Transit. He might have remained undiscovered for some time had it not been for a helpful arrow on the pavement, pointing to the van. The arrow itself might not have been cause for concern had it not been made up of severed fingers and toes. The rear doors were prised apart to reveal a toeless, fingerless scumbag with his arms and legs bound and his neck snipped open. His mouth had been gaffer-taped to keep him quiet, but his horror-struck face showed he had made quite an effort to scream. Across his lap lay a bolt cropper, a tool of his odious trade, its pinching blades covered in blood. In fact, the entire floor of the van was awash with the stuff, which meant he was still alive, his heart still pumping, as each of his digits came off.

The perp's identity was plain: in the road, beside the van, was a black donut of burnt rubber.

The other murder, committed Friday night on the local by-pass, gave the investigating detectives a whole new headache.

When he came into headquarters on Saturday morning, DCI Nelson already had a headache. His wife's sleeping pills had left him feeling horrendously hungover. It got worse when he realised he had badly miscalculated how last night's murder would be interpreted.

The passing motorist had identified a big man as the assailant. But big as in fat. And not wearing black; wearing two- or three-colour leathers. The exact colours were unknown – it had been the briefest of glimpses, at night, under a splash of orange streetlamp – but the witness had seen enough to throw doubt on it being the ZZ-R rider. Besides, there was no calling card, no donut scorched into the tarmac at the scene.

An isolated incident? Someone copying the copycat? No one could say for sure, but Nelson knew he could not lump it in with the other murders without arousing suspicion. He had already overheard one young constable joking that the latest incident was 'probably down to our own biking fat man'.

So, reluctantly but sensibly, Nelson was forced to launch a separate inquiry.

Still, how could it possibly lead back to him? How could anyone seriously suspect him, and why would anyone have reason to? Murders were generally solved because the victim was known to the attacker. In other cases, without a bloody trail leading directly to the killer's door, or a spontaneous confession, results were far harder to come by. Nelson had washed any trace of evidence down the drain, and was he about to break down and tell all? Hardly. The guilt he had expected to feel was wonderfully absent.

In fact, as his headache disappeared, he began to feel quite the opposite. He found himself wanting to grin. He felt gleeful, fulfilled. In those moments of lunatic fury last night, he believed he had made contact with his true nature for the first time in his life.

The Angel of the Lord had visited his just and vengeful touch upon the interloper.

Michael had wished a man dead, and now the front page of his local weekly newspaper carried a photograph of that man, above a caption which read: *Murdered Detective, Adam Ash*. There was little in the way of an accompanying story. The police were not releasing any details until preliminary investigations were complete. A spokesman would only comment that it appeared to be a motiveless attack on an officer with an exemplary record, and that it was a devastating loss both to his colleagues and to the community in which he had served.

As he donned his garb in the vestry, Michael kept telling himself he should be feeling guilty. But all he felt was euphoric. He was a conduit for Divine retribution. He had pointed the finger, and God had zapped the man. A sort of Old Testament smart bomb. So why should he feel bad? Would God have struck down a blameless soul? Of course not. Adam Ash must have been a black-hearted sinner who deserved to die. What evil would have spawned from that heart had it been allowed to continue beating? How terribly would he have hurt Angie Kellett had their relationship progressed?

Back to the mundane, Michael could not find his dog collar. He had not worn it since Wednesday, when he had hung it on a hook, the hook he was now looking dumbly at, because it

259

was bare. He could not imagine where the collar had disappeared to.

There was no time to search. In ten minutes, he would have to be at the west door to greet his congregation. He found a spare collar and put it on.

A few days ago, he had believed he would never take another Sunday service. Now his doubts had evaporated. His faith was implicit. He belonged in the Church. It was more than a career, more than a vocation, it was his destiny, and he could feel it unfolding on a universal scale, crossing dimensions his parishioners would not even breach in their dreams. He could feel the shifts taking place, in his mind, his body, his soul.

His journey had begun, and he would wait patiently for the next signpost in the certain knowledge that there was only one possible destination for a man so well connected: Heaven.

And the real miracle? He would not have to wait for the afterlife to get there. He could attain heaven on earth, because he knew the secret of life.

Love. Love was the key to open the gates of Paradise, and he had in his heart all the love in the world for just one person.

FORTY-FIVE

———◆———

Ten days passed. Tom hardly ate or slept. His eyes went dark and hollow. He pulled in two holes on his belt. He was alone during the weekdays, with his landlady in Manchester working. He tried to think of the cottage as his own literary retreat, a place of peace and solitude, without interruptions, but whenever he came face to face with Angie Kellett in the evenings, his delusion shattered, and he raced back upstairs to immerse himself in his story and forget.

And the words kept tumbling from his mind and landing in perfect running order on the page. Sentences flowed one after the other. Paragraphs followed on without a stutter. He barely had to pause for thought between chapters. He estimated the third novel in his Miltonian Trilogy was already one-third complete. Inside two weeks. It was incredible.

The price for all this was high. Tom felt almost completely detached from reality. During those times when he did break from writing, he felt disorientated. Without the fiction, the facts confused him. How had he got to this disastrous point in his life? How could he have been so wrong about so many things?

These were questions he never answered. He simply swapped one horror story for another and returned to the writing.

He certainly needed to. Seemingly to keep pace with Tom's lightning productivity, Milton had upped his own, striking five times since Tom's instalment at the Kellett residence, with a body count of eleven. It was the biggest ongoing news story since the Gulf War, and Angie had very kindly kept Tom informed of events.

Now, only one violent episode remained to be acted out. Tom's copy of *Man on a Murder Cycle* was a mass of missing print.

He wondered what would happen when the book had been exhausted. Would the biker demand a manuscript of the unpublished

261

sequel so that he could continue straight on with his spree? Or would he store his ZZ-R in a lock-up somewhere and vanish into thin air until the sequel was available in the shops? Both were equally horrendous propositions for different reasons. If the sicko wanted a manuscript immediately, that would mean Tom would have to carry on writing all day every day to maintain a safe gap until the police caught up with him. On the other hand, if he was happy to wait for the hardback, what would that do to Tom's sanity, knowing it was all going to start again in a year's time? But could anyone so mental be that coldly calculating as to cease all murderous activities for twelve months? Sadly, Tom imagined *only* someone so mental could be that coldly calculating.

Occasionally, Tom contemplated suicide to escape his problems, but the thoughts were too peripheral to manifest themselves as direct action. Whilst he had something to occupy his mind, they would stay away, like distant marauders he could hear but not yet see.

On that Wednesday night, Tom was scrawling away when he received a tap at the bedroom door.

'Yes?' he said weakly, flooding with renewed shame in anticipation of another close encounter with Angie Kellett.

She entered the room in her bathrobe and slippers. 'How's it going, Tom?'

He put his pen down and nodded. 'Okay,' he said, not meeting her eyes.

'Gosh, you've done all that?' she said, surprised, looking at the pile of finished sheets on the desk.

'I'm getting on with it,' he muttered, still nodding.

'You are, aren't you?' Then she affected some compassion. 'Don't you think you ought to give it a rest for tonight? Get some sleep?'

'I'm all right.'

'You're not, you're knackered. You look half dead.'

Tom mustered a smile. 'I'm all right.'

'But you're hardly sleeping. I go to the loo in the middle of the night and your light's still on. I can hear your pen scratching away.'

Tom was sceptical of this sudden concern. 'Don't tell me you care. I couldn't stand any sympathy from you.'

'And you wouldn't believe it.'

262

Tom didn't reply. He still wouldn't look at her.

Her voice hardened. 'I don't want you keeling over, Tom. It would be dangerous for the both of us if that happened. You must keep writing.'

'I know.'

'So go to bed, and tomorrow have a lie-in.' She sounded more matronly now, an acceptable compromise between the sweet and the sour.

'I might,' he said.

'You will,' she said. 'Come back to it refreshed. Don't burn yourself out.'

He turned his eyes up to hers for the first time in the conversation. He could feel tears trying to brim, but he would have preferred she saw him dead rather than crying. He willed them back down.

'Trouble is,' he said evenly, trying not to betray his emotion, 'I don't sleep when I do go to bed.'

'I commiserate. I know how that feels.' She reached into her robe pocket and produced a brown plastic pill bottle. 'These were Andrew's. I take a couple every so often.' She set them down by his elbow. 'You can take two tonight.'

'I don't want any sleeping pills,' he told her, though he did, very much, and a part of him wanted a whole bunch of the little darlings, way in excess of the stated dose. He just felt it would be immoral to accept her help when he so deserved his pain.

Angie folded her arms and let her weight transfer to one leg, causing her hip to thrust out defiantly. 'I'm not arguing with you, Tom. Take a couple.'

Tom sighed for effect and took the bottle. He unscrewed the child-proof cap and shook two green capsules into the palm of his hand. He threw them into his mouth and washed them down with some pineapple juice from a half-full litre carton on the desk.

'Good,' she said, receiving the bottle back from him. 'And if they're still under your tongue, you might as well swallow them once I've gone, because if your light isn't off in twenty minutes, I'm taking the bulb out.' She retreated to the door. 'You're going to be in the dark anyway, so you might as well sleep.'

'They're gone,' he said obediently, regretting their rapport could not have been warmer.

'Good.' Then she frowned. 'I see you took the photo down.'

Tom looked at the wall in front of him. He shrugged and withered inside. 'I had to.'

'Mmm. Goodnight.' She left him alone, with the door open.

A minute later she returned. 'And, Tom, for goodness sake, use the bed. Undress, get under the duvet, and sleep with your head on the pillow.'

He nodded and she disappeared, but he knew her last command could not be obeyed. He might have taken Andrew Kellett's pills, but he could never snuggle down under a dead man's duvet.

He continued writing for fifteen minutes before his brain suddenly called last orders and dropped its shutters. *Whoa! What a sensation!* He felt wonderfully muzzy and thoughtless, and when he stood up his movements seemed terribly slow and ponderous. There was no question: he was about to sleep, and sleep soundly. He had no choice. This was a chemically induced tiredness that no amount of fear or guilt or self-loathing could fight through. At that moment he just didn't care. About anything. The bed looked so good, so comfortable and cosy. So what if Andrew Kellett had slept in it? Who cared?

Tom undressed to his underpants, put the light out and climbed into the single bed, pulling the duvet up to his eyes which were already shut and seemingly sealed with glue.

Within seconds, he was gone.

That evening, as Tom Roker was away with the fairies, uniformed officers were visiting the local skinhead fraternity in their favoured haunts.

It was anathema to Nelson to be giving antisocial fuckwits information which might save their lives, but as one of his detectives had suggested it during a team briefing, he had not been able to just sweep it aside with his usual withering glare. After all, it was a logical course of action considering the final chapter of violence in *Man on a Murder Cycle*.

Seedy fascist pubs and the homes of known skinheads in the area were all targeted. Not unexpectedly, the visiting bobbies were greeted by grunting idiocy and blind disregard for the facts. Those skinheads actually gifted with the power of speech put it to little use, launching a barrage of insults to rise above the sea of two-fingered and Nazi salutes. Believing that 'The Filth' were no use to anyone, it was taken for granted they had nothing to say worth listening to. The Knucklescraping New Order could sort out their own protection, thank you very much, and did not need help from an organisation that was happy to regularly employ persons of a Non-Caucasian persuasion.

When this was reported later on, Nelson was quietly gratified. He did not like skinheads, and did not relish wasting precious resources on saving their miserable lives. As much as he hated foreigners himself, he was reluctant to see any beaten up outside his own personal custody. He was government-sanctioned, so that was okay. Besides, skinheads gave racism a bad name. Even middle-class Britain, the heartland of insidious racial prejudice, reacted badly to such overt aggression. All those red Doc Martens, green bomber jackets, snarling faces, crass tattoos, and bald, empty heads; it was enough to make anyone question their secret loathing, and that was bad for the future of White Power.

But, as an exercise, he supposed it had served its purpose. At least the police had been seen to be wise before the event, so no one could accuse them of giving insufficient warning. And perhaps inside one lone shaved dome, the odd synapse might crackle into life, remember, and avoid disaster before it struck. But Nelson seriously doubted it. So far, none of the biker's victims had seen it coming, not even Ash, and he didn't expect it would be any different for the last lot, warning or no warning. The biker was too swift, too assured, and Nelson had recently come to admire the man for that. Nelson knew what it was like to kill. It was easy to lose yourself in the moment, and that meant it was easy to make mistakes. There were too many people who might notice too many details.

A registration plate, for example. If the passing motorist on the opposite carriageway had shown the presence of mind to momentarily stop and note even a partial index, Nelson's Triumph would have sooner or later appeared on the computer. Or what if the index were unknown but the witness recognised the exact make of bike? A checklist of local Triumph Trophy ownership would have inevitably thrown up his name. Then it would only take one of his nosey, curtain-parting neighbours to confirm his evening jaunt for the two things to form some pretty damning circumstantial evidence.

It was so frighteningly easy to get caught.

Yet this ZZ-R rider had claimed multiple victims in a series of attacks and had not left a single unintentional clue behind. He always managed to evade capture, even when helicopter surveillance was on the scene within minutes, and although members of the general public could say in which direction he went, nobody was ever around when he got where he was going to see him garage the bike.

Nelson had very mixed feelings. He hated the biker for Ash, but he had to marvel at the man's homicidal genius. In fact, had Nelson's own reputation not been at stake, he might well have been egging the crazy fucker on.

FORTY-SIX

———◆———

Tom's first peep into Thursday let in images of a strange room.
He closed his eyes and tried to locate himself. It was difficult. His
pill-coloured dreams had taken him far away, to a parallel universe
where Tom Roker was a man who lived in perfect contentment with
a loving wife and daughter. This *doppelgänger* had never been a
writer, had never entertained thoughts of fame and fortune. He had
different values. He lived humbly, counting his blessings instead of
hurting people in a bid to buy more of what he didn't need. He lived
in a world without the Skunk, and did not encounter evil because he
had none within him. He shone with goodness and it was reflected
back at him.

Lucky sod, Tom thought as he opened his eyes and the dream
dissolved in his head like mist, and he recognised the room he
was in and the reason he was there.

'Shit.'

Outside his window, a strong wind was tangling noisily in the
barren horse chestnuts. The room was more gloomy than normal,
and Tom sensed it was late, perhaps as late as four p.m. His head
felt clear, free from chemical interference, and he figured that
would not have been the case had it been very much earlier. He
rolled over and lifted the curtain. The sky was darkening already.
Either that, or it was an especially miserable day.

Then again, weren't all days miserable of late?

'Stop it. Buck up,' he told himself. 'You can beat this.'

The words rang hollow, but at least they rang; there was still
a fight in him. He tried to convince himself he felt a whole lot
better for his rest, and he did, but, now that he *was* more refreshed,
reality had come into sharper focus, which only made him feel
more inclined to stay where he was: in bed.

However, when Tom turned away from the curtains and looked into the room, what he saw had his feet on the carpet before he was aware he had even moved.

'Oh, you *bitch*!' he shouted.

Strictly speaking, it was not just what he saw that caused alarm, it was what he didn't see.

On the carpet at the foot of his bed he saw the contents of his holdall tipped out – his clothes, his sponge bag, his copy of *Man on a Murder Cycle* – but he didn't see the manuscript of the sequel among them. On the surface of his desk he saw his pen and his second depleted pad of A4, but he didn't see the pile of handwritten pages he had left beside it.

He stood still for several seconds, battling his panic with a generous and undeserved dose of anti-paranoia. Maybe Angie had borrowed them last night for some bedtime reading. Hadn't she said she had trouble sleeping herself? Maybe they were on her bedside table, nice and safe and neatly boxed off. Or maybe she'd been reading them over breakfast. Maybe they were on the kitchen sideboard next to a drained mug of tea.

And maybe the world was flat.

Wearing only his undies, he bolted from his room into hers and ran round her bed, swearing when he couldn't find his work. He ran out onto the landing and quickly downstairs.

Angie was relaxing in the lounge. 'Ah, Tom,' she said with a disturbingly off-hand air, 'I wondered when you'd surface.'

Standing in the doorway, he was dimly aware of his near-naked state, but he wasn't bothered by it; his heart was thudding with heightened fear for the consequences of what he guessed she was about to say.

Her demeanour had clearly changed. She was no longer one half of a mutually dependent partnership, grudgingly accepting his presence in her home for the sake of her own personal safety. She was the smug and grinning schemer, oozing revenge from her pores like a pungent overdose of garlic. She was, in fact, the person Tom had originally expected she would be.

He had been conned.

'Where are they?' he demanded.

'Go and get dressed. I can't talk to you like that. You're making me feel sick.'

'*Where?*'

She was not even mildly intimidated. 'Get dressed. Go on. You can't make threats wearing Y-fronts, it doesn't work.'

Tom fumed, mostly to cover his growing apprehension. Whatever time of the day it was, Angie was not wearing her work attire. He checked the video clock. 15.44. So neither was she about to leave for work. Obviously, she had spent her day waiting patiently for him to wake up, which suggested she thought the wait would be worth it.

'Upstairs, there's a good boy.'

Tom glowered at her, but he was starting to feel the chill anyway, so he dashed back up to his room.

As he dressed in double-quick time, he reviewed his dilemma. If his worst expectations were true, then she had taken his work and destroyed it. Why, when that also laid her open to danger, was beyond him, but he thought he was right to prepare himself for just such a revelation. Then again, how much damage had she really caused? Okay, he didn't have a copy of the past two weeks' work, but inside another fortnight it could be recreated. The loss was minimal. As for the sequel, she had caused no harm at all, because there was a duplicate at his house in Fulham, secure in a fireproof safe.

He decided, on his return to the lounge, that he could afford to be fairly smug himself. He even took the time to make a cup of coffee before joining her, sitting opposite in the armchair beside the TV.

'You look pleased with yourself,' she observed wryly. 'Can't imagine why.'

He blew on his coffee. 'Because, madam, you're not as clever as you think. I take it you've stolen my work and destroyed it.'

She nodded.

'I suppose I can't complain. I'd be a hypocrite if I did.'

She nodded.

'But don't you think you've done a stupid thing?'

She shook her head.

'You're in danger as well,' he said with a cruel smirk. The gloves were off. He could quit kowtowing.

She shook her head.

Tom felt his brave front begin to crumble. 'No?'

'No.'

Tom put his coffee on the carpet. 'We're in the same boat,'

he said, hearing his tone of voice appealing for her agreement.

A twisted smile cracked her face. 'No, Tom. Not at all. In fact,
I don't think anybody's ever been in the same boat as you're in
at this precise moment.'

'Someone wants to kill me, Angie. It's bad, but it's hardly a
world first.'

'Oh, I beg to differ. You don't know *who* wants to kill you.'

With mock bravado, Tom said, 'And I suppose you do.'

Angie moved off the settee and took Tom's coffee for herself,
then settled comfortably again. 'I might as well have this. I've
got a few things to tell you, and you're going to have difficulty
swallowing once you've heard them.'

Tom gulped and found the problem was already with him.

'The spirit of my dead brother is acting out the violent scenes
from his novel in the physical guise of his fictional creation,
Milton the Biker.'

Angie let her claim hang in the air for a minute. She sipped at
Tom's coffee as he stared at her. His initial fear of what she might
say evaporated from his heart as gradually as the incredulous smile
bloomed on his face.

'That's right,' he finally humoured. 'And the tooth fairy shot
JFK.'

'Hmm. I knew how you'd react, so I thought I'd say that
first, so you can get your scoffing out of the way before I list
the facts.'

Tom began to chuckle. 'Facts? Oh, well, whatever you say,
fruitcake.'

'You think I'm lying. That's okay.'

'Well, you've lied already, haven't you? You got me here under
false pretences. Whoever this killer really is, you're obviously
not in any danger from him or you wouldn't have destroyed
my work.'

Angie smiled at his naivety. 'I think I gave you enough hints
that I wasn't exactly being straight with you.'

'Oh? How d'you figure that?'

'Ulterior motives, Tom. I told you right from the start I had
ulterior motives for you being here.'

'Yes; so?' Tom said defensively, feeling miffed that he was

evidently still missing the point. 'You told me what they were. You wanted me to write a third book.'

Angie curled her legs underneath her. 'Oh, Tom. Poor Tom. How can you have no morals yourself but expect them from other people?'

Tom tried to prevent the stupidity he felt from showing on his face.

With infuriating serenity, Angie sipped at her drink. 'And how can a writer with a supposedly good grasp of the English language not know what ulterior motives are? Ulterior motives are motives people don't reveal to anyone. So when I said I had some, why would you then believe I'd tell you what they were?' She shrugged at the simplicity of it all. 'I was lying, Tom. I lied.'

Something inside Tom was shrivelling up as she spoke. Hope, perhaps. Angie had stolen more than his work, she had taken his last chance to redeem himself. He had wanted to think he was saving her life, that he was making sacrifices for someone else, for a change. Of course, he was saving himself in the process, but he had genuinely believed there was also a higher purpose involved.

A cold wind blew outside, shaking the window panes, rattling the ivy across the front of the cottage, bellowing in the trees like distant thunder.

'Okay, so you lied,' he said. 'But what's all this bollocks about your brother? You think it's going to scare me? It's farcical.'

'I agree. I didn't believe it myself for a while.'

Tom eased his discomfiture by barking a laugh. 'Angie, come on, stop it. Why don't I pack my bag and leave? You've had your revenge. You've had me writing day and night for two weeks, all to no avail. I'm shagged out. I've lost weight. I look like shit. My head's a mess. I don't even know what day of the week it is. Well done. Look at me; I'm pissed off. All right? Can we call it a day now?'

Calmly, Angie continued her tack. 'That's what I'm telling you, Tom. It's not up to me to call it a day. It's up to Andrew. There can be only one logical conclusion to what you've done, and, by burning your work, I've brought it closer.'

Tom held his hands up and gave a facetious grin. 'Well, must be going. I do have other patients to see.' He stood up and headed out of the room.

'He'll get you, wherever you go.'

Tom rounded on her viciously. *'Listen! I've had enough!'* he screamed, and punched the door. He instantly quietened. 'I'm going home,' he said softly, and trekked upstairs to pack.

Angie was standing at the foot of the stairs when he descended. She looked spent; not as though the bombshell she had intended to drop had missed, but as though she was truly sorry she had been forced to drop it in the first place. She backed away and leaned against the wall. The hallway was dark, but she had switched on the porch lantern, and its glow reached through the pane in the front door to gently illuminate her face.

Tom said, 'I'm sorry I shouted.'

'Doesn't matter.'

He sat down on the stairs. 'This might sound strange, Angie, but I'm going to miss you.'

She did not return the sentiment. She eased down the wall and sat hugging her knees to her chest, her back against a tepid radiator.

'I understand your resentment towards me, Angie. I've done some awful things and I'm afraid you've been caught up in them. I'm sorry.'

'I know you are.'

Tom thought it was the sweetest thing he had ever heard.

'And you've got me all wrong,' Angie said. 'I admit, at first I was dying to tell you what I knew, but when I started to say it I realised . . . there's no enjoyment in any of this. The whole thing's a nightmare and I just want it to end.'

'So how does this . . . stuff about your brother help matters?'

'Please believe me, Tom. I'm not crazy and I'm not trying to scare you.'

Tom decided to stay silent; she deserved to have her say, however outlandish her words might be. He owed her that much.

She met his eyes with a sad smile. 'If I'd wanted to scare you, I'd have let you go back home not knowing whether I was going to tell the police about the fingerprints you left behind when you broke in. Anyway, I happen to think you're scared enough already. Some madman has threatened to kill you, and you know he's not bluffing. How could I beat that? By telling you a ghost story? I wouldn't waste my breath. If I wanted to hurt you, you'd already

272

be in prison, with your life and your career in ruins. If you think about it, you must know that. So if I haven't done it, and I didn't bring you here to write a third novel, you should appreciate there's more to this than meets the eye.'

'Your ulterior motive,' Tom said.

Angie nodded.

'So?' Tom asked.

'Wait,' she said, then climbed to her feet, edged past him and went upstairs.

Tom listened to the wind batter the porch door. A few moments later she trotted back down. She stood before him clutching a copy of *Man on a Murder Cycle*. There was a baseball cap over her short blonde hair. Even in the dim light, Tom could make out the red *ZZ-R* stitched into the black cotton.

She handed him the book. 'Open it.'

He did. Inside, there was a livid Biro hole where his name should have been. Beneath the title was the comment, *Like it*, and an inscription: *Angel, Making it right . . . Milton.*

The confusion in his eyes pleaded for answers.

Angie obliged. She sat down in front of him and told him everything. She hopped from one incident to another, in chronological disorder.

She explained how the book had been left for her on the doorstep; how the handwriting was identical to Andrew's and she could prove it; how Angel had been his secret name for her in childhood; how Milton had known to phone her at Carol Morgan's, when he had first used that special name; how she had come by the baseball cap she was now wearing, and how she had been mysteriously returned to her home on the night in question; how no one else could have known to commit the back to front hat murder during the bank raid; how Andrew's body at the undertaker's had apparently tipped itself onto the floor and ripped its eyes and mouth wide open; how subsequent events had led to Stapely's death and the theft of the hearse; how the location of its final burnt-out resting place happened to be right behind a motorcycle showroom from which specific items had been stolen, namely a turbocharged ZZ-R, a set of black leathers and a black helmet; how Andrew's body had disappeared and had never been recovered; how she first had a premonition of Andrew's death whilst standing alone on Alderley Edge; and, perhaps most chillingly, how the scars on the killer's face in the bank video exactly replicated the scars she had witnessed on Andrew's face at the undertaker's.

Tom's silence continued, but this time it was not self-imposed; her words had beaten him into submission. He actually had a great deal he wanted to say, but none of it could prevent him from arriving at one catastrophic conclusion: Angie was not lying to him; not about this. Although he had never been prone to gobbling up the whacko fantasies which seemed increasingly to abound as the Second Millennium loomed, there had to be a point when even the most logical of minds could be classed as insane if it stubbornly dismissed the paranormal when faced with overwhelming proof of its existence.

He unzipped his holdall and dug a hand inside. He produced his own copy of *Man on a Murder Cycle* and offered it to Angie. She reached out and took it, opened it and carefully leafed through, but Tom very soon understood that she was not going to see anything more – or less – than page after page of black print.

'What am I meant to be looking for?' she asked, flicking on.

'Never mind. You won't find it.'

She looked up. 'What?'

'I mean, why search for something that's right there in front of you?'

'Tom?'

'*I* can't find it because it's *not* there. *You* can't find what I can't find because, to you, it *is* there.'

'Pardon?'

'It's all right, I'm rambling. I'm also making perfect sense.' He gave a brief, self-deprecating chortle. 'Welcome to the madcap world of Tom Roker.'

Angie returned the book, which Tom opened up midway through, then leafed several pages ahead before turning his chosen pages to face her.

'Can you read that?' he asked.

'Course,' she answered with an amused frown.

He spread the book on his lap and stared at it. After a moment he announced with some levity, 'Well, I bloody well can't.'

'What are you talking about?'

'To my eyes, these are blank white pages without a single word on them.'

'Don't be daft.'

Tom closed the book. 'All the violent episodes have disappeared, except the final one, of course, because that hasn't happened yet. Each time Milton acts out a murder as written, the words just peel off the page.'

'Come off it, Tom.'

Tom gave a crooked smile. 'You surprise me, Angie. Are you really saying that you can believe everything you've just told me, but you can't believe this?'

Angie considered, and had to accept his reasoning. 'Point taken. So what do you think? Andrew's letting you know that you're directly linked to the things he does as Milton? That it's all your fault?'

Tom shrugged. 'Something like that.'

'But what about Carol Morgan? She's as guilty as you are. Is she having the same problems?'

'Don't know. I haven't told her my troubles, and I assume she'd have called me if she was missing great chunks out of her books.'

'Books plural? How many copies have you got?'

'Personal copies? Twelve. And they're all the same.'

'That was my next question.'

'I know.'

'Okay . . . have you actually seen the text disappearing?'

'No. I haven't been watching the pages, waiting. But if I had been keeping a vigil, I expect I'd have seen the words just vanish one by one, line by line.'

A silence descended and the conversation died.

After a while, Tom sneaked a sly peek at Angie. She was all securely bunched up: knees folded tightly to her chest, arms cradling them. Her head was downturned now, her face completely covered by the peak of her cap. She could have been staring at the carpet, but he guessed her eyes were closed. He no longer regarded her sexually. He was glad of that. Finally, the weight of his remorse had squashed his libido.

Instead, he felt desperately protective towards her. She had no one, and he had caused the death of her only brother to be a thousand times more distressing than it needed to be. Through his selfish actions, he had protracted her grief and warped her mourning. Perhaps, because of him, she *couldn't* mourn. Because

275

of him, her brother was not at peace, and until he was, he suspected her mourning process could not even begin.

Tom tried to derail his morbid train of thought by listening to the gale outside. Sheets of rain had started to thrash at the windows.

'It's a nice sound,' Angie said suddenly, speaking into her jeans in a muffled voice. 'Rain on glass.'

'It is. As long as you're inside looking out.'

She raised her head. 'I hadn't thought of that.'

Tom realised he had just wrecked her pleasant little moment. He had taken it and instantly thrown it back at her all mangled up. Typical.

'Angie, what did you mean when you said there was only one logical conclusion to what I'd done, and that you'd brought it closer?'

'I mean until Milton is revenged upon you personally, Andrew's soul can never be at peace. And although I'm not eager to see anyone else die . . .' She bowed her head again, hiding her face. 'Well, I wouldn't shed any tears over your death if that's what it took to bring it to an end.'

Tom had difficulty catching his breath. 'I see.'

'Sorry.'

'No, don't be. I understand.'

She lifted her face. 'I hope you do.'

'But I'm sorry, Angie, I'm not in my grave just yet, and I'm afraid I don't intend to surrender myself to that sick fuck out there – no disrespect to your brother – so that he can put me in it.'

'Not much of the martyr in you, is there, Tom?'

Without apology, Tom said, 'It's human nature. I don't want to die.'

Angie got to her feet and looked coldly down on him. 'Well, that's tough, because there's only one more scene to go, then Milton's going to come for you, and there's nothing to keep him away now I've destroyed your work. Even if you get writing this very second, you won't earn yourself more than a day or two. He can kill faster than you can write. Why are you smiling?'

'I told you earlier, Angie: you're not as clever as you think. All you've done is screw up two weeks' work.' His smile widened into a mischievous grin. 'You see, I have a copy of the sequel in my safe at home.'

Angie shook her head. 'No, you don't.'

'Yes, I do.'

'You don't.'

'I do.'

'You did.'

'I . . . pardon?'

'It *was* there, now it's not.'

Tom felt distinctly light-headed. 'What?'

She slipped a hand into her back pocket. 'You might want these if you're going home.' She tossed something to him which jangled lightly in the air.

He examined what he caught. 'My keys,' he said like an imbecile.

'You've got a nice place in Fulham.'

Tom was aware his features had gone slack, but he couldn't pull himself together. 'You . . . drove all the way to London last night?'

'And back again. It's not so bad at night,' she said, chattily. 'Not so much traffic.'

'How d'you know where I live?'

'Driving licence in your wallet.'

'And you found my safe?' Tom asked in a tiny voice.

'Found it, opened it, emptied it, as Edmund Blackadder might say.'

Tom put his hands to his face. 'Fuck,' he said defeatedly through his splayed fingers, and dug his nails into his brow. 'You bitch.'

He sat on those stairs for thirty minutes, frozen by the immensity of his situation. Angie left him to it, and drove into the nearby town to do some shopping.

The barrage of foul weather outside seemed like a bad omen, a portent of doom straight from a cheap horror flick. All that was missing was the occasional fork of lightning and crack of thunder.

Tom felt he was close to losing it. Milton could at that moment have been shuffling a few skinheads off their mortal coils, a prelude to Tom's own demise, and Tom was doing nothing to delay it. He was just sitting there, uselessly twiddling his thumbs, sobbing silent tears which rolled down his cheeks to dampen his thighs.

He missed his ex-wife and daughter more painfully in that half-hour than ever before. Maybe it was the prospect of never seeing them again. He could not understand why he had wasted all those years. Why had he never followed up on his plans to visit? Time was so precious. He knew that now he had none left.

Suddenly, he powered to his feet. 'No! I'm still alive and I'm going to stay that way!' He *was* going to hug his Charlotte again. He would put his illegitimately earned money to good use and fly to see her every few months, and if his funds were dwindling he would make a final trip from which he would not return. He would rent a room close by, live hand-to-mouth if necessary, working for cash in crappy jobs to cheat US Immigration.

Whether any of this would actually come to pass was a moot point. It gave him the boot up the arse he needed, the incentive to plough ahead, in spite of the odds. He picked up his holdall and hurried back up the stairs.

In Andrew Kellett's room, he slung his coat on the bed, pulled his pad and pen from his bag and sat down at the desk. If Angie came home and complained about his continued presence, well . . . fuck her. He could not afford to squander four hours travelling down to London. Anyway, he doubted she would involve the police; the last thing she wanted was him safely locked away.

In a pool of light from the Anglepoise, Tom touched the point of his Biro to the paper and waited for the inspiration to flow. It had been on tap for him for two weeks, and he had a book-and-a-third to plunder for ideas.

Now that he knew who Milton was, he guessed there would be no break in the killing. Milton would not wait for any sequel to go to publication. Probably he would not have to read it in print at all; he would simply tune in psychically to whatever Tom had written, and act on it whenever he saw fit.

But however nightmarish that scenario seemed, in this war Tom still considered it to be a joyous piece of intelligence, because it meant that provided he kept one step ahead – or one violent scene ahead – Milton would not get to him, and, at that precise moment, Tom did have that one priceless scene in hand.

He retrieved *Man on a Murder Cycle* from his bag and set it open on the desk at the final relevant section.

But even as he smoothed the palm of his hand across the pages to keep them flat, the words began to disappear.

FORTY-SEVEN

They were new to the area. A hardcore National Front cell sent to leaflet and canvas, beat and maim. A nomadic posse with a rusty old minibus, who were currently installed in a rented rundown terraced property two miles from Manchester University's halls of residence.

It had been decreed by their Council of War that racial attacks in that particular zone had fallen to an unacceptably low level, and it had to be rectified.

The Filth, as yet, had not cottoned on to their tenancy. Ordinarily, premature detection by the authorities was something of an inconvenience. Tonight, an infinitely more disabling spanner would be dropping into their works, and they would come to understand that a cautionary word from PC Plod was sometimes in their best interests.

For now, though, they were happy, amusing themselves with another of their regular, though more passive, pastimes.

They had chosen an Indian takeaway at random from *Yellow Pages*, phoned in an order that would feed an army, given a false name and number, and then laughed themselves stupid, which meant a welcome boost to their collective IQ.

It was hysterical to imagine a bunch of thicko wogs charging around a stifling kitchen at their behest, cooking up a huge order that would never be picked up, and would eventually be chucked in the bin, which, of course, was where foreign shit deserved to end up.

It didn't dawn on them that a telephone number was requested so that suspiciously large orders could be verified. It didn't cross their minds that whilst they were cackling their heads off, a return call was being made to the number they had just given on the pretext of checking the order, and that if the number was unobtainable or false, not a single onion bhaji would be brought out from the fridge. And lately, with the option of call-tracing, it had become an even easier task to sift out any bogus customers, with the added bonus of being able to relate the joker's real number to the police if one in particular persisted in trying it on.

Still, if you didn't know all that, you could think it was a fucking good laugh, and among the multitude of things they didn't know, they didn't know that.

They also didn't know that a homicidal maniac was presently three streets away.

Milton had deferred to common sense. He revelled in his noise-pollution, but, sadly, a rorty race exhaust had to come second to the requirements of stealth.

He cruised slowly along the street on his ZZ-R, his road-legal end-can emitting a disappointingly respectable growl.

It was six o'clock. Dinner time.

His headlight bore into the darkness, illuminating thousands of slanting silver needles. The rain was icy, the wind a nuisance for a man on two wheels, but he was whistling inside his helmet; it was fun at night with the black visor, a real challenge.

He turned one corner, rode on between the parked vehicles, turned another and pulled into the kerb behind a white Bedford minibus with a cross of St George on the bumper. He parked and dismounted. Rain was dribbling like tears down his visor. He wiped it with the palm of a gloved hand.

'Nice,' he said, surveying the drab building. Its paint was peeling, and the brickwork needed pointing. A couple of windows were cracked right across. The front garden, such as it was, consisted of a few broken paving stones, between which foot-high weeds had been allowed to flourish.

He approached up the short path to the solid-wood door. To his left, he could see in through a bay window. It was draped on the inside only by ancient and ripped lace nets. Four baldy youths were deposited about the floor. The room was unlit but for the brightly flickering electric blue of a television set. Milton raised his visor. On the TV itself, he could see somewhat more explicit porn than *Electric Blue*. He peeked in for a while, and listened to the muted sound of overblown moans, unrealistic dialogue, and a meanderingly tuneless seventies soundtrack, all overlaid by the Neanderthal grunts and howls of the male viewers.

Which was all well and good, but he didn't want to be accused of a tardy delivery. So he rang the bell, provoking an uncouth exchange in the front room.

'Shit. Freeze it, will you, Kev?'

'No.'

'Fucking freeze it!'

'Fucking hurry up then!'

The TV fell silent. A moment later, someone tramped down the hallway – Doc Martens on bare floorboards – but the door stayed shut. Good security. Can't be too careful when you're as vilified as an outbreak of rabies.

'What?' said the testy yob.

Milton was at his most agreeable. 'Having a party, eh?' he almost sang.

'Who is it?'

'I've got your food.'

'Food?'

'The stuff you eat.'

'Didn't order any.'

The television burst into unscheduled life.

'*Freeze it!*'

Kev did.

'I love parties,' said Milton.

'Piss off.'

'No can do!' Milton called cheerily. 'You ordered, you gotta pay the price!'

'We didn't order any fucking food.'

'Twenty poppadoms, mango chutney, onion, lime pickle, and yoghurt dips, six vegetable samosa, six meat samosa, six chicken tikka starters—'

'Wrong house, wanker. We don't eat foreign shit in here. Now fuck off!'

Milton heard the skinhead's steps retreat down the hall, followed by the resumption of the porno flick. He bent down and shouted through the letter box.

'*Two chicken dopiaza, one chicken jalfrezi, one lamb dansak, two mixed bhuna . . .*'

Inside, the video was put on hold again.

'*One prawn vindaloo, one beef madras, one beef korma, one vegetable rogan josh . . .*'

Milton could hear threats of death mumbling towards him with heavy bootfalls.

'*Ten pilau rice, a side order of aloo gobi, two of tarka dhal . . .*'

The door was being unlocked from top to bottom; bolt, chain, key, bolt.

'*One bombay duck, three garlic nan, four plain nan . . .*'

The letter-box was pulled away from him, and the unshaded hall lightbulb sent the skinhead's shadow hurtling outside, only to be swallowed up by the figure in black leather who was now standing tall.

'*And a* – oh, there you are . . . and a partridge in a pear tree.'

'Listen, cunt, fucking do one!' snarled the skinhead, a wiry individual in jeans, white T-shirt and braces. His arms were covered in jingoistic tattoos. One hand was balled into a fist, the other was white-knuckling a Stanley knife.

Milton flipped his visor down and helmet-butted him on the nose, splitting it straight down the bone which snapped and flattened. The skinhead squealed and dropped his weapon, staggering backwards to collapse on the stairs. There was a commotion in the front room, but Milton maintained his composure, unclipping and removing his helmet.

The scarred, skunk-like apparition in the hallway stopped the rest of the Master Race in their tracks. They saw their fallen compatriot and made appropriately indignant noises, but none was eager to step in and help.

Milton flashed them a septic smile, then windmilled his helmet and smashed it down against the shaved and semi-conscious skull resting on the fifth stair up, causing a fatal fracture.

The other three, screaming in frightened fury, charged at the intruder.

Milton squatted, set his helmet on the threadbare carpet and picked up the Stanley knife. As six fists rained down on him, he stayed on his haunches and whipped the small blade repeatedly back and forth at groin level.

It was a few seconds before the skinheads realised that all was not well with their nether regions. What was that warm stuff drenching their legs?

One of them whimpered and recoiled, deserting his mates. He

gawped wide-eyed at the shredded, blood-soaked denim at his crotch. '*Fucking hell!*' he wailed, cupping his slashed genitalia in his hands and fleeing onto the street and into the night.

Milton kept slicing like a master-chef until the other two ceased their ineffectual punches and retreated out of arm's reach. They reacted much the same as the first man, caterwauling and trying to hold together whatever bits and pieces they had left in their pants.

But these two were going nowhere. Milton stalked them into the front room, then into the corner where the TV was still on pause.

'Kneel,' he ordered, and they did.

The place was a sty. Empty beer cans, chip trays, crisp packets, cake wrappers, cigarette ends.

'I want an ambulance . . . *please*,' whined the bloodiest of the two, cowering and shaking.

'Hmm,' Milton mused. 'Well, you'll hardly create that special atmosphere if you don't tidy up a bit.'

'*What?*' the skinhead sobbed.

'Even with subtle lighting, comfy chairs and a nice Yucca, there's no guarantee.'

'*Please.*'

'You see, true ambience is an almost magical qual—'

'*Ambulance!*' shrieked the skinhead. '*Fucking ambulance!*'

Milton slapped his forehead with the heel of his empty palm. 'Oh, *ambulance*. No, sorry. You might live if I call an ambulance.'

Just then, the video-pause expired and the tape ran on. Some actress-singer-model-dancer continued deep-throating some athletic stud.

'Bet you'd like to be him, wouldn't you?' Milton asked salaciously.

The petrified skinhead began screaming lustily.

'Wouldn't you?' Milton repeated.

The skinhead was mesmerised by the way his blue jeans had completely changed colour.

'*Wouldn't you?*'

'*Yes!*' the skinhead bawled.

So Milton clawed a hand round the back of his head and rammed his face through the television screen, pressing his neck onto the lower shards.

'There we go!' Milton said with elation. 'Now you're actually in a porno film.'

The TV sparked and hissed and crackled. The skinhead stopped crying. He went limp, then seemed to deflate on his knees with his head still in the set.

Milton's remaining captive appeared to be in shock. He was rocking like a metronome, and humming in a monotone. Blood was pooling between his legs.

Milton tapped him on the head. 'And how's Adolf?'

'Go fuck yourself.'

'Oh, you are still with me. Good.'

'You're fucking dead, you cunt.'

Milton raised his hairless eyebrows. 'Is it that obvious? I'm not starting to smell, am I?'

'You think you're mean? Wait around. We've got six mates down the chippy. See how you cope with them.'

'No,' Milton politely declined. 'I would, but I only wanted the four of you. Ten would be exceeding my quota for the evening.'

'Shit, you're fucking mad.' He started to moan, inspecting his dripping hands like Lady Macbeth. 'Oh, Christ . . . what have you done to me?'

'Well, I've had a pretty good stab at castrating you.'

'*Fucker!*'

'Oh, I see. That was rhetorical.'

The skinhead stared at his friend who was now seriously into television. 'Kev,' he lamented.

'I know. What a tragic waste of a talented life. He might have been a future ambassador to the West Indies.'

The skinhead fixed Milton with venomous eyes. 'You cunt.'

'Yeah, yeah, we've done that bit.'

For the first time in his life – and the last, as it would transpire – the skinhead was overjoyed to hear the sound of distant sirens. He even managed a tiny wincing smile.

'That's it. Chin up,' said Milton.

'Fuck . . . off.'

Milton's dark eyes narrowed and his unlovely features became severe. 'No, I mean lift your chin up.' He edged the tip of the blade closer to the skinhead's right eye until he obeyed and tilted his head backwards.

'Ah, there it is,' Milton said, looking at the skinhead's throat.

A line of blue dashes encircled his neck, with the invitation to *CUT HERE* etched just to the left of his Adam's apple.

Milton drew his arm back, preparing the Stanley knife for its final bloodletting. 'Now that is what I call a risky tattoo . . .'

FORTY-EIGHT

If there had been any lingering doubts in Tom's mind as to the truth of Angie's earlier claims, this would have quashed them. To have seen the text just vanish like that confirmed it: this was no case of selective blindness. With his pulse racing and his brain swimming, he had effectively watched Milton commit his last scripted murders. And Tom might as well have been there at the crime scene, for he had not been able to stop himself from picturing every detail.

When the chapter ended, his focus came to rest at the spot where the last word had disappeared from the page. In the Epilogue, Milton now sped off into the night pursued by the police. The reader could safely assume they never caught up with him.

Tom cursed Andrew Kellett for leaving the ending so open. What was wrong with surrounding Milton with police marksmen and then perforating him? It was highly irresponsible to suggest that such gross evil could triumph in the world.

'Look who's talking,' Tom said to himself.

He tore his eyes away from the novel and angrily knocked it off the desk. His pen was still poised on a pristine sheet of A4. He needed just one sentence to begin his first chapter. Just one. Then a second would follow on, then a third and a fourth, and that was how it happened.

Just one sentence. Just one.

Words buzzed through his head, but fell short of forming a coherent sentence. He jumbled them around, added some, swapped a few, started to write, then crossed it out. This was no time to be pedantic, but each set of words he tried just trailed off into garbage.

'Come on . . . don't.'

He was talking to that ton weight in his mind, the one he had struggled to lift so many times in the past. The one that would stay suspended if inspiration were immediately available, but after fifteen non-productive minutes would drop and flatten the merest possibility of any developing. And frustration was the blade which severed the rope and made it plummet. This time it was worse. Simple frustration was the least of his worries; dying horribly at the hands of a Psycho From Hell was a more pressing concern, and it had vastly accelerated the normal process.

Five minutes later, after many words scribbled and all of them deleted, the block came down.

A news flash interrupted the back-to-back playlist promised by the DJ. Angie turned up the volume to drown out the pounding rain and the whack-whack of her wipers.

The report, though sketchy, contained all the pertinent information. There had been an incident involving a group of skinheads. Enough said; any fan of Tom Roker's could have filled in the details.

Angie switched the radio off after that. She needed silence to clarify her feelings. In spite of all the hurt Tom had caused, to her and to many others, she felt winded to know he was soon going to be dead himself. Of course, there were thousands of people on the planet at that very moment who would not live to see another dawn, but this was different. Most of them would not see the Grim Reaper coming, and those who did were to some extent prepared for him. When bullets flew, the soldier accepted that one of them might have his name on it; when food ran out, the famined masses could feel their strength ebbing away; when the patient received his terminal prognosis, he at least had time to say goodbye; when the capital offender was finally hooked up to the lethal IV, he had spent years on Death Row attuning himself to his fate. And for all of these people, right up to the very brink of the abyss, there was always hope: a peace accord, humanitarian aid, remission, a stay of execution.

Not for Tom. He was a dead man. A perfectly healthy human being with a life-expectancy measurable in hours. It was a mind-boggling thought.

She wondered if Milton would allow Tom to reach London before striking, or whether he would stage a spectacular and derail the train to get to him as quickly as possible. She did not relish either thought.

Tom Roker was a sad character; a tragic figure of Shakespearean proportions. In his search for glory he had unwittingly engineered his own undoing. She had told him she would not shed any tears over his demise, and that was true, but neither would she take any pleasure in it. She only wanted her brother's spirit released, to be at peace with his late wife and daughter.

She arrived home two minutes later and parked the Mini half on the boggy verge. She lugged her carrier bags up to the front door and let herself in. She immediately sensed she had company. There were no tell-tale sounds, but some instinct told her she was not alone.

'Tom?' she called up the stairs.

'Hiya, babe!' came the strangely upbeat reply.

Bemused, she dumped the shopping and climbed the stairs.

In the back bedroom, Tom was slouched in the director's chair. His eyes were vacant and glassy. His grin was inane and quite out of place. Or it would have been had there not been an empty bottle of Bailey's on the desk.

'Good evening, gorgeous,' he slurred at her.

'Why are you still here?'

'I've been writing, my Angel.'

'Don't call me that.'

'My sincere *apperlowgies*. I am here because I have been plying my trade.' He pointed to a page of A4. It was filled with furious obliterations. 'Bear in mind, that this is only the first draft.' He barked a laugh then handed her another sheet. 'I am, however, immensely proud of *this*.' On it was a complex and seriously disturbed collection of doodles. On a much larger scale, it would probably have won the Turner Prize for Art. 'Unfortunately I have written it in an alien alphabet for which I possess no exact translation. But I am able to tell you the gist of it, and that is: yours truly, Tom Roker, is fucked.'

Angie wiped some rain from her face and leaned back against the wall. She shook her head sorrowfully. 'You heard about the skinheads.'

He closed his eyes. 'Sort of. Sorry I drank your drink.'

'Forget it.'

'I'm . . .' his head lolled forward '. . . sorry.' With his chin on his chest, he instantly fell into a sodden doze.

Angie stared at him, and could feel the final unwritten chapter drawing to its natural conclusion. Out there, somewhere, Milton was tearing through the dark towards them. But she felt no compulsion to remove Tom from the premises; her own life was not at risk, she felt sure of that. On the night she had taken a tumble from her mountain bike, she believed that Milton – or the part of him that was Andrew – had actually saved her.

She watched Tom for five minutes, then crept out of the room. There was no point in waking him. What limited time he had left was best spent in blissful ignorance. He was out of it now, self-sedated in preparation for his imminent execution.

Downstairs, she unpacked her purchases then sat silently in the lounge with a coffee.

It was not long before the unexpected happened: creaking floorboards above her, then a decidedly careful descent of the stairs. Tom appeared in the doorway. His fringe and the hair at his temples were damp, his eyes were brightly bloodshot.

'I've just made myself ill,' he said. 'I need to think straight. Can I get myself a coffee?'

'Here, have mine,' she offered.

'Thanks.'

He accepted the mug, then shocked Angie by sitting next to her on the settee. Perhaps he craved a moment of togetherness with someone. She twisted to face him as he took a big gulp of caffeine.

'Why do you want to think straight, Tom? I'd have thought that was the last thing you wanted.'

He looked amazed. '*What?* Angie, if I can't write, I have to figure out some other solution.'

'Why don't you take another couple of sleeping pills? Sleep until the time comes. Make it easy on yourself.'

'What are you talking about, woman? Milton's going to kill me.'

'Yes, he is. And there's no solution to that.'

'You're wrong,' he said adamantly. 'I'll . . . you're wrong.'

She bowed to his naive optimism. 'Well, I'll say this much for you, Tom: you're no quitter.'

'I know.' He summoned a faint smile, tinged with irony. 'If only I had been . . .'

Both of them spent the following hours clock-watching; Angie downstairs, whilst she finished another trashy novel, and Tom in his den upstairs, whilst he tried in vain to start one. Two sets of ears were on red alert, listening into the howling, pouring night for the sound of an approaching motorcycle.

Tom's block worsened as the evening progressed and a sickly hangover set in. His emptied-out stomach griped and his head felt stuffed with humming cotton wool. He cursed his idiocy for resorting to booze.

As the minutes ticked by, he felt himself sinking deeper into the blackness and further from the light. He doodled aimlessly until a fresh sheet of A4 was covered, then he doodled on the doodles until there was not a trace of white paper beneath.

As midnight drew nearer, Tom's foreboding enlarged like a tumour on his soul, engulfing his pitiful remnants of hope. He suspected that with Milton's evident sense of the dramatic, he would choose midnight as a fitting moment to unleash the wrath he had specially reserved for the person who had caused him to haunt this corporeal dimension.

With fifteen minutes to go, Tom experienced the mythical calm before the storm. A trance-like tranquillity swept through him. He suddenly forgave all the people who had ever wronged him, and sought God's forgiveness for the numerous ills he had brought upon others.

After muttering a self-indulgent farewell to Charlotte and his ex-wife Helen, he decided to try to go out on a moral high note. With movements that felt floaty and detached from the physical, he made his way into Angie's bedroom. He settled softly on her bed, picked up the phone and punched a familiar sequence on the button pad.

'Hello,' Peter Morgan said into the receiver.

'Hi, it's Tom, is—?'

'Peter, put the phone down,' Carol said brusquely, having picked up the extension.

Tom politely waited for the click before resuming, but Carol beat him to it.

'Tom, I tried to call you. We've done the deal with Pyramid. You won't believe what we got.'

'Uh-huh. Carol, listen, we're in big trou—'

'Guess what we got.'

'Carol—'

'Guess.'

'Just tell me.'

'Guess.'

'Twelve pounds fifty.'

'Four million.'

'Yeah, course we did.'

'Seriously. Four million pounds. Pyramid had a lot of competition so they upped their offer.'

Tom was more intrigued than interested. 'Four million for one book? That's bloody silly-money.'

There was a brief pause, then she said defiantly, 'It's not for one book, Tom. It's a two-book deal. And they've bought exclusive rights to the Milton character.'

Tom sighed. 'They can't have the sequel, Carol. I told you.'

'Yeah, I know what you said, but—'

'That's not the reason. They couldn't have it even if I wanted them to. I had two copies and they're both gone. They've been destroyed.'

There was a lengthy silence.

Tom broke it by saying, 'Believe me, Carol, this inconveniences me far more than it does you.'

'Tom . . . what if there was another copy?'

'There isn't.'

'What if there was?'

'There isn't, so the question is irrelevant. And, anyway, we have a far bigger problem to worry about. I called because—'

'I photocopied the manuscript,' Carol cut in loudly.

'Pardon?'

'Before I gave it back to you. It's safe.'

There was no reason for her to lie, and he was quite able to believe in such underhand tactics; he would have done the same himself in her position.

His understatement surprised even him: 'I'm not best pleased with you, Carol.' But what surprised him even more was that he sincerely meant it. Though a surviving sequel would ensure his own survival, at least temporarily, he nevertheless took it as terrible news. It even overshadowed the dread he had felt building up inside him throughout that evening, prior to his strange internal blossoming of peace.

Perhaps he did possess a soul, after all.

He stood up from the bed. It made him feel more authoritative. 'Carol, if you let Pyramid Pictures have my manuscript, I will go straight to the police and give them chapter and verse on our sordid little secret.'

She sent him a snort of derision. 'No, Tom, you wouldn't do that. You forget: I know you. You're selfish. You don't know the meaning of self-sacrifice.'

'I'm learning fast.'

'You're bluffing. You've got too much to lose.'

He scrunched the telephone flex in his fist. 'I've got *nothing* to lose.'

'Wealth, reputation, liberty—'

'*Nothing*.'

She laughed at him. 'Go on, then, I'm listening. Explain this Road-to-Damascus transformation. This'll be your best yarn yet.'

Tom lightened up. 'All right, Carol. For purposes of what I'm about to tell you, it's probably useful if you do assume I've moved into the Fantasy genre. As long as you hear me out, I don't mind what you think.'

'Once upon a time . . .' Carol prompted sarcastically.

So Tom took his cue and proceeded to tell her everything he had learned from Angie about the true identity of the man who called himself Milton. Carol interrupted his opening gambit several times with withering sneers, but soon settled into what Tom hoped was rapt attention. He would only know after he had finished whether she had simply been humouring him with her silence.

'And they all most definitely did not live happily ever after,' Tom eventually wound it up.

Five seconds later, Carol responded, and much to Tom's gratification, her tone was serious and considered.

'So . . . in your copy of *Man on a Murder Cycle*, every violent event has now vanished from the page?'

'Yes.'

'My God,' she whispered.

'I know.'

'And you think I'd have been next in line for the chop after you?'

'Without the sequel, maybe so.'

'Then it's a damn good job I saved it, isn't it?'

Tom shook his head; he felt ill and exhausted. 'No, Carol. The sequel might save us, but it condemns thirty or forty other people to die, and die horribly.'

'Hmmm. Still, that's not my fault.'

'Carol, you have got to destroy the manuscript. We have to save these people. They can't pay for *our* sins with *their* lives.'

She tutted thoughtfully and drew a deep breath. 'All right, Tom. I'll get the manuscript now and I'll burn it.'

'It is the right thing to do,' he said. 'You're a good woman, Carol Morgan.'

There was another beat of five seconds before Carol exploded with laughter, real gut-wrenching, bellyaching gales of amusement.

Tom nearly smiled, at her perfect deceit and his own gullibility. He did not shout her down; he guessed he should have expected as much. He had believed Angie, but why should Carol believe him? There was clearly a chasmal difference between the credentials of the two story tellers. Angie was a bereaved innocent who had concrete evidence to exhibit and no discernible reason to lie, and he was a proven world-class cad and bounder who could offer nothing more than a worthless assurance of his honesty and who had been suffering career delusions for years.

Glumly, he said, 'Yes, I can imagine how all that sounds. But the fact still remains, if you hand over the sequel I will bring the roof down on us both.'

'The problem with having a dishonest reputation,' she countered haughtily, 'is that the credibility of everything one says is tainted.'

Tom gave up. He did not wish to be ridiculed by a suicidally ignorant woman he had never really liked. 'Ah, what the hell, Carol, give it to them. But bear in mind, if I am telling the truth, it means you won't live long enough to enjoy the proceeds. Milton's gone through the first novel in a matter of weeks. He'll do the same with the second. He'll be knocking on your door before the money's even wired to your account.'

'As you say: *if* you're telling the truth.' She sniggered. 'But you're not, are you, Tom? You want the sequel back from me so you can take it to another agent, negotiate a ten per cent deal, and cheat me out of my fifty. Well, it won't ha—'

He hung up the phone. What was the point? She would still be in denial when Milton produced the knife to disembowel her.

So Tom had been granted a reprieve, not that he wanted one. But aside from his sudden saintly compassion for Milton's next batch of victims, he was concerned for someone closer to home. How would poor Angie react when she discovered her trip to London had been a waste of petrol, and that her wayward brother would again be ticking off completed visitations from his new itinerary?

Easy. She would have no reaction whatsoever, because he would not be telling her. By the time she learned the facts from the news reports, he would be back in Fulham.

As for Carol, shopping her to the police would achieve nothing. If he believed in the supernatural world, and he did, he also had to believe it did not receive information via normal channels; Milton would not need to see anything in print or on film to be able to home in on his next victims, or to know exactly how they had been scripted to meet their Maker. So what did it matter who got their hands on the sequel? And ratting on his agent for the hell of it seemed very petty under the circumstances. He no longer felt spiteful or vindictive, only weary.

He returned to his room and lay down on the bed. He relaxed as much as he could, then launched an interrogation of his conscience. Now was not the time to be lying to himself. His death had only been delayed, and not by more than a few weeks. For his own peace of mind on that terminal day of reckoning, he had to know now if he was still deluding himself. Had he embraced his fate through simple lack of choice, or through genuine regret at the wickedness of his recent actions? The first would damn him beyond salvation, the second might at least have St Peter scratching his chin in contemplation when Tom arrived snivelling at the Pearly Gates.

Soul-searching, he fell asleep.

FORTY-NINE

———◆———

Carol stood in the dark, staring through her balcony windows. Thunderheads were rolling menacingly across the distant cityscape, their towering edges luminescent with moonlight.

So at least some clouds had silver linings.

Her grip on the tumblerful of gin was just short of breaking strength.

That bloody man. She was surprised she hadn't heard him come a cropper as they spoke; all those lost marbles of his rolling around the floor at his feet. For goodness sake, what was all that crap about Milton? Unfortunately, that only reinforced her assessment: if he was unreliable in one department, why should she believe anything else he said? Like when he had latterly invited her to hand over the sequel to Pyramid with impunity.

But what could she do? She would be sued off the face of the earth if she failed to produce the contracted sequel.

The man was unhinged; of that much she was certain. Not because he wanted her to believe his story, but because she got the feeling he believed it himself. Although she had not been able to check his expression for authenticity, nothing in his timbre denoted a conscious lie, and she knew how difficult that was to achieve. Her encounter with the Kellett woman had demonstrated how uncooperative the voice could be when forced to join in a ridiculous pretence. Her own vocal diffidence that day had grated like fingernails down a blackboard.

The irony was exquisite. Just as Tom finally became the hot property he had threatened to be eight years ago, he was hit smack between the eyes by the Crazy Stick. The animal of genius, host to the parasite of madness; sad but all too common.

Even his madness had a joyful invention to it. Concocting a

horror story around recent real-life events, his diseased imagination seamlessly weaving fact and fiction. Moreover, he was safe in his fantasy because none of it could be disproved. According to him, the main evidence came in the form of strange textual disappearances, but they were only visible – invisible – to him. It was the perfect paranoid delusion.

Carol downed her gin, set her glass on the coffee table and headed for bed. Perhaps it would all be clearer in the morning.

In the bedroom, Peter was still awake, reading a Western novel. He glanced up at her and tried a quarter-smile which turned her on her heels in emotional retreat. She couldn't stand the doe-eyed hurt which shone up in him at bedtime. His nightly attempts at reconciliation made her quietly furious, because he seemed to have no idea how unbridgeable was the gap between them.

She locked herself in her office. Peter would never presume to barge in on her, but she enjoyed sending him the message of an audible snick of the bolt.

The room was windowless. Deprived of sun or moon, she felt out of time, capsuled in her own little world. A comfort in the past, these days it only made her anxious. She didn't want her world to be little, she wanted to explore new horizons and feel there was nowhere on this earth beyond her reach.

Settled in her chair, she hoisted her legs and dumped her feet on the desk. Her satin kimono split and swished off her thighs like curtains.

She stared down at her exposed mound of pubic hair, and slipped her fingers into the black curls, but a furtive fiddle was the last thing on her mind. The thought of sex made her shiver with revulsion. She had soiled herself by screwing Tom Roker. Eight years before, despite being newly married to Peter, there had been an inevitability to her fling with Tom. It had seemed like good, clean, uncomplicated fun; a natural part of celebrating their success with *Hidden Blade*. Of course, it had been morally wrong, and she had regretted the betrayal, but she had never viewed the affair as sordid. But this second time, in spite of a defunct marriage and nothing to lose, had made her feel terrible. It had not happened out of fun; they had both been angry and frightened. Nor had it been natural; she had engineered it through her taunts. Neither could she think of it as a celebration; whatever financial rewards lay ahead for them both, their partnership was not a happy one.

She removed her hand from her crotch, hitched up the kimono and covered her legs, tucking the satin firmly between her knees.

More disturbing than the sex, however, was the strange nagging idea that the episode itself had not yet drawn to a close, that the repercussions had missed her, but that they had gone on ahead to be absorbed into some future event which she would soon catch up with.

The telephone rang at half-past midnight. By the time Tom emerged sufficiently from his slumber to register that it was the phone that had woken him, the call had been answered. He lay rigid on the bed, his head groggy but for one crystal certainty: it was Milton on the line, and in a few seconds Angie would shout for him to take the call upstairs.

'*Tom!*'

Tom shifted himself, sat on the edge of the bed and put his face in his hands. He wondered what Milton might want to discuss. With the sequel still in existence, talk seemed premature and redundant. Perhaps he was phoning to gloat; to rub Tom's nose in the blood soon to be spilt, and make Tom plead for it not to happen.

'*Tom!*'

'*I know!*' he bellowed down to her.

'It's . . .' There was a pause. '*Take it in my bedroom!*'

He stood up and wandered through; he was in no hurry to start this particular conversation.

He lifted the handset to his ear. 'Yes?' he said flatly.

'*Tommy!*' came the exuberant greeting, and there was no mistaking the voice; that rasping hoarseness, as though the larynx had been scoured with coarse sandpaper, and bits of grit had been left embedded.

'What?'

'You can put the phone down now, Angel. Me and Tommy need to have some private boys' talk together.'

'Tommy and I,' Tom corrected daringly.

'Angel, hang up.'

The downstairs line clicked dead.

'Getting a bit cheeky, huh, Tommy?'

'What d'you want?'

There was a gravelly exhalation, then Milton said: 'We're in a bit of a quandary, aren't we, Tommy?'

'How's that?' Tom asked, sitting down on the bed.

'What to do about this sequel.'

Tom frowned, then realised his suspicions had been right concerning Milton's motive for calling. 'I see. You want me to beg, get all frantic hoping I might be able to stop you from killing again if only I can say the right words?' Tom huffed. 'I don't think so. I'll spare myself the disappointment. You'll do what you want, regardless.'

'Might, might not.'

What Tom did next he knew was extremely stupid, but the flush of glee at the thought of doing it was too much to deny.

Very gently, he set the phone back on its cradle.

His heart threatened a coronary in the five seconds it took for Milton to call back.

'Kellett residence,' he announced with false nonchalance.

'Tommy, if you'd like me to pop by and turn that handset into a suppository, hang up again.'

Tom kept quiet and kept the phone to his ear.

'Wise choice. Now listen. I want to go away. I've made my point and I'm willing to call it a day. There is one person in this world I *don't* want to hurt, and as long as I stick around, that person will continue to suffer. So I will forgo the sequel . . .'

'On one condition,' Tom suggested, noting Milton's telltale rising inflection.

'That you write me a final chapter. Something you think I might enjoy. Something I can really get my teeth into. And that's not a hint; I'm not Hannibal Lecter.'

Tom experienced a sense of renewed hope, a pale dawn on his black horizon. And over that lightening horizon, his beloved Charlotte was waiting for him, her youthful innocence a balm for his tortured soul.

But he *couldn't* write. He had already tried and failed, and the block would only get worse with this added pressure.

'So . . . wanna call it quits?' Milton said.

'I do. God, I do, I really do, and I'm sorry for everything I've done, for making you do what you've done, but I . . . I . . .' Tom stuttered to a halt. He could feel the rictus of horror on his face. What cruel fate had made his salvation so simple and yet put it so far beyond his present capabilities?

'Tommy?'

'I'm blocked,' Tom moaned as he felt the sobs rise in him. 'Please believe me. I'd write if I could but I can't. And I don't want to be responsible for killing anyone else. Why can't you just kill me? Get it over with. I won't fight.'

'Oh, Tommy, you'd fight all right. I'd make you fight. I'd murder you slowly, lovingly, and that much pain makes a person kick and punch.'

Tom gulped quietly.

Milton continued, 'I suppose you could always pass out, but then I suppose I could always bring you round. Yep. Rest assured, Tommy, I'd make the whole thing last for years.'

'Years?' Tom echoed tremulously.

'Well, okay, days. But that would be in real-time. In Roker-time, it would feel like years.'

Tom shivered uncontrollably but spoke against his natural fear. 'I don't care. Come and get me, you fucking headcase.'

'Nah. The choice is one specially commissioned chapter with one death . . . or the entire sequel and all who sail in her.'

Tom's bravado vanished in a puff of panic. 'But what about Angie? You said you didn't want to hurt her any more.'

'Then don't make me,' Milton reasoned pleasantly. 'You've got six hours. That's plenty of time to construct a cosy little scene of violence and mayhem. And don't worry too much about descriptive prose; you know, how the rain sounds on the window-pane or whether my victim's got any knickers on. I'm not without imagination. You know what's important to me. Get that bit right and all will be well with the world. I won't kill again.'

'How do I know I can trust you?' Tom asked, as though this point of honour actually meant something.

'You don't,' was the inevitable reply. 'And you won't. You'll spend the rest of your days wondering if I was lying, checking over your shoulder, waiting for me to pounce, jumping every time you hear a motorbike. It'll be your personal ongoing epilogue, Tommy; something to remember me by.'

Tom was fit to scream. 'But I'm blocked.'

'Ex-Lax. Works for me.'

Tom clutched at straws. 'But I don't know who you want me to kill.'

'Kill who you like,' Milton said, then laughed. '*Kill who you like*. Hear that? Silly me. You're hardly going to kill who you like, are you? If you're going to kill anyone, you'll probably want to kill someone who you *don't* like. Anyway, enough of this chit-chat. It's good to talk, but in your case it's better to write.'

'But—'

'Lick your Bic, Tommy, you've got six hours.'

'But—'

'Oh, what the heck, you're a buddy, let's round it up to the nearest hour. Let's say done and dusted by seven. Can't say fairer than that.'

'But—'

'Meter's running.'

Carol was beginning to realise that human nature was a bit of a lemming. It acted instinctively, often against all reason, charging ahead towards plainly idiotic conclusions, just to see what lay over the edge. It was the geek-eyed kid in us, staring drop-jawed at the heavens, searching for Santa's sleigh, and doing it all year round. It was a gullible Womble, collecting up the discarded disbeliefs of a proudly rational public, and examining them to see if a crumb of truth might actually be contained within. It was Fox Mulder on a mission.

Because ever since speaking to Tom, Carol had been fighting a growing urge to pull a hardback off the shelf and check it for missing text. It was impossible, of course, that such an occurrence might have occurred, but human nature required that she check, out of curiosity, if nothing else. Clearly, she would open up the novel, find everything where it should be and give herself a mocking smile, tutting at the farcical thought processes which had caused her to make the inspection, and ignoring the peculiar sense of relief at having proved the impossible was still not possible.

She reached behind her, above her head, and plucked *Man on a Murder Cycle* from the crowded shelf. She opened it in her lap and turned a few random pages.

'What the . . . ?'

She leafed through some more intermittently empty pages, then closed the book and set it reverently on the desk.

Impossible.

So what had happened was . . . was that . . . yes, Tom Roker had privately commissioned Neptune to produce several specially incomplete editions. Why he might have done this was a more difficult question, though she guessed that freaking her out would be reason enough for a petty prick like him.

No, she would not give it the slightest headspace. She was not about to renege on a multi-million pound film deal just because Tom Roker had slipped beneath a white bedsheet and had gone *Whoooooooo* down the phone at her.

She dropped the novel in the waste bin down by her side.

'Screw you, Thomas. Screw you.'

Needs must when the Devil drives.

From somewhere deep in his reserves, Tom had found the inspiration to write. But Tom knew that the Devil didn't drive, he rode, and Tom had sent him biking down south to Rotherhithe.

It had not taken very long to decide who should be sacrificed. Wittingly or not, Milton had provided all the clues. By telling Tom not to bother with too many details, like the sound of the rain on a window or whether the victim was wearing any knickers, Milton had put Tom firmly in mind of a recent event. And suggesting Tom kill someone he didn't like, well . . . what more did he need to hear? Besides, if it was the wrong decision, why had it suddenly broken his block?

No, this felt absolutely right. The words were flowing again, a long-overdue comeuppance was being duly served, and he was saving innocent lives in the process. Even Peter might applaud the content of Tom's final chapter; there was no love lost in the Morgan household of late.

Shortly after completing his first page of A4, he heard Angie go to bed. He had expected she would grill him on the gist of his telephone conversation with Milton, but she was obviously fed up with the whole business and had long since accepted her impotence to change any of it.

So in the quiet of the night, Tom wrote like a man possessed, always dimly aware that a major part of him probably *was* controlled by an evil spirit. Not an alien soul that had conquered from the outside, but his own, which had quietly transformed itself over the years into something quite grotesque.

FIFTY

The early morning alarm call Carol Morgan had planned for herself did not materialise. What came in its place left her doubtful she had woken up at all.

The night before, she had elected to sleep on the settee under a spare duvet. She was so close to dumping her old life and all it contained, and sleeping alone in a different room was symbolic of that coming severance. She had slept fitfully, tossing and turning. Confused images tumbled around her head; fantastic dreams of gold bullion weaved with nightmare visions of dark avenging angels. Her eyes had half opened on the lounge clock every thirty minutes, each time hoping she had put more than half an hour behind her in this longest of nights.

Until shortly before seven a.m., when she peeked out of her troubled mind to glimpse the clock again, and found something blocking her view. The nightmare had materialised in front of her, a hulking silhouette against the eerie city lights in the balcony windows.

Her mouth had opened and a cold leather palm had clamped it silent, followed by the more permanent remedy of a length of gaffer tape wrapped twice around her head.

For the first few seconds, she had struggled to place her dilemma. Was it in the waking world or still in her sleeping mind? Her brain had flicked back and forth between the two options like channels on a remote control, but too many senses were being drawn into the picture for her to deny that this ride was as real as it got.

As raw panic seized her, she peed herself, and began to thrash and kick at him, squealing like a rodent through the tape. Bundled in the duvet, her feet struck with cushioned ineffectuality. She popped one arm out from her cocoon to punch him, but his own gloved fist made

303

contact first. A dull explosion at her left temple sent her halfway back to Dream Town, which was exactly half as far as she would have liked. Already she was overwhelmed with a fear she could not believe, and would have willingly swapped all her promised riches for the simple gift of unconsciousness just to escape the freakish face grinning down at her.

Reeling from the blow, Carol drifted on the periphery. The duvet was torn away from her. The loose material of her kimono seemed to fly like surreal orange flames for a moment before settling. She looked down at her form, exposed in all the wrong places, and soaked with urine in the very worst. Oddly, she wasn't frightened of sexual violation, nor of death itself. What she dreaded was a piling on of more and more fear. She was already overdosing on the stuff.

Suddenly, the gaffer tape was untacked noisily from its roll and harshly ripped into lengths. Carol prised open her eyes to see her ankles being bound tightly, then her wrists, then her arms to her body. Her skin crawled with goosebumps as she heard the central heating roar into life for its morning stint, but Carol doubted she would live long enough to feel the apartment warm up, and knew that no amount of heat could ever remove her present chill. Then, as her eyes became accustomed to the gloom, and her assailant's face became more distinct, she thought she could feel her soul begin to freeze.

He tipped a sackful of rope onto the carpet, and Carol noticed there was a noose fashioned into one end.

Propped by fists, supported by elbows set squarely on the desk, Tom's exhausted head danced gently on his neck in a deep doze. Beneath his chin was a pile of twenty-six finished pages, his scrawl of handwriting growing more ragged as the chapter developed. The final sheet was barely legible.

Never mind. Milton would understand.

It had only taken two hours to complete the required work, but Tom had decided not to sleep. At any rate, he had made a supreme effort to keep awake. Over the past hour, he had begun to lose the battle. He had wanted to witness the final blankings as they happened, to know for sure that the exercise had been a success. But he was just too tired.

His peace was not to last.

One of his elbows was abruptly swept from the desk, destroying his finely balanced head-support. Full consciousness arrived too late to prevent his face from crashing into the desk top nose-first.

Blood leaked out of his nostril onto page number one.

'What the hell have you done now?' Angie demanded from behind his chair.

He lifted his head and looked at her, then returned his attention to the page and knew precisely what he had done: he had missed the start of the chapter. The spilled red drops had landed on an emptying sheet of white paper. When he had nodded off only minutes before, it had been crammed full of Biro.

'Thank God,' he mumbled to himself.

'What have you done?' Angie wanted to know. 'Why can't you let it be over? Let him have you?'

Tom turned in his chair to face her. 'No, you don't understand, Milton wanted this. This *is* the way to end it, he told me.'

Angie squawked with laughter. 'And you believed him? Christ, you're naive. This won't be over till you're in your grave. He's playing with you, offering hope where none exists. You're dead, Tom. Sooner or later. So why let more people suffer? Be a man, for pity's sake. At least die with some dignity, even if you've never lived with any.'

Tom was engrossed in the dwindling chapter again. If he ignored Angie, perhaps she might go away. He pushed the blank first page to one side, put his sleeve to his dripping snout, and began following the reductions on page number two.

After a moment, Angie said over his shoulder, 'Are they blanking?'

'Yes.'

'I can't see it.'

'They're blanking.'

Where was that protective husband of hers? Useless git.

Belated questions were filling her frantic mind.

Was Peter dead in the bedroom? Did she care? Of course she did, but only because she needed someone to save her. Apart from that, did she care that he might not be breathing? No, not much. And just who the hell was this scarred intruder in black leather? Clearly, it was *meant* to be Milton, but *who* meant it to be Milton? Tom? The Kellett woman? Both of them in cahoots? If so, why?

What did they hope to gain? A sick laugh for themselves? Heart failure for her? Not for a second did she think it might really *be* Milton, in the flesh, off the page.

Pretty quickly, such questions became academic. There was only one salient fact: Carol Morgan was in mortal danger. Although the man would not stop his crazy grinning, there was no joke involved in all of this. She could feel his homicidal intent rolling in waves around the lounge.

Trussed up on the settee, she stared horrified as he pulled the balcony windows wide open and set about knotting two pieces of rope to the handrail of the ornate iron railings outside. One length was short, with a trail of about seven feet. The other was long, extremely long, perhaps up to eighty feet of it coiled on the token width of balcony like a snake-charmer's basket, topped with the noose, more threatening than any hooded cobra.

The pre-dawn air infiltrated the room and goosebumped her goosebumps. The satin draped her contours like a cold sweat. She was hyperventilating now, the two wee holes in her nose unable to satisfy the demands of her terrified lungs.

He moved confidently, lazily, pausing occasionally to stare over the awakening city, like Tarzan first surveying civilisation. It seemed he was in no rush, that there was no way he wouldn't have all the time he needed for whatever he had planned. The sky was deep and heavy around his massive silhouette. On the horizon, the night was beginning to lift, offering a rim of steel blue above the familiar Lego shapes of London.

As he finished up and came for her, she limply struggled in her bindings. He snatched her off the settee as though she weighed nothing more than polystyrene, and carried her to the balcony. He placed the noose over her head and tightened it gently like a necktie. The second rope he looped under her arms and secured beneath her breasts, providing a two-foot length between her and the railings. She guessed it was some sort of safety rope, but she did not imagine it would ultimately save her from very much.

Then he manhandled her over the edge, carefully settling her bare feet on the lip of balcony which protruded beneath the railings on the drop-side. Windows in the wall of the flat beneath glowed yellow through their curtains. The world was getting up, just as she was being put to sleep. She could hear London humming into life. Nine floors down, the swollen Thames slid by in a darkness she dared not peer into. She whimpered behind her gag, a plea for leniency to cure even the hardest heart.

But not his.

He leaned her out over the river as far as the rope would give. Having hated his every touch, she now prayed he wouldn't let her dangle in the breeze on her lonesome. He released her and she swayed helplessly over the Thames, all gaffered up like an Egyptian mummy. The salty pungence of the river filled her nostrils and made her want to gag. Where it wasn't bound by tape, her kimono flapped in the wind. Her feet were practically numb but she was afraid to shift them on the concrete lip. The safety rope creaked where it was knotted to the railing, and in the unfriendly gloom her eyes inspected it for any frays.

The rope was good, but she felt her chances of survival were still slim-to-none. Which was confirmed when the man produced a combat knife from inside his jacket. The blade was double-edged, razor sharp one side, viciously serrated on the other. He rolled the handle round in his fist several times, causing the steel to flash dully, appearing to choose: one swift merciful swipe, or a sawing motion so she could watch with growing apprehension as each fibre split and curled.

'Time for confession,' he whispered roughly, eyes glittering madly. He put the razor edge to her cheek and sliced the silver tape, peeling it back from her mouth.

Carol felt blood-warmth rise through her skin where the blade had nicked, but she was more concerned with gulping in all that free air now available to her tortured lungs. Partially recovered, she sent it back out in a dreadful begging scream.

'*Peeeeeete! Peteeeeeeeer! Pee—!*'

She shut up in shock as her attacker joined in the clamour, bellowing hoarsely for 'Petey' to join them. She realised that Peter must be dead, for why else would the madman have allowed her to vocalise her fear? No, there was no one in the apartment to help, and, as for the neighbours, blood would have to be oozing through their light fittings before they deigned to get involved.

But Peter wasn't dead. With a stubbled chin and wild hair, he came tearing out of the bedroom in his Marks and Spencer's jim-jams, punching the wall switch to illuminate the lounge. His eyes changed from bleary to wide awake as they fixed on his wife's predicament.

'Ah, you must be Petey,' said Milton, lowering his volume. 'My name's Milton, this is your beloved wife Carol, and she wants to tell you a story.'

Peter staggered forward, his eyes blazing up with rage and tears.

'Don't!' Carol said, and, as if to make the point crystal clear, Milton lay his blade against the safety rope.

Peter stopped.

'Park your arse,' Milton said amiably, indicating the settee. 'Just mind the piss-patch.'

Peter hesitated. 'What's going on? What d'you want? Why are you doing this?'

'Hush now, Petey. Your spouse will elucidate. Over to you, Caz.'

Peter sat down on the edge of a dry cushion.

'Please bring me in from here, I'm scared,' Carol sobbed. Her legs were shaking so badly she thought they would give way, and she didn't trust the chest rope to hold if that happened.

'Hmmm . . .' Milton considered. 'Nope. I want you to tell Petey here about your somewhat unconventional acquisition of *Man on a Murder Cycle*. Then we might review your situation *vis-à-vis* the brand new sport of neck-attached non-elasticated bungee-jumping.'

Carol moaned some more, mostly from the bone-cold shivers, then began to spout like a stoolie squealing to the Feds. She still couldn't decide exactly who this leather-clad man might be – perhaps an aggrieved friend of Andrew Kellett's – but he had proved his credentials, he wasn't bluffing, and if she could live through this ordeal by offering a simple confession, then that was fine by her.

'Petey, are you getting all of this?' Milton interrupted her once, and Peter nodded.

Perhaps she had done Pete a disservice. Roles reversed, would she have lied to save his life? Because she knew that most of what she was saying was actually fairly incomprehensible, garbled by fear and warbled by cold. If Peter wanted her dead, he only had to admit that he wasn't following her monologue as clearly as he should. In fact, by lying, he was placing himself in peril; she felt no doubt that this intruder could squish two heads just as economically as one.

Clearly, Peter did not want her dead; his half of their love was still alive. So he played along like a trained negotiator, listening intently and nodding in all the right places.

In those few minutes, she loved him too. By adopting the same wimpish, non-confrontational stance she had always detested, he was more than likely saving her skin. She imagined most men would have had their Stallone head on by now, planning a dumb move which would get them both killed.

She finished her story with an apology to the man in leather, for good measure.

Milton said, 'And that's the truth, the whole truth, and nothing but the truth?'

'Yes, yes, that's it,' she stuttered.

'You wouldn't like to take this opportunity to add anything else? Think about it.'

Carol did think about it; she did not want any foolish oversight to queer her chances at this late stage. But nothing came to mind.

'No, honestly, I swear, that's it,' she said.

Milton began applauding daintily with the tips of his fingers. 'Well, thank you for sharing that with the group, Caz, I know how difficult it must have been for you.'

'Can I come in, then?' she asked hopefully.

'Please let her in,' Peter said softly.

'You'd like her to come in, would you, Petey?'

Peter nodded.

'Why? Do you think she deserves to live? You heard her confession. Why shouldn't I cut this rope right now? Know what would happen if I did? With this much drop of rope, we wouldn't have a lynching, we'd have a decapitation. But don't you think that's perfect justice, Petey? Think of the poor headless farmer in Kellett's back garden. Great payback, huh?'

'Please,' Peter said. 'I don't know who you are, but—'

'Think of me as the Executor of Andrew Kellett's will.'

'Okay . . . okay, but you have no quarrel with me. Please don't punish me, and you will if you take my wife away from me.'

'Convince me not to.'

'I love her,' Peter offered simply.

Carol felt like thumb-gouging her husband's eyes. What a dildo; using love as an argument with a heartless psycho. Way to go, dickhead.

'I can relate to that,' Milton said sympathetically, though Carol kept the whooping celebrations to herself for the moment. It was *just* possible she might be witnessing the employment of sarcasm. 'So I should spare her because you love her?' Milton asked.

'Yes.'

Milton looked out at Carol's distraught features. A thick dark dribble from her cut cheek was coagulating in the chill breeze.

'Petey . . .' He turned back into the room. 'Petey, you do know she doesn't love you, don't you?'

Carol opened her mouth to object but Peter's reply made her planned fib redundant.

'I know that. It doesn't matter,' he said quietly.

'And you do know·she was going to leave you as soon as she got her millions?'

'I expected she would.'

'And you wouldn't like me to kill her? Not even a teency-weency little bit?'

Peter stood up with saggy, inoffensive movements. 'I still love her. If it really is up to me, then I'd like you to let her live.'

Carol guessed she had entered the final minute of her life. No way was this dilly-dallying anything other than bullshit. She was dead whatever Peter tried, verbal or physical.

'Okay, Petey, she's all yours,' Milton said, and slipped the knife through an iron loop in the railings so it stuck there by its handle. He winked at Carol and spoke to her in an undertone. 'Here's where we depart from the script for a moment.'

Carol did not understand the comment, but put it down to the ramblings of a psycho, and she cried out with relief as Milton headed across the lounge towards the apartment door. He passed Peter, then stopped and backtracked several paces to whisper something in his ear. Peter's expression did not alter. It was calm and impassive as he received whatever information Milton had to impart. Carol didn't know what was said, and didn't care; as long as the bad man left her alone.

'Peter, get me in from here!' she yelled, fearing the bad man would change his mind and spin on his heels at the apartment door. *'Quick!'*

But Milton continued on his way and left the apartment, closing the door behind him.

Peter walked unhurriedly to the balcony. He leaned over and took his wife by her strapped arms and pulled her in vertical.

Carol was sobbing her heart out. 'Thank you, Peter, thank you, I love you, I love you, I'll change, I will, I love you, I love – What?' Peter had whispered something in her ear and Carol couldn't quite believe she had heard the words she knew she had heard. The lapping water nine floors below seemed louder than ever.

She wanted to deny the charge, but she knew her expression had already confessed.

Peter removed the combat knife from its slot in the railings and kissed her lightly on the forehead. 'I said: fuck Tom Roker, did you, dear?'

Then he pushed his wife back out over the Thames, and as the line went taut, he severed it.

Carol screamed for eighty feet before developing acute and irreversible brain-lung communication failure.

Tom crumpled all twenty-six blank sheets into a large ball and dropped them in the waste bin. He could think of nothing to say.

Angie could. 'And you think that's finished it, do you?'

Tom shrugged. 'He said.'

'Well, I hope you're right, but I wouldn't go booking any summer holidays, if I were you.'

Tom gave another lethargic lift of his shoulders, but it was a lie; it was still panic stations in his head. He no more believed Milton had quit killing than he believed Angie would drop to her knees and blow him. A week might go by, boring and uneventful, a month, a year, five years, maybe ten, but Tom would never be able to relax. Evil did not simply run its course and evaporate into the ether. It had to be destroyed. Otherwise it had to be endured, and Tom could easily imagine Milton stalking generation after generation of Roker descendants, until the name of Tom Roker became a curse, never spoken out loud and only brought to mind by the fiercely brave or the supremely ignorant.

This whole affair had moved into a different sphere, and Tom felt like weeping. He had created a monster, out of control and out of this world. He was beyond help. Only in the movies were there dust-covered tomes lurking at the back of high library shelves, containing incantations for the banishment of the Powers of Darkness. No one of his acquaintance happened to be a white witch on the side, that fabled amateur sleuth of the supernatural. Shit, he had never even met anyone who owned a pack of Tarot.

He turned in his chair, but there was nobody there. He had been so lost in his morbid thoughts, he had not noticed Angie leave the room. The only human being who could at least understand his plight had abandoned him, and who could blame her?

Tom closed his eyes and shook his head. 'Oh, Christ, where do I go from here?'

Immediately he had said it, he knew the answer.

FIFTY-ONE

<hr>

They sat huddled like spies in one of the rear pews.

The parish vicar was everything Tom had expected: from the cheery smile as he had approached up the church path, to this, the expansive pause before he delivered his pronouncement on all Tom had told him. The man was interested, caring, a perfect listener, and did not appear to sit in judgment, either on Tom's awful moral track record to that day, or on the verity of recent supernatural events. The man seemed aglow with compassion; not as though he would swallow any cartload of crap dumped at his door to avoid antagonising the troubled dumper, but as though he could genuinely sift the wheat from the chaff, and had done so now by way of some God-patented divining mechanism.

'So you believe your life to be in danger?'

Tom gave a solemn nod. 'Mine and many others.'

'And are you and Miss Kellett . . .' Michael smiled benignly '. . . together, as it were?'

Tom understood the question, but wondered how the answer might be relevant. Then he wondered whether the vicar really had been listening; how on earth could Angie have fallen for a man who had all but wrecked her life?

'It is important,' Michael said, evidently reading Tom's doubtful expression. 'Your relationship with Miss Kellett surely affects how her deceased brother will ultimately deal with you. And I must have all the information if I am to have any hope of resolving this unfortunate situation.'

'No,' Tom said definitely, 'we're not together.'

'Good. I mean, that simplifies matters.'

'So how do we proceed?'

Michael glanced thoughtfully at a gargoyle, perched seven feet up a supporting pillar. Someone had shoved a half-smoked cigarette in its mouth.

'Well, Mister Roker, I know of no text to which I can refer. Generally, the troubled souls of departed relatives exist only in the minds of the living, and a few kind, reassuring words from me often have the desired—'

'We are not talking about a troubled soul, forgive my interruption.'

'Indeed.' Michael absently brushed a shower of dust from the prayerbook shelf. Tom watched the grey fluff descend into the darkness at his feet. 'Indeed,' Michael repeated. 'To all intents and purposes, you have brought the realm of Hell to this earth, and our battle is with Lucifer incarnate.'

At this official pronouncement, Tom gulped, and fear brought sarcasm. 'Phew. And there was me thinking it was serious.'

Amazingly, Michael let out some jolly laughter. 'Take heart, Mr Roker. You are in God's house, and I am an appointed representative. The Lord does watch over his flock, I can assure you of that.'

Tom exhaled a shaky breath. 'No offence, but please tell me you have a plan, and not just blind faith.'

Practically gloating, the man in the dog collar said, 'You don't know the things I've seen, Mr Roker.'

Tom became instantly peeved at what he assumed to be some extraordinary oneupmanship. 'No, I don't. But I've told you the things I've seen, so unless the things you've seen are going to have some practical bearing on the things I've seen, I might as well take my problem elsewhere.' He stood up and stared along the nave at the altar crucifix beneath the east window. Tears brimmed.

'I want you to write another chapter,' Michael said softly.

Tom yelped with bitter amusement, and the sound echoed hollowly in the empty heights of the clerestory.

Michael continued calmly. 'I want you to write a chapter which describes a meeting between myself and Milton. He would appear to thrive on the product of your imagination, especially when you provide him with a confrontational set-piece. So that is exactly what you must write.'

Tom slumped back onto the bench. His shoulders sagged and his head lolled forward until his chin touched his chest. 'I've had it with writing,' he mumbled into his coat. 'I can't.'

'Then I am very much afraid I can't help you,' Michael said with no discernible sympathy.

Several minutes passed. Tom was trying to gee himself up for another slog at the A4. It seemed a fantastical proposition, like performing open-heart surgery, untrained, with the lights out.

Eventually, Tom spoke, and each word was heavy with shame; that he might seriously be entertaining yet another murder by proxy. 'Milton won't come unless I write a death for him.'

'I realise,' Michael said martyrfully.

Still speaking into his coat, Tom said, 'I'm not sure you do. I'd need to describe your untimely demise. And I'd need to make it fun for him. Which, uh . . . wouldn't be much fun for you.'

Michael gently squeezed Tom's forearm to make him look up. 'Mr Roker – Tom – you must write what is required. I shall not come to any harm, believe me.'

Tom searched the vicar's eyes for a glimmer of doubt, but there was none to be seen.

'Perk of the job,' Michael said, and winked.

A selfish hope – all too familiar – warmed inside Tom's chest.

Michael's voice was rich with The Word. 'I shall dispatch this demon to the very deepest pit of Hell, from which he will never again emerge. He will learn that for every force of evil, there is a greater force of good. So . . . go . . . write.'

Michael's fingers had dug into Tom's forearm like the claws of a ravenous predator, and Tom decided there was quite clearly a gossamer divide between religious fervour and a one-way ticket to the Rubber Room. He just had to trust that, in this case, his saviour was patrolling the sane side of the border.

Tom stood up and pulled away out of Michael's gnarly grip. 'As soon as the chapter's complete, I'll let you know where and when it's set for.'

Michael nodded vaguely.

Tom dithered. 'Okay . . . thanks.'

Michael, however, had elevated himself onto a higher plane, and did not hear what the mortal earthling had uttered.

Michael sat down in the vestry with a mug of tea. He believed every word Tom Roker had said. It certainly explained the macabre occurrence at the undertaker's last summer. But in the final analysis it didn't matter whether Andrew Kellett truly had come back from the dead, only that his sister believed in his reincarnation as fervently as Tom Roker claimed she did. If so, Michael had the ideal opportunity to redeem himself in her eyes and capture her heart. By freeing her brother from his earth-bound bondage, she would owe a debt of gratitude greater than she could repay with mere words. On the other hand, if the whole affair did turn out to be so much unfounded tosh, at least he would have shown willing; he would have cast himself as the dashing hero, selfless to a fault.

Either way, how could she not fall in love with him?

The red Mini Cooper was gone from outside the cottage. Tom walked across the churned-up verge and tracked muddy shoeprints along the footpath to the porch door.

He hoped Angie had ventured into work today. She had been increasingly absent lately, and he felt responsible. He didn't want her to lose her job; it was perhaps her only link with normality, and he feared for her sanity almost as much as he did his own. But he supposed it was difficult to smilingly laud the merits of various holiday destinations when her corpse of a brother was touring her own locality, himself on vacation from that hottest of hot-spots.

Tom let himself in, hung his coat on the newel post and reluctantly plodded upstairs.

More sodding words. He couldn't believe it. Did his salvation really lie in writing *more*? It was a sick, sick world. Then again, what perfect payback. He had wanted to write, he had positively craved the old, easy, lucrative flow of prose, and now it seemed his grasping hand was destined never to let go of the cursed pen which produced it.

He entered the back bedroom, and immediately, and too late, a hulking black shape on the desk behind the door caught the corner of his eye.

He spun round and squealed. '*Jesus Christ!*'

'You flatter me.'

Tom scurried backwards and fell on the bed. At that moment, a fatal heart attack would have been a godsend. He was dimly aware that he might have peed himself, then he wondered if he hadn't somehow been stabbed instead, which would make the wetness blood, not urine.

'Tommy Roker . . . you *genius*!' Milton said sycophantically.

'Can I have your autograph? *Please*. Or dare I ask for a signed piccy? Am I going too far if I ask for a hug?'

Unconnected to Tom, a strange moaning noise was nevertheless coming from his mouth. He wanted to switch it off, but he couldn't. His brain was occupied, downloading all the information it had stored up concerning the grinning, white-maned, black-eyed, scar-faced monster presently squatting on the desk with its bum perched lightly on the word processor monitor.

'Come on, let's bond,' Milton said.

As Tom's nemesis climbed down from the desk and plucked him off the bed for a hug, Tom's brain computed its result: Oh, bollocks. It was an oddly muted conclusion given the input, but he guessed that his mind had blown a couple of its weaker synapses in the few seconds since he had walked through the door. Probably to calm him down. A self-administered quasi-sedative. Prepare him for execution.

Milton squeezed him tightly, but not harmfully. Tom's nose was pressed flat against Milton's jacket, and Milton creaked all over; tiny leather noises. The smell in Tom's nostrils was pleasantly sniffable, but it nearly made him retch. He was being cuddled by the undead.

Tom wasn't moaning any more, but he realised Milton was; the sort of overly ecstatic sound people made on sick-making Sunday evening TV shows which reunited long-lost relatives who probably had damn good reason to remain thousands of miles apart if only the show's researchers had bothered to check.

Suddenly, Milton released the hug and held Tom by his shoulders at arm's length. 'You know, Tommy, I think I might fancy you.'

Tom felt greyness fill his head. He fainted.

FIFTY-TWO

———◆———

He came to in the kitchen. Milton had laid him across a counter so that his head was resting on the electric stove. In the light of Milton's last comment before Tom had fainted, Tom prayed that Milton hadn't just laid him, full stop. But he wasn't sore anywhere, so perhaps he was okay. He calculated from the still wet urine stain at his crotch that he had been unconscious for only a few minutes.

'Why is my head on a cooking ring?' Tom asked bravely.

Seated on the opposite fitment, Milton smiled innocently. 'No reason.'

'Can I get off?'

'Feel free.'

Tom sat upright, allowed his brain to adjust, then eased himself onto the floor. He briefly considered making a run for it, but even if he got away, where could he hide that Milton wouldn't find him?

'Why have you come here?' he said.

'I think I have more right to be here than you do.'

Tom conceded with a nod. 'Are you going to kill me?'

'No.'

Tom chuckled humourlessly. 'I don't believe you.'

'Haven't you heard it said that ghosts can't lie?'

'You're not a ghost.'

'And whose fault's that?' Milton said pointedly, then let out a gruff laugh. 'Tommy, can you believe you're having this conversation? This is one for the next novel, eh? Huh? Eh?'

Tom stared Milton straight in the eyes for added emphasis. The black pools glittered back at him, too close together, almost threatening to spill into each other. 'There won't be another novel,' Tom said. 'I won't be writing another word.'

318

'How will you ever pay for anything by cheque?'

Tom ignored him; he was querying the truth of his own assertion. He had just remembered that Michael needed one more chapter from him. That was allowed, wasn't it? If it saved lives?

Then it dawned on him that there was a simpler way: now he was here, why not just ask Milton to meet with Michael? Surely Milton wouldn't turn down the chance of a freebie kill.

'Are you doing anything this evening?'

Milton raised his non-existent eyebrows. 'Nothing I can't reschedule. Why?'

'D'you want to have tea with the local vicar?'

The non-eyebrows lifted higher. 'Two like-minded people getting together, sharing a frank exchange of views? I'm all for it.'

Tom was a little taken aback. He shifted nervously on his feet. 'You'll go?'

'Tell me where and when, I'll be there.'

'Oh. I hadn't thought where, or when.'

'How about eleven-thirty for midnight, the stone outcrop, Alderley Edge?'

Tom went and sat on a kitchen stool for support. His head was spinning again. It didn't feel right. He would have felt much better had he needed to persuade Milton. It felt as though Michael had lost control of the situation before it had even developed.

'Right, I'll let him know,' Tom said. 'Are you going now?'

'Not yet. I have something I'd like to run by you; see if it trips up.'

Before Milton could explain, there was a knock at the front door. Tom experienced the instinctive desire to scream for help, but unless it was Godzilla calling, there would be no contest: Milton, one; Caller, dead.

'I'll get that,' Milton said, jumping off the fitment.

'What if it's Angie?'

'Then she's a silly sausage for not using her keys,' Milton said as he left the kitchen, pulling the door to behind him.

Tom got up and put his ear to the crack, and heard Milton open the front door, then the porch door.

'Yes, hello,' said the male caller, 'I was uuuhhhhhhh . . .' Tom imagined the poor man trying not to gawp at Milton's features. '. . . uuuhhhhhhhwondering if you'd be interested in a religious tract.'

319

'You mean for a religious train to run along?'

'Uh . . . no, a religious tract.' The final 't' of tract was heavily stressed.

'A religious tractor? Do I look like a religious farmer?'

In spite of everything, Tom smiled.

'Uh . . . no, a . . . a tract, a pamphlet, a magazine.'

'Oh, a religious magazine. Called?'

'Are you interested?'

'Called?'

There was a pause.

'*The Watchtower*.'

'I see, no I'm busy.'

'Too busy for God?'

'Too busy for you. Unless you are God, but you're not exactly how I pictured the Supreme Being.'

'It's not expensive.'

'You want me to *buy* it?'

Tom wondered how long the banter would continue before Milton tired of it and sent the Witness up to see Jehovah.

'Well . . .' continued the Witness, with the sect's customary and sterling disregard of blatant rejection, '. . . perhaps you'd like to attend one of our meetings.'

'No, actually I'd hate that.'

'It's very informal.'

'I don't think you'd want me there.'

'Just for an hour.'

'Listen,' Milton intoned with a patience Tom would not have credited. 'Tell you what: I'll take your *Watchtower* if you'll take one of my religious publications.'

'Oh, a fellow worshipper! Marvellous! I'm sure we can find some common ground. We are all Jehovah's children, after all. And you'll come to the meeting?'

'Careful. Ask me again and I'll be there.'

'I hope you will be. So what is your tract?'

'*Beelzebub Monthly*. Have you seen the January issue?'

'Sorry? Beel– Uh, I have to go.'

'Well, if you must. Fuck off and toodle-pip. But don't be a stranger! You come on back real soon, y'all hear?'

Tom heard the porch door close, followed by the inside door, then thunderous bootfalls returning to the kitchen. He scurried away from his listening-post and jumped back on the kitchen stool.

Milton entered, tittering to himself. 'I love that lot. Fucked-up or what? They make me feel sane.' He hopped back on the counter.

'Why didn't you kill him?' Tom wanted to know.

With mock-hurt in his voice, Milton said, 'But, Tommy, I promised I wouldn't kill again. Or did you think I had my fingers crossed.'

'Hmm. So what did you want to run by me?'

'Oh, yes.' Milton smoothed a gloved palm over his white mane to the nape of his neck. 'As I'm sure you've learned lately, nothing good in this life is free. There's always a price. Well, I've done you a couple of whopping favours. I wiped out a copper who was about to suss you, and a literary agent who . . . well, pissed you off, basically. And you haven't even said thank you.'

'Thank you.'

'Don't mention it. Thing is, you haven't actually paid for *any* of the trouble you've caused. Now have you?'

Tom shook his head minutely and felt fear roll queasily in his stomach.

'Which brings me to my proposition, which I think is a fair one, considering.' He left a deliberate pause.

'I'm listening.'

'Three people are left who can point the police in your direction: you, but you lack the conscience to do so; Angie, who is too kind-hearted to do so; and me, and I'm going to do so.'

Tom did an unconscious double-take. 'What?'

'Yes, in five minutes I shall phone the Plod and ask them to come and take your fingerprints to compare with certain ones already in their possession. And I shall specifically ask for DCI Nelson, who I gather is not your biggest fan.'

'He'll kill me,' Tom muttered in horror. 'He knew I was lying.'

Milton gave a wide, sparkle-eyed grin. 'Yup. He certainly has the capacity for such violence. He offed someone himself the other night.'

Tom felt his face go slack. '*What?*'

'Poor chap in a Peugeot. Beat him to a pulp with a Stoplock.'

Tom shifted forward on his stool so that he was basically standing up. His neck hairs bristled with excitement; that someone else might be almost as deep in the shit as he was, and someone he could bargain with if need be.

Then he wilted. 'Yeah. Sure he did. I suppose you were there, were you, HandyCam rolling?'

'I get around.'

'Just happened to be passing, did you?'

'I was miles away. But I was there.' He winked. 'I'm not subject to your laws.'

Understanding, Tom said, 'Legal or otherwise.'

Another wink in response.

Tom chewed his lips for thirty seconds. He didn't want to go to jail. He certainly didn't want a homicidal detective carting him off there. He had already passed through his self-sacrificial period, emerging the other side neither incarcerated nor in a coffin. He wasn't the type to prostrate himself a second time. He had survived. Now he wanted health and freedom. He wanted to see his daughter again. 'Bit of a hollow victory,' he said, having the police lock me up. Beelzebub would not be pleased.'

'Absolutely.' Milton pushed himself off his perch and clumped over to the back door. 'Crap view these days,' he said, stroking the solid oak-stained door. 'Once upon a time there were fields as far as the eye could see. This used to be glass, you know.' He turned to Tom. 'Did you know that? This door used to be glass?'

Tom looked away.

'Oh, of course you did. Silly me.'

Tom snapped. 'All right, fuckhead, what's the deal?'

Milton dropped his mouth cavernously open. '*Wow!* Reckless *bastard*! Insulting me down the phone is one thing. But to my face—'

'You don't have a face. Look in the mirror.'

This time Milton's expression flickered with something nasty. He quickly resumed a smile, but his gravelly voice betrayed his continuing pique. And so did what he said: 'You keep up the insolence, Tommy-my-man, and I'll carve a similar pattern into your physiognomy.'

Tom thought it prudent not to answer back. Milton approached and stood over him, and Tom shrank back onto his stool.

'The deal, Tommy, is this: I will leave you alone and leave Nelson in his ignorance. For this, I will exact a one-time-only payment from you. Payable now. Credit facilities not available.

322

Zero APR. Offer cannot be repeated. Only one per household. No cooling-off period.' Saying this, Milton cackled hysterically. When he quietened, he corrected himself. 'Forgive me, but there will for damn sure be a cooling-off period.'

This maniacal gibberish washed over Tom and left him dizzy with apprehension, because he knew that, to Milton, it all made perfect sense, and that it would presently be translated into plain English in a way he would not much enjoy.

Milton stepped over to the electric stove and switched on the front two cooking rings. Tom watched with an accelerating heart as the black circles brightened to a fierce, glowing orange. Heat reached his face, but he guessed that was just his brain, boiling with fear.

'And here,' Milton announced, swirling around dramatically to confront Tom, 'is where you can make your payment. I have my cashier's hat on and the counter is now open for business.'

Tom was frozen on the stool. Adrenalin surged through him, which curiously always made his back ache. His heart was pumping crazily, thudding in his chest like a separate entity, scared in its own right.

'What is the payment?' he barely managed to ask.

'Eight fingertips, two thumbtips,' was the horrendous reply. 'A hand on each ring. Funny that, because a lot of people have a ring on each hand. I digress. Payment complete when your prints melt off onto the stove.'

Tom was sobbing by now. A tragic accident was one thing, but knowing in advance that a perfectly healthy portion of the anatomy was soon to be destroyed made him limp with racking sadness. 'Oh, Christ, no.'

'Oh, Christ, yes. Step right up.'

'Don't do this.'

'Okay,' Milton said happily. 'Do you realise that nine nine nine is six six six upside down?'

Fifteen seconds of pain or fifteen years in prison. Tom had a choice. Hypothetically, the decision was easy. But staring at the burning instrument of his torture, with those fifteen seconds imminent, he found his clear-cut decision became blurred. He tried to look past his impending agony; this evening he would be carefully bandaged up, soothed by emollient, high on painkillers, comforted by pretty nurses in a warm hospital bed. It would all be over. The

323

alternative would drag on and on and on and on and ruin whatever was left of his life. He would exist in a cycle of misery, every day regretting his cowardly refusal to face the pain and hold onto his freedom.

'Think of it this way,' Milton said. 'If you lose your fingertips certain police evidence won't be incriminating any more. So I'm actually providing a service. I should charge.'

Tom used his fury at Milton's evident relish to propel himself over to the hob. *'Just do it!'*

So Milton did. He snatched Tom's hands and slapped them flat on the rings, clamping his own huge gloved palms on top of them. On contact, Tom instinctively tried to lift his hands away, and although he was allowed to arch them to clear the palms, Milton still maintained the requisite pressure to keep the tips of Tom's digits firm against the heat.

Having fleetingly choked on his agony, Tom now spewed it out in a glass-shattering ululation. Smoke curls erupted from his burning flesh and reached his nostrils as the sickliest personal stench. Crazed with terror, the sense of mental detachment was so great, he almost thought his hands weren't his, but were twin Things from the Addams Family, about to scurry off the hob like deformed prawns being cooked alive.

There was a fresh flood of urine at his crotch, then, mercifully, he fainted again.

324

FIFTY-THREE

The pain in Tom's fingers was excruciating; the worst physical pain he had ever known. They throbbed hysterically and felt ten times their normal size, like the laughable cartoon aftermath of Jerry having dropped an anvil on Tom's paws. Before the Paramedic had put temporary dressings on them in the ambulance en route to the hospital, Tom had inspected the damage. He had looked away before the nausea could cause him to pass out a third time. The wounds were glistening and seeping, red crater-like sores filled with pustular yellow.

Now, lying in a cubicle in the local Accident and Emergency, they were revealed again. A handsome young Indian doctor – Dr Baveeta according to his name tag – was peering critically at his injuries. Then he glanced at the patient record.

'All right then, Mr . . . oh. Tom Roker. You're not the novelist, are you?'

Tom nodded.

'Not having the best of times recently, are you?' he said pleasantly.

'No.'

'So, how did this happen?'

'I burnt them on the stove.' True enough.

But an inquisitive pinch of skin appeared between Baveeta's eyes. His bedside smile was genuine, but there was now a crooked quality to it.

'This was an accident, yes?'

Tom nodded at the floor.

'Mr Roker, you have third-degree burns.'

'Will I need skin-grafts?' Tom asked, through genuine concern and in an attempt to sidetrack the doctor from his evident suspicions.

Baveeta paused, then answered the question. 'Fortunately, no. The cuticle and outer layer of the true skin have been destroyed, but the deeper papillae are unharmed. There will be enough skin cells surviving to ensure natural multiplication.'

Tom winced at a sudden burst of electrifying pain. He barely stifled a curse.

Baveeta cringed in sympathy. '*Un*fortunately, the papillae contain the nerve-endings, which are now exposed. Third-degree burns are consequently extremely painful.'

Through gritted teeth, Tom said, 'This I know.'

'But this is still preferable to fourth degree, for which you would certainly have required skin-grafts.'

'So I'm lucky?' Tom said, quite seriously.

'Only if you suspect it could have been worse.'

Tom missed the doctor's subtle dig at his 'accident' explanation. 'Yeah,' he said.

Baveeta silently busied himself, cleaning the burns with a mild antiseptic. At its touch, Tom's eyes flared and began to water. Had he uttered anything more than a closed-mouth squeak, his reaction would have been classed as crying. Afterwards, fresh dressings were applied: open-weave gauze impregnated with soft paraffin and antibiotic.

'Would you like a painkiller?' Baveeta offered finally.

'That would be nice.'

'And I'll get the nurse to bring you some sweet tea. It'll help to combat any delayed shock.'

'Thank you.'

'You're welcome,' Baveeta said, wheeling his stool backwards and standing up. He peeled off his Cellophane gloves. 'And, in future, you might want to consider cooking by microwave.'

Tom attempted a laugh, but it came out as a noiseless, guilty shrug.

'Is there anyone at home who might look after you?' Baveeta asked.

Tom thought of Angie. 'No.'

'Ah.' The doctor considered this. 'Well, we'll have you in overnight. Keep an eye on you. It'll also give you a chance to organise some sort of homehelp until the bandages come off. You won't even be able to open a door for a while. I'll call the Bed Manager. Don't go away.'

Baveeta disappeared through the curtains. Tom heard him collar a nurse, followed by some incomprehensible whispering; no doubt instructions regarding the painkiller and tea.

Tom regarded his new dressings and shook his head. Milton . . . vindictive son-of-a-bitch. Knowing exactly how long to fry the fingers; to pass through second degree but stop short of fourth, for that perfect, raw-nerved result.

An optimist would have looked on the bright side: at least he was in the clear over the break-in last summer. No prints, no proof. But in Tom's world since last summer it seemed there had been only darkness. In Tom's world, an optimist was certifiably deluded, a pessimist was a realist, and a realist was depressed.

Tom jolted on the bed. He sat stiffly upright. The pain was bad, but it was not the stimulus. He had remembered Michael, perhaps the only person who could possibly lead him out of this nightmare. He was probably at the church right now, packing his bag with The Old Unimproved Exorcist Kit – crucifix, holy water and Bible – and awaiting Tom's visit to confirm the time and place. But Tom was about to be confined to bed, and he didn't know the name of the church to telephone, if indeed the church contained a telephone, nor did he know the name of the main road through the village on which the church was situated.

Mindful of his handless state, he carefully climbed off the bed and peeked through the curtains. No angel of mercy was striding his way, so he struggled his overcoat onto his shoulders like some Mafia Don, nipped out of the cubicle and headed for the street.

Tom asked the taxi driver to wait as he dropped by the church on his way back to Angie's. He kicked the vestry door, keeping his hands hidden from sight, thrust deep into his coat pockets. He didn't fancy having to explain his injuries; an innocent explanation simply would not come to mind.

Thankfully, Michael was there, relaxing like a man without a care in the world. Tom didn't know whether to take heart from this apparent nonchalance, or worry like hell for the man's safety.

Michael received notification of the time and place with a nodding, knowing smile. Alderley Edge at midnight; it didn't surprise him. Michael said that the place was fabled to possess mystical powers going back to the legendary Merlin the Wizard. It was an apt spot for a battle against the Dark Forces. Tom neglected to point out that Milton the Whacko was a whole different proposition, and was sadly not in the slightest bit mythical. Instead, Tom wished him well, thanked him and left without offering to shake hands.

The taxi driver seemed none too pleased about having to dip into Tom's front trouser pocket to get his fare. Tom apologetically held up his useless hands, but the cabby plainly resented fiddling in another man's crotch, especially when that crotch felt disconcertingly damp.

Angie's Mini was still absent from the verge, and, checking his watch, Tom realised she would be away for several hours yet. It was only two-twenty in the afternoon, though the day seemed a lot older than that. Since seven a.m., he had brought about the death of his agent, talked exorcism with a parish vicar, shared some quality time with the living dead, lost his fingertips, and been in an ambulance. Not even Butlins could cram more into a day.

And there were plenty more hours to be filled.

With his fat Tubigripped fingers he somehow managed to let himself into the cottage, but the effort caused silent tears of pain to roll down his cheeks.

Ten minutes later, he was sobbing noisily as he left the cottage and posted the keys back through the letterbox. Collecting his belongings, bundling them into his holdall, and finally changing his piss-reeking trousers for a clean pair, Tom thought he had experienced suffering beyond anything a human being should be asked to endure. A dog in his wretched condition would have been put down. That he actually deserved to suffer, and that he should have been grateful he was still alive because it was his fault that so many other people weren't, had been relegated to a mere triviality. He was hurting in too many ways, and it felt blissful to weep some of it away.

Now he was going home, which was no comfort at all. A house he had bought in a different lifetime, now an empty shell; furnished like a home, but empty for all that. He had outstayed his welcome at Angie's, not that he had ever been welcome. Rather, he had outlived his usefulness, to her and to himself. And after midnight tonight, with God's grace and Michael's trust in that grace, Angie would also be free of Milton.

FIFTY-FOUR

Angie was spending another day sending people off on holiday. It was likely to be one of her last days doing so; she had been reprimanded by her boss that morning for taking too much time off work.

But how could she summon a fear of unemployment? How bad was not working when most of the people she had known were no longer living?

Soon, her boss would wish she had not shown up at all. Angie was deliberately inputting wrong departure times, from inaccurate airports, to unfancied destinations.

'So that's two weeks' self-catering in Ibiza, flying from Manchester International on the 16th of June,' she had said to one dizzy young couple before lunch. She only wished she could see their faces when their confirmation arrived in the post: six months' full board in Bogota. Such outlandish mis-instruction, however, was a harmless prank compared to the subtle alterations she had made to some holiday plans that day. The dupes who would leave on the correct flight to the proper resort, but would then find themselves transported to the Hotel El Cheapo when they had supposedly booked into five-star luxury. A cock-up which, in high season with no available alternative accommodation, the on-site tour reps would have no chance of rectifying.

And did she feel bad about this? No. Her primary aim was her own entertainment, to brighten up her day by ringing the changes, however much that was against company policy, and possibly against the law. The holidaymakers' crushing disappointment was simply an unavoidable by-product. She was sneaking some genuine glee into her otherwise false smile, and that was reason enough for her. Besides which, hadn't her clients read the reports: that the annual vacation could perversely be one of the most stressful events in a person's life? So what did they expect?

Miracles, was the answer to that. Two weeks that made sense of the other fifty. The carrot that kept the rat racing. Forget last year's disastrous fortnight, this year it was going to be *different*.

Sure. Week one, tense as hell, suffering the stress hangover of an unenjoyable, probably unchosen, career. First few days of week two, sickly-tired as the stress begins to melt through the system. From then on, fun and relaxation could have been on the cards if only they'd booked for a month, but strictures of work wouldn't allow it. So the last few days are actually spent getting stressed back up to level, wondering why yet another annual holiday has failed to work the oracle, peeling crimson, crusty flaps of skin from each other's shoulders, having burnt a dose of latent skin cancer into their cells to meet up with in later life, and generally cursing the laid-back, healthily-tanned locals for being born in an altogether more pleasant country.

Life. *Jesus*.

FIFTY-FIVE

An icy wind gusted through the mainline station, hurtling down the tracks like an invisible express, stopping for no one. Tom shuddered and hunched his shoulders against the blast. His hands throbbed with molten pain in the warmth of his pockets. At the counter, one of the station staff had obligingly dipped inside Tom's coat, found his wallet and pulled out a credit card for payment. His signature had been a joke, but had thankfully been accepted. It had all felt a little undignified. When he needed a pee, Tom decided he would have to manage on his own.

The West Coast InterCity was due in five minutes, which probably meant he had another twenty to wait. The heating in his carriage would more than likely be kaput, and no doubt the automatic dividing door nearest to him would be stuck in that maddening limbo which has it opening and closing the entire way for no apparent reason, shushing frantically to and fro like a reject from the Star Trek Props Department.

A few minutes later, absolutely on time, the grimy yellow snout of a 125 appeared round the bend, down the line.

In the next second, Tom realised his journey was about to be infinitely more nightmarish than his imagined scenario.

'Hands up, Roker, it's the law,' said Nelson as he sidled up to Tom. 'Want a finger of Fudge?' he asked, producing an orange packet. 'Go on, take it.'

Tom kept his hands out of sight. 'I'm not hungry.'

'You don't need to be for chocolate. Go on, hold out your hand. Uncle Kenny has some sweeties for you.'

'I don't want any,' Tom said stiffly.

There was an uneasy break in the conversation. Nelson whistled something tuneless, but the wind stole most of its sound before it could really irritate.

'I hate stations,' he said suddenly. 'All those fond farewells. The platform awash with tears.'

Tom gave him a look. 'I think you'll be okay this afternoon,' he said dryly.

A hundred metres away, the train thundered into the station, buzzing the tracks in front of them.

'I think you're right,' Nelson agreed. 'I can't say I'll miss you. Nor you me, eh?'

'Very intuitive. That'll be your police training.'

'*And I don't blame you!*' Nelson shouted as the locomotive roared by. '*I've been on your case, haven't I? I hold my hands up to that!*'

Tom's ears pricked at yet another reference to hands. He waited for the engine noise to fade before speaking.

'Nelson, you're not catching this train, are you?'

'Are you leaving town?'

'Yes.'

'Then I'm catching this train.'

'Fine,' Tom said, stepping back against the station building. 'Then I'll get the next one.'

Nelson joined him. 'Then so will I.'

The train squealed to a coffee-spilling halt. People drained from its side like parasites abandoning a dying host. Doors slammed in an irregular pattern along the platform, and Tom was reminded of the shotgun blast which had launched the farmer's head into the lower branches of the horse chestnut. The last passenger was about to descend from the door directly in front of him. If it closed, Tom knew his wrecked fingers might never get it open again. Which would mean another hour. In the cold. With Nelson.

'All right,' he said, striding forward with Nelson hot on his heels, 'come to bloody London, I don't care.' He climbed aboard without using the handrail, still with his bandaged mitts in his pockets, and made it into the train without mishap. He hoped he appeared more smartarse than suspicious.

He hurried down the gangway, his eyes ignoring the table seating, searching for an isolated spot to escape from Nelson. Halfway along he fixed on one. A vacant window seat with an occupied aisle seat beside it, both facing the seatbacks in front.

'Anyone sitting here?' he asked.

'No,' said the elderly gent, getting up to allow Tom in.

333

There was no way round it. He would have to pull his right hand from its den to get the bag off his shoulder and stored away. But what the hell. How could seeing wraps of white crêpe bring any enlightenment to Nelson's bulbless investigation? Nelson was simply on another fishing trip. So Tom tugged both hands free from his pockets, lowered his right shoulder and let his holdall slide off and drop to the floor. He kicked it into the nearest luggage space.

Nelson stared at the bandages for a moment, but made no comment.

Tom winced as he used his palms to weakly grip the seatbacks, then shuffled in crabways and sat down. Nelson loitered in the aisle.

The old gent tutted kindly at Tom. 'My goodness. You poor chap. What have you done to yourself?'

Nelson shoved a warrant card in the old fellah's face. 'Police. Would you sit somewhere else? I need to talk to this man.'

The old gent turned his milky eyes up to Nelson, then beamed at him. 'By all means, of course, sir.' He collected his coat and case and wandered off.

Nelson dumped himself heavily into the vacated seat, and patted Tom's knee. 'Bloke like that,' he said, nodding towards the departing OAP, 'last of a dying breed. Part of a bygone era, when people had respect for the law.'

Tom ignored him. He was acutely aware of the bulky white gloves resting in his lap. And for the first time since Nelson had approached him on the platform, Tom suddenly recalled Milton's tale of the fat bad cop with the Stoplock. Was it true? Had Nelson killed a man?

The train jolted forward twice and began to roll smoothly on its way.

Tom had to say it: 'If you behaved properly, people might treat you better.'

Nelson sneered. 'What would you know? It's society that's changed, not us. We respond to what it gives us. And most of the time, it gives us no end of shite. There's the CPS who need fucking video evidence before they'll even go to court. The judges give a slap on the wrist when they should throw away the key. Lawyers push their clients through legal loopholes to get them acquitted so they can go out and rape again. Then there's Joe Public, who cries blue murder if some piece of scum violates his

334

precious home, but won't get involved when it happens to someone else. And then . . .'

Tom shrieked as Nelson lightly pinched his fingers. Nearby passengers turned in their seats. Nelson glowered at them and they quickly resumed their own business.

Nelson continued: '. . . then there's the likes of you, who seem to think they're above the law. Well, maybe *outside* the law's a better way of putting it. Like you think we couldn't solve the case even if you did let us in on the facts.'

Although Nelson was clearly grasping at straws, he had just succeeded in picking one up. Tom would have been quietly impressed had his wounds not been raging.

'Why don't you tell me,' Nelson urged conspiratorially, 'before someone kills you?'

Tom gave him a sideways stare. Was that a threat from Nelson? *Was* he a murderer? Tom kept his counsel.

'You see, Roker, I've always known you're in over your head, but when Doc Chocolate called me about the peculiar nature of your injuries this afternoon, I knew you'd just been dragged right under. Then when I got to the hospital and you'd done a runner, I guessed you'd finally had enough, and that you'd be running all the way back home. And there you were, waiting for a train. So I'm not stupid, am I? You tell me what's going on, I won't just scratch my head, I'll do something constructive about it. And you'll thank me for it, because I reckon your fingers are just a warning, right? Next time, whoever it is . . . he'll kill you. Am I right?'

Slowly, Tom began to shake his head. 'Nelson, I don't appreciate you hurting me just now. If you think *more* violence is going to solve anything, you're as deranged as—' He checked himself and shut up.

'As . . . ? As who? Give me a name,' Nelson pleaded. 'One piddling fucking name, that's all. Then you can go home. You'll never see me again.' His tone became desperate, and edged with threat. 'Come on, Roker, spill your guts.'

Tom smiled faintly at the irony. 'That's it, you see. If I did tell you, *no one* would ever see you again. At least not in one piece. He'd spill *your* guts.'

'*Who?*'

Outside the train, it went black. Track sounds beneath them

became amplified, and Tom swallowed to repressurise his ears. Then daylight again. Green fields, grey skies.

'You're wasting your time, Nelson. You might as well go to the Himalayas and look for the Yeti.'

Nelson manoeuvred in his seat to face Tom; not an easy thing for such a large man to do.

'Roker . . . you can tell me what I need to know willingly, or I can crush your fingers and make you talk that way. I don't want to but I will.'

'Yeah. A man's gotta do what a man's gotta do. And in my condition I can hardly stop you. But just listen to me, will you? Nothing I can say will help you crack this case; nothing can bring Sergeant Ash back. I expect you're already pencilled in to die. If you interfere, he'll go over your name with a black Biro, and a day later he'll be crossing it out. Do you understand? I'm not protecting him, I'm protecting you.'

'You don't think I'm a big boy? I can't take care of myself?'

Tom tried to think how best to get the message across.

'Have you seen *Terminator 2*?'

Nelson indulged this apparent tangent. 'Yes.'

'You know the liquid metal terminator in it?'

'What about it?'

'If one of those things wanted to kill you, do you think you'd get away?'

'No. What's your point?'

Tom struggled. This was going to sound ridiculous. 'Well . . . you're up against something on a par with that.'

'Don't talk crap.'

Tom shrugged and looked out of the window. Several minutes passed.

'All right,' Nelson finally allowed. 'Go on.'

Even in that short time, Tom had to pull himself back from the brink of sleep. His head felt swimmy he was so tired. 'Hmm? What?'

'I said go on.'

'Go on what?'

Agitated, Nelson said, 'I mean, you've got my attention. Explain why this biker is on a par with a relentless, nigh-on indestructible killing machine.'

Tom couldn't be bothered. Fatigue had swept through him like a debilitating virus. He turned away again to watch the countryside roll by, but his leaden eyelids immediately blocked the view. 'Because he is,' he quietly replied.

Then his eyelids snapped wide open and he thought his eyeballs would pop from his skull. Fire leapt inside his fingers and up his arms, tripping every pain sensor in his brain. Startled breath wheezed fiercely into his lungs, but instead of releasing it in a sound to wake the dead, Tom clamped his mouth and absorbed it all internally. He could almost feel his arteries furring up. But he wouldn't give Nelson the satisfaction of hearing him scream a second time.

Nelson let go of Tom's fingers. Incensed, Tom thrust his face up to Nelson's. His invective came out in a scratchy whisper.

'You fucking arsehole, Nelson. You're like some Wild West lawman with a score to settle, you're so *aggrieved* by it all, aren't you? You're so bloody righteous. Good old Nelson, out there rounding up the baddies. Well, you're a fucking hypocrite.' He was speaking too fast for his brain to vet the words before they were out. 'I've felt your violence and your temper, but I suppose I should be grateful; at least I'm still alive, unlike that poor sod in the Peugeot.'

In the beat that followed, Tom's brain caught up with his words. Perhaps this was one tale he should not have told. He was just glad to be in a carriageful of people. Especially as he could see now that Milton hadn't lied. Although he was trying to, Nelson could not conceal his shock, and something in his eyes admitted it was the shock of discovery, not the shock of having a scandalous, unfounded accusation levelled against him. Without the carriageful of people, Tom realised he would have been a goner.

Nelson squinted at him, his whole face tense with fury. 'And where did you hear shit like that?'

Tom could see no harm in telling the truth. Anyway, he couldn't think of an alternative explanation. 'From the man you're after.'

Nelson snorted, belatedly deciding to offer some semblance of innocence. 'Roker, that story was on the news. He hears it, he's feeling guilty, so he shifts the spotlight onto someone else. And you believe him?'

Tom had to smile. 'Nelson, the last thing this man feels is guilt.'

'Right, I forgot, he's a cyborg.'

'No, he's the undead.' There, he'd said it.

Nelson appeared to freeze for a moment, then cracked up with roaring laughter.

But Tom persisted. 'He saw you do it, Nelson. He wasn't there, but he saw you. He has powers. I think the technical term for it is Remote Viewing.'

Still overtly amused, Nelson shook his head. 'Novelists. You live in a fantasy land. Chief witness for the Crown: a murdering zombie with ESP. Get writing, Roker, I'm sure it'll be another bestseller.'

'Yeah, I sound deranged,' Tom said, 'I know. And I might be. I've seen enough to send me down that road. But if I am, he made me that way. He came first. If I do have any mental illness, he's the reason, not the product.'

Nelson dismissed it with a wave of one fat-fingered hand. 'Tell it to your shrink, Roker.'

'He saw you. He did. You took a Stoplock and you killed him.'

Nelson's smile vanished, swiftly followed by the blood from his face. He blinked once but that was all. He was totally silent, totally still. He looked like a mannequin. Even the pallid skin tone was right.

Wow. Something had struck a chord. Tom wondered what. The answer quickly dawned; there was no other explanation.

Tom spoke slowly, confidentially, formulating his theory as he went. 'The weapon you actually used to kill him wasn't in the news, was it? I mean, I might be wrong – I haven't read a paper or watched TV in ages – but the police often hold back a few pertinent details, don't they? Helps sift out any bogus callers they might get.' Tom was really enjoying himself now. 'So how do I know about it? How does the biker? And if *you* didn't see *him* on that night, you need to ask yourself how the hell he managed to see you, and see you close enough to identify your weapon.'

Tom waited for a response, or a punch and several crushed fingers.

What he got was a barely audible grunt before Nelson got up from his seat as though in a trance, and wandered off along the carriage, crashing against seat-sides with the train's rocking momentum.

Thirty seconds later, the train driver slammed on the brakes, hurtling folk forward in their seats, flattening buffet customers in the gangway, throwing table detritus onto suits and dresses, and pouring luggage down from the racks.

When the wheels finally finished squealing and everything came to a standstill, Tom pressed his cheek to the cold window and just glimpsed a flash of yellow down the side of the train, the internal colour of the carriage door, as it was pushed open. A moment later, Nelson was seen to disembark, heave his bulk over a fence and set off staggering across a boggy field.

FIFTY-SIX

The leafless branches above Michael's head rattled in the wind as he cycled his old Raleigh racing bike towards Alderley Edge. He was dressed in black, with a dog collar and cassock. He had deemed it appropriate to wear the garb of his calling on this special night. He was about to lock horns with the AntiChrist. Jeans and pullover didn't cut it. His cassock trailed behind him, flapping and twisting. He felt like Batman.

He carried no bag of goodies with him. No Bible, no holy water. Not even a torch, and the batteries in his bicycle lamp had long since died. A silver crucifix hung around his neck, but it was nothing he would not have ordinarily worn with the rest of the outfit. He did not sense the need for other accoutrements. God would provide all the back-up he needed.

As the day had dragged on, Michael had become increasingly certain that his journey tonight would not be wasted. His sixth sense was on red alert. He felt wired, crackling with something akin to static electricity. It was more than the excitement of a true vocation finally revealed. It was the prospect of Angie's personal thank you to him. Each time he pictured it, coupling on the purple altar cloth, basking in the sun-bright colours of the East window, his groin would perform delirious little somersaults that made him shiver.

He pedalled hard. It was eleven-fifteen and he had another mile to go. With time in hand, he could check the lie of the land and talk pre-fight strategy with the Angel of the Lord. He glanced up. Above the disturbed and tangled canopy, the sky was starless. The heavens were hidden from his sight.

The path he had to take led to darkness. Michael lifted his racer over the stile and climbed over himself. Breathing heavily from his

340

exertions, he contemplated the view ahead, peering into the gloom. Two hundred yards away, the stone outcrop was only visible as a wide break of midnight blue in the black treeline. Either side of the outcrop, woods undulated along the Edge, dropping steeply down to the floor of the Cheshire Plain. In the woods themselves were caves, unexpected plummets, mini-valleys with sheer rock walls, and rain-filled scars in sandstone clearings. By day it was a playground. By night it was a perilous collection of topographical ways to kill a person. And that was without Satan lurking in the shadows.

A panic gripped Michael briefly, then flew off with the wind. He was left feeling wary, which was no doubt reasonable under the circumstances, but it was not a feeling he had at all anticipated. Forgetting to bring a torch now seemed extremely stupid.

He reassured himself; God would give a sign of His protection not when His servant needed it, but when it was appropriate. It was a simple matter of faith. He began to wheel his bicycle, treading carefully over the exposed roots he remembered from his previous, less ominous visits on warm summer days. Now, his shoes squelched in pools of mud, and the howling gale bombarded his eardrums, making them roar like sea-shells. He was listening out for a motorbike, but would have been hard pressed to hear Armageddon kick off.

At the outcrop, he laid his racer on its side and waited. He kept a safe distance from the Edge. He could see where the pale orange rock abruptly fell away, and he didn't want to do the same. He began turning 360 degrees on the spot, scanning all directions, including the air above the Edge; perhaps Milton was visiting this dimension on a Fly-Ride holiday.

Exposed above the Cheshire Plain, the wind felt ten times stronger. Each time it eased for a few seconds, strange scurryings in the nearby undergrowth made him jump. He was ashamed of himself. He could not deny: wary had become terrified. It was probably nothing more sinister than a family of cutesy bunny rabbits.

Probably. Which meant it was *possibly* something else.

Back on the road a car streaked by, lighting a tunnel of trees ahead of it before disappearing down the hill towards the village of Alderley Edge.

Michael imagined himself inside that car. A business man, warm and snug in a Jag, a classical CD in the machine, on his way back

341

from a conference in London, mere minutes from his warm bed and welcoming wife and angelic, dreaming children.

Oh, *Jesus wept*, he wanted to be that man. He wanted to be *any* man who had a loving family at home; a family that cared what happened to him on that wretched slab of rock.

He looked at the light framework of his bicycle on the ground. Could he get away from this place before the moment of confrontation? Even if there was not to be a confrontation, could he get away before he went mad with the fear of it? Where was his haloed protector? And where was his faith without that manifestation? His eyes darted left and right, chasing black shapes in his periphery that he knew weren't there. Never before had he experienced the sheer power of darkness to overwhelm. It stretched for thousands of miles around, and millions above. He felt it like a physical force gathering against him, weighing down on him, making him the epicentre of an evil plot to destroy him.

'I'm going,' he said breathily to no one in particular. He reached down and plucked his bicycle upright, but before he could run, the wind died and a distant whisper drifted to him through the lull.

'*Miiiichaaaeeel.*'

He spun on his feet towards the source. It had come from the woods. He wanted to flee, but he couldn't move. It seemed the voice had transformed him from terrified to petrified. He squinted into the wood's impenetrable black guts, expecting some ghastly demon to vomit forth and shred him with its claws.

Suddenly, there was a pale blob in the blackness. Heart thudding, Michael strained his eyes and identified it as a face.

'Oh, praise God,' he whispered shakily, because hovering above the face was a white halo, just as there had been outside the church that night.

But, next moment, the halo began to move whilst the face stayed put. Left to right, up and down, then waggling comically like a plate-spinner's plate about to fall. It stilled, lowered past the face, shifted slightly right, then sharply left, frisbeeing out of the undergrowth, carried through the air by the wind.

Horrified, Michael watched his missing dog collar land in a puddle.

'*Michael!*' Milton rasped, and charged out of the woods.

Rather unhelpfully, Michael's vice-like grip on his bicycle would not loosen. The rest of his body had gone from stone to jelly, but his fingers were curled tightly around the handlebars.

Eventually, when Milton had covered half the fifty yard distance between them, his boots hammering down on the sandstone bluff, Michael managed to throw his bike on the ground and set off running towards the woods opposite. The prospect of crashing headlong into a tree was very real and highly unappealing, but short of jumping over the Edge there was nowhere else to go; his late reaction had allowed Milton to pass the mouth of the path which would have led him back to the road.

But perhaps God *was* watching over him, because Michael somehow kept to his feet, dodging every tree, and the footfalls behind him were miraculously fading, and when they had faded sufficiently, he would be able to stop and hide, safe in the knowledge that if he couldn't hear where Milton was, Milton would have no idea where *he* was.

For now, he sped ahead. He had a place of refuge in mind, somewhere he could stay until morning, out of the elements. Milton would expect his prey to keep moving, but running was a mug's game. At some point, exhaustion would stop a runner in his tracks. That being the case, it seemed wise to pre-empt the exhaustion and hole up in a place of his choosing. Otherwise he might collapse out in the open where Milton could stumble across him.

Well, the theory was sound.

It was a small pit in the ground, an old, man-made amphitheatre. Two sides of sloping grass and two of sheer rock walls. In one of those rock walls was a machine-bored cave, a circular tunnel extending horizontally about a hundred and fifty feet into the ground. Michael had known about it since childhood and had ventured in only once for a dare when he was thirteen. Drawn by his torchlight, moths had fluttered off the walls and scared the hell out of him, scaring him out of the cave in the process.

Now he was being scared *into* the cave.

Michael ducked his head as he hurried inside, brushing his fingertips against the side walls to keep him centred. It was pitch black. Nothing, but nothing, was visible ahead. For all he knew, Milton could have been in there already, standing five feet in front of him, waiting, and Michael would only have known it when he bumped into him and smelt leather.

For this reason, Michael assumed he would be safe. Who would expect him to seek shelter in the darkest, most goosebumping place on the Edge? Being pursued by the undead, wouldn't he head for the lights of the nearest village?

A hundred feet in, Michael bumped into something and smelt leather.

On waking, Michael was surprised to discover he wasn't dead. He was lying on his right side with his bicycle between his legs. His hands were gaffer-taped to the handlebars, his fingers left free for the brakes, and the same silver bindings secured his upper thighs to the thin racing saddle, which was on nodding terms with his colon, so firmly was the crack of his bum in contact with it. He expected to see his feet taped to the pedals, and was puzzled to find they weren't. His head ached and stung, and he could feel the congealed blood matted in his hair from where Milton had smashed him unconscious against the cave wall, but that seemed to be his only injury. He was not quite naive enough to believe it would be his last.

The wind had calmed, but he could still feel a gentle breeze. Trees and bushes rustled lightly. All down the right side of his body, small stones dug into his skin. He could smell them: chips of limestone. He had been carried to the visitors' car park, off the main road; for what purpose he could not begin to imagine, and his ignorance was likely to be his only blessing, and shortlived at that.

He lifted his head clear of the ground. Several small stones had stuck to his temple and cheek and they now dropped off, one by one.

Ten feet away, a black motorcycle was parked on its sidestand. A chariot from Hell. On the petrol tank was a black crash helmet.

Suddenly he was being manhandled upright.

'Both feet on the ground, please, Mick,' Milton said in the kindly manner of a motorcycle instructor with a novice. 'Though when we get going, obviously you should keep them up.'

'Get going?' Michael said feebly as he planted his shoes on the stony surface of the deserted car park.

Milton bent down and picked up some rope from the ground. 'I never go anywhere without a length of rope and a roll of gaffer tape. Bloody useful, I can tell you.'

'For what?' Michael squeaked like a fool, as though he wasn't about to find out.

344

'Ooh, all sorts,' Milton answered, before proceeding to tie one end to the front of the Raleigh. 'By the way, did you like the trick with the dog collar?'

'What are you doing?'

'Nothing for nosies.' And the other end was attached to the pillion grabrail of the ZZ-R.

'You can't scare me,' Michael blatantly fibbed. 'I'm one of The Chosen. The Lord will stay your murderous hand.'

Milton paused to stare into the night sky. 'Cutting it a bit fine, isn't He?'

Michael began whining. 'But I'm not the one you want. Go and kill Tom Roker. It's his fault.'

'Wrong,' Milton said, plucking his helmet from the tank. 'What's happening to you now, preacher man, is very much down to you.' He clumped back over to him. 'Know why?'

'No.'

Milton sniggered. 'Did I get away with that? Calling you preacher man? It's the sort of thing I think people expect from me, but I really can't say it with a straight face. It's just too Clint Eastwood.'

'What in Christ's name are you talking about?' Michael cried in confused terror.

'You're very, shall we say, *fond* of Angie Kellett. Aren't you, Mick?'

Michael offered a dumb expression, but now knew what it was all about. Somewhere inside Milton was the angry spirit of Andrew Kellett, and, last summer, Michael had tried to rape his sister.

'Yes, we're on the same wavelength,' Milton said, nodding. 'But, you know, Mick, you lost your place in heaven a long time ago. Fooling yourself with your so-called vocation. A career hypocrite, that's you. A lifetime in denial. Let's hope the Buddhists are right about reincarnation, eh? Means you'll get another crack at the whip. Course, first you'll have to work your way back up from a threadworm.'

There was no defence. Dead centre on his forehead, Michael felt a sudden, intense heat. He frowned at Milton, who simply grinned back. Then the heat was gone and a warm fluid dribbled between his eyes. The flow became heavier. He could feel it splitting into three streams. One ran straight to the tip of his nose and dripped off, the other two fell either side of the bridge, to trace like tears down his cheeks. He went cross-eyed to identify what it was, and saw a darkness that could only be one thing. Milton was laughing now, a guttural sound that made Michael's flesh crawl.

'Bad blood,' Milton said to him, and laughed some more.

Michael whimpered in response. What was happening to him?

Milton raised a gloved hand and crossed himself – forehead, sternum, shoulder, shoulder.

Michael understood: his scar was bleeding; the cut he had inflicted upon himself last summer at Angie's, when he had taken a shard of picture glass and scored a crucifix between his eyes. He even recalled the photograph in the frame, though he could not remember seeing it at the time: Andrew Kellett on his motorcycle.

Now the cross was purging itself.

Milton slipped his helmet on, muffling his laughter, then flipped open the black visor. 'We'll take it easy at first. Let you get the hang of things, then we'll crank it up a bit. Oh, and when that happens, you might want to keep your feet off the pedals.'

The noise of the ZZ-R drowned out Michael's screaming protests. Exhaust fumes floated back and swam around his head, making him feel even more nauseous. Milton's taillight came on, and the ZZ-R edged forward towards the car park exit.

As they eased out onto the road, Michael blinked to clear his bloody veil, but he was effectively blinded. They picked up speed. Fifteen miles an hour perhaps, though it felt like fifty. The pedals flew round and Michael lifted his legs away from the bike, like a kid coasting down a hill. He probably looked like he was enjoying himself.

He wasn't, and it seemed undignified to go to his death sightless. He squeezed both brakes gently, hoping Milton might feel a slight tug behind him.

After a few seconds, Milton slowed and pulled over. Michael rode over a lump of rock, lost his balance, and fell with the bicycle into a mud-filled roadside ditch. Milton put the ZZ-R on its sidestand, got off and walked back to him. Michael and bicycle were righted, then Milton lifted his visor and cocked his head questioningly to one side.

'What now?'

'I can't *see*!'

Milton huffed theatrically, went back to his bike, unlocked and lifted the seat, and returned with an oily rag and the roll of gaffer tape. He draped the rag over the handlebars and then inspected the tape, circling it in his hands before finding the end and struggling to unpick it from the roll.

'Take your gloves off,' Michael said.

'Good idea.'

That done, Michael received a wipe down with the rag, then had it pressed to his forehead and gaffer-taped in place with three wraps round his head. Milton left the remaining roll dangling over Michael's left ear, and trudged back to his bike without a word.

Off again. Michael's vision was still hardly 20/20, but at least he could see enough to anticipate curves in the road. Ahead, Milton's headlight barrelled into the night, illuminating a broken white line which could only lead to a dead end.

The hill led down to the outskirts of Alderley Edge village. Amazingly, Michael stayed on two wheels, at speeds, he reckoned, of up to 50 m.p.h. At the foot of the hill, Milton slowed and turned left, pointing his bike away from the shops.

They kept to between forty and fifty through weaving country lanes. Michael wasn't dressed for a midnight blast into the wilds. The rushing air felt like ice, and he juddered and moaned like a man in cold turkey. Wind-induced tears swept across his temples and into his earholes. He was half blinded – yet again. His cassock cracked and flapped and twisted behind him, and the hanging roll of gaffer tape kept thwacking against the side of his skull.

At four miles, a solitary car passed by. At five, they passed a sign for the M6, and Michael began to wonder how 70 m.p.h. might feel. Then he remembered that Milton was not exactly the law-abiding motorist, and from the awesome sound of the motorcycle ahead, perhaps *one hundred* and seventy was closer to the mark.

Oh, Lordy Lord.

A mile further on, Milton turned down the motorway slip road, and Michael resigned himself and made his peace.

They joined the motorway at sixty, scooting straight across into the empty outside lane. It was beyond reason, but Michael, with his eyes now coursing rivers into his ears, remained upright, and the whole affair warped in his mind from dangerously real to gigglingly unreal. It was *The Way-Out Whacky Races*, and he was Mick Minister, hot on the heels of Dick Dastardly and Penelope Pitstop.

The next surge of acceleration was so abrupt that as the ZZ-R wheelied past the ton, Michael's front wheel was also jerked clean off the road.

He bowed his head and closed his eyes and was on the deck and dead before the first of his bones were exposed by the friction of the speeding tarmac.

FIFTY-SEVEN

Information received. There were two things to do with it: act on it or ignore it. Nelson had yesterday received information that he was the man wanted for the brutal murder of a motorist, and the witness to his crime was . . . undead. Yeah, yeah. So would he act on it? Would he shop himself to his colleagues? Would he appeal to any zombies passing the crime scene that night to come forward and identify him? Sure.

But neither could he ignore it. Someone out there knew it was him. Whoever they were, however they knew, it didn't matter. They knew, and they could talk. If they had been downstairs in custody, Nelson could have arranged a nice little suicide for them. If he had known whose door to knock on, he would have done so, then would have knocked on their heads with a baseball bat. But the person who did know was the very person he had not been able to apprehend in over eight months, and now he wasn't at all sure he *wanted* to catch him. Nelson had made some enemies on both sides of the law. It would only take one copper with a grudge against him to pursue matters and push forensics to find a connection.

Poring over the latest victim report, Nelson had to smile. If it really was down to a killer zombie, it was good to know that death did not diminish a person's sense of humour. A ton-up vicar on a pushbike. Fucking hysterical.

Nelson, however, did not believe in zombies, or anything else that he couldn't readily pop into an existing file. Which meant he had a problem, because apart from the 'Remote Viewing' Roker had suggested, he could not figure out how anyone outside the investigation could have known about the Stoplock. Even the motorist on the opposite carriageway had stated his ignorance on that specific detail.

He realised he would just have to wait and see. He couldn't crack the case, and, with recent developments, was now loathe to. It was simple. Either the biker would one day disappear for good, or he would eventually become blasé and get himself arrested. On the evidence to date, it seemed unlikely that the biker's wrists would ever be troubled by the steely crush of handcuffs.

But if it did happen, Nelson vowed he would not let the knowledgeable bastard make it into court.

Angie resigned before they could sack her. She phoned in that morning and gave her notice, then gave notice she would not be working her notice. The manageress grunted her acknowledgment and didn't force the issue.

It felt like another chapter in her life was closing, and she had to do her part to help it close. Another skin was sloughing off; more dead cells left in her wake.

Tom was gone, and she missed him. Her reaction might have seemed inappropriate had she not understood the psychology; she knew no one else she *could* miss, and everyone needed to experience that poignant emptiness to feel alive. Besides, they had shared too much for her *not* to miss him. She certainly didn't hate him. For all the damage he had wrought, she believed he had not wilfully set out to cause any of it. He had been a fool, then a catalyst, and now she suspected he was dancing on the edge of madness. He was to be pitied more than despised.

The fact of his departure begged certain questions. Did he think he had solved the problem? Had he truly solved the problem? Or had he simply given up?

At lunchtime she tuned into local radio, and the leading item on the news informed her that the situation was as dire as ever. Milton was still gadding about, doing his thing.

Angie wept. Not for Michael, for herself. Because whatever Tom had done, whatever he thought he might have achieved, it wasn't over yet.

As a token comfort in a life of trouble, waking up in his own bed felt good. The whole house seemed more like a home than in years. Tom supposed it was all a matter of perspective; having just stayed in a building where death was practically built into the brickwork, he could now appreciate the comparatively happy history of his own

350

place. True, he had lost his wife and daughter, but to another man, not to the Grim Reaper.

The news from up North reinstated his general downer. The vicar had failed. Tom knew this without listening to any radio, watching TV or reading a paper. Within half an hour of rising, a bombardment of bad vibes had convinced him: Michael was dead. Rationally, he might have expected as much. Telepathically, he knew it as a fact.

Where that left him, God alone knew. And God alone knew how he would manage on his own without the use of his fingers.

His burns were on fire again. Thankfully, an overdose of tiredness and a couple of paracetamols had seen him through the night. The child-proof cap had proved difficult until he had smashed the bottle under his heel, releasing the pills that way. Picking up two of the little bleeders had been another lesson in frustration.

He wandered downstairs to the kitchen and made a mess as he made a coffee, scattering granules all over the counter. As it cooled, he bent down and chased two more painkilling tablets around the floor with his bandaged mitts, but this time did not have the patience to succeed. So he lowered his face to the tiles and kissed them into his mouth. The dust and fluff were a bonus. Standing again, he lifted his coffee mug between the heels of his palms and took a swallow, helping the medication and assorted floor muck down his gullet. He felt a bit like a Thunderbirds puppet in his tragic lack of dexterity.

Remembering his answering machine, he took his coffee through to the front living room. He really didn't care who might have called whilst he was away. They would all be people from his old life, and if he was to be allowed a new life, they would not be a part of it. It was idle curiosity that prompted him to press the replay button.

The first message was from Carol, with information concerning the film deal, information he now had since he had called her from Angie's. It was strange hearing her voice, knowing she was dead and that he was to blame.

Then the simpering tones of a life insurance salesman. Did Mr Roker need some? Oh, yeah, mate, bloody funny.

Next, Roger Mercer. 'Tom, Roger. Re Pyramid: we need to talk. Call me.'

Followed by a voice that caused his heart to skip a beat and his

mouth to drop open. 'Hello, Tom, it's Helen. I'm just calling . . .
to check you're okay. You've made the news over here. There's,
uh . . . someone acting out scenes from your book, is that right? It
sounds awful. Umm . . . yeah, Charlotte's doing fine. She's worried
about you, of course, but, uh . . . she's . . . she's fine. Listen, give
me a ring, you've got the number. I know Charlotte would feel
a lot better if she could hear your voice. And, uh . . . we could
chat. You know, about . . . things. Anyway, call soon. Bye, Tom.
Take care.'

Emotions surged inside him. His chin began rippling. His legs
became weak. Helen's voice was the release he needed. He wanted
his family. He missed his daughter. He sank into an armchair, broke
down and bawled his head off.

When the storm had passed, Tom felt almost as crappy as before.
The crotch of his pyjamas was sodden with fallen tears. He reached
across to the phone and knuckled the button to return the tape to
the start of Helen's message.

He listened again and the tears stayed away. She sounded
genuinely concerned, and not just for him, also for herself; as
though she was scared of losing him. But hadn't she lost him
years ago? Did he have the right to hear anything more than
indifference in her voice? No. He didn't have the right to hear
her voice at all. Whilst they were man and wife, he had virtually
ignored her to concentrate on his precious writing. So how much
meaningful communication could he reasonably expect from her
today, when she had a new husband in a new country?

For all that, he knew his Helen. Her tone had always conveyed
more than her words, like a secret code only he could crack, and
those awkward pauses said something else again. Helen was highly
articulate, never lost for words. He had never known an occasion
when she had struggled to maintain a flowing sentence. She kept
her silence and her speech entirely separate. If she could not express
herself perfectly, she would say nothing. So to hear the hesitancy in
her voice, her sentence structure fragmented by pauses and dumb
little noises, it was obvious that her heart, or mind, or both, were
in desperate turmoil.

And perhaps Tom had finally turned a corner. Maybe, just maybe,
he was on a different road now, leaving Selfish Street behind him in
the past. Because, despite his own multitudinous headaches, they

paled beside the thought that a crisis might be affecting the lives of Helen and Charlotte. He suddenly realised there were at least two other people in the world whose happiness meant more to him than his own.

He grabbed the phone, gritting his teeth against the flaring pain the action brought. He jabbed a finger at the international code for the States, squeaking with each digit. Then he stopped and depressed the cut-off.

He had to think. He couldn't just launch back into their lives, babbling emotionally, talking rekindled flames and joyous reconciliations, on the basis of a hunch. Okay, they might not be happy, but that didn't mean they were inviting him to cheer them up by re-forming the family unit.

Instead of phoning out, someone rang in, and Tom picked up.

'Tom! Roger. Four mill, two books. Good deal, eh? We're all going to be rich.'

'Except Carol,' Tom said.

Roger tried to sound downbeat, but the effort was more evident than the sorrow. 'Er, yeah, yeah. Just unbelievable. Couldn't believe it. Carol dead. Murdered. Ghastly. Fantastic for sales, though. Really helps. So when can I have the sequel?'

'What . . . ? You haven't seen it?' This was unexpected but excellent news, because whatever Milton decided to do, Tom did not want his further antics glorified on screen or in a published work.

'No.'

Thinking fast, Tom said, 'Well, you wouldn't have, because there isn't one.'

'Pardon?'

'It doesn't exist.'

'What? But Carol said—'

'Carol lied.'

'She lied? Why?'

'Greed.'

Roger took a moment to consider, then said hopefully, 'But you can still write one.'

'No. I've had my fill of Milton.'

'Well, just give them a treatment. A one-page synopsis. That'll do for now.'

353

'It's not going to happen, Roger.'

'I understand,' Roger said; 'you're upset. Your agent's dead—'

'A fucking *score* of people are dead, you callous shit.'

Roger cleared his throat. 'I'm as distressed as the next person, I really am. But . . . Tom, business is business. The contract has been signed.'

'Not by me.'

'No, by Carol.'

'So what's the problem? They can't sue a corpse.'

'They're *Yanks*, Tom. They'll find a way to sue *me*.'

'Shit happens, Rog.'

Roger tried to sound calm. 'Tom . . . Tom,' he said, then spent five seconds floundering in silence. 'Tom . . . please let me speak. Can I? Will you let me?'

Tom shrugged to himself. 'Go ahead.'

'Tom . . . once this motorcycle maniac is in prison, you'll feel different. I know you will. I guarantee you will. All I want, is if Pyramid talk to you, you say . . . I don't know . . . you've had to rewrite. Yeah, you've had to rewrite, but the sequel is most definitely in the pipeline.'

Tom stayed quiet. Roger waited. Tom stayed quiet.

'Tom?'

'Oh, I'm allowed to speak now, thanks. Trouble is, Roger, no sequel will ever emerge from any pipeline because I will never write one.'

'But you might.'

'I won't.'

'You don't know that.'

'I do.'

'But if *you* don't write a sequel, someone else will.'

'I can't help that. I just don't want my name attached to it.'

'Tom . . . fuck's sake, it's a done deal.'

Tom felt sorry for the man. He was denying him a once-in-a-lifetime coup.

'Listen, Roger, why don't you tell them the manuscript was stolen when Carol was murdered. They know what's happening over here with the biker. Say he killed her and stole it. As far as they're concerned, it's all grist to the mill. More bad news making great publicity.'

'D'you think that'll work?'

'Better than the truth, yes. You can suggest they have the first novel for a million – their original offer – and throw in character rights for free. As you say, there are plenty of scriptwriters in Hollywood; they'll get a sequel from someone.'

Roger swore. 'It doesn't look like I have much choice, does it? I think you're being a fool, though.'

'No, I have been a fool, and now I'm trying to rectify it. That's what this is all about.'

Roger groaned. 'I don't understand, but I don't suppose I'm meant to. So, assuming this does work out like you say, and they send me a cheque, what should I do? Take my ten per cent and send you the remainder so you can forward what's owed to Carol's estate?'

Tom thought about it. His fifty-fifty deal with Carol was a secret. If he wanted, he could ignore it and let Peter Morgan have just the usual agent's cut.

'Roger, take your ten . . . then send the rest to Peter Morgan.'

'Sorry? Come again?'

'I don't want any of it.'

Roger tested him with a laugh.

'I don't,' Tom said.

'You're having me on.'

'I don't want it.'

'You're serious, aren't you?'

'Yes.'

'So can't I have it, then?'

Tom smiled. 'Nice try, Rog.'

'Nah . . . hold on. You're saying you want Peter Morgan to have nine hundred thousand pounds that you earned? You are joking.'

Tom would have preferred to make Angie Kellett a joint beneficiary, but he couldn't risk it. If he handed her a cheque, he would in effect be handing her proof of his guilt should she suddenly wake up one morning and belatedly feel compelled to tell all to the police.

'Every penny,' he said.

'*Why?*'

'That's my affair.'

The silence from Roger's end was priceless. Eventually, when he was able to speak, he said, 'Jesus, Roker. What's your middle name? Fucking *Camelot*?'

'Give it to Peter Morgan,' Tom repeated, and hung up.

FIFTY-EIGHT

It was early evening before Tom made the critical call. He had spent the day slobbing in front of the telly, absorbing none of the garbage it spewed into his living room. He had swapped his pyjamas for sweatshirt and sweatpants to avoid the impossible feat of buttoning up.

Mid-afternoon, he had telephoned the local medical centre to arrange for his wounds to be examined and re-dressed.

But that was tomorrow, and tomorrow seemed a long way off. Between now and then he would make the most important phone call of his adult life. Perhaps it would work out as nothing more than a few terse words with his ex-wife and a weepy exchange with his daughter. If it did, he knew he would handle it the same way he had handled everything recently: very poorly. It might even signal the end for him. He still reserved his right to suicide, even if he had not yet felt the final trigger-pull inside his head to make him do it. After all, he may have been mistaken. Perhaps there was no subtext to Helen's message. Perhaps it had been a call made purely on Charlotte's behalf to check on her dad's wellbeing, and Helen's awkwardness was the natural discomfort of having to speak to a machine, and, worse, a machine that spoke for an ex-husband she had hardly spoken to since their divorce.

Still, Helen had requested a return call, and, apart from a few more tears, he had nothing left to lose by obliging.

He switched off the television and dialled. As he did, he tried to squash that illogical bud of hope that had never completely died out of his heart. When he couldn't do that, he told himself to ignore it; to stop clinging onto that pathetic, shattered dream of Tom Roker as husband and father.

The connection was made. Helen's end gave a mellow warble: distinctly un-British. After a further three, it was picked up.

'Hello.'

Tom swallowed. 'Hi, are you having a nice day out there?'

Her reply was not instant and he feared he had somehow offended her with his very first comment. Then he heard a smile in her voice.

'Tom. Hi. My day's going okay. How about yours?'

Chirpily, he said, 'Fair to bloody.'

'Yeah, I figured as much. That's why I called.'

'*Figured?*' Tom said. 'Picking up the lingo, eh?'

She laughed, but there was a sadness in the sound.

'Hel, are you okay?'

'You're the only one who's ever called me Hel.'

'Are you okay?'

'Terry and I are divorcing,' she said swiftly, as though she would choke on the words if she didn't spit them out.

'Oh . . . shit, Hel, I'm sorry.'

She was not cruel enough to question his sincerity on that score.

'So what are you going to do?' he asked, trying to keep the self-interest out of his voice.

'I don't know; d'you want to speak to Charlotte?'

She had shut the door on the subject, and Tom knew there was no breaking it down. 'Please, yeah, I'd love to.'

A moment later he was crying again: Charlotte had said hello to him.

'Dad, what's wrong?' Her accent was pure US.

'I miss you, darling, that's all,' he spluttered.

'I miss you, too, but you can catch a plane, can't you?'

Tom had to pull himself together, for his daughter's sake. 'I can, yes, and I will, very soon.' He wiped his eyes dry on his sleeve.

'When? Tomorrow?' she said eagerly.

Tom warmed to her innocence. 'No, I'm very busy at the moment, sweetheart; now's not a good time.'

'You mean the man who's killing people?'

'Uh, no, no, it's not that. Don't worry, that doesn't affect me. The police'll get him. Anyway, how are you doing?'

'I wasn't feeling very well today so Mom kept me off, but I'll be okay tomorrow.'

Tom computed the information. 'Oh, of *course*, I was forgetting about the time difference. You should be at school at the moment, shouldn't you?'

'Yeah, I think I'd be in math right about now. But I'm okay to miss a day. My grades are good. Especially English. I think I get that from you.'

Tom giggled. 'Maybe. I'm pleased you're doing so well.'

'You know, Dad, if you can't come to us, we can come to you. We both want to.'

Tom held the phone away from his ear and gave it a queer look, as though some vindictive circuitry had scrambled her meaning. In the background he could hear Helen reprimanding her big-mouthed daughter, her voice growing louder as she approached the phone to snatch it away. He gripped the phone tightly. 'Charlotte, sweetheart, what did you say?'

Helen answered. 'Ignore her, Tom. She's simplified matters in her own mind and decided the three of us should get back together. She's a kid, it's how they think.'

'And how do you think, Hel?'

'I think . . . it's not as simple as that.'

Tom was in mental agony. He had been after this huge catch for years – the one that got away – and now it was on the end of his line again he was scared to reel it in. What if he made the wrong move and lost it for ever? How would he cope, knowing he had come so near?

Gently, he said, 'Okay, but if it was simple, how would you feel then?'

'Oh, Tom, I don't know. Charlotte's had a rough ride. We both have. I just want us to be happy.'

Make or break. 'And do you think I could make you happy?'

'You did, for a long time.'

'And I screwed up.'

'Honestly, yes.'

Tom felt the line snap and his hope swim away. He very nearly put the phone down.

'But, you know, Tom . . . I still love the person you used to be. I'd come back to that Tom Roker. God, I'd never have left that Tom Roker.'

Tom hardly wanted to speak. Perhaps it would be better just to savour these sentiments rather than open his mouth and make Helen regret opening hers.

'I've stopped writing,' he forced himself to say.

'Is that true or what you think I want to hear?'

'Both.'

'Why?'

'All this business with Milton.'

'Who?'

Tom grimaced. 'He's the bloke the police are after.'

'You *know* him?'

'No! Shit, no, I just . . . call him that. It's a nickname. You obviously haven't read the book or you'd understand.'

'Oh. So what are you going to do if you don't write?'

It was a fair question, and he had no idea. 'Well . . . get into the other side of it, I suppose. Editing, proofreading, whatever. I've got contacts.' That was good; that was his career change sorted. 'Are you interested?' he asked, as though he was flogging double-glazing.

'There's nothing keeping us here,' she said, monumentally. 'When could we come?'

It was extraordinary; one telephone call had changed the course of his life. He wanted to shout out, '*As soon as you can!*' but that would have been the selfish Tom talking. He was not safe to be around. Until he was, if he ever was, it was best they stayed thousands of miles away. If he loved them, he would keep that distance between them.

'I love you,' he said. 'I love you both.' His chest tightened. 'That's why I can't let you come over yet. I don't know what this nutter has in mind. I can't put you at risk. Do you understand?'

'Had you said anything different, I'd have been very disappointed.'

Tom felt like the only kid in class with the right answer. 'Can I ask . . . why are you and Terry splitting up?'

'Tom, you had a mistress—'

'Wha—?' Tom's stomach dropped to his feet; Christ, had she known all along about his cheating weeks with Carol?

'—and that was writing,' she continued. 'Terry, on the other hand, is screwing his eighteen-year-old secretary.'

Phew. 'Oh, Carol, I'm so sorry,' Tom said with immense understanding.

'Carol?' Helen queried.

'Sorry?'

'You called me Carol.'

Tom's stomach crashed through the floor into the foundations. 'Er, yeah, I did, didn't I?'

'Why?' she asked, making no attempt to mask her suspicion.

Tom thought swiftly, but his excuse was ready-made. 'She was murdered yesterday.'

Helen gasped. 'My God!'

'I've been thinking about her a lot since then.'

'I thought these were copycat killings; only the scenes in the novel. Has it got that close to you?'

Tom reverted to type, and span a yarn. At least it was only verbal. 'No, don't worry. The police don't believe it's connected. I'm sure the media will be adding it to the biker's tally, but I've been told that really isn't the case.'

'Oh . . . good.'

Tom hopped back to the main issue. 'So I'll call you when it's all died a death. Sorry, poor turn of phrase. I'll call when I feel it's safe for you both to be here. Are you going to be at the same number?'

'Yeah. For the time being. Terry and I are amicable – if you call ignoring each other amicable. We've pretty much left the argument phase behind.'

Tom wasn't sure how to respond. Comforting his ex-wife over the failure of her second marriage, when he had long prayed for such a result, felt distinctly disingenuous. 'Well, that's a blessing, at least.'

'Mmm. Obviously, if we do move out, I'll let you know.'

'Thanks.'

'But, Tom, are you sure you can give up the writing? I know what it means to you.'

'Meant,' he corrected. 'And it's already done. It's over.'

'You're sure?'

'Helen, I used to think that anyone who gave up their dreams had lost the guts to fight for them. I used to think they were pathetic. Now I understand – they just don't want them any more. They haven't settled for second best, they've just realised what's important in life.'

'Grasshopper,' she mocked. 'Such wisdom.'

Wisdom? Perhaps. But Tom didn't know whether it was his own wisdom or something he'd read in a book.

'I swear on my life,' he added to quell his own doubts.

'Would you swear on ours?'

Now she was asking.

'Sorry, Tom, but I need to know you're sincere about this. I need to know where your head is. By all accounts, you've been through a lot lately. Your giving up the writing may just be a temporary adverse reaction. When everything calms down, how will you feel then?'

'If you knew the full story, you wouldn't be asking that. You'd know I will never again sit down at my desk with a view to writing another novel. Never.'

'And you'd swear on our lives?' she persisted.

Tom winced. He didn't like the thought of swearing on anyone's life, but if that's what it took to convince her . . .

His mouth went dry as he spoke the words. 'I swear on your life and the life of my daughter, I will never write again.'

FIFTY-NINE

The days passed, and they were joyfully bland. The days turned into weeks and the weeks stretched into months. Winter vanished like a bad dream. Spring blossomed and slipped warmly into summer.

Over these months, Tom telephoned Helen and Charlotte every week, twice a week, but there was nothing to tell. After Michael's murder, the killings stopped. Milton had gone away. With no further gore to report, it wasn't long before the media attention fizzled out. Tom's burns healed, and his fingertips were left printless. For a while they served as a reminder, but he could feel his mind healing with them, and soon he was spending more time anticipating the future than dreading a return to the past. He dared a little more each day to believe that Milton had told the truth, that he had received his punishment in Angie's kitchen, had paid for his mistakes and balanced the account.

Finally, one glorious morning in mid-July, Tom decided he had waited long enough. It was time to start over. He called his family and gave them the go-ahead.

Pack your cases and head for the airport. Come on home.

Peter Morgan was a rich man. Two months after Carol's death, he had received a cheque for nine hundred thousand pounds, and a note from Roger Mercer, saying that Tom Roker insisted he keep it all. He had dreamed of such a windfall for years, so, in a state of near-delirium, he had immediately deposited the cheque in a newly opened high-interest account.

Four months on, he had not withdrawn a single penny. It was like a worthless wad of Monopoly cash he fantasised over but knew he couldn't spend. Some evenings he would gaze at his pass-book for a solid hour. £900,000, it said. A fortune. All the things he could do with it. The places he could go. The toys he could buy.

And the guilt he could feel if he gave in to temptation.

It wasn't his. Had Carol been alive, it would not have been hers either. She had been handling stolen goods. By her own admission, Tom Roker was a thief, and if it wasn't true then why had he not kept the money for himself?

It was clear: she had not lied under coercion. Peter was rich because Roker was feeling guilty; for screwing Carol and for involving her in his illicit plans, which had ultimately led to her death.

He was being paid off. It was compensation for the loss of his wife, and perhaps a bribe to keep his mouth shut. At the end of the day, it was blood money, and however strongly Peter yearned to be free of the rat-race, he could not use this money to make it happen.

Had there been no one else to give it to, he knew he would have felt differently, but since Carol's confession, the name Angie Kellett had stuck in his mind. The poor woman who had lost her brother, her grief then compounded by Roker's botched break-in which had left a headless body in her back garden.

He had not passed on this knowledge to the police. It seemed less complicated that way. Thankfully, one of his neighbours had confirmed seeing the scarred biker leave the apartment, otherwise Peter himself would have been in the frame. The police had made the obvious connection to Carol's involvement with *Man on a Murder Cycle*, but, further than that, they hadn't a clue. Hardly surprising, really. Even with all the extra information Peter possessed, who the biker was that he thought he had an axe to grind remained a mystery.

This evening, Peter's frustration had reached a crescendo. He needed to move on. He longed for resolution. The money was like a decree nisi on his life which could not become absolute unless he gave it up. Tonight, he could not get Angie Kellett out of his head. Shortly after Carol's death he had rooted through her office and had discovered a photocopy of a letter from Andrew Kellett regarding his manuscript. In front of him now, on the coffee table, he had for the first time placed the pass-book next to the letter alongside the telephone.

His eyes shifted from one set of digits to the other, from

the deposited amount in the pass-book to the phone number on the letter.

A soft breeze washed in through the open windows and cooled his brow. Outside, the descending sun had left the sky shot through with red – the promise of a bright tomorrow. Peter stared at the heart-warming hues, nodded to himself and picked up the phone. As he dialled, he felt like a nervous teenager pursuing his first would-be girlfriend. When Angie answered and he spoke, his voice quivered so badly certain words were almost without sound.

'Hello, is that Angie Kellett?'

'Yes, who's this?'

'My name's Peter Morgan.'

'Peter . . . ?' she queried. '*Morgan*,' she clicked.

'Carol Morgan was my wife.'

'Uh . . . yeah.'

'I don't suppose you mourned her passing,' he said amiably.

'I'm sorry for your sake,' she evaded. 'I know what it's like to lose a loved one. So what do you want, Mr Morgan?'

'I was wondering if we could meet. You wouldn't have to travel; I'd come up North.'

'Meet? Why?'

Peter stared at the pass-book. He silently read the amount, shook his head dolefully, and got on with the rest of his life.

'Because, Miss Kellett, I think I have something that belongs to you.'

Early retirement loomed like chemotherapy: a nasty way to cure the cancerous end of his career. Nelson had been urged by his superiors to accept the inevitable. He had, they said, 'lost his way a little'. Nelson knew a euphemism when he heard one, and did not appreciate people pussy-footing around. He had therefore not reciprocated in similar euphemistic fashion. The air was, in fact, as blue as the rooflights in the car park.

With time to reflect, however, he had realised they were not about to set any alternative offer on the table. Plus, the financial incentive to go was undeniably appealing; he had always fancied buying a cottage on the Welsh coast. The Welsh were the only drawback to that particular notion. The Algarve sounded nice as well, but then he would be among people who sounded *and* looked foreign. Perhaps splash out on a second bike, a big Harley.

Before any of that could happen, he would have to endure the indignity of retiring early 'on the grounds of ill health'. To Nelson, that was another euphemism, and seemed uncomfortably close to the bullshit verdict of manslaughter 'on the grounds of diminished responsibility', which generally meant that the accused was exceptionally pissed off with the victim, to the extent that 'frenzied knife attack' appeared in the media account of the incident. The moral being, if you want to kill someone, don't stab them once through the heart and get life imprisonment, stab them repeatedly all over the body and get five years, or three if the prison shrink has not seen fit to write 'subject tends to get exceptionally pissed off' anywhere in his reports.

Nelson was being kicked out, and kicked out for being quietly but demonstrably screw-loose. Suspects routinely complained of verbal and physical abuse and lines of questioning which strayed into the surreal. Also, Nelson was 'under-achieving in his communication skills', psych-speak meaning he no longer spoke to his fellow officers to pool information. Basically, he had become a loner, a loose cannon, and there was no place for such an individual in the modern police service. Nelson was not so far gone that he didn't know all of this, but he simply couldn't halt his one-man crusade to clear the scum off the streets. In failing to solve the motorcycle murders, he had lost his pride and, he imagined, his reputation.

It was trying to reclaim them that had truly ruined him, but this fact *was* beyond him.

SIXTY

The night before his family arrived in Britain, Tom couldn't sleep. He went to bed and closed his eyes but his heart was wide awake. He was not upset by his insomnia, he was glad of it. He was wonderfully excited, and would not have traded that feeling for any amount of refreshing slumber.

It was nearly midnight. Their flight was due to touch down at Heathrow just before ten the next morning.

Tom got up and paced the house, chain-smoking. He checked and rechecked Charlotte's bedroom, edging furniture an inch this way, an inch that. He hoovered for the third time. He rearranged the flowers which brightened and fragranced every room, including the toilet. He dusted spotless surfaces. He packed and unpacked the cupboards and the fridge, to make trebly sure he had bought in the correct provisions. With Charlotte now a vegetarian, Tom had shopped today in a strange new area of the supermarket, with multiple Linda McCartneys smiling up at him from the frosty depths. He stared through the Cellophane of a box containing something called Quorn Mince. It resembled bleached hamster droppings, but if it made his homecoming princess happy, it was okay by him.

He sat in the kitchen and smoked some more, then startled himself by recalling the distaste with which Helen had always watched him suck in a lungful. And what about his healthy veggie daughter? She would choke at the front door.

So Tom gave up the weed there and then. He collected his ashtrays from around the house and chucked them in the dustbin. He opened all the windows to clear the atmosphere, and threw his clothes in the washing machine on the hottest cycle. Then, for half an hour, he watched television with a mouthful of toothpaste.

367

As an afterthought, with his mouth stinging mintily, he dug out some old white emulsion from the garden shed and painted over the nicotine-stained walls of his study, from which his writing paraphernalia had already been banished to the attic.

His activities occupied him through to four a.m. when he flaked onto the living-room settee. Physically exhausted, he was still light years from sleep.

Six hours to go. Buzzing but bored.

Next to him was a pad of A4. He picked it up and inspected the top sheet. It was crammed full of scrawly blue Biro: his list of things to do before the big day. It all appeared to be ticked off, but he scanned down each line to be sure there was nothing outstanding.

Satisfied, he tore off the sheet, balled it and threw it across the room for a bin-in-one.

Without thinking, he took the blue Bic from beside him and began doodling around the punch-holes on the empty page. He was struck by an unsettling memory: of sitting at Andrew Kellett's desk and filling page after page with mayhem and murder, death and destruction. He shivered.

'What a nightmare,' he whispered to himself.

But the nightmare was over. Tomorrow would herald a new beginning, a second chance. He missed the writing, but not the genre he had worked in. It seemed evil to him now, breathing literary life into psychos. It was not in his heart any more to create such twisted narrative. He felt only love, more love than he could hold inside. He finally understood what drove the Mills and Boon brigade to churn out novel after novel, with only the names and places changing from one book to the next. He understood why so many people read them and would always be enthralled by them. Love was a timeless, tireless story. It could be retold a billion times over and would never lose its power to move. As a genre, love was the best, because it was universal. Everyone could identify because everyone had their own tale to tell.

Tom certainly did. Love lost and found. A family reunited.

His wife was a saint, his daughter an angel.

He had committed himself to paper before he knew it. The first sentence of a resurrected and a newly enlightened career.

And just as fast as he had written those words, one by one they disappeared from the page.

*   *   *

His heart drained of love and filled with horror. It began thudding like a council tarmac-flattener, but, pump as it might, a distinct lack of blood was reaching his head. Faintness turned his brain to cotton wool. He wailed his displeasure, and the eerie, unhuman sound he made only added to his sudden, copious goosebumps. He rejected the pad and pen, shooing them onto the carpet.

The telephone rang.

Four in the morning. Who could that be calling at this ungodly hour?

Someone ungodly perchance?

Tom crept along the settee towards the telephone table and lifted the receiver to his ear. He didn't say hello, and neither did Milton.

'It was a sleeping dog, Tommy, and you woke it. Now it's going to bite you where it hurts.'

That was it. The connection broke.

Tom found Angie's number through Directory Enquiries. He knew it, but could not unscramble his head to free it. He dialled, regardless of the time. The phone was by her bed; if she was home she would answer, just to silence it.

He gabbled loudly over her sleepy demands to know who the hell was calling.

Groggily, she said, 'What? What? *Tom?*'

Tom repeated himself, trying to calm down and speak coherently. 'Milton called. He's back. I only wrote one fucking line. He said he's going to kill me.'

'What? What are you talking about?' she said testily. 'D'you know what time it is?'

'Course I know what fucking time it is. What difference does it make what fucking time it is? What, you think four to five's a comedy hour for him, do you? He's having a laugh?'

'*Tom!* Stop swearing and stop shouting.'

Cowed, Tom awaited her life-saving advice.

'Tom . . . what do you expect me to do about it? I can't help you. I never could. He won't spare anyone on my say-so.'

Tom could not stop staring at the blank sheet on the carpet. 'One line, that's all I wrote – Jesus – and he's going to kill me for it.'

'Then he's going to kill you.'

369

Tom left a gap for Angie to correct her rash and clearly erroneous statement.

'I'm tired, Tom. I don't want all this back in my life. I'm sorry. It's too much. You're on your own.'

'*Don't hang up!*' he begged, sensing an imminent end to their conversation.

She yawned; not very encouraging. 'All right, Tom. What exactly did he say?'

The words were stamped on Tom's mind like a cattle-brand. '"It was a sleeping dog, Tommy, and you woke it. Now it's going to bite you where it hurts." That's all he said.'

'That's enough, isn't it?' she said unhelpfully.

'So?'

'So I reckon your opening analysis is pretty close to the mark.'

'You don't care, do you?'

'I'm past caring, Tom. Well past.'

For effect, he forced a sob up through his fear and anger. '*Angie . . . please . . . help me.*'

'You're a real nineties man, Tom,' she sniped, entirely unimpressed. 'So in touch with your emotions.'

'Well, *fuck you*! It's not just me you're condemning! My daughter's getting here tomorrow! She's going to lose her father, if you don't help!'

Angie's silence did not feel like the precursor to her hanging up; it felt worse.

'Angie?' he said in a wee voice.

'Your daughter?'

'And my ex-wife. They're flying back from the States. We're going to try again.' He could hear the hope in his voice, but could no longer feel it in his heart.

More silence, and this time Tom didn't dare break it.

Eventually, Angie said, 'Shit. I think I know what he means.'

SIXTY-ONE

———◆———

The police convoy sped west along the M4, taking up two lanes. No sirens, lots of lights. Tom was in the middle of it, in an unmarked black Scorpio. He was protected on all sides. By the Armco barrier to his right, by a squad car to the front, squad car to the rear, and by two in the centre lane to his left. Four motorcycle outriders kept accelerating ahead to halt traffic on the slip roads.

The low morning sun streamed in on him. Sandwiched between two plain clothed armed officers, Tom felt like a visiting head of state. The surrounding units were also armed. The whole operation was clearly well rehearsed and professional to a fault. Yet Tom did not feel safe.

What good were guns against someone who was already dead?

But his own longevity was not his uppermost concern. He was frantic about Helen and Charlotte. They were the ones in danger. The logic behind Angie's interpretation of Milton's cryptic message could not be questioned.

Andrew Kellett had lost his wife, Nina, and his daughter, Sally. After a long period of drink and depression and frightening rages, he had pulled himself round and written a novel, expressing and ordering all the feelings he had failed to cope with in the wake of his loss. He had not done it for the money, or for the notoriety. His reasons had been entirely different. It had been an exercise in self-healing. All except one page. And that one page had been more important than all the rest of it put together. That one page, the dedication page, the one Tom had destroyed by fire, had told the world how he felt about their lives, not how terribly he had been damaged by their tragic deaths.

Tom had stolen far more than a book.

But that wasn't all. Six months ago, Tom had sworn he would

never write again. He had sworn on the only two lives that mean anything to him. This morning, during a mental lapse, he had put pen to paper and with a single sentence had written off those two lives.

Now Milton was seeking the ultimate revenge; to bite Tom where it hurt. Because Milton knew where it hurt.

Payback on a par. Helen for Nina, Charlotte for Sally.

They swung off at junction 4, heading south along the two-mile section of the M4 which led to Heathrow. They passed the airport hotels at the end of the motorway and were waved through police checkpoints, manned by visibly armed officers. All other traffic was backed up solid. Tom was grateful for the fuss, but couldn't stop himself from feeling there was no point to any of it. He just glimpsed a Qantas 747 heaving improbably off the concrete a mile away, then the convoy descended beneath the northern perimeter road into the half-mile vehicle tunnel which fed directly into the heart of Terminals 1, 2 and 3.

Under the glaring strips of overhead lighting, the patrol car bounced their blue and red merry-go-rounds off one tunnel wall then the other, before rising into the sun again and onto the eastern inner ring road of the Terminals complex. Their speed dropped to a slow cruise.

'Mr Roker, if you see anything strange, let us know.'

Tom nodded to acknowledge the balding Inspector in the front passenger seat.

They skirted the bus and Underground stations to their right. To their left, outside the Terminal I pick-up and drop-off, Tom noticed a mass of Met pullovers and carbines.

Terminal 2 went by on their left, with the same heavy police presence, both inside and outside the concourse. Between Terminals 2 and 3 they broke off the ring road and drove down a restricted-access ramp onto the apron.

For a mile and a half to the west, half a mile to the south, and a mile to the east, the scene was one of concrete taxi-routes and runways, and unused strips and patches of grass. Odd, boxy little vehicles scurried about on predetermined paths, like ants working for the general good of the community. All sizes of plane in all colours of livery were taking off, landing, trundling and waiting. Jet engines droned and roared incessantly like audio torture.

In the shadow of the control tower they stopped.

'What are we doing?' Tom said.

The Inspector twisted himself round to explain. 'American Airlines five one two will be instructed to taxi to the Cargo Terminal on the southern perimeter. We will take the passengers off there and transport them back here by bus. Except your ex-wife and daughter. They will be taken under armed escort to a safe-house.'

Tom shook his head. 'There's no such thing. Not from this maniac. I want them out of the country.'

'That is another option.'

'That's the only option,' Tom said, his panic riling him. 'If they stay in this country more than ten minutes, he will get to them and kill them.'

'Mr Roker, please leave it to us. We know what we're doing.'

Tom flared. 'You might know what you're doing, pal, but you *don't* know what *he's* doing!'

'Please calm down, Mr Roker.'

'*Calm down?*' Tom unclipped his belt and leaned into the gap between the front seats. 'He knows *everything*, d'you understand? *Everything!*'

'Mr Roker, Mr Roker, be quiet.'

Tom obeyed, but only because he had finished anyway.

'Now, Mr Roker, we have taken your word that he is in possession of the relevant flight information concerning the arrival of your ex-wife and your daughter, although you cannot explain how he has come by this information. Still, we have mounted this operation in response. But please don't ask me to believe that he knows where all our safe-houses are located and which one in particular will be accommodating your family.'

No, he couldn't ask them to believe that. It was true, but to tell them so would be an utter waste of breath.

'I want them out of the country,' he merely reiterated.

'That is not a part of our operational directive.'

Tom frowned. 'What . . . directive?'

The Inspector indicated that the driver should get going. The driver flashed his headlights at the car in front. The convoy moved off, shortly descending into the half-mile cargo tunnel beneath the busy expanse of concrete.

'What directive?'

The tunnel lights flew past like flash photography.

'That is not something you need to know, Mr Roker.'

Tom sat back quietly and tried to figure it out for himself. They had surfaced before he offered his formulated suspicion.

'You're using them, aren't you?' he said, disgusted. 'They're bait.'

The Inspector remained face front. 'We will be housing them at a secure, heavily armed location. If our man does decide to mount an offensive, that will be his funeral.'

Tom blasphemed under his breath. They were so catastrophically wrong, it was hardly worth pointing out.

The Cargo Terminal was on their right. Planes were lined up with their tail-ends open and black gaps in their silver bellies. Conveyor belts were loading and unloading. Trolley-trucks rattled to and fro, carrying crates and boxes. Police marksmen lay on the Terminal roof, the muzzles of their telescopic rifles wandering over the surrounding area.

They drove to a sheltered position round the back of the building. Tom saw there was a lorry carrying a passenger staircase, a fleet of buses standing by, and more guns.

He scanned the terrain. They were less than a quarter mile from the southern perimeter. Juggernauts rumbled up and down the supply roads which connected the perimeter road to the Terminal and its adjacent warehouses.

'Hold on,' Tom said. 'You just used me as well, didn't you? We could have come in from the south to get here, same route as those lorries. We didn't need to drive through the passenger Terminals. You were trying to lure him out, weren't you, and so what if he took a pot-shot at me?'

'The glass in this particular vehicle is ballistically hardened, Mr Roker. You were never in any danger.'

Tom scoffed bitterly. 'I've always been in danger. And now every one of your men is in danger. For all your firepower and skills and organisation, if he wants to, he'll make sitting ducks out of the lot of you. And not one of you will see it coming.'

The Inspector looked at his watch. 'The time is zero-eight-hundred, Mr Roker. American Airlines flight five one two doesn't land until zero-nine-fifty. There's a VIP suite upstairs. Why don't you make yourself comfortable?'

Tom scowled at the Inspector's ignorance, then climbed out of the black Scorpio and was hurried across the tarmac, sandwiched between his grey-suited, fantastically aware, but ultimately deluded protectors.

SIXTY-TWO

———◆———

Half an hour to go before touchdown.

Tom was slouching on a stool at the bar of the plushly furnished VIP suite. He threw his head back and took another slug of Scotch. It burned pleasantly in his throat and restoked the fire in his stomach. By now he was pretty drunk. As for giving up smoking, that could wait for a better day; he was already well into his second vending pack of the morning.

A breakfast of booze and fags. Nausea lurched inside him. His breath was short and his palms sweaty in spite of the air-conditioning. He was heartily sick of being in situations that scared the crap out of him. Had he been a character in one of his own novels, he would have run out of ways to describe exactly how he felt.

The bartender looked on sympathetically. Tom had informed him of the circumstances which required this unprecedented police deployment. At least, he had explained as much as any sane man might reasonably believe.

Tom tapped his tumbler on the counter and indicated a refill. He swivelled on his stool to gaze blurrily across the suite and through the wall of windows that gave spectacularly onto the entire airport. The sunshine was dazzling, gleaming off the sleek metal bodies in their various stages of arrival and departure.

Where were Helen and Charlotte in that big blue yonder? A hundred miles out? Two hundred? Might as well be on Jupiter. They would never be a family again. Not whilst Milton was ali—. Undead.

He spun back to a replenished Scotch on a fresh coaster. 'Cheers,' he said to the bartender, and nearly added 'good health'. He took a sip and knew he didn't want any more. 'Landing's the most dangerous time, isn't it?' he blurted.

The barman nodded. 'And taking off. But it's all relative. It's infinitely safer than driving a car. Difference is, if you crash your car, three hundred people don't die, so it doesn't make world news.'

'I've already made world news,' Tom said sombrely. 'Anyway, I've heard it all before, everyone has. It might be safe; doesn't mean people aren't shit-scared when they get on a plane.'

'True,' said the bartender, then had an idea. 'Tell you what. I've got an airband scanner in the back. Why don't I bring it out and we can have a listen? When you hear how these guys talk to each other you'll realise there's nothing to worry about. They're consummate professionals. You won't even follow what they're saying they're so slick.'

Tom shrugged. 'Yeah, why not?'

The bartender disappeared through a door and returned a moment later with a handheld radio. He set it on the bar.

'There you go. You can twiddle this knob to flick through the frequencies. What flight are you interested in?'

Tom had to think. His mind was both sodden and puddled. 'Yeah, American Airlines flight number five one two from Denver.'

'Well, we'll stay with the frequency it's on for the moment. It gets a lot of traffic.'

The bartender switched the scanner on and Tom immediately heard a voice spouting fluent gobbledegook. He was able to pick out some figures and the odd word, enough to identify it as air traffic control, but the controller might have been speaking in tongues for all the sense Tom could make of it.

'Bloody hell,' he said, screwing his face up in drunken concentration.

'See what I mean? Easy as falling off a log for these people. There's no mystery to flying – not for them.'

Tom listened intently to more apparent gibberish, and the bartender kindly translated when Tom's face became too painfully puzzled.

A minute later, the bartender adjusted frequencies. There was a five-second burst of static before, like magic, Tom was treated to a confident American drawl and the exact communication he craved.

'*London Control good morning American five one two passing WELIN at flight level three one zero estimate BUZAD at three five, requesting descent.*'

'*American five one two Roger maintain flight level three one zero standard routeing to London Heathrow landing runway two seven right squawk ident on five four seven six, descent clearance in five miles.*'

'*Roger London ident five four seven six standard route for Heathrow two seven right American five one two.*'

Tom looked dumbly at the bartender for enlightenment.

'He's flying over Wellingborough Reporting Point at thirty-one thousand feet and reckons he'll be over Leighton Buzzard at nine thirty-five; few minutes' time. Control's told him to stay at that altitude for another five miles on the standard route in and that he'll be landing on the right-hand side of runway two-seven. American's repeated the instructions to check he heard them properly.'

'What's this squawk thing?'

'Oh, every flight's assigned a transponder code which it then squawks to identify itself. You'll hear more in a little while. He'll be given descent clearance, then later he'll tell control he's "established", meaning he's locked on to the Instrument Landing System which'll bring him in bang on target.'

Tom nodded, and decided he would finish his drink, after all.

Charlotte was gawping through the plane window, captivated by the thirty-one thousand feet of air between her and a landscape she could see in perfect miniature detail. In the seat next to her, Mom was fast asleep.

When the tannoy announcement was made, Helen woke up and Charlotte paid attention. In fact, the entire cabin pricked up their ears.

'Good morning, ladies and gentleman, this is your deputy sub-assistant trainee co-pilot speaking. The captain has given me control of the plane and we will soon be commencing our descent into London Heathrow. I didn't want control but I have to learn sometime. I'll certainly try not to do what I did in the simulator last week. Hmm. Anyway, for those of you with Labradors in the hold, the weather outside is very pleasant. The air temperature at Heathrow is colder than Denver but, hey, welcome to England. The No Smoking sign has been switched on, but I'd smoke if I were you; you're at thirty-one thousand feet encased in a highly flammable parcel of metal, so why worry about cancer? Finally, in case anyone was unsure, Toby and Nigel, our stewards today, are homosexual, and, yes, they do have the hots for each other. Thank you.'

'Mayday Mayday Mayday Drayton Centre seven-six-seven American five one two at three eight zero knots flight level three one zero on squawk ident seven five zero zero tyro, I say again, squawk seven five zero zero tyro carrying full house acknowledge.'

'American five one two squawk ident seven five zero zero tyro will notify Heathrow Emergency Services, switch to victor frequency one two one decimal five.'

'Shit!' said the bartender, 'that's the International Aeronautical Emergency Frequency.' He retuned to resume listening. 'And that squawk code indicates a frigging hijack situation. *Jesus.'*

Tom was instantly sober. Half of him was dazed by shock, half of him was dulled by an awful sense of *déjà vu*. He didn't need the bartender's exposition; the first word 'Mayday' had said it all.

'Milton . . . fuck,' he muttered to himself. 'What's "tyro" mean?'

'Means the pilot has no idea how to handle things.'

'American five one two specify exact nature of distress.'

'It's, uh . . . bad, Drayton. Climbing to flight level three five zero.'

'Negative American—'

'That's not a request.'

'Understood American but be aware there is crossing traffic range nine miles left to right flight level three three zero, a seven-four-seven, you should have visual.'

'Oh, shit, Milton. Don't do it,' Tom said.

'Do what?' asked the bartender. 'Who's Milton?'

'Uh . . . affirmative Drayton, American vacating flight level three one zero for three five zero.'

'Understood American standby, break . . .'

'What's going on?' Tom asked. 'Why's it gone quiet?'

'He'll be contacting the Jumbo to bring it onto the emergency frequency so both planes can hear each other.'

'Drayton Centre this is Speedbird six three niner pass your message.'

'See,' said the bartender.

'*Speedbird six three niner you have conflicting traffic climbing into your track descend to flight level two nine zero continue present heading until advised, conflicting traffic is a seven-six-seven on squawk seven five zero zero.*'

'*Roger that Drayton fully understood, Speedbird six three niner leaving flight level three three zero for two nine zero, thank you.*'

'No, don't do it,' Tom said, 'he's lying.'

'*Speedbird you should have the traffic in your two o'clock.*'

'*Looking . . . Negative Drayton.*'

'That because he's *lying!*' Tom shouted.

'*American five one two Drayton Centre . . . confirm flight conditions.*'

'*Drayton American speed three eight zero knots, now, uh . . . passing flight level three two zero for three five zero approaching BUZAD standard route to Heathrow.*'

'It's a *trap!*' Tom screamed. 'Listen to his voice, he's being made to lie!'

'*Speedbird Drayton you should have visual by now.*'

'*Drayton negative. Request radar information on American five one two.*'

'*Roger . . . track and flight level as specified, you should have him in sight.*'

Tom recoiled in his seat. '*No!* Now a machine's lying for him! Milton, you bastard, *don't!*'

'Who's Milton?'

'*Negative Drayton, we do not have the traffic.*'

'*Speedbird confirm present position.*'

'*Now passing flight level three two zero for two nine zero heading two three four degrees.*'

'*Roger Speedbird continue descent to flight level two nine zero report approaching for further.*'

'*Understood.*'

'For Christ's sake, American lied! He's not climbing! They're both heading for twenty-nine thousand!'

'They'll still see him,' said the bartender, confused by all the fuss. 'It's unlimited visibility up there.'

'They *won't* see him! He's not where he said! Not where the radar says!'

'Drayton this is American . . . message for Heathrow Tower, message reads: Foxtrot Uniform Tango Oscar Mike. Acknowledge.'

'Foxtrot Uniform Tango Oscar Mike. Ame—'

'American out.'

Tom repeated the message: 'Eff You Tee Oh Em.' And deciphered it with pitiful ease: 'Fuck you, Tom.'

'American acknowledge over . . . American five one two acknowledge over . . . Break, Speedbird six three niner any visual with American five one two in your two o'clock yet, over?'

'You're looking in the wrong place!' Tom screeched desperately. *'Get out of there!'*

'Negative – still looking.'

Tom sobbed. 'Why doesn't someone realise?'

'Drayton request secondary surveillance radar information, over.'

'None available Speedbird, American transponder switched off.'

'Marvellous Drayton, awaiting fur—'

A split second of static frazzle before total silence.

'Speedbird? Speedbird acknowledge. Acknowledge over. Speedbird acknowledge over! . . . Speedbird! . . . American! . . . Somebody bloody say something! . . .'

Grey and tearful, the bartender commandeered a bottle of brandy and went to the paying side of the bar where he proceeded to swig from it without paying. Tom sat next to him for ten minutes, staring blankly at the grave-like scanner.

In those ten minutes it all caught up with him. It was over; the struggle. He had received his just punishment. He was no longer in any danger from Milton. Milton could do nothing more to hurt him. Killing him would be merciful now, and Milton was not that kind of a guy. Knowing this, something inside Tom collapsed and his roof fell in. He felt his will to live crushed under its weight, the bud of hope wither in his heart. But there was no will to die to take its place; there was no will left in him at all. His humanness had ebbed out of him and he felt . . . nothing.

Slowly, not knowing where he was going or why he was leaving, Tom rose from his stool and wandered towards the exit.

Downstairs, outside, no one stopped his zombified progress. The news had reached them, and a pall of death had settled on their heads, bowing them to the ground.

Tom meandered towards the southern perimeter. A soulless shell, dead before his time.

SIXTY-THREE

In the week after American Airlines 512 and British Airways 639 collided in mid-air, raining bodies and fiery metal down on more innocent heads, Tom went walkabout.

Even now, fourteen months on, he still could not remember his long trek from London to Cheshire, nor knocking on Angie's door at three o'clock in the morning, nor the fact that he had lost his shoes en route. He could not recall taking any sustenance throughout the whole journey, but neither could he recall feeling hungry or thirsty at any time. If he had slept, he did not feel rested for it. If he had eaten, it had not been much; he had lost so much weight his skin clung to his bones as though it had been vacuum-packed onto his frame. He had no memory of Angie opening the door to him, nor of the expressionless lack of recognition she had reported seeing in his dark and hollow eyes. He had no idea how he had navigated his way there, nor where the impulse had come from to head in her direction. He could not remember Angie phoning the ambulance, nor his subsequent journey to the local psychiatric ward.

For three months there was no sign of improvement. No one visited. He didn't say a word to anyone. His face never cracked from its vacant blankness. His mind was impenetrable. He woke up when ordered, ate when told to, sat dutifully in the TV room of an evening, and obediently swallowed his medication throughout the day.

Then one night, after lights out, he began to cry, and he cried constantly for the best part of a fortnight. No one needed to ask why; they knew who he was and what he had suffered. They did want to know what had triggered this release, but Tom couldn't tell them because he didn't know himself. He only knew that he had suddenly noticed his face was wet and his heart was in agony.

Up to that point, he had been switched off with the plug out. He had not registered a single moment of his life since walking out of the VIP suite at the Cargo Terminal.

For the next six months, Tom fell into the blackest depression. He didn't want to do anything but mope and cry. He didn't want to eat, read a book, watch television, get out of bed in the morning or go to sleep at night. He didn't even want a cigarette, so he gave them up by default. His medication was increased. He cried less, but his true progress was nil. He often contemplated suicide but made no attempts. He was seen by a psychiatrist every three to four weeks. Christ alone knew how much good they thought that would do, but it was the way of the ward. They all kept taking their pills. The patients were not treated so much as managed. It seemed that if time wasn't the cure, no one had much of an idea what might be.

When Tom's tears eventually dried to an intermittent trickle, he started talking to his fellow patients and he told them everything. Absolutely everything. Some did not believe him and scoffed viciously. Some did not believe him and laughed like loons. Some did not believe him, but believed Tom believed it, so sympathised with his plight. Some said they did believe him, but Tom suspected they were just being polite. And some clearly did believe him, but were barking mad themselves and would have believed anything.

It didn't matter. Any of it. What he said, how they reacted. Even under medication, he could feel a futility to his existence that extended as far as his mind could reach. There were no life-saving oases on his horizon, or over it, and that was not a verdict tainted by the shadow of depression. By now, the worst of it had lifted and was rumbling darkly off into the distance.

As a child, he had imagined death as nothing but a terrifying blackness. As an adult, he had feared it would crowd in on him prematurely and snatch him away.

Now he understood. The blackness was not the danger. How could it have been? At the depths of his despair, he had been rendered harmless. The blackness had paralysed him. It had stolen his will to perform even the simplest of tasks. If he couldn't be bothered lifting a fork to his mouth, how could he summon the energy required to kill himself?

The danger lay in the dawn of recovery, the light by which all things became clear. When rationality took over and a future could be seen to exist.

Because, then, he could calmly decide whether he wanted that future. Not knowing what lay ahead, but based on what had gone before, did he really want to risk more of the same? Was there anything he still wanted to achieve in this life? Was there anyone he hoped to meet?

No. Nothing. No one.

It was not a sad decision. He did not feel at all like he might have expected. He was anticipating the end of his earthbound tenure, and he felt relieved. More than that – happy. He could give up the struggle. He didn't care for it any more. He had seen too much, learned too much.

Ignorance truly was bliss.

So, fourteen months after Tom had been admitted, he discharged himself into the late-summer sunshine and strolled off the hospital grounds with a faint smile on his face; an expression of wisdom gained too late, but gained nonetheless.

He breathed deeply in the balmy air, expanding his lungs. His smile widened, opened, and broke into laughter.

He felt free, unburdened, for the first time in . . . for the first time ever.

SIXTY-FOUR

———◆———

There was no earthly reason why Tom should have walked those five miles to Angie's house. He did need time to think, that was for sure; he had to decide on his means of departure from this world. But why he pointed himself in that specific direction, he had no idea. He would not receive a welcome. There would be no reminiscing with cocoa and biccies late into the night. He would encounter only hostility. His was a vilified name. Had she felt any compassion for him, she might have popped in to visit. Just once. But no. She had chucked him into the ambulance like a sack of garbage into a skip. She was hardly about to drop by the council refuse dump to see how the recycling was coming along.

Yet for some reason he felt compelled to call round.

Did he have some macabre desire to reawaken her anguish? Was he still deranged after fourteen months? He shook his head. Then nodded. Of course he was still screwed up, but that wasn't the reason.

He walked through the village, past the church and the chippy. Memories surged to the front of his mind. Poignant memories, of his life in ruins but the lives of Helen and Charlotte still intact; missing them terribly, but hoping to make the trip.

The sun raised thermals off the tarmac. He wiped a sheen of sweat from his brow and continued through the village until he came to the bottom of Angie's lane.

He stared at the For Sale sign in the overgrown front garden. The magenta ivy was creeping unchecked across the cottage windows, and the windows were curtainless. The grass of the verge was tall, unflattened for some time by tyres. Tom estimated that the building had been empty for at least the duration of that summer.

He was glad. Wherever she was, it had to be better than here. This place was a damned mausoleum.

Hot and fatigued, he sat on the front stone wall and stared down at his shoes, a pair of clumpy brown brogues, the uppers straining away from the soles. Oxfam rejects, donated to poor Mr Roker by the staff of ward P3.

He dug into his trouser pocket and brought out his London house keys. He jumped them noisily in his palm a couple of times, then hurled them across the road into a field. The fragrance of the countryside filled his nostrils, but he had no right to sample such an innocent pleasure.

From the village, a car motored up the lane. Tom kept his eyes to the ground until it slowed in front of him and the engine died. He looked up to see a suited young man climb from a mint green Vauxhall Tigra. The face beneath the crew-cut was red and full of apology.

'I am so sorry. I hope you haven't been waiting too long. I was held up with another couple. Mr Quinn, isn't it?' he said, extending his arm. 'Is your wife not with you?'

Tom loosely grasped the proffered hand. 'No, my wife's not here,' he answered automatically.

'Well, not to worry, she can come along and view it any time that's convenient for her. Please, this way.'

Tom followed the estate agent up the path to the porch door.

'As you can see, this is a highly desirable property. Peaceful and secluded yet convenient for rail travel to the city.' He brought out a set of keys and fiddled one into the lock.

'There is some remedial work which would need—'

'I'm not Mr Quinn.'

The estate agent froze, as though, if that wasn't Mr Quinn standing behind him, it had to be a mass murderer on the loose from a secure mental hospital who was masquerading as Mr Quinn. Not far wrong. He spun around. To his credit, he did try to maintain a smile. 'So, may I ask . . . ?'

'I was a friend,' Tom said. 'I wasn't aware she'd moved out.'

The estate agent stashed the keys safely back in his pocket. 'Oh, I see. Yes, they moved out last October.'

Tom made a face. 'They?'

'Yes. The Morgans. Peter and Angie. Nice couple. I believe they emigrated to Spain.'

'What?'

'Between you and me, I think they won the lottery. Certainly came into a substantial amount of money. Bought a villa near Marbella; didn't even need the proceeds from this place. Some people have all the luck, eh?'

Tom raised his eyebrows. 'Some people, perhaps. But not the Morgans, believe me.'

The real Mr Quinn showed up five minutes later, along with Mrs Quinn. Sitting on the front wall again, Tom heard Mr Quinn apologise for their tardiness and the estate agent gracefully accept the apology, tactically omitting to mention that he had been late himself. They all gave Tom a distasteful sidelong look, like he was part of the remedial work that would need sorting.

Fifteen minutes after that, the viewing concluded, the two cars drove off in different directions, and Tom was left on his own.

He wanted to kill himself. On one of God's finest summer days, Tom yearned to dispatch himself to God's opposite number. Well, he didn't exactly *want* to go to Hell, he just couldn't convince himself that his ultimate passage would be along a fantastic tunnel of light with Helen and Charlotte waiting serenely at the far end, their fingers poised on the latch of the Pearly Gates.

Despite this, he was not afraid of death, but it had to be quick. He did not want to give some passing Samaritan the opportunity of dragging him off to hospital for resuscitation.

But the method Tom had in mind *would* be quick.

As the estate agent had mentioned, a mainline railway ran through the village. Tom already knew this. On clear nights last summer, he had been able to hear the roar of the express trains, and later, in the small hours, the ponderous rumbling of the goods locomotives.

Tom planned to sneak down the embankment and hide behind a bush. He would listen for the local stoppers and let them pass, but when the tracks began to sing of a fast train coming, he would prepare himself for the leap. The horrified driver would manage to lose less than one mile-an-hour off his ton-plus speed before impact; plenty fast enough for the job.

It would be a bloody, violent death, and how appropriate.

One final sunset. That was his last request. Then he could catch the last train home.

Tom sat on the front wall until he gradually felt shadow and coldness engulf him. He looked over his shoulder to see a corona of lemon sunlight fuzzing the high foliage of the horse chestnuts. He got up and made his way through to the back garden.

Across the unkempt lawn he walked, under the cool canopy, to the drystone rear wall, where he leaned and stared nostalgically over the lush fields. The descending sun bathed him warmly. He shivered with a rash of goosebumps, and scanned the horizon. Somewhere out there was a lay-by with a phone box. A place in which he had forsaken his innocent failure for a naive success.

A man could travel the world and not be sated. But journey to the forbidden part of his own mind, and that one place could cause complete information overload.

For Tom, this view across the fields was the geographical equivalent of that mental location. For all the glory he perceived in this idyllic scene of natural beauty, it instilled in him only sorrow, because he would never have known it had he not strayed so far from righteousness.

In an instant, the happiness he had experienced on release from P3 was gone. He realised that his joy had only come from the decision to effect the ultimate of releases. Now that the course of his own life was decided, the destruction he had brought upon so many other lives returned to haunt him.

He hated himself. He would die bitter and livid. At least Andrew Kellett had managed to translate his pain into the written word, blunting it in the process. Tom would die with his, taking all that fury with him to the grave.

And he hated the world. Not the world he saw before him at that moment; not God's great Earth. But the world Man had fashioned into a consumer nightmare, the world which urged folk like him to struggle all their lives for a worthless prize, whilst losing their priceless gifts along the way. The world that could think of no better way of introducing little children to the technological miracle of computers than by teaching them how to fight and kill each other in so-called 'games'.

He turned his back on the fields to look at the trees and the cottage beyond them. That was a poor view as well. Not much of a feel-good factor in that little picture.

Perhaps he'd have to skip the sunset, head for the tracks in daylight, and trust nobody saw him trespass onto the railway and called the police.

He was about to move off when he glanced sideways and did a double-take. The door of the garden shed was ajar, and Tom had glimpsed something shining blackly just inside.

Slowly, he approached. Five feet away he stopped dead. A patch of sunlight bounced back at him from the mirror shell of a black crash helmet. It was sitting on a metal work bench. No doubt it was one of Andrew Kellett's spare lids. He stepped up and pushed the door. It creaked wide open, swirling a billion golden motes of dust, and Tom gasped at what he saw.

His strange desire to visit the cottage now made sense. He had not come for Angie, he had come for this.

Leaning on its sidestand was Milton's black ZZ-R1100 Turbo. Laid out on the bench beside the helmet were his leathers, boots and gloves.

But Tom's eyes came to rest on something else. On the seat of the big Kawasaki was a small black revolver and a note, with the message: *Make it right*.

He picked up the revolver and turned the black hole towards his face. Looking down the snubby barrel, he counted six chambers. Five were empty, but the one to the right of top showed the dull grey tip of a lead bullet. All he had to do was squeeze the trigger, raising the hammer and rotating the cylinder anti-clockwise – from his unfortunate point of view – then the hammer would fall and the bullet would fly.

It was better than the train.

Tom sank down to the floor and crawled underneath the bench. He settled himself with his back against a cobwebby wall and breathed in the musty, timberous atmosphere.

He stared into that lethal muzzle for ten minutes . . . half an hour . . . an hour. His finger was curled tightly round the trigger, waiting for his brain to impulse the required action.

The hours dragged by. He put his mouth round the barrel countless times, tasting the steel but never the lead. The sun dropped and reddened and Tom's hiding place darkened. He wasn't scared of dying, he just couldn't end it like this. Mourning his impotence to perform the task, he moaned lowly in his frustration, eventually uttering the lamentable cry: 'But it's not *right*!'

Suddenly, his mind burned white with comprehension. He emerged from his den and rose to his feet. His legs almost gave way, but he stood firm. He grabbed Milton's note from the seat.

'Make it right,' he whispered. 'Make it right.'

He nodded.

'Yeah, you bastard. I'm with you now.'

SIXTY-FIVE

These were the days life made sense. Cloudless skies. Sunshine from dawn till dusk. Biking weather. Hour upon hour of undiluted pleasure.

Even ex-DCI Kenny Nelson could forget his worries on a day like today.

But now it was night-time. The Triumph was locked away in the garage, covered in bug splats, and his wife was complaining that his dinner was ruined; he should have been home when he said he'd be home. Oh, piss off, woman.

When he was out of his leathers, Nelson did not enjoy his retirement. There could not have been a more disastrous way to end a career than his last twelve months in the job, and he wasn't at all certain he had left that period of his life behind. He knew from experience, if the case hadn't closed, the criminal had not got away with it. Not until the coffin lid was nailed down over him.

Nelson took a packet of chocolate digestives upstairs with him. He changed out of his bike gear and washed. Wearing one of his retirement presents, a dark green silk dressing gown with his monogram in gold, he propped himself up on the double bed to watch TV. He remotely flicked through the channels before settling on a current-affairs programme about the sharp rise in violent crime. He could hear the simultaneous boom of the same channel below him in the lounge, but he preferred to waste electricity rather than join his wife. On the screen, some multi-pipped senior officer was delivering the same spiel about underfunding in the police service, and a judicial system that allowed the bad guys to walk. It sounded like so much rhetoric, but Nelson could only nod in agreement.

One by one, the biscuits disappeared whole into his mouth. Crumbs dropped into his lap, and he brushed them onto his wife's side of the bed.

'*Kenneth! Telephone!*'

His wife's irritation punched up through the floor. Nelson had heard the telephone ring six times before she had silenced it – there was a phone beside the bed – but answering himself would have involved the interruption of his feeding frenzy.

'*Right!*' he bellowed as he picked up. 'Nelson,' he announced thickly, crunching away, hearing the downstairs line disconnect.

'Sir, this is DS Manion.'

Sir. At least his old underlings still faked some respect. 'Yes, what is it, Trish?'

'How are you enjoying your retirement, sir?'

'What is it, Trish?'

'Uh, well, I've had a call into the office from Tom Roker, wanting to speak to you.'

Nelson lowered the volume on the portable. 'Roker? What did he say?'

'Nothing. He only wanted to speak to you. I told him you weren't here any more, so he asked for your home number.'

'Did you give it him?'

'No, sir, I thought—'

'*Bollocks!*'

'Sir?'

Nelson breathed deeply. 'It's not your fault, Trish, I'm just . . . inquisitive as to what he might want after all this time.'

'I did take *his* number, sir. I told him all I could do was pass it on. The thing is, he was in a phone box, so if you are going to call it needs to be soon.'

'Give me the number, I'll ring him straight back.'

'Psychic Investigations, that'll be Kenny Nelson.'

'Very drole, Roker. What d'you want?'

On the dirty kiosk glass, Tom traced *FAT TWAT* with one of his printless fingertips. Outside, the sons and daughters of the well-to-do were playing at Crips and Bloods along the main street of the village.

'I want you to listen very carefully.'

'You shall say this only once,' Nelson quipped.

393

'Exactly. By the way, how's your retirement? Cut back on your motorist-battering, have you?'

'My retirement's fine. How's your wife and kid?'

Tom flinched and closed his eyes. His speech failed, as though all the stubbed toes of his life had ganged up to steal his breath.

'Roker?'

'God, Nelson . . . you are such a cunt.'

'I've learned to live with it.'

'Well, live with this: the star witness in the case of the Crown against the Cunt has just ridden back into town.'

It was Nelson's turn to be quiet.

'And at midnight tonight, he will be walking into your old headquarters to confess his sins. He might even mention one or two of yours whilst he's about it. Of course, if you haven't done anything wrong, or you're positive you covered your tracks, this information will be of no interest to you.'

'This information *is* of no *personal* interest to me, save for the fact he murdered young Adam Ash.'

'And we don't like murderers, do we?'

'That we don't. Especially when they're . . . undead, did you say?'

'Ah. Yeah. I was obviously a bit disturbed when I said that.'

'And you're not now? Tell me, Roker, where exactly are you phoning from? More to the point, how did you manage to dial with your arms in a straitjacket?'

Tom gave a wry smile, just for himself. 'You heard about me.'

'I hear everything.'

'Just like our mutual friend, then. Except he *sees* everything. *Saw* everything.'

'So why call me?' Nelson said. 'Why forewarn me? Wouldn't you like to see me go down for life?'

Tom watched a pizza delivery boy splutter down the dark street on a learner moped.

'Nelson, I'd love to give the evidence that *sends* you down. Unfortunately, I'm not the one who saw you that night. Plus, I have a bigger fish to fry. I want this bastard dead for what he's done. Even if that means you get away with it.'

'How can I help? I'm retired, remember?'

'Pull a few strings. Call in a few favours. Arrange a reception committee for midnight. Make sure someone opens fire. You won't be lacking a willing marksman. Find one who was friends with Ash.'

'And why should I believe a single word you're saying, Roker? You're a certified nut-job. I expect you're basket-weaving as we speak.'

'What, with my arms in a straitjacket?'

Nelson snorted with amusement.

'Come on, Kenny, you can't afford *not* to believe me.'

Still no reply, then, 'Midnight, you say?'

'On the dot.'

'Hmm. I might see what I can do.'

SIXTY-SIX

———◆———

Tom undressed and dressed again in the dark. The leathers were a baggy fit, but no one would notice from a distance, even through a telescopic sight.

By his wristwatch, it was twenty to midnight. He would be late. It seemed sound policy to keep them waiting. Fray their nerves, make their trigger fingers itchy.

He straddled the ZZ-R and planted his armoured boots on the shed floor. He eased the machine off its sidestand and retracted it with his left foot, then waggled his fingers in the gloves and felt like he had done over a year before with his burns all bandaged up: totally inept.

But this night, of all nights, he could not be clumsy. He had to appear one hundred per cent fluent in his handling of the motorbike.

What was likely to queer this was the simple fact that he had never ridden one before. He knew the theory from *Man on a Murder Cycle*, but he had absolutely no practical experience. He had planned to be late, but there was a real chance he would not get there at all.

He zipped the revolver inside his jacket, then slipped the helmet onto his head, flipped up the black visor, and clipped the chin strap.

Milton had conveniently left the key in the ignition, and Tom now pinched it awkwardly between his fat leather fingers, and twisted. The neutral light shone green. He gave it full choke. His right-hand thumb, poised above the starter button, depressed it.

The bike awoke, screaming blue murder through its naughty race exhaust. The shed shook, and quickly filled with the sweetly mingled grey fumes of petrol and expensive synthetic oil. Tom tried a switch by his left grip, and the headlight cut across the garden, illuminating the trunks in the copse of horse chestnuts. Left hand, clutch in. Left foot, clunk down into first gear. Now what? Okay, right hand open throttle whilst left hand gently let out clutch.

The front wheel of the ZZ-R edged onto the grass, then the entire machine emerged fully from its mothballs. Tom walked his boots either side to maintain balance, and continued in the same tentative fashion across the lawn, between the trees, all the way to the road.

Now came the real test. The public highway. Moving up through the gears and back down again. Not falling off.

But what a doddle; he rode like a natural. From one end of the lane to the other. He didn't get past third gear, but only because his speed didn't warrant it. Fourth, fifth and sixth would pose no problems, they would just be faster.

Not wishing to attract premature attention, he decided to head straight off without further practice.

Man and machine shattered the night. Plate-glass shop fronts trembled as he passed. Behind the black visor, Tom's eyes lit up with exhilaration. His sense of power was extraordinary. Why had no one introduced him to this before? The fear his grating presence could instil in people. It made him feel wicked, evil, unshackled from the laws of mere mortals. Free to express his darkest desires.

Perhaps Milton was not the grotesque aberration Tom had always believed.

Perhaps there was a bit of Milton in him.

Perhaps there was a bit of Milton in all of us.

SIXTY-SEVEN

—————◆—————

Tom was not Milton. Milton would have hurtled off to pastures new. Tom, despite his euphoria, was under no illusion. How far would his gleeful madness get him before he realised he wasn't a fictional character and that the farce had to end? Come to think of it, how far would he get before he ran out of petrol?

So he stuck to his plan and rode to the police station to meet his fate.

Turning slowly into the quiet side road that led to the cop-shop, Tom expected he would ride into a flood of arc lights and a hail of bullets.

Instead, a thickset figure rushed at him from behind a parked car and swung a baseball bat at his protected head. Tom instinctively ducked. The blow only glanced off the dome of his crash helmet but it was sufficient to unseat him from the ZZ-R. He crashed to the tarmac. The bike fell away from him and stalled as it smashed down against the opposite pavement.

Covered in armoured leather, Tom was not injured, but he could hardly see a thing; panicked breath had steamed up a view that was practically opaque to begin with. He jabbed his gloved fingers at the lower rim of the visor, raising it halfway.

The fat man was launching another attack, homing in on his stricken victim. He wielded the bat at chest level, pointing the bulbous end backwards over his shoulder, ready for a splitting crack to Tom's skull.

Tom's moment of release was upon him. In two seconds he would be unconscious from the impact, face down in the street. Seconds after that, Nelson would kick him over onto his back and aim a mighty, lethal blow at his Adam's apple, flattening his neck onto his spinal cord, effectively removing his head.

398

Make it right, Milton had told him.

But, somehow, this still wasn't right.

As the sculpted wooden stick flew at him, Tom rolled away into the gutter. Nelson growled his displeasure as he overbalanced with a follow-through he had not anticipated. Tom seized his chance, pulled off his gloves, unzipped his jacket and delved his right hand inside for the revolver. His palm closed on it and he whipped it out. Nelson steadied himself and returned to the fray, oblivious to what awaited him. Tom aimed dead-centre, almost point-blank, at the fat man's chest and pulled the trigger. The gun sounded a deafening report, and the fat man was stopped in his tracks.

Swaying on his feet, with an expression of insult more than pain or shock, Nelson stared down at the front of his black shirt.

Tom unclipped his claustrophobic helmet and yanked it off his head. In the cool night air, he fought to control his breathing.

'*Roker!*' Nelson said, astonished, though his voice sounded oddly unaffected by the physical trauma Tom should have inflicted. 'Well, I don't know what your fucking game is, pal, but it ends right here.'

'Huh?' Tom went, realising that Nelson appeared to be disappointingly right as rain.

'I think you missed,' Nelson said, hefting the bat from hand to hand.

But Tom hadn't missed; Nelson was too big a target. This was down to Milton. Not trusting Tom's intuition – that he would know how to make it right, that he wouldn't use the gun on himself – Milton had evidently loaded a blank cartridge into the cylinder.

With mock-kindness, Nelson said, 'Now I really do have to end this. I didn't come here for a police reunion, which is what I'll get if I hang around.'

Tom glanced down the road at the lights of the police station. No one had come out to investigate the gunshot. Maybe a Higher Power had corked their ears, and this was a game only two could play.

Nelson took a step forward and Tom threw the revolver at his face, catching him in his bared and snarling teeth. Nelson yelped and dropped his guard. Calculating he would not have time to stand up, Tom grabbed his crash helmet and arced it at the side of Nelson's left knee. The fat man yelped again, buckled and collapsed. Level now, Tom swung again and connected with Nelson's temple, knocking him sideways to sprawl on the road. Scrambling to his feet, Tom snatched the bat from Nelson's limp grasp, took it in both hands and raised it high above his head.

Only half-conscious, Nelson looked up and said pathetically, 'Don't.'

Tom smiled and opened a deep grey trench in the top of Nelson's skull.

SIXTY-EIGHT

———◆◆———

The ZZ-R had escaped its tumble unscathed but for cosmetic damage. Tom swiftly donned his helmet and pulled on his gloves, then found the immense strength to raise the 500-lb machine upright.

It started first press, and Tom fled raucously into the night.

What had happened did not change a thing. Tom had fought for his life not because he longed to grow old. He had done it to obey Milton's final command and break the curse.

Make it right. And dying at the hands of a psycho cop had not felt right. Sure, it had been a snap judgment to defend himself, but he believed it had not been born of the natural urge towards self-preservation. For Tom, that urge was alien. There was no percentage in the continued ebb and flow of his lungs.

Tom knew what was right. He knew exactly what he had to do to complete the cycle.

He followed signs for the M6, reversing the route by which he had first arrived at Angie's over two years before. He tackled the country lanes like a GP racer. The hedgerows streaked darkly by. It felt unreal, almost like an arcade video game, and Tom wondered whether all bikers got this sensation.

The ecstasy of speed was with him again. The rushing air blasted against him and roared inside his helmet. He tingled with excitement, shivered with cold, shook with fear. His teeth chattered until he clamped them together, then his jaw trembled. The turbocharger hissed beneath the tank, drowning the exhaust note.

His senses were being bombarded, and the sheer force of that onslaught might have stopped him, but above it all, untouched by it all, his wrath towards the world kept him going.

He finally reached the motorway, slowed, turned, and sped down the slip road to join it.

He wound open the throttle, felt the front wheel lift and settle again, then accelerated.

... 70 ... 90 ... 110 ...

After two miles, a sign: *Services 1 mile.*

... 130 ... 150 ... 170 ...

Services.

... 180 ...

Three.

... 190 ...

Two.

... 200 ...

One.

... 210 ...

Off.

... 220 ...

SLOW.

... 230 ...

EPILOGUE

———◆———

Simon Collins, junior partner at the Rotherhithe law firm of Moody, Carter and Collins, closed his copy of the *Telegraph* and chucked it on his disorganised desk.

It was more than two years since Carol Morgan had first employed his services, and during that time he had followed the unfolding events with great interest. On the day she and Tom Roker had sat in his office and signed the contracts for *Man on a Murder Cycle*, he had known something stank. Of course, he came into contact with plenty of people who stank, some literally, so he had not given it much thought. Then people had started dying and his antennae had really shot up.

But he had still not been able to figure out what part of the proceedings was rotten and giving off the stench.

He had kept abreast of the news, watching the biker's tally rise almost daily. Then Carol Morgan had been murdered, followed by Tom Roker's family in the worst single loss of life in aviation history, and now, after a quiet year or so, Tom Roker himself had snuffed it. Riding P155 OFF, the very motorcycle the police had failed to track down, he had exploded through the side of the Road Chef restaurant at the Sandbach Services at over two hundred miles an hour.

All sorts of theories abounded in the Press, but a lawyer did not deal in theories. He dealt in facts, or at least those matters which could be distorted to appear as facts.

And one indisputable fact was this: sitting uselessly in his locked safe at that moment was the sequel to *Man on a Murder Cycle*, a novel which had reputedly earned its author a million pounds from film rights alone.

And the most delicious fact was that this particular manuscript no longer *had* an author.

Collins was an author. Unpublished perhaps, but everyone knew he'd been writing for years. Who was to say that this would not be his breakthrough year?

Collins got up from his swivel chair and crossed his office. He bent down and unlocked the corner safe and removed the bulky brown package.

Back at his desk, he opened the parcel and tipped out the manuscript.

The first page read: *MOAMC SEQUEL – TOM ROKER.*

Collins reached and grabbed the black onyx cigarette lighter used by his clients. He sparked the flint and made fire, then held the title page above the flame and let it catch. When the tide of orange had crept halfway up the sheet, he dropped it into his metal waste bin.

The next page read: *For Helen and Charlotte. I wish I could turn back the clock. I love you.*

'Soppy bastard,' Collins said coldly, and produced another lick of flame from the desk lighter.

'Sorry, Mr Roker, but you're dead . . .'

Tom's dedication went up in smoke.

'. . . and life goes on.'